Son of the Morning

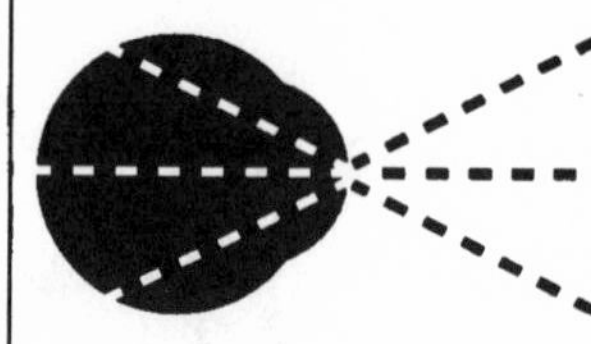

This Large Print Book carries the Seal of Approval of N.A.V.H.

Son of the Morning

Linda Howard

Thorndike Press • Thorndike, Maine

This book is a work of fiction. Names, characters, places, and incidents are products of the author's imagination or are used fictitiously. Any resemblance to actual events or locales or persons, living or dead, is entirely coincidental.

Published in 1997 by arrangement with Pocket Books, a division of Simon & Schuster, Inc.

Thorndike Large Print ® Basic Series.

The tree indicium is a trademark of Thorndike Press.

The text of this Large Print edition is unabridged.
Other aspects of the book may vary from the original edition.

Set in 16 pt. Plantin by Juanita Macdonald.

Printed in the United States on permanent paper.

Library of Congress Cataloging in Publication Data

Howard, Linda, 1950–
Son of the morning / Linda Howard.
p. cm.
ISBN 0-7862-1135-0 (lg. print : hc : alk. paper)
I. Title.
PS3558.O88217S66 1997
813′.54—dc21 97-13852

To Susan Bailey, my friendly banker
who answered all my questions about
ATMs, and didn't accuse me of planning
a robbery — thanks.

"How art thou fallen from heaven,
O Lucifer, son of the morning!"
— *Isaiah, 14:12*

Part One

Grace

Prologue

December 1307
France

The stone walls of the secret underground chamber were cold and dank, the chill penetrating wool and linen and leather, going straight to the bone. Two smoking torches provided the only illumination, and too little heat to make any difference. The pair of men revealed by the flickering light paid no attention to the cold, however, for such discomfort was of small matter.

The first man was standing, the other kneeling before him in a posture that should have been submissive, had it not been obvious that such an attitude was alien to that proud head, those broad shoulders. The man who was standing looked frail in contrast with the vitality of the other, and in fact the kneeling man's head was level with the chest of the first. Valcour was, indeed, frail in comparison to the warrior he had once been, and to the man who knelt before him, but age and despair had taken their toll. He was fifty-one, long past the age of vigor. His hair and beard were more gray than brown, his thin face lined from the burdens he had endured. It was time to pass along the responsibility, the duty, that had been his for all these long years. They would be safe with this fierce young lion, he thought. There was no better warrior in the Order, which was the same as saying there was no better warrior in Christendom, for they were — had been — a brotherhood of warriors, the best of the best, the cream skimmed from Europe's battlefields and tourneys.

No more.

Just two months past, on Friday, the thirteenth of October in this year of Our Lord 1307, a day that would surely be remembered through the ages as a day of darkness, Philip IV of France and his puppet, Pope Clement V, had given in to their greed and in one fell swoop effected the destruction of the greatest military order ever to exist: the Knights of the Temple. Some of the brethren had escaped, but others had already died horrible deaths, and more deaths would follow as those captured refused to recant their beliefs.

The Grand Master had received mere moments of warning, and had chosen to use those moments to secure the safety of the Treasure rather than of himself. Perhaps Jacques de Molay had sensed the approach of catastrophe, for he had already spoken with Valcour several times about keeping their enormous fleet of ships out of Philip's hands, but above all his concern, and that of the great warrior Geoffroy de Charnay, had been the safekeeping of the Treasure. After long hours of consideration the Guardian had been chosen: the true and fierce warrior, Niall of Scotland. He had been chosen very carefully, not just for his prowess with a sword, which was unrivaled, but for the protection that came with his very name. The Treasure would be safe in Scotland.

The Grand Master hadn't been certain his choice was the correct one, even given Niall's connections. There was something untamed and ruthless about the Scot, despite his unswerving loyalty to God and the Brotherhood, and the oaths he had sworn to both. Some of those oaths had been given unwillingly, the Grand Master was certain, especially the oath of chastity. Niall had been forced into the Brotherhood, for of course a monk could never be king; a king must have at least the possibility of children, for kingdoms were built on continuity. His illegitimacy should have been an unsurmountable barrier, but even at a young age Niall had been tall and proud, intelligent, cunning, ruthless, a born leader; in short, he had all the characteristics of a great king. The choices had been simple: kill him, or make it impossible for him to be king. Niall was loved by his father and half-brother, so there had really been no choice. The young man would be a servant of God.

It was a master stroke. Should Niall renounce his vows to the Temple, that too would render him unacceptable for the crown, for he would be dishonored. No, putting young Niall into the protection of the Temple had at once saved his life and now and forever removed him from consideration for the Scots throne — such as it was.

But if Niall had been unsuited for the life of a monk, he had been perfectly suited for that of a warrior. He had taken his lust for female flesh and turned it into fierceness on the battlefield, and if his eyes sometimes lingered overlong on that which was forbidden to him, still, to the Grand Master's sure knowledge he had never broken his vows. He was a man of his word.

That, and his fighting ability, was what had finally convinced de Charnay to choose Niall as the next Guardian, and though the Grand Master was the head of the Order, de Charnay was undoubtedly the most powerful Knight. Moreover, de Charnay had borne the responsibility for the safety of the Treasure for many years, and his was the final say. His choice was Niall of Scotland, and Valcour agreed wholeheartedly. The Scot would safeguard the Treasure with his life.

"Take them," Valcour whispered now to that bent black head, feeling the younger man's bitter rage and knowing no way to ease it. "No matter what happens, the Treasure must never fall into the hands of others. The Brotherhood has devoted itself to the protection of our God and His followers, and we must not falter in our duty."

The cold stone floor was hard beneath Niall's knees, but he scarcely noticed it. His thick black hair, cut short as was required, gleamed with sweat despite the chill of the underground chamber. Steam drifted from his body. Slowly he lifted his head, his eyes stark, and as black as night with bitterness. "Even now?" he asked, the bite of betrayal in the deep, softly burred tones of his voice.

Valcour smiled thinly. "Especially now. We serve God, not Rome. Methinks the Holy Father has forgotten there is a difference."

"The concept should come easily to him," Niall all but snarled. "He does not serve God, but rather licks Philip's arse every time the king presents it." His night-dark gaze wandered over the collection of artifacts that had been spirited out of the Temple in Jerusalem more than a century before. He studied them, and felt his bitterness growing. Good men had died horrible deaths protecting these . . . things. The King of France and the Holy Father were so intent on stripping the Order of its more earthly treasures, of gold and silver, but the Brotherhood's secretiveness centered around these things rather than mere gold. Oh, there was gold aplenty — Niall had it. But its only purpose was to provide for the safekeeping of the real Treasure, this disturbing and powerful group of —

Things. A cup, plain and scarred. A shroud, with its secrets embedded in the very fabric. A throne, unsettling and pagan — or was it? A banner, rich and compelling despite its age, reputed to hold strange powers in its frayed threads. And an ancient text, written in a mixture of Hebrew and Greek, which told of a secret, and of a power beyond belief.

"I could go back," Niall said, thinking of the text. He lifted his merciless warrior's gaze to Valcour. "Both Philip and Clement could fall under my sword, and this could be undone as if it never was, and our brothers would live."

"Nay," said Valcour. His face had the drawn, exalted look of someone who has gone beyond horror, beyond fatigue. "We must not risk discovery for our own sakes. *Only for the sake of God* may the secret be used."

"Is there a God?" Niall asked bitterly. "Or are we but fools?"

Valcour's thin, bloodless hand lifted, gently touched Niall's head in both a benediction and a restraint. He felt the steamy heat emanating from the warrior's muscled body, for Niall had just discarded his helm and still wore heavy armor. Would that he had a fraction of Niall's great strength, Valcour thought tiredly. The Scot was like iron, neither breaking nor wearing down no matter the hardships he faced.

His sword arm was tireless, his will unswerving. There was no greater warrior in the Lord's service than this formidable Scot with royal blood running through his bastard veins. Not just noble, but *royal.* 'Twas that blood that had won him entrance into the Order, for legitimacy was a requirement. Wisely, the Grand Master had decided that, in this case, blood ties were more important than rules.

And because of that blood, Niall would be protected. Clement would not be able to lay his bloody, greedy hands on the Scot, for he would be safe in his homeland, among the craggy mountains of the Highlands.

"We believe," Valcour finally said, in simple response to Niall's question. "And, believing, we've sworn our lives to protect. You are released from all your other vows, but on the blood of your brothers, you must swear to devote your life to the guardianship of these holy relics."

"I swear," Niall said fiercely. "But for *them.* Never again for *Him.*"

Valcour's eyes were troubled. Loss of faith was a terrible thing — and a common one, in these days of horror. More men would lose their faith, or their lives. Not all Brothers had remained true; some of them had turned their backs on the Order, and the God, they had served so faithfully but who had allowed this ungodly thing to happen to them. Friends, brothers, had been tortured, dismembered, burned at the stake, the Order shattered — all for the love of gold. It was difficult to believe in anything except betrayal, and vengeance.

And yet Valcour tried to keep a small, central part of himself pure, to keep his belief enshrined there, for without belief there was nothing. If he didn't believe, then he had to accept that so many good men had died in vain, and that he could not do, could not live with. So, because the alternative was so unbearable, he believed. He wished Niall could have that comfort, but the Scot was too uncompromising, his warrior's heart seeing only black and white. He had been on too many battlefields where the choices were simple: kill, or be killed. Valcour had fought for the Lord, but he had never been the soldier Niall was. The heat of battle did tend to make one's vision very clear, to distill life down to the simplest of choices.

The Order needed Niall, to fulfill its greatest, most secret vow. The Brotherhood was at an end, at least in this incarnation, but its sacred duty would continue, and Niall was the chosen protector.

"For whatever reason, then," Valcour murmured. "Guard them well, for they are the true treasures of our Lord. Should they fall into the hands of evil, then the blood of our brothers will have been shed in vain. So shall it be, then: if not for *Him,* for *them.*"

"With my life," said Niall of Scotland.

December 1309
Creag Dhu, Scotland

"Three more Knights have found their way here since last you visited," Niall murmured to his brother as the two men sat before a crackling fire in Niall's private chamber. A tall, thick tallow candle sat on the table where they had recently filled their bellies, its flame adding to the golden glow of the hearth fire. Except for that, the chamber was in shadows, and delightfully warm. No drafts crept through the stone walls to stir the air with icy breaths; the cracks and crevices had been carefully daubed with clay, and the tapestries were thick and heavy. The door to Niall's chamber was stout, and securely barred. For all that, the two men kept their voices low, and spoke in French, so that if they were somehow overheard they wouldn't be understood. None of the Scots servants spoke the language; most of the nobility did, but here in this impregnable fortress, in a remote corner of the Highlands, they had only the servants and men-at-arms with whom they had to concern themselves.

Both held heavy goblets filled with fine French wine, and now Robert sipped his in contemplation. He had seated himself in a huge, carved wooden chair, while Niall had drawn up a heavy bench and placed it at an angle to the fire, so that he faced his visitor rather than the flames. Robert watched the dancing flames as he drank his wine; when he glanced back at Niall, it took a moment for his vision to adjust, and suddenly he realized that was why Niall had placed the bench as he had. Even here, in his own castle, secure in his own chamber with his brother, Niall's instincts were those of a warrior and he had protected his vision. Should an enemy somehow take him unawares, he would not be hampered by limited sight.

The realization made Robert's mouth curl wryly. After years of battle with the English, he too had learned to protect his night vision, but here in this safe place he had allowed himself to relax. Not so Niall. He never relaxed; he was eternally vigilant.

"Have any of the Knights sought other refuge?"

"Nay. They remain here, for there is no other certain refuge. Yet they know they must go, soon, or by their very number they could bring to Creag Dhu the attention they wish to avoid." Niall's black gaze was piercing as he stared at his brother. "I have not asked for myself, for I have no wish to add to your troubles, but for them I must know: do you intend to enforce Clement's edict against us?"

Stung, Robert drew back. "Ye ask that!" he growled, angered enough to speak in Gaelic, but Niall's gaze didn't waver and after a moment he reined in his temper.

"You need the alliance with France," Niall said calmly. "Should Philip discover my identity, he would stop at nothing to capture me, including joining his forces to Edward's. You cannot risk that." What he didn't say was, *Scotland* needed the alliance; the distinction wasn't needed, for his brother *was* Scotland, all her hopes and dreams personified.

Robert drew in a deep, calming breath. "Aye," he admitted, returning to French. "It would be a crippling blow. But already I've lost three brothers to England's butchery; my wife and daughter, and our sisters, have been captives for three years already and I know not if I'll ever see them alive again. I'll not lose you, too."

"You scarcely know me."

" 'Tis true that we were not much in each other's company, but I *do* know you," Robert disagreed. Know him, and love him. It was that simple. None of his other brothers could have challenged him for the crown, but he and his father had known from the time Niall had been a tall, sturdy lad of ten that this illegitimate half-brother had the stuff of kings, uncommonly gifted with the boldness and intelligence that were Robert's own characteristics. For Scotland's sake, they could not risk an internal struggle between the brothers, and even had Niall grown up to prove loyal, such was his personality that folk would have flocked to him anyway. The circumstances of his birth had been kept secret, but secrets had a way of outing, as Niall himself had proven at that time by boldly approaching Robert and asking if 'twas true they were brothers.

It wasn't unusual for aspirants to the throne to clear the way by killing those who might challenge them, but neither Robert nor his father, the Earl of Carrick, had been able to tolerate the thought. It would have been like extinguishing a bright flame, leaving them in darkness. Niall burned with life's force, full of joy and deviltry, drawing people to him like a lodestone. He had always been the leader among the younger lads, fearlessly taking his followers into mischief and then just as fearlessly taking the blame onto his own shoulders whenever they were caught.

By the time he was fourteen, the lasses had begun following him, too, with their bright eyes and lissome bodies. Already his voice had deepened, his shoulders widened, his chest broadened as manhood settled easily on his tall frame. He had proven himself unusually adept at arms, and the constant practice with heavy swords had further strengthened him. Robert doubted the lad had spent many nights alone, for it wasn't just the young lasses who had pursued him, but the older ones as well, including some who were wed.

He had changed, though. Robert wasn't surprised, given the treachery that had befallen the Templars. His magnetism hadn't lessened, but it was harsher now, his black eyes remaining grim even if his lips smiled. As a lad he had been restless with inexhaustible energy, but now he was a man grown, and a fearsome warrior. He had learned the art of patience, and his stillness was like that of a predator waiting for its next meal.

Now Robert said deliberately, "Scotland will not join in the persecution of the Templars."

Again Niall's gaze bored into him, like a black sword in its sharpness. "You have my gratitude . . . and more, should you care to use it."

What Niall had left unspoken hung heavily in the shadowed room. The watchful black gaze never wavered, and Robert lifted his eyebrows. "More?" he asked, sipping again at the wine. He was curious about what "more" would entail. He scarcely dared to hope . . . perhaps Niall was offering *gold.* More than anything, Scotland needed gold to finance its battle to resist English domination.

"The Brethren are the best soldiers in the world. They must not gather here, yet I see no need for their skills to go unused."

"Ah." Thoughtfully, Robert stared into the fire again. Now he knew Niall's goal, and it was tempting indeed. Not gold, but something almost as valuable: training, and experience. The arrogant, excommunicated Knights no longer wore their red crosses, but essentially they were still exactly what they had been before the Pope and the King of France had conspired to destroy them: the best military men in the world. This endless war with England was stretching Scotland's poor resources so thin that they were, at times, literally fighting with their bare hands. As gallant as his people were, especially the wild Highlanders, Robert knew they indeed needed more: more funds, more weapons, more training.

"Blend them in with your armies," Niall murmured. "Give them the responsibility of training your men. Consult with them in strategy. Use them. In repayment, they will become Scots. They will fight to the death for you, and for Scotland."

The Templars! The very idea was dizzying. Robert's fighting blood sang through his veins at the idea of having such soldiers under his command. Still, how much could a handful of men do, no matter how well trained? "How many are there?" he asked doubtfully. "Five?"

"Five here," Niall said. "But hundreds in need of refuge."

Hundreds. Niall was proposing to make Scotland a place of sanctuary for the Knights who had escaped and gone into hiding all over Europe. If they were caught, they had the choice of betraying their Brethren, or enduring torture before being burned at the stake. Some had cooperated and lost their lives anyway.

"You can bring them here?"

"I can." Niall rose from the bench and stood with his broad back to the fire, his massive shoulders throwing a huge shadow across the floor. His thick black hair flowed over his shoulders, and in the Celtic fashion he had plaited a small braid to hang on each side of his face. In his hunting-plaid kilt and white shirt, with a knife thrust in his wide belt, he looked every inch the wild Highlander. His expression was grim. "What I cannot do is join them."

"I know," Robert said softly. "Nor would I ask it of you. I seek no details, yet I know that you are in greater danger than those you wish to aid, and not just because you are my brother. Whatever mission the Temple has charged you with is one no lesser man could accomplish. If ever you need my aid, or that of the Knights you wish to put at my service, you have only to send word."

Niall inclined his head with a motion that conveyed acceptance, and yet Robert knew that day would never come. Niall had forged a stronghold here in the wildest, most remote part of the Highlands, the rugged northwest mountains, and he would defend it against all threats. He had gathered about him a strong force of disciplined knights and men-at-arms, and turned Creag Dhu into an impregnable fortress.

Already the country folk whispered about him, even as they gathered closer to Creag

Dhu for his protection. They called him Black Niall. The Scots tended to name as black anyone with dark coloring, but the whispers about Niall said that it was his heart so described, not just his mane of hair and midnight eyes.

Robert, who knew Niall's ancestry, could see the resemblance between his half-brother and his own best friend, Jamie Douglas, the infamous Black Douglas, and the coincidence of coloring and name made him uneasy. Niall's mother had been a Douglas; he and Jamie were first cousins. Jamie was tall and broad-shouldered, though not as tall or strongly built as Niall. Should anyone see them together, would the resemblance be noted? Would it then also be noticed that Niall had the great physical strength of the Bruces, as well as the almost unholy handsomeness for which Nigel, another of Niall's half-brothers, had been so famous? Bruce and Douglas blood had combined in Niall to form a man of unusual looks and force, the type of man who strode the earth only once every hundred years or so. He did not go unnoticed. For his own safety, and for the sake of the mission charged to him by the ravaged Order, no one must ever know that the infamous Black Niall was the beloved half-brother of the King of Scotland, and the bastard son of the lovely Catriona Douglas, for Catriona's husband still lived and would stop at nothing to kill the result of his wife's infidelity.

Niall was also a Templar, excommunicated, and by order of the Pope under a penalty of death should he ever be captured. On the surface, his existence was precarious indeed.

On the other hand, it would take a fool to try to breach Creag Dhu's defenses. The Order had chosen its champion well.

Robert sighed. There was naught he could do for his brother except respect his secrecy, and offer his kingdom as sanctuary to the scattered, persecuted Knights. Little enough, given what Scotland would gain in return.

" 'Tis time I take my leave," he said, draining his goblet and setting it aside. "The hour grows late, and the lovely wench waiting for you below may become impatient, and seek another's bed." Niall had completely discarded his Templar's vows of poverty, chastity, and obedience, but most particularly chastity. Robert wondered now how his brother had ever endured eight years without a woman, for even though he was a man himself, he could still see the burning, intense sexuality of Niall's nature. If there had ever been a man less suited to monkhood, Robert couldn't imagine it.

Niall's mouth quirked. "Perhaps," he said placidly, without a shred of either jealousy or doubt, for there was no likelihood Meg would do so; she was thoroughly enjoying her current status as his favorite, though by no means only, bedmate.

Robert laughed and clapped his hand to the broad shoulder. "As I ride through the cold night, I will envy you *your* ride between warm thighs. God be with you."

Niall's expression didn't change, but Robert was instantly aware of a sudden coldness, and intuitively he knew his last remark was what had elicited that reaction. Troubled, he tightened his hand on his brother's shoulder. Sometimes faith was all folk, be they common or king, had to sustain them, and Niall had turned his back on that bulwark as the Church had turned her back on him.

But there was nothing to be said, no comfort to be offered except the promise he had already made. "Bring them here," he said softly. "I will make them welcome." Then Robert the Bruce, King of the Scots, pressed on a certain stone to the left of the great hearth, and a whole section opened inward. He took up the torch he had left just inside the hidden way, and held it into the fire until it was once more flaring brightly. He left Creag Dhu as he had entered it, in secret.

Niall watched as the door closed, immediately becoming invisible within the stonework. His face was impassive as he took the goblet his brother had used and wiped the rim clean, then filled it again with the fine wine. His own goblet was still nearly full; he set both of them beside the bed, then unbarred his door and went in search of Meg. His mood had darkened, despite the sanctuary Robert had offered to the fugitive Templars. The rage was always there, controlled after two years but never weakening. Damn Clement, damn Philip, and most of all, damn the God whom the Knights had served so faithfully, but who had abandoned them when they needed Him most. If he went to hell for such blasphemy, so be it, but Niall no longer believed in hell; he didn't believe in anything.

He would work out his black mood on Meg's lush, willing body, wrapped tight by her arms and legs. The rougher the love play, the more she liked it.

Finding Meg was no effort; she was lurking near the bottom of the huge, curving stone stairway, and came forward with a smile when he appeared at the top. Niall halted, merely standing there, waiting. Meg lifted her skirts and hurried up the stairs, the flickering torchlight intensifying the flush in her cheeks. Niall turned before she reached him, striding back to his chamber. Her quick, light footsteps followed, and he could hear her breathing as it too quickened, both from her exertion and from anticipation.

She was already shrugging out of her shawl, tugging at the laces to her bodice, as she followed him through the door to his chamber. He shut it and watched as she feverishly shed her clothes, revealing the lushness of her body to him. His shaft rose hard and pulsing, tenting the front of his kilt.

She spied the two wine goblets and a pleased smile curved her lips. He'd known she would take it as an expression of his besottedness with her, but let her think what she liked, rather than suspect he'd had a secret visitor, or that it was none other than the King himself. Though he was willing to soothe her ego with small gestures, and more than willing to return twofold the physical ease she gave him, his only interest in her was for the pleasure he found in her soft, bountiful body.

Naked, she took up one of the goblets and sipped the wine, doubly gratified to find it contained a fine vintage rather than the sour, watery ones to which she was more accustomed. The firelight played over the full curves of her bosom, turning her dark nipples to the color of fine wine themselves, deepening the shadows of her navel and the full nest of curls between her thighs.

He didn't want to wait. He approached and took the goblet from her hand, setting it down with a thud that sloshed some of the red liquid over the rim. She gave a little squeal of surprise as he lifted her and tossed her onto the big bed, but the squeal turned into laughter as he landed on top of her.

He kneed her thighs apart. "Are ye no going to remove yer boots, at least?" she asked, giggling. She reached up to tug at the laces of his shirt.

The smell of her was dark and rich, female. His thin nostrils flared, drinking in the scent. "Why?" he asked in a reasonable tone. "They're on my feet, not my cock." The giggles turned into full-scale laughter. Niall reached beneath his kilt and grasped his erect rod, guiding it to her wet cleft. He surged forward, sheathing himself, shuddering with relief, and Meg's laughter died a quick, strangled death as her body absorbed the force of the thrust.

The darkness within him receded, pushed back by sheer delight. So long as he had a woman in his arms, he could forget the betrayal, and the crushing burden of responsibility that weighed on his shoulders.

Chapter 1

April 27, 1996

A low, coughing rumble announced to the neighborhood that Kristian Sieber was home from school. He drove a 1966 Chevelle, lovingly restored to all its original gas-guzzling, eight-cylinder power. The body was a patchwork of different colors, as the parts had been taken from the corpses of other Chevelles, but whenever someone commented on the multicolored car, Kristian would grumpily say that he was "working on it." The truth was, the exterior didn't bother him. He cared only that the car ran the way it had when it was new, when some lucky, macho guy had thrilled every girl around with its growling power. In the instinctive, primal, murky way of males, he was certain all that horsepower would overcome his image as a nerd, and all the girls would flock to his side, wanting to ride in his supercar.

So far it hadn't happened, but Kristian hadn't given up hope.

As the rumbling car passed her house and turned at the corner, Grace St. John hastily took one last bite of the stew she had prepared for supper. "Kristian's home," she said, jumping up from the table.

"No kidding," Ford teased. He winked at her as she grabbed up the case that contained her laptop computer and the multitude of papers she had been translating. The sides of the supple leather case bulged outward, so crammed was it with notes and disks. She had unplugged her modem earlier, wrapped the cords around it, and placed it on top of the case. She cradled case and modem in her arms as she leaned over to reach Ford's mouth. Their kiss was brief, but warm.

"It'll probably take a couple of hours, at least," she said. "After he finds out what the problem is, he wants to show me a few new programs he has."

"It used to be etchings," her brother Bryant murmured. "Now it's programs." The three of them took most of their meals together, a convenience they all liked. When Bryant and Grace had inherited the house from their parents, they turned it into a duplex; Grace and Ford lived in one side, and Bryant in the other. The three of them not only worked for the same archaeological foundation, but Ford and Bryant had been best friends since college. Bryant had introduced Ford and Grace, and still patted himself on the back for the outcome of that introduction.

"You're just jealous because you can't hack

it," Grace said, poker-faced, and Bryant groaned at the pun.

Her hands were full, so Ford got up to open the kitchen door for her. He leaned down to kiss her again. "Don't get lost in Kristian's programs and lose track of time," he cautioned, his hazel eyes sending her a very private message that, after almost eight years of marriage, still thrilled her to her toes.

"I won't," she promised, and started out the door, only to halt on the top step. "I forgot my purse."

Ford picked it up from the cabinet and looped the strap over her head. "Why do you need your purse?"

"The checkbook's in it," she said, blowing a strand of hair out of her eyes. She always paid Kristian for his repair services, though he would gladly have done it for free just for the joy of fooling around with someone else's computer. His equipment was expensive, and his skill better than any she had seen at computer or software companies. He deserved to be paid. "Plus I'll probably buy him a pizza."

"As much as that kid eats, he should weigh four hundred pounds," Bryant observed.

"He's nineteen. Of course he eats a lot."

"I don't think I ever ate that much. What do you think, Ford? When we were in college, did we eat as much as Kristian?"

Ford gave him a disbelieving look. "You actually asking *me*, when you're the guy who once ate thirteen pancakes and a pound of sausage for breakfast?"

"I did?" Bryant frowned. "I don't remember that. And what about you? I've seen you down four Big Macs and four large fries at one sitting."

"Both of you ate as if you had tapeworms," Grace said, settling the discussion as she went down the steps. Ford closed the door behind her, his chuckle rich in her ears.

Thick, resilient grass cushioned her steps as she walked across their backyard, then angled her steps in a shortcut through the Murchisons' overgrown lawn. They had taken a month's vacation in South Carolina, and weren't due to return until the end of the week. It was a shame; in seeking warm weather, and spring, they had missed it at home.

It had been an unusually warm April, and spring had exploded in Minneapolis. The grass was green and lush, the trees leafed out, flowers were in bloom. Even though the sun had set and only the last bits of twilight remained, the evening air was warm and fragrant. Grace inhaled with deep delight. She loved spring. Actually, she loved every season, for they all had their joys.

Kristian stood in the Siebers' back door, waiting for her. "Hi," he said in cheerful greeting. He was always cheerful at the prospect of getting his hands on her laptop.

He hadn't turned on a light. Grace entered through the dark laundry room, passing through the kitchen. Audra Sieber, Kristian's mother, was sliding a tray of rolls into the oven. She looked up with a smile. "Hello, Grace. We're having lamb chops tonight; would you like to join us?"

"Thanks, but I've just finished eating." She liked Audra, who was comfortably fifty, slightly overweight, and completely understanding of her son's obsession with gigabytes and motherboards. Physically, Kristian was just like his father, Errol: tall, thin, with dark hair, myopic blue eyes, and a prominent Adam's apple bobbing in his throat. Kristian couldn't have looked more like the prototypical computer nerd if he'd had the words stenciled on his forehead.

Remembering his appetite, Grace said, "Kris, this can wait until after you eat."

"I'll fix a plate and carry it up," he said, taking the case from her arms and cradling it lovingly in his. "That's okay with you, isn't it, Mom?"

"Of course. Go on and have fun." Audra aimed her serene smile between the two of them, and Kristian immediately loped out of the kitchen and up the stairs, carrying his prize to his electronics-laden lair.

Grace followed him at a slower pace, thinking as she climbed the stairs that she really needed to shed the twenty extra pounds she'd gained since she and Ford had married. The problem was, her work was so sedentary; a specialist and translator of old languages, she spent a lot of her time with a magnifying glass going over photos of old documents, and very occasionally the actual papers themselves, but for the most part they were too fragile to be handled. The rest of the time she was working on the computer, using a translation program that she and Kristian had enhanced. It was difficult to burn many calories doing brain work.

Earlier that day she had been doing just that, trying to access the university's library to download some information, but the computer hadn't obeyed her commands. She wasn't certain if it was a problem with the laptop itself, or with the modem. She had caught Kristian at home for lunch, and arranged for him to take a look at it when his classes were finished for the day.

The delay had almost driven her mad with frustration. She was fascinated by the batch of documents she'd been translating for her employer, the Amaranthine Potere Foundation, a huge archaeological and antiquities foundation. She loved her work anyway, but this was special, so special that she was almost afraid to believe her translations were correct. She felt almost . . . *pulled,* drawn into the documents in a way that had never happened before. The night before, Ford had asked her what the documents contained, and she had reluctantly told him a little about them — just the topic. Usually she talked freely with Ford about her work, but this time it was different. She felt so strongly about these strange old documents that it was difficult to put it into words, and so she had been rather casual about the whole thing, as if it wasn't even particularly interesting.

Instead, it was . . . special, in ways she didn't fully understand yet. She had translated less than a tenth of the whole, and already the possibilities were driving her half mad with anticipation, swirling just beyond comprehension, like a jigsaw puzzle with only the border assembled. In this case, though, she had no idea what the finished product would look like, only that she couldn't stop until she knew.

She reached the top of the stairs and entered Kristian's bedroom. It was a maze of electronic equipment and cords, with just enough room for his bed. He had four separate phone lines, one each to the one laptop and two desktop computers he owned, and another to a fax machine. Two printers shared the duty among the three computers. One of the desktops was on, with a chess game displayed on the monitor. Kristian glanced at it, grunted, and used the mouse to move a bishop. He studied the results for a moment, before clicking the mouse and turning back to the puzzle at hand. He pushed a stack of papers to one side and moved another onto the bed. "What's it doing?" he asked as he opened the case and removed her laptop.

"Nothing," Grace said, taking another chair and watching as he swiftly unhooked the other desktop's electrical umbilical cords from power port and modem, and plugged in hers. He turned it on and it whirred to life, the screen flickering to a pale blue. "I tried to get into the university's library this morning, and nothing happened. I don't know if it's the unit or the modem."

"We'll find out right now." He knew his way around her menu as well as she did; he clicked onto the one he wanted, then double-clicked on the telephone icon. He dialed the number for the university's electronic library, and ten seconds later was in. "Modem," he announced. His fingers were practically quivering as they hovered over the keys. "What did you want?"

She leaned closer. "Medieval history. The Crusades, specifically."

He scrolled down the list of offerings. "That one," Grace said, and he clicked the mouse. The table of contents filled the screen.

He scooted away. "Here, you take over while I try to find out what's wrong with the modem."

She took his place in front of the computer, and he switched on a lamp on the desk, automatically pushing his glasses up on his nose before he began dismantling the modem.

There were several references to the military religious orders of the time, the Knights Hospitaller and the Knights Templar. It was the Templars she wanted. She clicked onto the appropriate chapter, and lines of information filled the screen.

She read intently, looking for one certain name. It didn't appear. The text was a chronicle and analysis of the Templars' contribution to the Crusades, but except for a few grand masters none was mentioned by name.

They were interrupted briefly when Audra brought a filled plate up to Kristian. He positioned it next to the disassembled modem and happily munched as he worked. Grace went back to the main list and chose another text.

Sometime later she became aware that Kristian had evidently either repaired her modem or given up on it, for he was reading over her shoulder. It was difficult to pull herself out of medieval intrigue and danger, and back into the modern world of computers. She blinked to orient herself, aware of the strangely potent lure of that long-ago time. "Could you fix it?"

"Sure," he replied absently, still reading. "It was just a loose connection. Who were these Templar guys?"

"They were a military religious order in the Middle Ages; don't you know your history?"

He pushed his glasses up on his nose and

flashed her an unrepentant grin. "Time began in nineteen forty-six."

"There *was* life before computers."

"Analog life, you mean. Prehistoric."

"What kind of gauges are in that muscle-bound thing you call a car?"

He looked chagrined, caught in the shameful knowledge that his beloved chariot was hopelessly old-fashioned, with analog gauges instead of digital readouts. "I'm working on it," he mumbled, hunching his thin shoulders. "Anyway, about these Templar guys. If they were so religious, why were they burned at the stake like witches or something?"

"Heresy," she murmured, turning her attention back to the screen. "Fire was the punishment for a lot of crimes, not just for witchcraft."

"Guess people back then took their religion seriously." Kristian wrinkled his nose at the electronic display of a crude drawing of three men bound to a center pole while flames licked around their knees. All three men were dressed in white tunics with crosses emblazoned on their chests. Their mouths were little black holes, opened in screams of agony.

"People are still executed because of religion today," Grace said, shuddering a little as she stared at the small drawing, imagining the sheer horror of being burned alive. "In the Middle Ages, religion was the center of people's lives, and anyone who went against it was a threat to them. Religion gave them the rules of civilization, but it was more than that. There was so much that wasn't known, or understood; they were terrified by eclipses, by comets, by sicknesses that struck without warning, by things we know now are normal but which they had no way of understanding. Imagine how frightening, and deadly, appendicitis must have been to them, or a stroke or heart attack. They didn't know what was happening, what caused it, or how to prevent it. Magic was very real to them, and religion gave them a sort of protection against these unknown, frightening forces. Even if they died, God was still taking care of them, and the evil spirits didn't win."

His brow furrowed as he tried to imagine living in such ignorance. It was almost beyond him, this child of the computer age. "I guess television would've given them a real spasm, huh?"

"Especially if they saw a talk show," she muttered. "Now *there* are some evil spirits."

Kristian giggled, sending his glasses slipping down his nose. He pushed them up again and squinted at the screen. "Did you find what you want?"

"No. I'm looking for mention of one particular Templar — at least, I think he was a Templar."

"Any cross-references you can check?"

She shook her head. "I don't know his last

name." *Niall of Scotland.* She had already found his name several times in the portion of the documents written in Old French. Why wasn't his surname recorded, in a time when family and heritage were so important? From what she had gleaned from her translations so far, he'd been a man of immense importance to the Templars, a Knight himself, which meant he was well born and not a serf. Part of the documents were also in Gaelic, strengthening the unknown tie with Scotland. She'd read up on Scotland's history in her encyclopedia, but there hadn't been any mention of a mysterious Niall at all, much less one in the time frame of the Templars' existence.

"Dead end, then," Kristian said cheerfully, evidently deciding they had wasted enough time on someone who had died even before the age of analog. His blue eyes sparkled as he moved his chair a little closer. "Want to see this cool accounting program I've worked up?"

"I don't think the words *cool* and *accounting* go together," Grace observed, keeping her expression deadpan.

Shocked, Kristian stared at her. He blinked several times, making him look like a myopic crane. "Are you kidding?" he blurted. "It's the greatest! Wait until you see — wait. You *are* kidding. I can tell."

Grace's lips curved as she deftly tapped keys, backing out of the university's library system. "Oh, yeah? How?"

"You always tighten your mouth to keep from smiling." He glanced at her mouth, then quickly looked away, blushing a little.

Grace felt her own cheeks heating and carefully glued her eyes to the screen. Kristian had a tiny crush on her, based mostly on his enthusiasm for her expensive, powerful laptop, but on a few rare occasions he had said or done something that bespoke a physical awareness of her as well.

It always disconcerted her; she was thirty years old, for heaven's sake, and was certainly not a femme fatale by any stretch of the imagination. She considered herself very ordinary, with nothing about her to inspire lust in a nineteen-year-old — though God knows, almost anything female and breathing could inspire lust in a nineteen-year-old boy. If Kristian was the stereotypical image of a computer nerd, she'd always thought she looked the typical shy academic type: dark brown hair, impossibly straight, which she had long ago given up trying to coax into curls and now wore pulled back into a single thick braid; light blue eyes, almost gray, usually framed by reading glasses; no makeup, because she didn't know how to apply it; sensible clothes, tending toward corduroy slacks and denim skirts. She was hardly the stuff of an erotic dream.

But Ford had always said she had the most kissable mouth he'd ever seen, and it flustered her that Kristian had looked so pointedly at her lips. To distract him, she said, "Okay, let's see this hotshot program." She hoped the Chevelle would work its macho magic soon, and lure into Kristian's orbit some smart girl who appreciated both horsepower and multitasking.

Looking grateful for the change of subject, he opened a plastic case and removed the diskette, then inserted it into the disk drive. Grace scooted to the side, giving him better access to the keys. He directed the computer to access the disk in the A drive, there was some electronic whirring, and a menu appeared on the screen.

"What bank do you use?" Kristian asked.

Grace told him, frowning as she scanned down the menu. Kristian zipped the cursor to the item he wanted, clicked on it, and the screen changed again. "Bingo," he crowed as a new menu appeared, this time of bank services. "Am I slick, or what?"

"You're illegal, is what you are!" Appalled, Grace watched as he chose another item, clicked on it, then typed "St. John, Grace." Instantly a record of her checking account transactions appeared on the screen. "You've hacked into the bank's computers! Get out of there before you get in big trouble. I mean it, Kris! This is a felony. You told me you had an accounting program, not a back door into every bank in the area."

"Don't you want to know how I did it?" he

asked, clearly disappointed that she didn't share his enthusiasm for the deed. "I'm not stealing or anything. This lets you see how long it takes each check to clear, so you can establish a pattern. Some places only deposit once a week. You can get a better handle on your cash flow if you know how long it takes for a particular check to clear. That way, if you have an interest-bearing checking account, you can time your payments so your average balance doesn't dip below the minimum."

Grace simply stared at him, amazed at the wiring of his brain. To her, money matters were a straightforward affair: you had *X* amount of money coming in, and you had to keep your expenses below that amount. Simple. She had long ago decided there were two types of people on earth: math people, and non-math people. She was an intelligent woman; she had a doctoral degree. But the intricacies of math, whether it dealt with finance or quantum physics, had simply never appealed to her. Words, now . . . she reveled in words, wallowed deliriously in the nuances of meaning, delighted in the magic of them. Ford was even less interested in math than she was, which was why she took care of the checkbook. Bryant tried; he read the financial section of the newspaper, subscribed to investment magazines — in case he ever had enough money to invest — but he didn't have a real grasp of the dynamics. After fifteen minutes of wading through one of his investment magazines, he was tossing it aside and reaching for something, anything, on archaeology.

But Kristian was a math person. Grace had no doubt he'd be a billionaire by the time he was thirty. He would write some brilliant computer program, wisely invest the profits, and retire happily to tinker away at more innovative programs.

"I'm sure it's a real boon to depositors," she said dryly, "but it's still illegal. You can't market it."

"Oh, it's not for public knowledge, it's just goofing around. You'd think banks would have better security programs, but I haven't found one yet that's much of a challenge."

Grace propped her chin on her hand and eyed him. "My boy, you're either going to be famous, or in jail."

He ducked his head, grinning. "I've got something else to show you," he said enthusiastically, his fingers darting over the keyboard as he exited the bank's accounting records.

Grace watched as the screen changed rapidly, flickering from one display to another. "Won't they be able to tell you've been in their files?"

"Not with this baby. See, I got in through a legitimate password. Basically, I put on an electronic sheepskin, and they never knew a wolf was prowling around."

"How did you get the password?"

"Snooping. No matter how coded the info, there's always a back door. Not that your bank has very good computer security," he said with obvious disapproval. "If I were you, I'd consider moving my account."

"I'll think about it," she assured him, with a baleful glare that had him grinning again.

"That's just part of the program. Here's the accounting system." He pulled up another screen and motioned Grace closer. She obligingly scooted her chair forward an inch or so, and he launched into the intricacies of his digitalized baby. Grace paid attention, because she could easily see it *was* a good system, deceptively simple to execute. He had programmed it to compare the current entry against past entries in the same account, so if anyone accidentally typed in, say, "$115.00" instead of "$15.00," the program alerted the user that the amount wasn't within the previously established range, and to check for an input error.

"I like that," she mused. She had always paid bills and done her bookkeeping the old-fashioned way, by hand and on paper. However, she was completely at home with computers, so there was no reason for her not to do their household finances electronically.

Kristian beamed. "I knew you would." His long fingers stroked the keys, downloading the program into her hard disk. "Its name is Go Figure."

She groaned at the sly corniness of it, the groan changing midway into a laugh. "Do me a favor. When you get busted for playing around in the bank's computers, don't tell the feds that I have a copy of the program, okay?"

"I'm telling you, it's safe, at least until the banks change all their passwords. Then you simply won't be able to get in. *I* could get in," he boasted, "but most people couldn't. Here, let me give you a list of the passwords."

"I don't want it," she said quickly, but Kristian ignored her. He rifled through a stack of papers and plucked out three sheets of closely printed material, which he stuck in her computer case.

"There. Now you'll have it if you need it." He paused, staring at the computer with the ongoing chess game. His opponent had made a move. He studied the board, head cocked slightly to one side, then he chortled. "Aha! I know that gambit, and it won't work." Gleefully he moved a knight and clicked the mouse.

"Who are you playing with?"

"I dunno," he said absently. "He calls himself the Fishman."

Grace blinked, staring at the screen. Naw, it couldn't be. Kristian was playing with someone who had probably chosen that Net name with malice aforethought, to trick people into making just that assumption. The real Bobby

Fischer wouldn't be surfing the Net looking for games; he could play anyone, anywhere, and get paid huge amounts of money for doing it.

"Who usually wins?"

"We're about even. He's good," Kristian allowed as he rehooked his other desktop.

Grace opened her purse and pulled out her checkbook. "Want a pizza?" she asked.

His head cocked as he pulled his mind back from cyberspace to check the status of his stomach. "Boy, do I ever," he declared. "I'm starving."

"Then call it in; this one's on me."

"Are you going to stay and split it with me?"

She shook her head. "I can't. I have things waiting for me at home." She barely controlled a blush. Ford would have roared with laughter if he'd heard her.

She wrote out a check for fifty dollars, then pulled out a twenty to pay for the pizza. "Thanks, buddy. You're a lifesaver."

Kristian took the check and tip, grinning as he looked at it. "This is going to be a good career, isn't it?" he asked, beaming.

Grace had to laugh. "If you can stay out of jail." She placed the laptop in the case and balanced the repaired modem on top of her unzipped purse. Kristian gallantly took the heavy case from her and carried it downstairs for her. Neither of his parents was in sight, but the sounds of gunshots and a car chase drifted from the den and pinpointed their location; both of the older Siebers unabashedly loved Arnold Schwarzenegger's action movies.

Kristian's gallantry lasted only as far as the kitchen, where the proximity to food reminded him of the pizza he hadn't yet ordered. Grace retrieved the computer case from him as he halted at the wall phone. "Thanks, Kris," she said, and left the same way she had entered, through the darkened laundry room and out the back door.

She paused for a moment to let her eyes adjust to the darkness. During the time she had been with Kristian, clouds had rolled in to block most of the starlight, though here and there was a clear patch of sky. Crickets chirped, and a cool breeze stirred around her, bringing with it the scent of rain.

The light from her kitchen window, fifty yards to the right, was like a beacon. Ford was there, waiting for her. Warmth filled her and she smiled, thinking of him. She began walking toward her home, stepping carefully in the darkness so she wouldn't stumble over some unevenness in the ground, the soft spring grass cushioning her movements in silence.

She was in the Murchisons' backyard when she saw someone in her kitchen, briefly framed by the window as he moved past it. Grace paused, frowning a little; that hadn't looked like either Ford or Bryant.

Oh, Lord, they had company. Her frown deepened. It was probably someone interested in archaeology or associated with the Foundation. College kids pondering a career in archaeology sometimes dropped by to talk, and sometimes she was the one they wanted to see, if they were having a problem with Latin or Greek terms. It didn't matter. She didn't want to talk shop, she wanted to go to bed with her husband.

She was reluctant to go in, though of course she would have to; she couldn't stand out there in the dark waiting for whoever it was to leave, which could be hours. She edged to the right, trying to see if she recognized the visitor's car, hoping that it belonged to one of Bryant's friends. If so, she could signal her brother to take his friend into his side of the house.

Her familiar Buick sat in the carport, and beside it was Bryant's black Jeep Cherokee. Ford's scratched and dented Chevrolet four-wheel-drive pickup, which was used for field work, was parked off to the side. No other vehicle occupied their driveway.

That was strange. She knew they had company, because the man she'd so briefly glimpsed had had sandy-colored hair, and both Ford and Bryant were dark-haired. But unless it was a neighbor who had walked over, she had no idea how he had arrived. She knew most of their neighbors, though, and none of them fit the description of the man she'd seen.

Well, she wouldn't find out who he was until she went inside. She took a step toward the house and suddenly stopped again, squinting through the darkness. Something had moved between her and the house, something dark and furtive.

A chill ran down her spine. Icy shards of alarm ran through her veins, freezing her in place. Wild possibilities darted through her mind: a gorilla had escaped from a zoo . . . or there was a really, really big dog in her backyard.

Then it moved again, ghosting silently up to her back door. It was a man. She blinked in astonishment, wondering why someone was skulking around in her yard, and going to the back door instead of the front. A robbery? Why would any thief with half a brain break into a house where the lights were still on and the occupants were obviously at home?

Then the back door opened, and she realized the man must have knocked on it, though softly, because she hadn't heard anything. Another man stood in the door, a man she knew. There was a pistol, the barrel long and curiously thickened, in his hand.

"Nothing," the first man said, his voice low, but the night air carried the sound.

"God damn it," the other man muttered, stepping aside to let the first man enter. "I can't stop now. We'll have to go ahead and do it."

The door closed behind them. Grace stared across the dark yard at the blank expanse of her back door. Why was Parrish Sawyer there, and why did he have a pistol? He was their boss, and if he'd called to let them know he was coming over, for whatever reason, Ford would have called her to come home. They were on cordial terms with Parrish, but they had never socialized; Parrish played in the more rarefied stratosphere of the rich and well connected, qualifications Grace's family didn't have.

"Do it" — that was what he'd said. Do what? And why couldn't he stop?

Puzzled and uneasy, Grace left the shadows of the Murchisons' yard and walked across her own. She didn't know what was going on, but she was definitely going to find out.

While she had been cooking earlier she had opened the kitchen window so she could enjoy the freshness of the spring day, and it was still raised. She plainly heard Ford say, "Damn it, Parrish, what's this about?"

Ford's voice was rough, angry, with a tone in it she'd never heard before. Grace froze again with one foot lifted to the first step.

"Where is she?" Parrish asked, ignoring Ford's question. His voice was indifferent and cold, and the sound of it made the hairs lift on the back of her neck.

"I told you, the library."

A lie. Ford was deliberately lying. Grace stood still, staring at the open window and trying to picture what was happening on the other side of the wall. She couldn't see anyone, but she knew there were at least four people inside. Where was Bryant, and the man she'd seen enter the kitchen?

"Don't give me that shit. Her car's here."

"She went with a friend."

"What's this friend's name?"

"Serena, Sabrina, something like that. Tonight's the first time I've met her."

Ford had always thought fast on his feet. The names were enough out of the ordinary that it gave the lie a bit of credence, where a plain Sally wouldn't. She didn't know why Ford was lying, but the fact that he was doing it was enough for Grace. Parrish had a pistol, and Ford didn't want him to know where Grace was; something was very wrong.

"All right." It sounded as if Parrish exhaled through his teeth. "What time will she be back?"

"She didn't know. She said they had a lot of work to do. When the library closes, I guess."

"And she carried all of the documents with her."

"They were in her computer case."

"Does this Serena-Sabrina know about the documents?"

"I don't know."

"It doesn't matter." Now Parrish sounded a little bored. "I can't take the chance. All right, stand up, both of you."

She heard chairs being scraped back, and she moved silently to the right, so she could see inside the window. She was careful to stand back, so if anyone glanced out the window she wouldn't be framed in the pool of light.

She saw Bryant, shirtless, his hair damp; he must have just gotten out of the shower, which told her that Parrish and the other man had arrived not long before. Her brother's face was drawn and pale, his eyes curiously blank. Grace moved another step, and saw four more people.

There was Ford, as pale as Bryant, though his eyes glittered with a kind of anger she'd never seen before. Parrish, tall and sophisticated, his blond hair expensively styled, stood with his back to the window. The man she'd seen earlier stood beside him, and another man stood just inside the interior kitchen doorway. The man at the doorway was armed; his pistol, like Parrish's, was silenced. The third man would also be armed, Grace thought, since the other two were.

She didn't know what was going on, but she was sure of one thing: she needed the police. She would call them from the Siebers' house. She took a cautious step backward.

"Go into the bedroom, both of you," she heard Parrish say. "And don't do anything stupid, like trying to jump one of us. I can't tell you how very painful it is to be shot, but I'll be forced to demonstrate if you don't co-operate."

Why was he making them go to the bedroom? She had heard enough to know that she was the one he really wanted, and he seemed to be concerned about the documents she carried.

If Parrish wanted the documents, all he had to do was say so; he was her boss, and she worked on the assignments he gave her. It would break her heart to give up the tantalizing papers, but she couldn't stop him from taking them. Why hadn't he just called, and told her to turn them over tomorrow morning? Why had he come to her house with a gun in his hand, and brought two armed thugs with him? None of this made sense.

She started to walk quickly back to the Siebers' house, but impulse led her around the corner of the house to where she could look into the bedroom window. She waited for the light to come on, waited to hear voices in the room, but nothing happened, and abruptly she realized Parrish had taken them to Bryant's bedroom, on the other side of the house. Given the configuration of the house when they had divided it, Bryant's bedroom was at the back of the house with the kitchen. Parrish would have had to take them up the hallway to the front of the house, then through the connecting door into Bryant's part of the house and back to the bedroom.

As quickly as possible Grace retraced her steps, taking care to remain in the deepest shadows. A water hose was curled like a long, skinny snake around the protruding outside faucet; she skirted it, and also sidestepped a big sifting board one of the men had propped against the house. This was her home; she knew all its idiosyncrasies, the little traps for the unwary. She knew where the squeaks in the floor were, the cracks in the ceiling, the ruts in the yard.

Light was already shining from Bryant's window. She pressed her back against the wall and sidestepped until she was right beside it. She moved her head around, slowly, trying to move just enough that she could see inside.

One of the men stepped to the window. Grace jerked her head back and stood rigidly still, not even daring to breathe. He jerked the curtains together, shielding the window and darkening the spill of light.

Blood thundered in her ears, and sheer terror made her weak. She still couldn't breathe; her heart felt as if it were literally in her throat, suffocating her. If the man had seen her she would have been caught, for she couldn't possibly have moved.

"Sit on the bed," she heard Parrish say over

her pounding heartbeat.

Grace's lungs were finally working again. She gulped in deep breaths to steady her nerves, then once again shifted position.

The curtain hadn't quite fallen together. She moved so she could see through the slit, see Ford and Bryant —

Parrish calmly lifted his silenced pistol and shot Ford in the head, then quickly shifted his aim and shot Bryant. Her brother was dead before her husband's body had toppled to the side.

No. *No!* She hung there, paralyzed. Somehow her body was gone, vanished; she couldn't feel anything, couldn't think. A dark mist swam over her vision and the unbelievable scene receded until it was as if she saw it at the end of a long tunnel. She heard them talking, their voices oddly distorted.

"Shouldn't you have waited? There'll be a discrepancy in the times of death."

"That isn't a concern." Parrish's voice; she knew it. "In a murder-suicide, sometimes the killer waits awhile before killing himself — or herself, in this case. The shock, you understand. Such a pity, her husband and brother conducting a homosexual affair right under her nose. No wonder the poor dear got upset and went a little berserk."

"What about the friend?"

"Ah, yes. Serena-Sabrina. Bad luck for her; she'll have an unfortunate accident on the way home. I'll wait here for Grace, and you two wait in the car, follow Serena-Sabrina."

Slowly the mist cleared from Grace's vision. She wished it hadn't. She wished she had died right there, wished her heart had stopped. Through the gap in the curtains she could see her husband sprawled on his back, his eyes open and unseeing, his dark hair matted with with —

The sound rose from her chest, an almost silent keening that reverberated in her throat. It was like the distant howl of the wind, dark and soulless. The pain ripped out of her. She tried to hold it back with her teeth, but it boiled out anyway, primitive, wild. Parrish's head snapped around. For a tenth of a second — no more — she thought that their gazes met, that somehow he could see through that small gap into the night. He said something, sharply, and lunged for the window.

Grace plunged into the night.

Chapter 2

She needed money.

Grace stared through the rainy night at the ATM; it was lit like a shrine, inviting her to cross the street and perform its electronic ritual. It was thirty yards away, at most. It would take her only a couple of minutes to reach it, punch in the necessary numbers, and she would have cash in her hand.

She needed to empty out the checking account, and probably a single ATM wouldn't have enough cash on hand to give her that amount, which meant she would have to find another ATM, then another, and every time she did the odds that she would be spotted would increase — as well as the odds of being mugged.

The ATM cameras would all film her, and the police would know where she had been, and when. A sudden image of Ford blasted into her brain, paralyzing her anew with shattering pain. *God, oh God.* The inhuman, involuntary keen rose in her throat again, rattled eerily against her clenched teeth. The sound that leaked out made a prowling cat freeze with one paw uplifted, its hair standing out.

Then the animal turned and leaped and vanished into the rain-washed darkness, away from the crouched creature who emitted such a ghostly, anguished sound.

Grace rocked back and forth, pushing the pain deep inside, forcing herself to *think.* Ford had bought her safety with his life, and it would be a betrayal beyond bearing if she wasted his sacrifice by making bad decisions.

A slew of late-night withdrawals, all *after* the estimated times of death, would cement her appearance of guilt. Kristian would know what time she had left the Siebers' house, and Ford and Bryant had been killed at roughly that time. They had both been partially undressed, and in Bryant's bedroom. Parrish had set up the situation with his usual thoroughness; any cop alive would believe she had walked in on a homosexual encounter between her husband and her brother, and killed them both. Her subsequent disappearance was another point against her.

The men with Parrish had been professional in their manner; they wouldn't have done anything sloppy like leave fingerprints. No neighbors would have seen strange cars parked at the house, because they had parked elsewhere and walked to the house. There were no witnesses, no evidence to point to anyone except her.

And even if by some miracle she convinced the police she was innocent, she had no proof

Parrish had killed them. She had *seen* him do it, but she couldn't prove she had. Moreover, to the cops' way of thinking, he wouldn't have had a motive, while she obviously had plenty of motive. What could she offer as proof? A batch of papers written in a tangle of ancient languages, which she hadn't even deciphered yet, and which Parrish could have gotten from her at any time simply by telling her to turn them over to him?

There was no motive, at least none she could prove. And if she turned herself in, Parrish would get the papers, and she would end up dead. He would make certain of it. It would be made to look as if she'd hung herself, or perhaps a drug overdose would cause a brief scandal about the presence of drugs in jails and prisons, but the end result would be the same.

She had to stay alive, and out of police hands. It was the only chance she had of finding out *why* Parrish had killed Ford and Bryant — and avenging them.

To stay alive, to stay free, she had to have money. To get money, she had to use the ATMs no matter how guilty it made her look.

Would the police freeze her bank account? She didn't know, but if they did they would probably need a court order to do it. That should give her a little time — time she was wasting by huddling behind a trash bin, instead of walking across the street to the ATM and getting out what she could, while she could.

But she felt numb, almost incapable of functioning. The thirty yards might as well have been a hundred miles.

The shiny black surface of the wet pavement reflected the distorted, surreal image of the lights: the brightly colored hues of neon, the stark white of the streetlights, the never-ending, monotonous progression of the traffic light through green, yellow, red, over and over, exerting its control over nonexistent traffic. At two A.M. there was only an occasional car, and none at all for the past five minutes. No one was in sight. Now was the time to approach the ATM.

But still she crouched there, hidden from view and partially protected from the rain by the overhang of the building and the bulk of the trash bin. Her hair was plastered to her head, her sodden braid hanging limp and rain-heavy down her back. Her clothes were soaked, and even though the night was still unusually warm by Minneapolis standards, the dampness had leached the heat from her body so that she shivered with cold.

She clutched a garbage bag to her chest; it was a small bag, the type sometimes used to line the trash cans in public buildings. She had liberated it from just such a can in the ladies' rest room of the public library. The computer and the precious papers were protected inside the case, but when it had started raining she had panicked at the possibility of them getting wet, and all she could think of using to protect them was a plastic bag.

Maybe it hadn't been smart, going to the library. It was, after all, a public place, and one she frequented. On the other hand, how often did the police search libraries for suspected murderers? It was impossible for Parrish to have gotten a good look at her through that tiny slit in the bedroom curtains, but he certainly guessed she was the one lurking outside the window and had seen everything. He and his men were searching for her, but even though Ford had told them she'd gone to the library she doubted they would think she had gone *back* to one to hide.

The police might not even have been notified of the murders yet. Parrish couldn't report them without bringing himself into the picture, which he wouldn't want to do. The neighbors wouldn't have heard anything, since the shots had been silenced.

No. The police knew. Parrish wouldn't take the chance of letting days go by before the bodies — her mind stumbled on the word, but she forced herself to finish the thought — were discovered. Was there any way for forensics to tell if the pistol had been fitted with a silencer? She didn't think so. All Parrish would have to do would be to call in a "suspicious noise, like gunshots," at their address, and use a pay phone so nothing would show up on the 911 records.

Both Parrish and his henchmen, and the police, were looking for her. Still, she had gone to the main branch of the library. Instinct had led her there. She was numb with shock and horror, and the library, as familiar to her as her own house, had seemed like a haven. The smell of books, that wonderful mingling of paper and leather and ink, had been the scent of sanctuary. Dazed, at first she had simply wandered among the shelves, looking at the books that had defined the boundaries of her life until a few short hours ago, trying to recapture that sense of safety, of normalcy.

It hadn't worked. Nothing would ever be normal again.

Finally she had gone into the rest room, and stared in bewilderment at the reflection in the mirror. That white-faced, blank-eyed woman wasn't *her,* couldn't possibly be Grace St. John, who had spent her life in academia and who specialized in deciphering and translating ancient languages. The Grace St. John she was familiar with, the one whose face she had seen countless times in other mirrors, had happy blue eyes and a cheerful expression, the face of a woman who loved and was loved in return. Content. Yes, she had been content. So what if she was just a little too plump, so what if she could have been the poster girl for Bookworms Anonymous? Ford had loved her, and that was what had counted in her life.

Ford was dead.

It couldn't be. It wasn't real. Nothing that had happened was real. Maybe if she closed her eyes, when she opened them she would find herself in her own bed, and realize it had only been a ghastly nightmare, or that she was having some sort of mental breakdown. That would be a good trade, she thought as she squeezed her eyes shut. Her sanity for Ford's life. She'd go for that any day of the week.

She tried it. She squeezed her eyes really tight, concentrated on the idea that it was just a nightmare and that she was about to wake up, and everything would be all right. But when she opened her eyes, everything was the same. She still stared back at herself in the stark fluorescent light, and Ford was still dead. Ford and Bryant. Husband and brother, the only two people on earth whom she loved, and who loved her in return. They were both gone, irrevocably, finally, definitely gone. Nothing would bring them back, and she felt as if the essence of her own being had died with them. She was only a shell, and she wondered why the framework of bone and skin that she saw in the mirror didn't collapse from its own emptiness.

Then, looking into her own eyes, she'd known why she didn't collapse. She wasn't empty, as she'd thought. There was something inside after all, something wild and bottomless, a feral tangle of terror and rage and hate. She had to fight Parrish, somehow. If either he or the police caught her, then he would have won, and she couldn't bear that.

He wanted the papers. She had only begun to translate them; she didn't know what they contained, or what Parrish thought they contained. She didn't know what was so important about them that he had killed Ford and Bryant, and intended to kill her, merely because they knew these particular papers existed. Maybe Parrish thought she had deciphered more than she actually had. He didn't just want physical possession of the papers, he wanted to erase all knowledge of their existence, and their content. What was in them that her husband and brother had died because of them?

That was why she had to protect the laptop. Her computer held all her notes, her journal entries, her language programs that aided her in her work. Give her access to a modem, and she could connect to any resource on-line that she needed in her work, and she could continue her translations. She would find out why. *Why.*

To have any chance of successfully hiding, she had to have cash. Good, untraceable cash.

She had to make herself walk to that ATM. And when she'd emptied it — assuming there was any cash left in it, given the hour — she would have to find another one.

Her fingers were numb, and bloodless. The temperature had remained in the sixties, but she had been wet for hours.

She didn't know where she found the surge of energy that carried her to her feet. Perhaps it wasn't energy at all, but desperation. But suddenly she was standing, even though her knees were so stiff and weak she had to lean against the wet wall for support. She pushed away from the wall, and momentum propelled her several unsteady steps before panic and fatigue dragged at her again, slowing her to a standstill. She clutched the garbage bag to her chest, feeling the reassuring weight of the laptop within the plastic. Rain dripped down her face, and a massive black weight pressed on her chest. *Ford. Bryant.*

Damn everything.

Somehow her feet were moving again, clumsily shuffling, but moving. That was all she required, that they move.

Her purse swung awkwardly from her shoulder, banging against her hip. Her steps slowed, stopped. *Stupid!* It was a miracle she hadn't already been mugged, wandering back alleys at this time of night with her purse plainly in sight.

She edged back into the shadows, her heart thumping from a surge of panic. For a moment she stood paralyzed, afraid to move as her gaze darted around the dark alley, searching for any of the night predators who prowled the city. The narrow alley remained silent, and her breath sighed out of her. She was alone. Perhaps the rain had worked in her favor, and the homeless, the druggies, the hoodlums, had decided to take shelter somewhere.

She laughed in the darkness, the sound small and humorless. She had grown up in Minneapolis, and she had no real idea which sections of the city she should avoid. She knew her neighborhood, her routes to the university, the libraries, the post office and grocery, doctor and dentist. In the course of her work, and Ford's, she had traveled to six continents and God knows how many countries; she had thought herself well traveled, but suddenly she realized how little she knew of her own city because she had been encapsulated in her own little safe, familiar world.

To survive, she would have to be a lot smarter, a lot more aware. Street smarts meant a lot more than locking your car doors as soon as you were inside. She would have to be ready for anything, an attack from any quarter, and she would have to be ready to fight. She would have to learn to think like the night predators, or she wouldn't make it a week on the street.

Carefully she slipped the ATM card into her pocket, then huddled once again under the overhanging roof. After depositing the precious, plastic-wrapped computer on her feet, she opened her purse and began ruthlessly sorting through the contents. She took out what cash she had, stuffing it into a pocket of the computer case without bothering to count it; she knew it wasn't much, maybe forty or fifty dollars, because she didn't normally carry much cash. She hesitated over the checkbook, but decided to take it; she might be able to use it, though a paper trail was dangerous. Ditto for the American Express card. She dropped both of them into the plastic bag. Any use they had, though, would be immediate and short-term. She would have to leave Minneapolis, and after she did, using either checks or a credit card would lead the police right to her.

There were several photos in the plastic pockets. She didn't have to see them to know what they were. Her fingers trembling, she pulled the entire photo protector out of her wallet and slipped it too into the bag.

Okay, what else? There were her driver's license and social security card, but what good were they now? The license would only identify her, which she wanted to avoid, and as for the social security card — a hollow laugh escaped her. She didn't think she had much chance of living to collect social security.

Any identification she left behind would undoubtedly be found and used by the street scavengers, which might help dilute the police search for her if they had to run down leads that had nothing to do with her. She left the cards, and on impulse dug the checkbook out of the plastic bag. After carefully tearing out one check and storing it in the same pocket with her cash, she dropped the checkbook back into her purse.

She left the tube of lip balm, but couldn't bear not having a comb. Another eerie, hollow laugh sounded in her throat; her husband and brother had just been murdered, the police were after her, and she was worried about being *unkempt?* Nevertheless, the comb went into the bag.

Her scrabbling fingers touched several pens and mechanical pencils, and without thought she took two of them. They were as essential to her work as the computer, because sometimes, when she was stumped on deciphering a particularly obscure passage or word, actually rewriting the words in her own hand would form a link of recognition between her brain and her eyes, and suddenly she would understand at least some of the words as she saw similarities to other languages, other alphabets. She had to have the pens.

There was her bulky appointment book. She ignored it, shutting it out of her thoughts. It held the minutiae of a life that no longer existed: the appointments and lists and reminders. She didn't want to see the scribbled notation for Ford's next dental cleaning, or the sappy heart he'd drawn on the calendar on her birthdate.

She left her business cards — she'd never

used them much, anyway. She left the small pack of tissues, the spray bottle of eyeglass cleaner, the roll of antacid tablets, the breath mints. She took the metal nail file, tucking it into her pocket. It wasn't much, but it was the only thing she possessed in the way of a weapon. She hesitated over her car keys, wondering if perhaps she could sneak back and get either her car or Ford's truck. No. That was stupid. She left the keys. With both the keys and her address, perhaps whoever found the purse would steal either the car or the truck, or both, and lead the police astray even more.

Chewing gum, rubber bands, a magnifying glass . . . she identified all of those by feel, and removed only the magnifying glass, which she needed for work. Why had she been carrying so much *junk* around? A flicker of impatience licked at her, the first emotion other than grief and despair that had seeped through the numbness that surrounded her. It wasn't just her purse; she couldn't afford to make any mistakes, carry any excess baggage, let anything interfere with her focus. From this second forward, she would have to do whatever was necessary. There couldn't be any more wasting of precious time and energy because she was paralyzed by fear. She had to *act,* without hesitation, or Parrish would win.

Grimly she tossed the purse on top of the trash bin, and heard a faint squeak and scrabble as a scavenging rat was disturbed. Somehow she made her feet begin moving again, shuffling across the littered alley, painfully inching from safety to exposure.

The headlights of an approaching car made her freeze just before stepping onto the sidewalk. It passed, tires swishing on the wet pavement, the driver not even bothering to glance at the bedraggled figure standing between two buildings.

The car turned right at the next intersection, and disappeared from view. Grace focused on the ATM, took a deep breath, and walked. She was staring so hard at the brightly lit machine that she missed the curb and stumbled, twisting her right ankle. She ignored the pain, not letting herself stop. Athletes walked off pain all the time; she could do the same.

The ATM loomed closer and closer, brighter and brighter. She wanted to run, to return to the safety of the trash bin. She might as well have been naked; the sensation of being exposed was so powerful that she shuddered, fighting for control. Anyone could be watching her, waiting for her to finish the transaction before mugging her, taking the money, and perhaps killing her in the process. The ATM camera would be watching her now, recording every move.

She tried to recall how much money was in the checking account. Damn it, she'd thrown away the checkbook without looking at the balance! There was no way she was going to go back to that alley and climb into the trash bin to search for her purse, even assuming she could manage the exertion. She would simply withdraw money until the machine stopped her.

The machine stopped her at three hundred dollars.

She stared at the computer screen in bewilderment. "Transaction Denied." She *knew* there was more than that in the account, there was more than two thousand — not a great amount, but it could mean the difference between death and survival for her. She knew there was a limit on what she could withdraw in a single transaction, but why had the machine balked at the second one?

Maybe there wasn't enough cash left in the ATM to fill the request. She started over, punching in her code, and this time she requested only one hundred.

"Transaction Denied."

Panic shot through her stomach, twisting it into knots. Oh, God, the police couldn't have frozen the account so soon, could they?

No. *No.* It was impossible. The banks were closed. Something might be done first thing in the morning, but nothing could have happened yet. The machine was just out of money. That was all it was.

Hurriedly, she stuffed the three hundred dollars into her pockets, dividing it up so that if she were mugged, she might be able to get away with emptying out only one pocket. She only hoped nothing would happen to the computer; she would hand over the money without argument, but she would fight for the computer and those precious files. Without them, she would never know why Ford and Bryant had died, and she had to know. It wouldn't be enough to avenge them; she had to know *why*.

She began walking hurriedly, desperation driving her numb feet. She had to find another ATM, get more money. But where *was* another one? Until now, she had used only the one located at her local bank branch, but she knew she had seen others. They were located at malls, but malls were closed at this hour. She tried to think of places that were open twenty-four hours a day, and also had ATMs. Grocery stores, maybe? She remembered when she had opened the account, the bank had given her a booklet listing all its ATM "convenient locations," but she wasn't finding them all that damn convenient.

"Gimme the money."

They materialized in front of her, lunging out of an alley so fast she had no time to react. There were two of them, one white, one black, both feral. The white guy jabbed a knife at her, the blade glinting ghostly pale in the rain-filtered streetlight. "Don't fuck wi' me, bitch," he breathed, his breath more lethal than the weapon. "Just gimme the money." He was short a few teeth and a lot of intelligence.

Wordlessly she stuck her hand into her pocket and took out the fold of money. She knew she should be scared, but evidently the human mind could sustain fear only to a certain level, and anything after that simply didn't register.

The black guy grabbed the money, and the other one jabbed the knife closer, this time at her face. Grace jerked her head back just in time to keep the blade from slicing across her chin. "I saw you, bitch. Gimme the rest of it."

So much for her grand scheme; they had probably been watching her from the time she crossed the street. She reached into her other pocket, and managed to wedge her fingers inside the fold so that she brought out only half of it. The black guy snatched it, too.

Then they were gone, pelting back into the alley, melting into the darkness. They hadn't even asked about the plastic bag she carried. They'd been after cash, not something that required extra trouble. At least she still had the computer. Grace closed her eyes, and fought to keep her knees from buckling under the crushing weight of despair. At least she still had the computer. She didn't have her husband, or her brother, but at least she still had . . . the . . . *damn* . . . computer.

The harsh, howling sound startled her. It was a moment before she realized it came from her own throat, another moment before she realized that she was walking again, somehow, somewhere. Rain dripped down at her face, or at least she thought it was rain. She couldn't feel herself crying, but then she couldn't feel herself walking, either; she was simply moving. Maybe she *was* crying, useless as that would be. Rain, tears, what difference did it make?

She still had the computer.

Computer. Kristian.

Oh, God. Kristian.

She had to warn him. If Parrish had any inkling Kristian knew about the files, much less part of their content, he wouldn't hesitate to kill the boy.

Pay telephones, thank God, were far more plentiful and convenient than ATMs. She fished some change out of the bag, desperately clutching the coins in her wet palm as she crossed one corner and hurried up the block, then turned at another street, wanting to put plenty of distance between her and the two muggers before she stopped. God, the streets were so deserted, something she would never have imagined in a metro area the size of Minneapolis–St. Paul. Her footsteps echoed; her breathing sounded ragged and uneven, unnaturally loud. The rain dripped from eaves and awnings, and the buildings towered high and close over her, with the occasional lighted window indicating some poor office prisoner pulling an all-nighter. She was a world removed from them, all dry and warm in their steel and glass cocoons, while she hurried through the rain and tried to be invisible.

Finally, panting, she stopped at a pay phone. It wasn't in a booth, they seldom were now, just a phone with three small pieces of clear plastic forming shelters on each side and overhead. At least it had a shelf for her to rest the bag on, propping it in place with her body while she held the receiver between her head and shoulder and fumbled a quarter into the slot. She couldn't remember Kristian's number but her fingers did, dancing in the familiar pattern without direction from her brain.

The first ring was still buzzing in her ear when it abruptly stopped and Kristian's voice said, "Hello?" He sounded tense, unusually alert for this time of night — or rather, morning.

"Kris." The word was nothing more than a croak. She cleared her throat and tried again. "Kris, it's Grace."

"Grace, my God! Cops are everywhere, and they said —" He stopped suddenly and lowered his voice, his whisper forceful and almost fierce. "Are you all right? Where are you?"

All right? How could she be all right? Ford and Bryant were dead, and there was a great empty hole in her chest. She would never be all right again. She was, however, physically unharmed, and she knew that was what he was asking. From his question, she also knew that

Parrish had indeed called the police; the quiet neighborhood must be in a turmoil.

"I saw it happen," she said, her throat so constricted that her voice sounded like a stranger's, flat and empty. "They're going to say I did it, but I didn't, I swear. Parrish did. I saw him."

"Parrish? Parrish Sawyer, your boss? That Parrish? Are you sure? What happened?"

She waited until the barrage of questions had halted. "I *saw* him," she repeated. "Listen, have they questioned you yet?"

"A little. They wanted to know what time you left here."

"Did you mention the documents I'm working on?"

"No." His voice was positive. "They asked why you were here, and I said you brought your modem over for me to repair. That's it."

"Good. Whatever you do, don't mention the documents. If anyone asks, just say you didn't see any papers at all."

"Okay, but why?"

"So Parrish won't kill you, too." Her teeth began to chatter. Oh, God, she was so cold, the light wind cutting through her wet clothes. "I'm not kidding. Promise me you won't let anyone know you have any idea I was working on anything. I don't know what's in these papers, but he intends to get rid of everyone who knows of their existence."

There was silence on the line, then Kristian

said in bewilderment, "You mean he doesn't want us to know about that Knight Templar guy you were trying to track down? He lived seven centuries ago, if he existed at all! Who the hell cares?"

"Parrish does." She didn't know why, but she intended to find out. "Parrish does," she repeated, her voice trailing off.

She listened to his breathing, the sound quick and shallow, amplified by the phone. "Okay, I'll keep my mouth shut. I promise." He paused. "Do you need any help? You can borrow my car —"

She almost laughed. Despite everything, the sound bubbled up in her throat and hung there, unable to work its way past restricted muscles. Kristian's mechanical monument to testosterone was a sure attention-getter, the one thing she most wanted to avoid. "No, thanks," she managed to say. "What I need is money, but the ATM I just tried ran out of cash, and I was mugged as soon as I walked away from it anyway."

"I doubt it," he said.

He doubted that she was mugged? "What?" She was so tired she could barely move or think, but surely he couldn't mean that.

"I doubt it was out of money," he said. Suddenly his voice sounded older, taking on the cool intensity that meant he was thinking of computers. "How much did you take out?"

"Three hundred. Isn't that the limit for each

transaction? I remember the banker said something about three hundred dollars when we set up our account."

"Not three hundred per transaction," Kristian patiently explained. "Three hundred per *day*. You could make as many transactions as you wanted, until the total reached three hundred for that twenty-four-hour period. Each bank sets its own limit, and the limit for your bank is three hundred."

His explanation fell on her like words of doom. Even if she found another ATM, she wouldn't be able to get more money until this time tomorrow morning. She couldn't wait that long. If the police could freeze her account, they would definitely have it done by then. And she needed to get out of Minneapolis, to find some safe hiding place where she could work on the documents and find out just why Parrish had killed Ford and Bryant. To do that, she had to have money; she had to have access to a phone, to resource material.

"I'm sunk," she said, her tone leaden.

"No!" He almost yelled the word. More softly he repeated, "No. I can fix that. How much is your balance?"

"I don't know exactly. A couple of thousand."

"Find another ATM," he instructed. "I'll get into your bank's computer, change the limit to . . . say, five thousand. Empty out your account, then I'll change the limit back to the original amount. They'll never know how it happened, I promise."

Hope bloomed inside her, a strange sensation after those past nightmare hours. All she had to do was find another ATM, something easier said than done when she was on foot.

"Look in the phone directory," he was saying. "Every branch of your bank will have an ATM. Pick the closest one and go there."

Of course. How simple. Normally she would have thought of that herself, and the fact that she hadn't was a measure of her shock and exhaustion.

"Okay." Thank heavens, there was still a directory chained to the shelf. She opened the protective cover. Well, there was part of a directory, at least, and it contained the most important part, the Yellow Pages. She thumbed through them until she reached "Banks," and located her own bank, which had sixteen of those so-called convenient locations.

She estimated it would take her half an hour to get to the nearest one. "I'm going now," she said. "I'll be there in thirty to forty-five minutes, unless something happens." She could be picked up by the police, or mugged again, or Parrish and his goons might be out cruising the city, looking for her. None of the things that could happen to her would be pleasant.

"Call me," Kristian said urgently. "I'll get

into the bank's computer now, but call me and let me know if everything went okay."

"I will," she promised.

The thirty-minute walk took almost an hour. She was exhausted, and the laptop gained weight with each step she took. She had to hide every time a car went past, and once a patrol car sped through an intersection just ahead of her, lights whirring in eerie silence. The spurt of panic left her weak and shaking, her heart pounding.

Her familiarity with the downtown area was limited to specific destinations. She had lived, gone to school, and shopped in the suburbs. She took a wrong turn and went several blocks out of her way before she realized what she had done, and had to backtrack. She was acutely aware of the seconds ticking away toward dawn, when people would be getting up and turning on their televisions, and learning about the double murder in her quiet neighborhood. The police would have photographs of her, taken from the house, and her face might be on hundreds of thousands of screens. She needed to be somewhere safe before then.

Finally she reached the branch bank, with the lovely ATM on the front of it, all lit up and watched over by the security camera, so if someone got killed right there they'd have a tape of the murder to show on the evening news.

She was too tired to worry about the camera, or the possibility that another couple of jerks might be watching her. Just let someone else try to mug her. The next time, she would fight; she had nothing to lose, because the money meant her life. She walked right up to the machine, took out her bank card, and followed the instructions, asking for a full two thousand.

The obedient machine began regurgitating twenty-dollar bills. It coughed up a hundred of them before it stopped. Oh, blessed automation!

What with the three hundred she had already withdrawn, she didn't think there could be much left. She didn't try to find out the exact amount, not with two thousand dollars in her hand and time pressing hard on her. She darted around the corner and hid herself in the shadows, hunkering down against the wall and hurriedly stuffing bills inside the computer case, in her pockets, in the cups of her bra, inside her shoes. All the while she scanned the area for movement, but the streets were quiet and empty. The night predators would be heading for their lairs now, turning the city back over to the day denizens.

Maybe. She couldn't afford to take any chances now. She needed some kind of weapon, anything, no matter how primitive, with which she could protect herself. She looked around, hoping to find a sturdy stick, but the only things littering the ground were small pieces of glass and a few rocks.

Well, weapons didn't get much more primitive than rocks, did they?

She picked up the biggest ones, slipping all but one into her pocket. That one, the biggest one, she kept clutched in her hand. She was aware of how pitiful this defense was, but at the same time she felt oddly comforted. Any defense was better than none.

She had to call Kristian, and she had to get out of Minneapolis. She wanted nothing more than to lie down and sleep, to be able to forget for just a few hours, but the luxury of rest would have to wait. Instead Grace hurried through the streets as the sky began to lighten, and the sun began to rise on her first day as a widow.

Chapter 3

"It shouldn't be difficult to find her," Parrish Sawyer murmured, leaning back in his chair and tapping his immaculately manicured nails against the wooden arm. "I'm sadly disappointed in the Minneapolis Police Department. Little Grace has no car, no survival skills, yet still she's managed to elude them. That really surprises me; I expected her to run screaming to a neighbor, or to the first policeman she could find, but no, instead she's gone to earth somewhere. Annoying of her, but all she's doing is delaying the inevitable. If the police can't find her, I'm confident you can."

"Yes," Conrad said. He didn't elaborate. He was a man of few words, but over the years Parrish had found him extremely reliable. Conrad could have been either his first or last name; no one knew. He was stocky and muscular and didn't look very bright; his bullet-shaped head was covered by short dark hair that grew low on his forehead, an unfortunate apelike resemblance that was only heightened by his small dark eyes and prominent brow ridges. His appearance, however, was deceiving. His chunky body could move with amazing speed and finesse, and behind his stolid expression was a brain that was both astute and concise. Best of all, Parrish had never seen Conrad exhibit any distressing signs of conscience. He carried out orders with admirable, machinelike precision, and what he thought of them no one but himself ever knew.

"When you find her," Parrish continued, "bring the computer and the papers to me immediately." He didn't give any instructions on how to deal with Grace St. John; Conrad wouldn't need direction on anything that simple.

There was a sharp, slight incline of the bullet head, and Conrad silently left the room. Alone, Parrish sighed, his fingers still drumming out his frustration with the situation.

It had turned unaccountably messy. Nothing had gone as planned. They should have been there, all three of them; he had made certain all three vehicles had been present before going in. But Grace hadn't been there, and neither had her computer or the documents. Moreover, Ford and Bryant had been remarkably good liars; Parrish hadn't expected it of them, and he didn't like being surprised. Who would have thought two nerdish archaeologists would have sized up the situation so accurately, and in an instant formulated a very believable lie?

But they had, and he'd made a very bad mistake in believing them. Such gullibility wasn't at all like him, and the sense of having been made a fool of was irritating.

Unfortunately, it seemed Grace had been just outside the house, watching and listening. That strange little sound he'd heard outside the window had probably been her; leaving a gap in the curtains, even a tiny one, had been another uncharacteristic mistake. Some days were just a *bitch.*

He and Conrad's team had quickly withdrawn, leaving no fingerprints or other sign of their presence behind, and the scene in the bedroom had looked pretty much as they had planned. Any cop walking in on that, two men half-naked together in a bedroom, both of them shot in the head, and one's wife missing — well, it wouldn't take a genius to figure it out. Minneapolis's finest had reacted just as he had expected; they were being circumspect, keeping details from the media, but Grace was their prime suspect.

He had thought she would seek help immediately, so he had returned to his luxurious home in Wayzata to wait. He wasn't worried about her accusations; after all, why would he kill two people in order to steal some documents he could obtain by simply asking for them? He was a respected and well-connected member of the community. He was on two hospital boards, he gave regularly and generously to all the politically correct charities, and several of the richest families in Minnesota had hopes — useless ones, of course — of enticing him into the fold by way of marriage. Moreover, he had an alibi in the form of his housekeeper, Antonetta Dolk. She would swear he had been working in his study all evening, that she had even taken coffee to him. Antonetta could pass any lie-detector test devised by man, a useful ability in a housekeeper, and one he valued far more than dusting. She worked, of course, for the Foundation; he had surrounded himself with people loyal only to him.

To think that the documents had surfaced after so long! They had come out of an insignificant dig in southern France, a dig that had produced so little, and nothing that appeared of any great age, that the documents hadn't drawn any attention. Certainly no one whose job it was to evaluate all finds and report anything interesting to him had found anything intriguing in documents that seemed to be only a few centuries old. He would have to take care of the bungler — another job for Conrad. If the documents had been correctly evaluated, they would never have been photographed, stored, and the photographs sent to Grace St. John for routine translation. None of this would have happened, and the information would be in his hands instead of Grace's.

It was Ford who had alerted him to the content of the obscure documents, and therefore caused his own death. Life could be so ironic, Parrish thought. Ford's chance comment about Grace's latest project, something about the Knights Templar, had set events into motion.

Parrish had quickly checked the assignment records and traced the original documents to their storage location in Paris. The French could be so difficult about allowing artifacts, even not-so-old ones, out of the country. Parrish had sent his people in to retrieve the papers, only to find that they had been destroyed, apparently by fire — though nothing else in the vault had been damaged. Nothing remained of the documents except a fine, white ash.

Grace St. John had the only existing copies. And according to the assignment record, she had been working on the translation for three days. Grace was good at her job; in fact, she was the best language expert on staff. He couldn't take the chance that she had already deciphered enough of the documents to know what she had; she, and everyone else who knew what she'd been working on, had to be eliminated.

Strange that Grace should prove more difficult than either Ford or Bryant. How long had he known her? Almost ten years? She had always seemed such a shy, mousy type, no makeup, her hair scraped back in an unflattering braid, slightly overweight. Her complete lack of style was an affront to his sensibilities. For all that, several times over the years he had been tempted to seduce her. Likely he had been bored, between women; little Grace presented something of a challenge, with her ridiculous middle-class morals. She "loved" her husband, and was faithful to him. But she had perfect skin, like translucent porcelain, and the most astonishingly carnal mouth he'd ever seen. Parrish smiled, feeling the blood pool in his groin as he considered the uses to which he could put that mouth, so wide and soft and pouty. Poor old Ford had certainly lacked the imagination to enjoy her as he could have!

She would be as helpless in the streets as any child. Anything could have happened to her during the night. She might already be dead.

If so, one problem would be conveniently solved, but he sincerely hoped she was still alive. She would keep the papers with her, and when Conrad found her, he would find the papers. If any of the human trash that prowled the streets at night killed her, however, her computer would be taken and fenced, and the papers thrown away. Once the copied documents disappeared into the maw of the night world, they would likely never surface again. They would be gone, and with them the long-searched-for, critical information. There would no longer be a purpose in the Foundation, and his plans would be reduced to so much ash, just like the original documents.

That couldn't be allowed to happen. One way or another, he would get those papers.

Grace couldn't sleep. She was exhausted, but every time she closed her eyes she saw Ford, the sudden, horrible blankness of his eyes as the bullet snuffed out his life, saw him toppling over on the bed.

It was still raining. She sat huddled in a metal storage building, hidden behind a lawn mower that was missing a wheel, a greasy tool box, some rusting cans of paint, and several moldy cardboard boxes marked "Xmas Decorations." The eight-by-ten building hadn't been locked, but then there wasn't anything in it worth stealing, except for a few wrenches and screwdrivers.

She wasn't certain exactly where she was. She had simply walked north until she was too tired to walk any farther, then taken refuge in the storage building behind a 'fifties-style ranch house. The neighborhood was showing signs of raggedness as its lower-middle-class respectability slowly deteriorated. No cars were parked in the carport, so she had taken the chance that no one was there. If any neighbors were at home, the rain had kept them indoors, and no one shouted at her as she walked slowly across the backyard and opened the flimsy metal door.

She had scrambled over the clutter until she

reached a back corner, then settled down on the dirty cement. She had sat in a stupor, staring at nothing. Time passed, but she had no grasp of it. After a while she heard a car drive up, and several car doors slammed. Kids yelled and argued, and a woman's voice irritably told them to shut up. There was the squeak of a storm door opening, then the slam of another door, and the human clatter was silenced behind walls that held warmth and normalcy.

Grace leaned her head on her knees. She was so tired, and so hungry. She didn't know what to do next.

Ford and Bryant would be buried, and she wouldn't be there to see them one last time, to touch them, to put flowers on their graves.

Her throat worked, closing tight on the surge of grief that made her rock back and forth. She felt herself flying apart, felt her control shredding, and she hugged her arms tightly as if she could hold everything together that way.

She had never even taken Ford's name, Wessner, as her own. She had kept her maiden name, St. John. The reasons had been so practical, so modern; her degree had been awarded to Grace St. John, and there was her driver's license, her social security, so much paperwork to be changed if she changed her name. And, of course, Minneapolis was in the vanguard of political correctness; it would have been considered hopelessly gauche by the academic crowd if she had taken Ford's name.

The pain was almost unbearable. Ford had been willing to die for her, but she hadn't been willing to use his surname as her own. He'd never asked, never even mentioned it; knowing Ford, it hadn't been important to him. He'd been so *grounded;* their marriage had mattered to him, not what name she used. But suddenly, to her, it mattered. She yearned for that link to him, a link she would never have now, any more than she would ever have his children.

They had planned to have two. They had talked about it, but put parenthood off while they both built their careers. After this past Christmas, they had decided to wait another year, and Grace had continued taking her birth control pills.

Now Ford was dead, and the useless pills had been left behind in a house to which she would never return.

Oh, God, Ford!

She couldn't bear this. The pain was too great. She had to do something or she would lose her mind, run screaming from this filthy little metal building and stand in the middle of the street until she was either arrested or killed.

Jerkily she pulled the computer case from the plastic bag. The light in the building was a dim, muted green, too poor to do any translation work off the copies themselves, but she had already had some of them transferred to disk and she could work on the computer. She was too tired to get much accomplished, but she desperately needed a few minutes of distraction. She had always been able to lose herself in her work; maybe this time it would save her sanity.

She didn't have much room, crammed in the corner the way she was. She repositioned the boxes of Christmas decorations, sliding one in front of her to use as a desk; she knew from experience that the laptop generated too much heat to rest it on her legs. She slapped down the mouse pad, then opened the top of the computer and pushed the switch on the side. The screen lit and the machine made its musical electronic noises as it went through the booting process. When the menu appeared on the screen, she moved the cursor down to the program she wanted and clicked the mouse. She already knew which disk she wanted, and had it ready to slide into the A drive.

The disk contained the section she had been working on before, when curiosity had led her to do more research on the Knights Templar. The language was Old French, something she was so familiar with that she should be able to work even with her mind so numb.

She accessed the file, and the words filled the screen. The letters were indistinct with age, strangely formed, and medieval people had been very creative spellers. There hadn't been any standardized spellings back then, so people had used whatever sounded right to them.

Grace stared at the screen, slowly scrolling as she read and reestablished herself in the work. Despite everything, she could feel her concentration gathering, her focus narrowing as the documents pulled her into their power. The name popped out at her again, "Niall of Scotland," and she took a deep breath. She eased down into a cross-legged position on the concrete, moving closer to the computer as she automatically fished out a pen and the pad that was always in the computer case for taking notes.

Whoever this Niall of Scotland had been before joining the Order, he had quickly become renowned as its greatest warrior. She skimmed over the cramped lines on the screen, jotting down notes on sections she couldn't quite make out, or on words that were unfamiliar to her. She didn't notice her heartbeat speeding, or feel the increased oxygen boosting her concentration. Instead she felt as if she were being sucked into the screen, into the epic account of a monk who had lived and died almost seven hundred years before.

Niall had been "of great size, three *elnes* and five more." Since this document was in French, Grace decided the measurement would more likely have been a Flemish *ell*, twenty-seven inches, rather than an English one of thirty-seven inches. And though Niall had been Scots, the Scots *ell* was something like forty-five inches, which meant that by Scots measurement three *ells* and five inches would have placed him close to twelve feet tall. The Flemish *ell* was more reasonable, making the man stand about six feet four, tall for his time but not freakishly so. Medieval people had been of varying sizes, depending on their nutrition during childhood. Some knights had been ridiculously small, their suits of armor looking as if they had been made for children, while others had been big even by modern standards.

According to this paean, Niall had been unsurpassed in swordsmanship and the other arts of war. There was account after account of battles he had fought, Saracens he had killed, fellow Knights he had saved. Grace felt as if she were reading a tale of a mythical hero along the lines of Hercules, rather than a Middle Ages record of an actual Templar. Granted, the Templars had been superb soldiers, the best of their time and the equivalent of modern-day special forces. But if the Templars had been such good soldiers, why had Niall of Scotland been singled out for excessive praise? She assumed she was reading actual records of the Knights Templar, and while outsiders would understandably be impressed by the great Knights, the Knights themselves would take such exploits for granted. It seemed unlikely they would aggrandize the accomplishments of one.

She scrolled down, and there was a break in the narrative. The text picked up on what seemed to be a letter, signed by someone named Valcour. He expressed concerns about the safety of "the Treasure," and the importance of protecting this, which had worth "greater than gold."

Treasure. Grace stretched her back, rotating her shoulders to ease the kinks. She didn't know how long she had been staring at the computer, but her feet were asleep and her neck and shoulder muscles tight with strain. There had been something about a treasure in the material she had read on Kristian's computer, but she had been skimming, looking for any mention of Niall of Scotland, and she hadn't read it closely. She did remember that the Knights Templar had been an extremely wealthy order, so much so that kings and popes had borrowed gold from them. Their treasure had been gold, so how could its worth be "greater than gold"?

She had been holding fatigue at bay by the sheer force of her concentration, but now it hit her again, pulling at her limbs and eyelids. Her hands were suddenly clumsy as she exited the program and removed the disk, fumbling it back into its protective sleeve. She turned off the computer and scooted back, almost groaning aloud as she stretched out her numb legs and renewed blood flow surged painfully through her veins.

Clumsily she edged herself around, propping herself up against the boxes of decorations. She could feel sleep coming, rushing toward her like a black tide of unconsciousness. She welcomed it, desperately needing the surcease. Her eyelids were too heavy to remain open a second longer. Her last thought was "Niall," and she had a brief picture of him, tall and powerful, swinging a six-foot sword with one iron-hewn arm while enemies fell dead all about him, before she slipped completely beneath the tide.

1322

Six hundred and seventy-five years away, Niall awoke with every nerve alert, his head lifting from his pillow. A single candle guttered in its holder, and the fire in the hearth had almost burned out. He had been asleep for almost an hour, he estimated, relaxed by some energetic love play. He had heard — what? Only the slightest whisper of sound, different but somehow nonthreatening. Normally, if he was awakened suddenly he had a dagger in one hand and a sword in the other even before his eyes were fully opened. He hadn't reached for his weapons, which meant his battle-trained senses hadn't detected any danger.

But something had awakened him, and the sound had been near. He looked at the woman sleeping beside him, softly snoring, the noise little more than a snuffle. That wasn't what had disturbed him.

They were alone in the chamber, the thick door securely barred, and the secret door beside the hearth was closed. Robert never came without first sending a message. But Niall felt as if someone had been there, and the sudden presence of a stranger had jerked him awake.

He got out of bed, his movements so silent and controlled that Eara slept on undisturbed. Though he could *see* no one was in the chamber with him except for the woman in bed, still he prowled the perimeter, trying to detect a scent, a whisper of sound, anything.

There was nothing. Finally he went back to bed and lay awake, staring into the night. Eara still snored beside him, and he began to feel irritated. He should have sent her to her own pallet after they had finished. He liked sleeping with women, liked the warmth and softness of their bodies beside him, but tonight he would have preferred being alone. He felt a vague need to concentrate on the elusive sound that had awakened him, and Eara's presence was distracting.

He tried to remember exactly how the noise had sounded. It had been soft, almost like a sigh.

Someone had called his name.

1996

Conrad gripped the punk's greasy hair, jerking his lolling head back. He studied the effects of his work. Both of the punk's eyes were swollen nearly shut, his nose was a bleeding mass of crushed cartilage, and instead of missing just a few teeth he now had few left. That had been nothing more than the softening up, though. The real persuasion had taken the form of broken ribs and fingers.

"You saw her," he said softly. "You robbed her."

"No, man —" The words were mushy, almost unintelligible.

That wasn't the answer Conrad wanted. He sighed, and twisted one of the broken fingers. The punk screamed, his body arching against the tape that held his ankles strapped to the chair legs and his wrists lashed to the wooden arms.

"You saw her," he repeated patiently.

"We don' have the money no more!" the punk sobbed, his minuscule store of courage already depleted.

"I am not interested in the money. Where did the woman go?"

"We got th' hell outta there, man! We din' hang around, y'know?"

Conrad thought about it. The punk was

probably telling the truth. He glanced at the crumpled body behind the chair. Too bad the young black man had used very bad judgment and pulled a knife on him. Perhaps he would have noticed something this cretin hadn't.

To be certain, he twisted another finger, and waited until the screams subsided. "Where did the woman go?" he asked again.

"I don' know, I don' know, I don' know!"

Satisfied, Conrad nodded. "What was she wearing?"

"I don' know —"

Conrad reached for a finger, and the punk shrieked. "No, don't, stop!" he screamed, blood and mucus streaming from his broken nose. "It was rainin', all her clothes was dark —"

"Pants or a dress?" Conrad asked. It *had* been raining, and if the woman had been out in it all the time she would have been soaked. He wasn't unreasonable; he didn't expect this idiot to notice colors at night, and in the rain.

"I don' — pants. Yeah. Maybe jeans, I dunno."

"Did she have a coat, a jacket?" The weather had turned colder, which wasn't unexpected. It was the warmth that had been unusual for Minneapolis, not this more seasonable chill.

"I don' think so."

"Short sleeves or long?"

"Sh-short, I think. Not sure." He gulped in air through his mouth. "She was carryin' a garbage bag, kinda hid her arms."

No jacket, and short sleeves. She had been wet to the skin, and she would now be very cold. Conrad didn't wonder what was in the garbage bag; it was a commonsense solution to keeping papers dry. Mr. Sawyer would be pleased.

She had gotten money from an ATM, and this piece of excrement had promptly robbed her. She was without funds, without any means of coping. Conrad thought he should be able to find her within a day, if she hadn't sought out the police by then. Though Mr. Sawyer had everything under control even if she made accusations against him, Conrad preferred to find her himself. It would be easier that way.

He looked at the human trash in the chair. The punk had no redeeming qualities. He had no skills, no morals, no value.

A bullet was too expensive for exterminating vermin, and too quick. Conrad reached out his gloved hand and closed it on the punk's throat, and expertly crushed his trachea. Leaving him suffocating in the chair, Conrad walked out of the abandoned house in the worst part of the city. He moved silently, unhurriedly. Screams were common in the neighborhood. No one paid him any attention.

Chapter 4

Distance, Grace learned, was relative. Eau Claire, Wisconsin, wasn't all that far from Minneapolis if you were driving, a matter of an hour or two, depending on where you were in Minneapolis when you began and how fast you drove. In a plane, it was nothing more than a hop. On foot, and having to hide during the day, it took her three days.

She didn't dare take a bus; with her long hair and carrying a computer case she would be too easily recognized. She didn't know, but she thought it would only be common sense for the police, knowing she didn't have her car, to check all public transportation leaving the city. Parrish would likely be hunting her, too, and he wouldn't have to compare her appearance to a photo in order to recognize her.

She operated in a vacuum, because that was the only way she could manage. Things she had always taken for granted, basics such as food, water, warmth, a toilet, were now an effort to obtain. At least she had money, and there were always convenience stores, though she knew she should avoid them because of their surveillance cameras. Food wasn't much of a problem; she simply wasn't hungry.

She looked homeless; she *was* homeless. She walked north for a while, then cut east, paralleling state roads whenever she could rather than walking on the shoulder where she would more easily be seen. She hadn't realized before how little human presence there was between Minneapolis and Eau Claire; if she had been on the interstate, there would at least have been a motel or truck stop every few exits, but away from the interstate there was nothing but a few houses and the occasional service station.

At ten-thirty on her second night on the run, she went into a service station and asked for the key to the rest room. The attendant looked up with bored, hostile eyes and said, "Get lost." It took her more than an hour to find another station. The second attendant wasn't as polite, and threatened to call the cops if she didn't leave.

The need to urinate was excruciating, exacerbated by her constant shivering. Grace's face was blank as she silently turned and left the station. She walked across the parking lot, aware of the attendant watching every step she made. Just as she was about to step onto the shoulder of the highway, she looked back and saw that the man had returned to the magazine he'd been reading when she went in to ask for the key. She made a sharp turn, skirting the edge of the parking lot, and circled around behind the station. She *had* to relieve herself, and she wasn't about to do it on the side of the road.

Gravel crunched as a customer drove up, and she heard a man saying something to the attendant, then the answer, but she couldn't understand what they were saying. Sheltered by the back wall, she carefully placed her precious trash bag out of the splash area, and unzipped her jeans.

Footsteps approached, scraping on the gravel.

There was no place to hide. A dim bulb over each of the rest-room doors stole even the advantage of darkness from her. There was nothing to do but run, and hope the approaching customer wouldn't get too good a look at her.

She grabbed for the trash bag and her gaze swept over the rest-room door, the one with "Ladies" painted on it in big block letters. There was a hasp attached to the door, and an open padlock hung from it. The door wasn't even locked!

The footsteps were close, almost to the corner. She didn't hesitate. Leaving the trash bag where it was, she darted into the dark little room, and pressed herself against the painted block wall. She didn't even have time to close the door. The customer walked past, and a second later a brighter light came on as he flipped the switch in the other rest room. The door slammed.

Grace sagged against the wall. The rest room was nothing more than a tiny cubicle, just large enough to accommodate a toilet and a washbasin. The walls were concrete block, the floor was cement. The smell wasn't pleasant.

She didn't dare turn on the light, though she closed the door until only a two-inch crack remained. Jerking down her jeans, she perched over the stained porcelain toilet just as her mother had taught her to do, and then she couldn't hold back any longer. Crouched there like an awkward bird, her legs aching from the unnatural position, tears of relief sprang into her eyes and she stifled a humorless laugh at the ridiculousness of what she was doing.

In the rest room next door there was a long, explosive sound of gas releasing, then a contented "Ahhh." Grace clapped a hand over her mouth to hold back the hysterical giggle that rose in her throat. She had to finish before he did, or he might hear her. The competition was the strangest in which she'd ever engaged, and no less stressful because she was the only one who knew it was in progress.

She finished just as a loud, gurgling flush sounded. Quickly she reached for the handle and pushed it down, the noise of the second covered by that of the first. Then she didn't dare move, because the man didn't pause to wash his hands but immediately left the rest room. She froze, not even daring to take a breath. He walked right by without noticing that the door that had been standing open when he'd gone into the rest room was now almost closed.

Grace inhaled a shaky breath and stood for a moment in the dark, smelly little rest room, trying to calm her nerves.

The rest room wasn't the only thing that smelled. She could smell herself, the stink of fear added to almost three days without a shower. Her clothes were sour, the effect of being rain-soaked and drying on her body.

Her stomach rolled. She didn't mind being dirty; she did mind being unclean, which was something else entirely. She was an archaeologist's wife — *widow,* an insidious little voice whispered before she could silence the thought — and had often accompanied him on digs, where dust and sweat had ruled the day. They had always cleaned up at night, however. She didn't think she had ever before gone so long without bathing, and she couldn't bear it.

She opened the rest-room door another inch or so, letting in more light. The sink was as stained as the toilet, but above the basin hung a towel dispenser, and beside the faucet sat a pump bottle of liquid soap.

The temptation was irresistible. Perhaps she couldn't do anything about the smell of her clothes, but she could do something about the smell of her body. Turning the faucet so a small stream of water came out, being as quiet as possible, she washed as best she could. She didn't dare undress, and she had only the rough brown paper towels to use for both washing and drying, but she felt much fresher when she had finished. Now that her hands were clean, she cupped them and filled them with water, and bent over to drink. The water was cold and fresh on her tongue, sliding down her dry throat and soothing the parched tissues.

"What's this shit?"

The irritable words speared her with shards of panic. Grace whirled, forgetting to turn off the water. It was the attendant's voice, and next she heard the unmistakable rustle of plastic as he picked up the trash bag containing her computer and all the documents.

A low growl sounded in her throat and she jerked the door open. He was standing with his back to her, holding the bag open as he looked inside it, but at her movement he turned. A mean look entered his eyes as he recognized her.

"I told you to get the fuck off this propitty." He reached out and grabbed her arm, roughly hauling her out of the rest-room doorway and shoving her several feet forward. Grace stumbled and almost fell, going down hard on one knee before she regained her balance. A rock dug sharply into her knee, making her gasp with pain. Another hard shove in the middle of her back sent her sprawling on the ground.

"Worthless piece of shit," the man said, drawing back his booted foot. "You won't leave when you're told, I'll kick your ass off."

He was skinny, but with the wiry, hardscrabble strength and meanness of a junkyard dog. Grace scrambled away from the swinging boot, knowing that it would break her ribs if the kick landed. He missed and staggered, and that made him even angrier. She crawled frantically to the side and he followed, drawing back his leg for another kick.

He was too close; she knew she couldn't move fast enough to escape this time. Desperately she lashed out with her own foot, catching him on the knee. He was standing on one leg, the other drawn back, and the blow sent him lurching off balance. He fell heavily on his side, and he dropped the plastic bag with a thud.

Grace bounced to her feet but she wasn't fast enough; cursing, he regained his own feet, looming over her and the bag between them. She spared a quick look at the bag, gauging her distance to it.

"You little bitch," he spat, his face drawn tight with rage. "I'll kill you for this."

He lunged forward, his hands outstretched to grab her. Desperately Grace tried what had worked before: she dropped to the ground and kicked with both feet. One foot landed harmlessly on his thigh, but the other connected solidly with the spongy tissue of his testicles. He stopped as if he'd hit a wall, a strange, high-pitched wheezing sound escaping from his throat as he folded over, both hands clasping his crotch. She grabbed the plastic bag, scrambling away even before she was upright, and then she ran. Her feet pounded on the hard parking lot as she circled the building and raced across the highway. She didn't stop even when darkness swallowed her and the gas station was nothing more than a pinpoint of light far behind.

Gradually she slowed, her heart pounding in her chest, her breath rasping painfully in her throat. She had to assume the attendant would call the cops, but she doubted they would look very hard for a vagrant, since nothing had been taken and the only damage was to the man's family jewels. Still, if a county deputy was cruising the highway and saw her, he wouldn't just drive on by. She would have to leave the highway whenever she saw a car coming, and hide until it was gone.

She had been relatively clean. Now dirt smeared her hands and face again, and her clothes were coated with it. She stopped, dusting herself off as best she could, but she was aware that, if anything, she looked even worse than before.

The situation had to be corrected. She didn't need a public rest room as much for the toilet as she did for water, and the opportunity to clean herself up, though she hadn't yet been able to bring herself to squat in a field or a ditch to relieve herself. That time would probably come, she thought numbly. The next time she had the opportunity she would steal some toilet paper, just in case. Still, if she wasn't to encounter over and over the same reaction she'd met with tonight, she would have to look, if not respectable, at least as if she had a place to live. The plastic trash bag was great for protecting the computer from rain, but it marked her as a homeless person, a vagrant, and store owners wouldn't want her on their property.

She would have to find another place to wash off, to make herself as presentable as possible, and then she would brave a discount store to buy a few clothes and a cheap bag of some sort. Simple things, but they would make life much easier; she would be able to use public rest rooms without attracting notice, for one thing. What she really needed was a car, but that was out of the question unless she stole one, and common sense said that stealing a car would attract just the kind of attention she most wanted to avoid. No, for right now she was better off walking.

The struggle and flight had sent adrenaline pumping through her system, warming her, but she felt shaky in the aftermath. Her knees wobbled as she marched along the dark highway, carefully holding the bag to her chest with both arms. She couldn't believe what she'd done. She had never hit another person before in her life, never even considered fighting. But she had not only fought, she had won. Dark, feral triumph filled her. She had won purely by luck, but she'd learned something tonight: how to use whatever weapon was available, and that she could win. The boundary she'd crossed had been a subtle, internal one, but she could feel the change deep inside, a strength growing where there had been only numbness, and fear.

Light shifted in the leaves of the trees ahead, signaling the approach of a car around a curve. Grace made a sharp turn away from the highway, unable to run because the darkness kept her from seeing the unevenness of the ground, and even a sprained ankle now could mean the difference between living and dying. She hurried toward the shelter of the tree line, but it was farther away than she'd thought, and the car was moving fast. The lights became brighter and brighter. The ground rose sharply, unexpectedly, and her feet slipped on the wet weeds. She fell facedown, landing hard on the computer case, jarring her shoulder. She glanced to her right, urgency pumping through her, and the car rushed into sight.

Grace dropped her head to the ground and lay still, hoping the sparse weeds were enough to hide her.

She felt as if the headlights pinned her to the earth like spotlights, so bright were they. But the car sped past without even slowing, and she was left behind in the blessed darkness, her clothes growing cold and wet, weeds stinging her face, her chest hurting from hard contact with the computer case. Once again she climbed to her feet, her movements clumsy as the various hurts she'd absorbed began to make themselves felt.

But every step took her farther from Minneapolis, from her home, her life — no, she had no home, no life. Every step was taking her closer to safety, away from Parrish. She would come back and face him, but on her own terms, when she was better able to fight him.

She ignored the cold, and the aches. She ignored the bruises, the strained muscles, the great empty place where her heart had once been.

She walked.

Scanners were wonderful inventions. Conrad learned a great deal from listening to the police bands. He knew all the codes, understood the cop slang. It was to his advantage to understand how cops think, so he had invested a great deal of time in studying them. Beyond that, a well-informed person had to know what was happening in the law-enforcement world, for so much of what happened in any given day was never reported by the media, which went after only the dramatic or the weird, or whatever bolstered the current politically correct causes. He recognized addresses of trouble spots to which the cops returned time and again to referee domestic problems, he knew where the drug deals went down, which street corners the whores worked. He also listened, with increased attention, whenever they answered calls to places that were out of the ordinary; their voices would be tighter, the adrenaline pumping because this was *different*.

The metro area was never quiet, never still. There was always trouble working. It was more peaceful out in the rural areas, and the county scanners picked up much more routine radio messages. Those scanners had to reach out for greater distances, and even though the payback in information was much less than what he gleaned from the city scanner, he was a prudent man, and had invested in more powerful scanners with special boosters for the rural areas. If anything happened within a sixty-mile radius, he wanted to know about it.

Conrad liked to lie in bed with all the scanners on, listening to the flow of information. The constant sound was soothing, connecting him to the dark underbelly of life that he'd deliberately chosen. He left the scanners on all night, and sometimes he thought he absorbed the crackle of words even in his sleep, because any urgent code would bring him immediately awake.

Not that he slept a lot, anyway. He rested, in a sort of suspended twilight state, but he didn't need much real sleep. He found physical rest more satisfying than mere unconsciousness; half dozing, he could enjoy his own total relaxation, the feel of the sheets beneath him, the gentle stirring of air on his hairy body. That was the only caress he enjoyed, perhaps because it wasn't sexual. Conrad was totally uninterested in sex; he didn't like waking with erections, didn't like feeling as if his body was not under his control. He considered sexual activity a weakness; neither women nor men appealed to him, and he disliked the sleazy promiscuity that seemed to pervade society. He never watched sexy thrillers on television, though he very much enjoyed reruns of *The Andy Griffith Show*. It was good, clean entertainment. Perhaps there were still places like Mayberry in the world; he would like to visit one someday, though of course he could never live there. Mayberrys were not for him; he just wanted perhaps to sit on a bench on the courthouse square, and breathe the air of goodness for a minute or two.

Conrad closed his eyes, and routed his thoughts from Mayberry to Grace St. John. *She* belonged in a Mayberry. Poor woman, she had no idea how to function in the world he listened to on the scanners, night after night.

Where had she gone, after that witless vermin had robbed her? Had she found a hiding place, or had she fallen victim to someone else? He hadn't been able to pick up the thread of her movements, but he had no doubt that he would eventually succeed. He had feelers out all over Minneapolis, and he *would* find her. Conrad had no doubt in his ability; sooner or later, all those he sought fell into his hands.

He was surprised by a slight sense of concern for her. She was just an ordinary woman, like millions of other women; she had lived quietly, loved her husband and her job, done the laundry, the grocery shopping. She should have no problems too serious to be solved with anything more than a dose of Mayberry common sense. Unfortunately, she had become involved in something that was far outside her experience, and she would die. Conrad regretted it, but there was no alternative.

One of the county scanners crackled to life. "Ah, attendant at Brasher's service station reports a vagrant who refused to leave the premises and attacked him when he tried to make her leave."

Her? Conrad's attention perked.

After a moment, a county deputy somewhere in the night clicked his radio. "This is one-twelve, I'm in the area. Is the vagrant still there?"

"Negative. The guy isn't hurt much, didn't want any medics."

"Ah, did he give a description?"

"Female, dark-haired, approximate age twenty-five. Dark pants, blue shirt. Height five-ten, weight one-eighty."

"Big woman," the deputy commented. "I'll swing by Brasher's and take his statement, but it's probably nothing more than a scuffle."

And the attendant had probably lied, Conrad thought, throwing back the sheet and getting out of bed. He switched on a lamp, the light mellow and soothing, and unhurriedly began dressing. He wanted to give the deputy plenty of time to dutifully take the attendant's statement and leave.

Five-ten, one-eighty? Possible, but it was equally likely the attendant had been the loser in the encounter, and he didn't want to admit he'd been bested by a woman who wasn't quite five-foot-four, and who weighed a hundred thirty-five pounds. It looked better if he added six inches and forty-five pounds to her size. The hair, the age, the clothes, were about right, so it was worth checking out.

He arrived at the service station an hour later. It was quiet, well after midnight, no other customers. Conrad pulled up to the gas pump with the sign "Pay Before Pumping" posted on the side, and walked toward the small, well-lit office. The attendant was on his feet, watching, the expression on his thin, ferrety face an incongruous mixture of suspicion and anticipation. He didn't like Conrad's looks, few people did, but at the same time he wanted an audience to listen to a retelling of his adventure.

Conrad took out his wallet as he walked, fishing out a twenty. He wanted information, not gas.

Seeing the money come out, the attendant relaxed.

Conrad stepped inside and laid the twenty on the counter, but kept his hand on the bill when the attendant reached for it. "A woman was here tonight," he said. "The twenty is for answers to a few questions."

The attendant eyed the bill, then darted a glance back up at Conrad. "A twenty ain't much."

"Neither are my questions."

Another glance, and the attendant decided it wouldn't be smart to try to get more out of this ape. "What about her?" he mumbled sullenly.

"Describe her hair."

"Her hair?" He shrugged. "It was dark. I already told the deputy all this."

"How long?"

"About an hour ago, I guess."

Conrad controlled an impulse to crush another trachea. Unfortunately, this idiot wasn't street trash; if he were killed, questions would definitely be asked, and Conrad didn't want to lead the cops in Grace St. John's direction. "Her hair. How long was her hair?"

"Oh. Well, it was in one of them twisted things, you know, whaddaya call it?"

"A braid?" Conrad offered helpfully.

"Yeah, that's the word."

"Thank you." Taking his hand off the twenty, Conrad left the office and walked calmly back to his car. No other questions were needed. The woman had definitely been Grace St. John. She needed to get out of Minneapolis, out of the state. She was headed east, probably to Eau Claire. It was the next city of any size in that direction. She would feel more anonymous in a city, attract less attention.

He might be able to find her en route, but at night she would have the advantage of being better able to hide when a car approached. Perhaps she was moving during the day, too, but he thought not. She had to rest, and she would be afraid to go out in the daylight. Would she try to hitch a ride to Eau Claire? Again, he didn't think so. She was middle-class, suburban cautious, taught from childhood how dangerous it was to pick up a hitcher or thumb a ride herself. She was also smart; a hitcher was noticeable, and being noticed was the last thing she would want.

The gas station attendant must have hassled her in some way, or she would never have risked drawing attention by scuffling with him. She would be cold, upset, possibly hurt. Perhaps she had gone to ground somewhere nearby, trying to get warm, crying a little, too discouraged to go on. She was close, he knew, but he had no way of finding her right now short of bringing in tracking dogs, and wouldn't *that* draw attention! He wanted this kept as quiet as she did. It would be better all around if no cops or media were involved beyond the present level.

He estimated how long it would take her to reach Eau Claire. At least two more days, and that was if nothing else happened to her. She was staying off the interstate highway, and secondary roads would give her more points of entry into the city. That made his job more difficult, but not impossible. He could narrow down her most likely routes to two, and two was a very manageable number. He would need backup, though. He wanted someone who wasn't trigger-happy, someone who could adjust without panic if things didn't go according to plan. He thought over the men who were available, and settled on Paglione. He could be a bit thickheaded, but he was steady, and Conrad would be doing all the thinking anyway.

Poor Ms. St. John. Poor little woman.

Chapter 5

By the time she reached the outskirts of Eau Claire, Grace knew she had to find something to eat. She wasn't hungry, hadn't been hungry, but she could feel herself getting increasingly weaker.

The cold wasn't helping. Spring had flipped her skirts to show her petticoats of flowers and greenery, luring everyone into a giddy hope they had seen the last of winter, but as usual she had just been teasing, the bitch. Grace couldn't look at weather's vagaries with her usual complacency. She shivered constantly, though now her shivers were weakening, another indication of her body's need for fuel. At least it wasn't snowing. She had fought off hypothermia the way all the street people did, with newspapers and plastic bags, anything to hold in her lessening output of body heat. Evidently the pitiful measures weren't so pitiful, because they had worked; she was still alive.

Alive, but increasingly uneasy. She couldn't go on like this. Even more than her precarious survival, a lack of opportunity to work was gnawing at her. If she couldn't work, she couldn't learn for what Parrish had been willing to kill them all. She had always believed the old adage that knowledge was power, and in this case knowledge was also her best path to vengeance. She needed a stable base, long hours without interruption, electricity. Her computer batteries were good for about four hours, and she had already used them for two. She craved work, craved the one part of her former life she had brought with her. To get that, she had to reenter the civilized world, or at least the fringes of it. It was time to put her strategy into effect.

She needed to clean up again before appearing in any store. She sought out another service station, but she'd learned to bypass the attendant altogether. Instead she left the road and approached from the back; if the restroom doors were padlocked, she moved on until she found a station where they weren't. At least half of them were left unlocked, perhaps because the attendants didn't want to be bothered with having to keep track of the keys. Of course, most of the rest rooms left unlocked were incredibly grungy, but that no longer bothered her. All she needed was a flushing toilet and a sink with running water.

Finding such a station didn't take long. She stepped into the dank little cubicle and turned on the light, a low-watt naked bulb hanging from the ceiling, out of reach of anyone inclined to steal the bulb unless they brought a ladder with them into the rest room. Her image floated in the streaked, spotted mirror, and she stared dispassionately at the unkempt, hollow-eyed woman who bore so little resemblance to the real person. After taking care of necessities, she took off her clothes and washed. The rest room had no towels or soap, but after encountering that lack of amenities the first time she had solved the problem by taking a supply of paper towels from the next station, and lifting a half-used bar of soap from another. Most places used liquid soap in a dispenser attached to the wall, to prevent what was evidently rampant soap theft, so she felt lucky to have found the bar.

She neatened her hair, undoing the braid and vigorously combing the long length, almost shuddering with relief as the teeth dug into her scalp. Her hair was so dirty she hated to touch it, but washing it would have to wait until another day. She rebraided it with the speed of experience, securing the end with a clip and tossing the thick rope of hair over her shoulder to bang against her back.

There wasn't much she could do with her clothes. She wet a paper towel and sponged the dirtiest places, but the results were minimal. Shrugging mentally in a way she couldn't have done three days before, she tossed the paper towel into the overflowing trash can. She had done what she could. There were worse things in life than dirty clothes, like being mugged, or a snarly man trying to kick in her ribs, or being chased by neighborhood dogs — or watching her husband and brother being shot to death.

Grace had learned how to shut off those last memories whenever they sneaked in and threatened to destroy her, and she did so now, turning her thoughts to practical matters. What would be the best place to buy a change of clothes? A Kmart or a Wal-Mart, maybe; they would still be open, and no one would notice what she bought.

The problem was, she knew absolutely nothing about Eau Claire, and even if she had the address of a store she wouldn't know how to get there.

She dismissed taking a cab as too expensive. The only other alternative was to ask directions. The idea made her stomach tighten with panic. She hadn't had any contact with people since her encounter with the service station attendant. Alone, concentrating on survival, she hadn't spoken a word in two days. There wasn't anyone to speak to, and she'd never been one to talk to herself.

Time to break the silence, though. She worked her way around the station, watched the attendant for a while, and decided that he wouldn't be the one with whom the silence was broken. She didn't like his looks. Though pudgy where the other man had been lean, there was something about him that reminded her of the look in the man's eyes when he'd tried to kick her. Birds of a feather, perhaps. She wasn't going to take the chance.

Instead she cut across a field toward another road, taking care in the darkness. She ran into a wire fence, but she was lucky: it was neither barbed nor electrified. It was falling down, and wobbled precariously under her weight when she scrambled over it. The condition of the fence meant there were no cattle in the field, though she really wouldn't have expected cattle so close to town. Still, it was reassuring to know she wouldn't suddenly find herself facing an irritated bull.

As she climbed the fence on the other side of the field, a dog began barking off to her right. As soon as her feet hit the ground she immediately angled to the left, because sometimes dogs shut up and lost interest if she moved away from their territory. The maneuver didn't work this time. The dog barked even more frantically, and the sound came closer.

She leaned down and swept her hand over the ground until she located a few rocks. The dog was innocent, performing its instinctual duties by barking at an intruder; she didn't intend to hurt the animal, but neither did she want to be bitten. A rock bouncing nearby was usually enough to send the animal in retreat. She threw one at the sound and said "Git!" in a voice as low and fierce as she could make it, stomping her foot for added emphasis.

She could barely make out the movement in the dark as the animal skittered back, away from the abruptly aggressive motion she had made. She took another step and said "Git!" again, and the dog evidently decided retreat was the best course of action. It went one way, and Grace went the other.

Well, at least she had broken her silence, even if it had been to a dog.

"I think I saw her," Paglione reported by cellular phone. "I'm pretty sure it was her. I just caught a glimpse of someone kinda slipping around behind a service station, you know?"

"Did you see where she went?" Conrad started his car. He had chosen highways 12 and 40 as the most likely for her to enter Eau Claire; he had elected to watch highway 12 because it was the busiest, leaving Paglione to cover 40. The two highways would intersect only a few miles from his present position.

"I lost her. I think she cut through a field. I haven't been able to pick her up again."

"She's headed for Eau Claire. Work in that direction. She has to hit a highway or street again somewhere."

Conrad folded the phone and laid it beside him on the car seat. Excitement hummed through him. He was close to her, he knew it. He could feel her, an interesting prey because her elusiveness was so unexpected. But soon he would have her, and his job would be done. He would have triumphed once again. He let himself feel the thrill for a sweet moment, then firmly put the emotion aside. He didn't let anything interfere with the job.

A Kmart sign soared into the night sky, drawing Grace toward it. She had crossed fields and vacant lots, negotiated backyards, and faced down several more dogs. The animals had been pets, rather than watchdogs, but still it had been tricky to work her way through the ever-thickening maze of houses without drawing undue attention to herself.

At the back of the Kmart parking lot loomed a Salvation Army collection container, piled around with discarded furniture and broken odds and ends. She skirted the container, having learned that a surprising number of people routinely went through the donations and took the best of the discards, leaving only the junk. She needed a safe place to stash her bag, but hiding it in the heap of donations was out of the question.

She walked around to the back of the building, taking care to stay in the darkest shadows. Beside the shipping and receiving bay was a pile of empty cardboard boxes, but the area was brightly lit with vapor lights. That would be an ideal hiding place, except for the lights. She continued on around the building to the lawn and garden section, with flowerpots and bags of grass seed stacked high against a chain-link fence. The exit gate was closed for the night, but a few people still braved the chill to pick out the latest in imitation earthenware plastic pots.

Ducking down behind a stack of grass seed, Grace carefully placed the plastic bag against the fence. The pavement was black, and the shadows dense enough that the bag was virtually invisible unless someone stumbled over it. Panic twisted her insides at the thought of letting her computer out of her possession, and she crouched there, taking another long look around to make sure no one was watching her. There was a small copse of trees behind her, and the crickets were setting up their usual racket, which told her no one was moving about in the trees.

Eau Claire wasn't Minneapolis, she told herself. It was less than one-sixth the size of Minneapolis–St. Paul. The city would have its share of bums, drug addicts, and homeless, but she was far less likely to be observed here. The Kmart parking lot wasn't exactly a hotbed of intrigue, especially this close to closing time.

She couldn't wait any longer. She got up and walked purposefully around the fenced-in area, not looking back, taking strong strides as if she had every right in the world to be there, which she did. She wasn't going to steal anything, she was going to pay for it with the cash she had in her pocket.

An employee had been stationed at the doors to watch the customers as they entered. He gave Grace a hard look and turned to the service desk, and she suspected he would have her followed by another employee to make certain she didn't steal anything.

She pulled a shopping cart free of the line. Let someone follow her; she didn't care.

"Attention, shoppers." The announcement rang out over the loudspeakers. "The store will close in fifteen minutes."

Walking as fast as she could, she pushed the cart toward women's clothing. She grabbed a pair of jeans in her size, a sweatshirt, a denim jacket, then darted over to the underwear section. A pack of panties went into the cart, followed by a pack of socks. Looking at the overhead signs in the store, she located the shoe department, and set off for the back of the store; on the way she passed through the men's clothing section, and she grabbed a baseball cap as she went by. When she reached the shoe department, she swiftly selected a pair of white athletic shoes. They would be better for walking than her loafers, which were much the worse for wear.

Okay, now for a bag. Luggage was at the front of the store, sandwiched between the sports department and the pharmacy. Grace gave the selection a quick survey and chose the cheapest of the medium-sized duffel bags offered. On her way to the checkout counters, she also tossed in a toothbrush, toothpaste, and shampoo.

Five minutes after entering the store, she wheeled the cart up to a checkout counter. She didn't look around to see if anyone was watching. The counter was lined with boxes of chewing gum and candy bars. Her stomach growled, and she stared at the selection. She had to eat something, and she loved chocolate, but somehow the thought of candy was sickening. Nausea twisted her stomach, making her swallow the mini-flood of saliva that threatened to overflow.

Peanuts weren't sweet. Peanuts were nice and salty. The customer ahead of her finished checking out, and Grace shoved the cart forward. She grabbed a pack of peanuts and tossed it onto the counter, then began unloading her selections.

The bored, sleepy-looking cashier rang up the items, stuffing them in crinkly plastic bags. "One thirty-two seventeen," she muttered.

Grace gulped. A hundred and thirty-two dollars! She looked at the two plastic bags and the duffel. If she were to be more efficient in hiding, in traveling, she needed every item there. Grimly she dug in her pocket and pulled out the wad of bills, counting out seven twenties. When her change was returned, she took the duffel in one hand and the two plastic bags in the other, and used her body to nudge the cart toward the lines of nested carts waiting for another day's flood of shoppers.

There was a vending machine in front of the store. Grace got a soft drink from it and dropped it into one of the bags.

Her heart was pounding as she strode back around the lawn and garden section. It was empty now, except for an employee covering plants for the night. When his back was turned she quickly ducked down behind the stacked bags of seed. Releasing the duffel, she swept her free hand over the dark, cold pavement, searching for her trash bag. Her fingers encountered only grit and dampness. Sheer horror immobilized her. Had someone been watching her after all, and stolen the bag as soon as she'd disappeared into the store? She crouched in the shadows, eyes dilated, her breathing hard and fast as she tried to think. If someone *had* been watching her, he must have been hidden in the woods. Had he gone back there? Could she manage to find him? What would she do, attack anyone she saw carrying a bag? The answer was yes, if she had to. She couldn't give up now.

But had she come far enough down the fence? Was she in the right location? The store's bright lights had ruined her night vision, and perhaps she had underestimated how far from the corner she'd left the bag. Carefully setting aside the rustly Kmart bag containing her new clothes, she crawled along the fence, not really daring to hope she had simply miscalculated the distance but making the effort anyway.

Her outstretched hand touched plastic.

Relief poured through her, making her weak. She sank down on the pavement, gathering the reassuring weight into her arms. Everything was still there, the computer, the disks, the papers. She hadn't lost them, after all.

She shook the weakness away. Hastily she collected the duffel and unzipped it, stuffing both her new clothes and the computer into it. Then she melted into the trees, losing herself in the night before she dared stop to eat the bag of peanuts and drink the soft drink.

After she'd eaten and rested, she stared through the trees at the bright signs that beckoned her. Kmart had closed, but down the street shone the lights of a fast-food joint and a grocery store. The thought of a hamburger made her feel queasy, but a grocery store . . . she could buy a loaf of bread and a jar of peanut butter, the makings of many meals, the purchases themselves so ordinary no one would remember her or what she'd bought.

Do it all tonight, she thought. She had already done so much: spoken, if only to a dog, gone among people again, bought clothes. The customers who frequented grocery stores at night were stranger on average than the day crowd; she'd often heard cashiers talking about the weird things that happened at night. She would be just another of the weirdos, and no one would pay much attention to her. Resolutely Grace lifted the duffel and began walking up the street to the grocery store.

Obviously she couldn't enter the store carrying the bag, though. She stood across the street and surveyed the situation. The street behind the store was residential, lined with houses and cars. A ten-foot-high chain-link fence ran around three sides of the store. On the left side of the store was a receiving bay and a huge, jumbled stack of empty cardboard boxes, prefab housing for a wino, or for a woman on the run. Even a cardboard shelter felt good during the cold nights.

She thought of the denim jacket in the suitcase, and laughed silently, humorlessly, at herself. She was cold; why hadn't she put on the jacket? A silly reason came to mind. She was dirty, and the jacket was new. She didn't want to put it on until she'd had a bath and changed into her new, clean clothes. The teachings of a lifetime were holding sway even though she'd been shivering for three days.

Tomorrow, she told herself. Somehow she would manage a bath, a real bath, and wash her hair. Tomorrow she would put on her new clothes.

For tonight, she just had to buy sandwich makings, and be on her way.

Some odd caution kept her from crossing

the street right then; instead she went up to the corner, crossed with the light, then worked her way back. She kept to the back edge of parking lots, worming her way around smelly trash bins, slipping into the shadows of trees whenever she could. Finally she was behind the grocery store, but something about it made her uneasy. Maybe it was the fence, restricting her choice of escape direction, if escape became necessary. She had planned to leave the bag there but changed her mind, instead carrying it toward the front. There weren't any cars parked in back, which meant the employees all parked in front too, probably along one side of the lot in order to leave the most desirable center-aisle spots for the customers.

Grace lurked at the side of the building, waiting until the lot was momentarily empty of customers either arriving or leaving, before bending down until her head was just below the level of a car hood and darting to the side row of parked cars. Crouched in front of the first car, she put her hand on the hood and found it cold; the vehicle had been there for hours, so she'd guessed right about where the employees would park. She slid the bag beneath the car, between the front tires. The store hadn't closed at nine so it should be open at least until ten, if not all night, and the employees would stay later than that. She would be back long before the owner of the car.

As an added caution, she didn't immediately straighten up and walk toward the store. Instead she crab-walked down the line of cars until she reached the last two. Then she moved between them, stood, took a deep breath, and braved the public exposure of a grocery store.

"Got her," Paglione reported. "I thought I spotted her walking down the street, but then I lost sight and all of a sudden she popped up in a grocery store parking lot. She's in there now."

"Give me the directions," Conrad said calmly. By this time, he and Paglione knew Eau Claire fairly well, having spent more than a day simply driving the streets, studying maps, memorizing the layout of the city. As he listened to Paglione's voice in his ear, he realized he was less than a minute from the grocery store.

He smiled.

Grace moved swiftly through the brightly lit aisles, focused on two things and two things only: bread and peanut butter. Her appetite was nonexistent, and none of the calculated displays caught her attention. She would buy food because she had to eat, but that was the only reason.

The peanut butter was, as always, on the same aisle with the ketchup and mustard. She grabbed the biggest jar available, then set out for the bakery section, only to be sidetracked by a sudden realization that she needed a knife to spread the peanut butter. A box of plastic utensils sprang to mind; that's what she would have bought before, but fragile plastic, designed to be disposable, would soon break and she would have to buy more. It would be cheaper simply to buy a real knife. She backtracked to the previous aisle, where she found the kitchen supplies. There was a row of plastic-sealed knives hanging from hooks. She took the first one she came to that wasn't serrated, because cleaning peanut butter from all the little teeth would be a pain. Her choice was a paring knife with a four-inch blade, and the print on the cardboard backing guaranteed its sharpness. Knife and peanut butter in hand, she hurried to the bakery section and grabbed a giant-size loaf of bread.

Looking at her watch, she saw that she had been in the store for one minute and twenty seconds, a personal record for her, but that was eighty seconds her computer had been left unguarded.

There were two checkout counters open. At one, a bachelor was unloading a couple of microwave dinners, a six-pack of beer, and an economy-size bag of potato chips, standard fare for the unclaimed male. At the other, a bent old gent was carefully counting out his money for a bottle of aspirin. Grace chose the second counter, placing her items on the belt just as the clerk gave the receipt to the old guy, who smiled sweetly.

"Wife's got a headache," he explained, a product of an earlier age when friendliness to strangers was something to be expected, not feared. "Not an aspirin in the house. Can't understand it, she's usually got a bottle for this and a bottle for that, something for any ailment a body could produce, but tonight there's not a single aspirin." He turned his head and winked at Grace, his eyes twinkling cheerfully. He didn't mind the errand, the usefulness.

The swift-moving clerk rang up Grace's three items while the old man fumbled his wallet into his pocket. "Twelve thirty-seven. Kill a tree or choke a bird?"

Grace blinked. "I — what?" She handed over thirteen dollars.

"Paper or plastic?" the clerk translated, grinning a little, and the old man chuckled as he toddled off.

"Plastic," Grace said. The night shift was definitely a little off kilter. She felt a tiny spurt of amusement, a hint of life in the desolation of her heart and mind like a faint, fragile heartbeat to show she still lived, after a fashion. Her lips curved involuntarily, the elusive smile fading almost as soon as it had formed, but for a moment the life had been there. She turned her head to watch the old gentleman as he approached the automatic doors, and through the big plate-glass windows she saw two men getting out of a beige Dodge sedan parked in the center of the lot.

The man nearest the store paused and waited for the other to come around the car, then they walked together toward the store. One was dark, powerfully built, vaguely simian in the shape of his head; the other was of medium height and build, ordinary brown hair, just . . . ordinary. Slacks and jackets, neither natty nor threadbare. Neither of them would stand out in a crowd, not even the ape-man. He was just another guy who was a little too hairy, a little too bulky, nothing unusual.

But they were walking together in a subtle sort of lockstep, as if they had a definite goal, a mission.

"Your change is sixty-three cents."

Absently Grace took the change and slid it into her pocket. Archaeologists picked up a lot of anthropology stuff, because the two went hand-in-hand in understanding how people had lived, and Grace had lived with two archaeologists, brother and husband, absorbing a lot of their conversations over the years.

Two men, walking together in a purposeful manner. Men didn't do that unless they were working together as a team, to some definite end. This was different from the more casual, walking-in-company-but-not-*together* gait of males who didn't want to send the wrong signal to any watching females.

She grabbed the bag from the startled clerk and darted back into the store. The clerk said "Hey!" but Grace didn't hesitate, merely took a quick glance not at the clerk but at the two men, who must have been watching her, because they broke into a run.

She dropped to the floor and scrambled down an aisle, knowing the two men couldn't see directly down it from their angle of approach. Her heart rate increased, but oddly she didn't feel panic, only an elevated state of urgency. She was caught in an enclosed area, stalked by two men who could catch her in a pincers movement unless she moved fast. Her chances of outrunning them were small, because they had to be Parrish's men, and Parrish wouldn't hesitate at giving the order to shoot her in the back.

A woman pushed a shopping cart into the aisle at the far end, her attention focused on the stacks of soft drinks. Her purse was unguarded in the cart's child seat, a red sweater draped over it.

Grace moved down the aisle, not running but walking fast. The woman wasn't paying any attention; she turned to pick up a carton of soft drinks, and as Grace walked by she snagged the red sweater from its resting place.

Quickly she turned the corner into the next aisle and pulled on the sweater, leaving her hair caught beneath the fabric. Her long braid was too identifiable, but the red sweater worked in reverse, because she hadn't been wearing one and the men's gazes would, she hoped, slide over anything so attention-getting.

She hooked the plastic bag over her arm like a purse and walked calmly toward the front of the store. She schooled her expression to the absorbed passivity of the grocery shopper, seeming to examine the contents of the shelves as she walked past them.

Up front, she could hear the checker telling someone, probably the night supervisor, that a woman had gone back into the store instead of out as shoppers were expected to do.

A man, the average-looking, brown-haired one, crossed in front of the aisle. His gaze barely touched on Grace, sliding right past the red sweater. Her heart jumped into her throat, but she kept a steady, unhurried pace. Her skin felt tight, fragile, no barrier at all to a bullet. The man had crossed out of sight but perhaps he was sharp, perhaps he had seen through her improvised disguise and was simply waiting for her at the front of the aisle, just out of sight. Perhaps she was walking right into a death trap.

Her legs felt weak; her knees shook. Three more steps took her out of the aisle, into the front checkout area. She didn't turn her head, but her peripheral vision caught the movement of the man, walking away from her as he looked down every aisle.

Run! Her instinct was to bolt, but her legs were too shaky. Her mind held her back, whispering to hold on, that every second without being noticed was an extra second for hiding. Shopping carts had been pushed up to block the entrances to the checkout counters that weren't open, and she nudged one aside, slipping into the narrow space that funneled customers to the exit. She angled to the left, to the set of doors nearest the line of cars where she'd left the computer. The automatic doors opened with a pneumatic sigh and she walked out into the night chill, heart pounding, unable to believe it had worked. But she had gained, at best, only a minute.

She ran for the row of employees' cars, diving for their shelter. Lying down on the pavement, she crawled under the car, wedging herself with her computer between the front wheels.

Sharp, loose gravel bit into her, even through her clothes. The smell of oil and gasoline, of things mechanical, seemed to coat her nostrils with a greasy film. She lay very still, listening for two pairs of footsteps.

They came within ten seconds, moving a bit fast, but the men were professional. They weren't doing anything to attract undue attention. They weren't yelling, they apparently didn't have weapons drawn, they were simply searching. Grace listened to the steps coming close and then retreating, and she huddled closer to the wheel, tucked into as small a ball as she could manage. They were quartering the parking lot, she realized, trying to spot her among the scattered cars.

"I can't believe she slipped past us," one voice said, the tone rather aggrieved.

"She has proven surprisingly elusive," a second, deeper voice replied. There was a subtle formality to the phrasing, a mild deliberateness as if the speaker thought of every word he spoke.

Something else was said but the words were indistinct, as if the speaker were walking away from her. After a few moments the voices grew plainer.

"She made us. Man, I can't believe that. She took one look and bolted. She musta slipped out through the receiving bay, no matter what that kid said about nobody coming by."

"Perhaps, perhaps not." The second voice was still mild, almost indifferent. "You said she had a suitcase when you saw her on the street."

"Yeah."

"She didn't have it just now."

"She must've stashed it somewhere. You figure she's gone back for it?"

"Undoubtedly. She would have hidden it fairly close by, but the location would be secure enough that she felt safe leaving it while she went into the store."

"Whadda we do now?"

"Fall back to our observation points, and refrain from discussing our plans in public."

"Uh, yeah."

A car started close by, presumably the beige Dodge, but Grace didn't move. Their withdrawal could be a trick; they could park somewhere close by and return on foot, waiting for her to show herself. She lay on the cold pavement, listening to the sporadic comings and goings of customers. The adrenaline level in her body began to drop, leaving her lethargic. The sweater was a thick one; she felt warmer now than she had in three days, and with warmth came drowsiness. Her eyelids were heavy, a heaviness that she fought. She could afford rest, but not inattention.

Her body had its own agenda. Three days and nights of struggle, of little or no rest, no food, and moments of sheer terror that overlaid a base of profound despair, had taken their toll on her. She was exhausted and weak, strained to the breaking point. One moment she was awake, fighting sleep, and in the next moment the fight was lost.

The grocery store closed at midnight, and it was the sudden dousing of the parking lot lights that woke her. She lay very still, jolted from sleep but unaware of where she was. Her surroundings were totally alien, she was crowded against something massive and dark and the smell was awful, like motor oil . . . she was under a car. Awareness hit her and in panic she looked around, but no one was leaving the store. The employees would have to close up, perhaps do some cleaning, before they would leave.

Though a peek at her watch told her the time, she had no idea how long she'd slept, because she didn't know how long she'd lain there before dozing. Her carelessness frightened her. What if whoever owned the car had left work early?

Don't borrow trouble, she told herself as she gathered her possessions and inched out from under the car. She had enough problems without worrying about something that hadn't happened.

She hoped that while she had slept, enough time had lapsed that her two pursuers had given up hope of spotting her in this area. She didn't dare stay any longer; she had to risk being seen. But the night was darker now as fewer cars were on the street, houses had darkened, stores had closed.

She was stiff from the cold and her cramped position under the car. She moved slowly, staying in a crouch to keep out of sight behind the parked cars. But finally there were no more cars, only a naked expanse of parking lot. She moved fast, then, almost running as she scuttled along the edge of the pavement, the duffel banging against her left hip and her food supply bouncing against her right. As soon as she cleared the fence she swerved into deeper shadows, and was swallowed by the night.

Chapter 6

Grace broke into a house.

She had chosen a hiding place well before dawn, in a lower-middle-class neighborhood where there weren't likely to be security systems, only nosy neighbors. She had watched the houses, picking out the ones that didn't have toys, bicycles, or swing sets in the yards. She wanted a house without children, a house where both husband and wife worked and no one was at home during the day. Children would complicate the issue; they got sick at inconvenient times and disrupted schedules.

The darkness had barely begun to lessen when the houses began coming alive, windows brightening with lights, the muted sounds of radios and televisions seeping through the walls. The scents of coffee and bacon teased her. She didn't know what day it was, weekday or weekend, if children would be going to school or playing in the yards and street all day. She prayed for a weekday.

People began leaving, the exhaust of cars and pickup trucks leaving plumes behind in the chill morning air.

Carefully Grace took note of how many people left each house.

Finally she selected her target. The husband left first, and about twenty minutes later the wife drove off with a clatter of lifters marking her progress.

Still Grace waited, and her prayers were answered. Children began appearing, carrying books and backpacks, their voices loud with a shrill giddiness induced by the approaching summer vacation. These past few days of chilly weather hadn't cooled their enthusiasm. Soon school would be out, the weather would be warm, and a long summer stretched before them. Grace envied them the simplicity of their joy.

The bus arrived, the street emptied. Silence ruled the neighborhood again, except for the occasional departure of a few whose workdays didn't start until at least eight o'clock.

Now was the time, when the street was mostly empty but there was still enough customary noise in the neighborhood that people were less likely to notice the little extra noise made by the breaking of glass.

Grace slipped around to the back of her targeted house, concealed by the neatly clipped hedgerow that separated the property from its neighbors.

As she'd hoped, the upper half of the back door was glass panes. Someone was still home in the house on the left, but the curtains were drawn so no one from that side was likely to see her. The house on the right was a 'fifties-style ranch, with a longer length but shallower depth than this one; anyone looking out a window wouldn't be able to see the back of this house.

Hoping for an easy way in, she looked around for a convenient place to hide a key. There weren't any flowerpots, and the doormat yielded nothing. Breaking the glass was more difficult than she'd expected. Television and the movies made it look so easy, panes shattering at a tap from a pistol or a blow from an elbow. It didn't work that way in real life. After bruising her elbow, she looked around for a harder weapon, but the yard was neatly kept and no handy rocks were left lying around. There were bricks, however, carefully laid to form the border of a flower bed.

With the red sweater held over the glass to muffle the noise, Grace pounded the brick against the pane until it shattered. After replacing the brick, she took a deep breath, then reached in and unlocked the door.

It took every nerve she had. Walking into that strange, silent house shook her. When she put her foot over that threshold, she officially became guilty of breaking and entering, she who had always been so conscientious that she'd actually obeyed the speed limit.

She wasn't there to steal anything, except hot water and a little electricity. The close call in the grocery store had made it imperative that she begin blending in with the population, and also work up some disguises. She could no longer look homeless; she had to look . . . homogeneous. Blend in or die.

Her heart pounded as she stripped out of her filthy clothes and put them in the unknown lady's washing machine. What if she had miscalculated, what if either the lady or her husband *hadn't* left for the day, hadn't gone to jobs, but instead one of them was just on an errand and would return any minute? At the very least the cops would be called, if a strange woman was found naked, and showering, in their house.

But she hadn't dared try to rent a motel room, assuming no one would let her take a room the way she looked and smelled, even if she paid cash. And perhaps Parrish's men were checking motels; a clerk would definitely remember her. Just this once she needed to take a bath and wash her clothes where she couldn't be seen, where no one would notice her, and after this she would look more respectable. She would be able to go into a laundromat and wash her clothes, to go into stores and buy the things she needed to disguise her appearance, to lose herself in the immense sea of respectability.

She should have hurried through the shower. She knew she should, but she didn't. She stood under the spray of water, feeling the grit wash off her skin, feeling her greasy hair soak up the moisture. She shampooed twice, and scrubbed herself until her skin was bright pink all over, and still she didn't want to get out of the shower. She stood there even when the hot water began to go and the spray grew chilly. She didn't turn off the water until it was so cold she'd begun shivering, and she did so then only because she'd been cold for three days and she was tired of it.

It was such a relief to feel clean again that she almost wept. Almost, because somehow the tears wouldn't quite come. Had she cried for Ford, for Bryant? She couldn't remember. She had crystal-clear memories of a lot of things about that horrible night, but she couldn't remember tears. Surely she had cried. But if she hadn't . . . if she hadn't cried for them, then she couldn't cry for something as ultimately mundane as being clean. Crying for less would minimize them, and that she couldn't bear.

Roughly she rubbed the towel over her bare skin, then wrapped the damp fabric around her head. She didn't want to abuse the owners' unknowing hospitality any more than necessary, and using two towels instead of one was a definite luxury.

Then, almost trembling with eagerness, she unzipped the duffel and took out her new clothes. The jeans and sweatshirt were very wrinkled, the denim jacket less so. Grace peeled the hard plastic bubble away from her kitchen knife and tested its sharpness by cutting the tags off her purchases. The knife easily sliced through the plastic loops and she thoughtfully regarded the shiny blade. Not bad.

She tossed the garments into the clothes dryer to get out the wrinkles, and brushed her teeth while the dryer did its thing. She eyed her reflection in the mirror, a little puzzled. She looked different, somehow, and it wasn't just the exhausted starkness of her expression. The pallor was expected, as were the circles under her eyes. No, it was something else, something elusive.

Shrugging aside her puzzlement, she turned her attention to more practical matters. Her long hair took forever to dry on its own, so she used the blow dryer lying next to the sink.

Her thick braid was too identifiable. She should cut her hair. She thought of looking for scissors, but the thought didn't transfer itself into action. Ford had loved her long hair, he had played with it —

The pain was like a mule kick in the chest, destroying her. She sagged against the wall, her teeth clenched against a keening wail as her body doubled over from the impact. *Oh God oh God.*

She could feel herself shattering inside, the enormity of loss so overwhelming that surely she couldn't keep living, surely her heart would simply stop beating from the stress.

Except for the savage need for vengeance against Parrish, she had no reason to live. But her heart, that sturdy, oblivious muscle, didn't feel her grief and continued without pause its preordained pumping mission.

No. No. She couldn't do this. Grieving was a luxury she couldn't afford; she had known from the beginning it would tear her apart. She had to put it away until after she had taken care of Parrish, when she could approach Ford's memory, and Bryant's, and say, "I didn't let him get away with it."

Drawing in deep, shuddering breaths, she straightened her aching body. The pain was real, so intense it actually permeated her muscles. With shaking hands she finished drying her hair, though she was at a loss what to do with the thick mass except rebraid it. For the time being she left it loose, hanging down her back, and retrieved her clothes from the dryer.

The garments were hot, almost too hot, but she relished the heat. Quickly she pulled on clean panties and socks, then dressed before all the heat could dissipate. The sweatshirt felt like heaven; she sighed as the warmth enfolded her. Her bra was in the washer, but she didn't really need one. She'd never been bosomy, and the sweatshirt was thick.

The jeans were loose, almost too loose to stay up. She'd chosen her usual size, but perhaps the label was wrong. Frowning, she unzipped the fly to check the inside tag. Nope, the size was right. The cut must be unusually large, unless she'd somehow lost about ten pounds. Realization dawned. After four days without food, without much sleep, walking all night long, under constant stress, of course she had lost weight.

Reminded of the need to eat, she got her loaf of bread, now sadly mashed, and the jar of peanut butter. After resetting the washer to put her filthy clothes through one more sudsing, she sat down at the battered kitchen table and smeared the peanut butter on one slice of bread. An entire sandwich would probably be wasteful, because her throat was closing up at the prospect of eating half of one.

With the help of a glass of water, she doggedly began eating. Swallowing was an effort, and her stomach, accustomed to emptiness, lurched in sudden nausea. Grace sat very still and concentrated on not vomiting. She had to eat or she wouldn't be able to function, period.

After a minute or so she took a sip of water, and another small bite.

By the time the washer had gone through its cycle again, she had managed to eat the half sandwich.

She washed the glass and returned it to the cabinet, cleaned the table of any crumbs, washed her knife, and put the bread and peanut butter back into the duffel. The knife . . . she tried putting it in her belt loop, but the handle wasn't big enough to prevent it from sliding through. She didn't want to put a naked blade in her pocket, but neither did she want to wrap it up so securely that she'd have to waste precious time unwrapping it if she needed the knife in an emergency, such as fighting for her life.

She needed one of those knife scabbards, the kind that slipped over a belt. Come to that, she needed a belt with or without a scabbard, because the jeans were seriously loose.

What she *really* needed was a switchblade, so she wouldn't have to worry about belts or scabbards.

It struck her that she had come a long way in four days, and not just the distance between Minneapolis and Eau Claire. Four days ago she couldn't even have thought of using a knife on anyone, even to defend herself. Today she wouldn't hesitate.

Going back into the kitchen, she unrolled a couple of paper towels and folded them twice before wrapping the bulk around the knife blade and sliding it into her front right pocket, leaving the handle sticking out and covered by the sweatshirt. If she needed the knife, it would slide right out. She'd have to be careful and not puncture herself before she could get something safer, but for now she felt better.

That done, she put her clothes in the dryer along with the bath towel she had used, threw in a sheet of fabric softener, then returned to the bathroom to do something with her hair.

As she passed the open duffel she automatically glanced at it to reassure herself of the computer's safety, and the sight of the bulging bag stopped her cold. A hunger grew in her, a need that had nothing to do with food or warmth. It wasn't physical at all, but it gnawed at her just the same. She wanted to *work*. She wanted to sit for hours poring over text, making notes, referring to her language programs, tapping in information. She wanted to find out what had happened to Niall of Scotland, all those centuries ago.

The battery pack was weak, almost depleted. She could have been recharging it while she showered, but she'd let an hour go by. Still, she could set up the computer and work on the household current, just until her clothes were dry.

She resisted the urge. She might have to leave in a hurry, and she didn't want to make things more difficult by having her belongings scattered about. If she began working she might lose track of time, which had happened more than once, and she had things to do today. She had been traveling at night and hiding during the day, but that had to change. They were hunting her at night, they knew that was when she'd been moving, so she had to alter her habits as well as her appearance.

Using some bobby pins she found in the bathroom, she twisted her hair up and pinned it on top of her head. Knowing from experience that the slippery strands would soon slide right out of the pins, she jammed the baseball cap on her head to hold everything in place.

It wasn't much of a disguise, but added to the change of clothes it just might do. She needed sunglasses and a wig, two items she intended to acquire as soon as possible, and she would be able to vary her appearance. She made a mental note to look for a knife scabbard, too.

The men following her would expect her to keep moving, to follow her previous pattern. She didn't intend to do so. After bettering her disguise with a wig, she would rent a cheap motel room there in Eau Claire and stay for a couple of days. She needed to rest, she needed to stabilize, and she needed to work. More than anything, she needed to lose herself in work.

The plan worked. After tidying the house, removing all signs of her invasion, she let herself out and locked the door, then tossed a rock through the window to provide an explanation for the broken glass. It took her a while to find a store that sold cheap wigs, and an equally long time trying them on before she managed to slip the frizzy blond one under her sweatshirt. She bought one, a dark red pageboy, and while the clerk was ringing up the sale she slid the money for the blond wig under the edge of the cash register. If the men following her were really good, they might connect her to the red wig, but no one would know about the blond one.

She was wearing the blond wig when she rented a room. The motel was only a step above sleazy, officially in the run-down category, but the plumbing worked and the bed, though the mattress was lumpy and the sheets dingy, was still a bed. Except for her nap under the car she hadn't had any sleep, but she resisted the urge to lie down. Instead she took off the itchy wig and set up the laptop on the rickety table and forced herself to stay awake by plunging into the intricacies of language use that had died out before Christopher Columbus was born.

Grace loved her work. She loved losing herself in the challenge of accurately putting together the torn or shattered remnants of early man's painstaking efforts to communicate thoughts, customs, dreams — reaching out to the future with hammer and chisel, or with quills dipped in dye, and in the act of creation going beyond the forever *now* of time, setting down the past for the sake of the future, uniting the three dimensions of existence. Writing had begun when mankind began thinking in abstracts, rather than just physically existing. Whenever she studied a worn, broken piece of stone, puzzling over the figures so roughly etched into the surface and almost worn away by time and the elements, she always wondered about the writers: who had they been, what had they been thinking that was important enough for them to crouch for hours over a bit of stone, legs cramping, back and arms aching, as they cut the images into the stone with little more than the sharpened edge of another piece of stone?

These documents about the mysterious Niall of Scotland were much more sophisticated than that. They had been written with ink on parchment, parchment that had survived the centuries remarkably intact, though not unscathed. She would love to get her hands on the originals, she thought. Not because they would be any plainer; no, it was always best to work with reproductions, to avoid additional damage to the ancient parchment. There was just something unusual about these papers, though in archaeological terms they were far too recent to be of interest. Seven hundred years was nothing to a science devoted to deciphering life from millions of years ago.

There was such a hodgepodge of languages here! Latin, Greek, Old French, Old English, Hebrew, even Gaelic, yet the documents all seemed to be connected in some way. She wasn't proficient in Gaelic, and deciphering the documents written in that language would take considerable research and study on her part. She was better in Hebrew, better still in Greek, and completely at ease in the other three languages.

She had worked before in the Old French

sections; this time, after inserting the CD, she pulled up a section in Latin. Latin was such a tidy, structured language, extremely efficient; easy reading, for her.

Five minutes later she was rapidly making notes, her brow furrowed in concentration.

She had underestimated the age of the documents by about two centuries. The oldest of the Latin papers seemed to have been written in the twelfth century, which would make them almost nine hundred years old. She whispered a phrase, testing it on her tongue: "Pauperes Commilitones Christi Templique Salomonis." The syllables rolled with a measured cadence, and a chill ran up her back. *The Poor Fellow-Soldiers of Christ and the Temple of Solomon.* The Knights of the Temple. Templars.

What she'd read in the library's files came back to her. The Templars had been the richest organization in medieval society. Their wealth had exceeded that of kings and popes; they had, indeed, operated the first rudimentary banking system in Europe, handling the transfer of funds and extending loans to kings. Their original reason for existence had been to protect the Christian pilgrims on their way to the Holy Lands, and the warrior monks had become the best-trained, best-equipped fighting force of their time. They had been so feared and respected on the battlefield that they were never ransomed when taken prisoner by the Muslims, but put to death immediately.

They had, for a time, been quartered on the site of King Solomon's Temple in Jerusalem. During that time, they had evidently done extensive excavation on the site, and from that time until the Order had been destroyed, they had been the most powerful and wealthy force in Europe. Their treasure, supposedly taken from the ruins of the great Temple, had been rumored to be enormous.

Their treasure had been their downfall. Philip of France, in debt to the Templars, had devised a unique way of repaying the debt: he and Pope Clement V conspired to have all the Templars arrested and condemned for heresy, a charge that allowed the property of the charged to be confiscated. In a surprise move against the Knights on Friday the thirteenth, in October of 1307, thousands of Knights and their retainers had been arrested, but no treasure was found — or had ever been found. Moreover, shortly before that, the Grand Master of the Knights had ordered many of their records destroyed.

Or had he? She seemed to be looking at some of them right now.

The name jumped at her again. Niall of Scotland. Her pen dug into the paper as she wrote out the translation. "It has been ordained that Niall of Scotland, of Royal blood, shall be the Guardian."

Of royal blood? She hadn't been able to find a Niall in Scotland's history, so how could he be of royal blood? And what had he been guardian *of?* Had it been a political position or a military one?

She needed a library. She would prefer the Library of Congress. She could get into it with her modem and computer if the motel room had a phone, which it didn't. Tomorrow she would find a library in Eau Claire and do what research she could, make notes of the books she would need. She would like to find a Gaelic/English dictionary, because the papers written in Gaelic would likely be the most informative about this Niall of Scotland, but the Eau Claire public library might not have such an exotic item in its inventory.

The Chicago library system probably would, though, given the Irish heritage of such a large part of the city's population. New York, Boston . . . those were other likely places accessible by computer.

She ejected the CD and carefully stored it, then exited the program. The computer was great, but she wanted the feel of paper in her hands, to give her the illusion of handling the originals. She pulled out the thick sheaf of copies, tracing her finger over the slick, smooth texture of modern paper. These too would fade over the centuries; sometime in the future other people would puzzle over the remaining scraps, trying to piece together what twentieth-century life had been like. They would try to restore videotape and retrieve the images from it, they would have CDs, books, disks, but only portions of the vast number would survive the centuries. Languages would have changed, and technology would be vastly different. Who knew what present time would look like from a distance of seven hundred years?

She stopped at a sheet written in Old French. Taking her magnifying glass to help her see the faded marks more clearly, she began reading. This page was an account of a battle; the handwriting was thin, spidery, the words crammed together as if the writer had wanted to make use of every inch of paper.

"Though the enemy numbered five and Brother Niall was but one, yet he slew them all. His mastery of the sword is unequaled among the Brethren. He fought his way to the side of Brother Ambrose, who lay sorely wounded, and lifted his fallen fellow Knight onto his shoulder. Burdened by Brother Ambrose, he slew three more of the enemy before escaping, and bearing the wounded Knight to a place of safety."

Grace sat back, restlessly running her fingers through her freed hair. Her heart was pounding. How could an ordinary man have done that? Outnumbered five to one, Niall had nevertheless killed all five opponents and rescued his fellow Knight. Then, carrying a grown man who had been wearing chain mail and probably weighed, armor and all, more than two hundred fifty pounds, he had still managed to kill three more opponents and escape with his burden.

What kind of man had he been? A powerful one, both in battle and in authority, but had he been mean-spirited or generous, jolly or dour, quiet or boisterous? How had he died, and, more important, how had he lived? What had led him to become a warrior monk, and had he survived the destruction of his Order?

She wanted to keep reading but a yawn took her by surprise, and weariness swamped her. She checked her watch, expecting to see that about an hour had elapsed, but instead more than three hours had gone by. It was late afternoon, and she didn't know how much longer she could stay awake.

Why should she? This was the safest she had been in four days, hidden behind the disguise of a blond wig and a fake name. She was clean and warm; there was water to drink, food to eat, and a working bathroom. There was a bolted door between her and the rest of the world. The sheer luxury of it made her almost boneless with relief.

The temptation was more than she could withstand. After carefully repacking the laptop and the papers, and making certain her money was secure, she turned out the lights and slipped off her shoes. She couldn't relax her guard more than that, not after four days of only fitful naps, but that was enough.

A sigh shuddered from her lips as she stretched out on the bed. Every muscle in her body ached from the release of tension, the chance to relax and rest. Turning on her side, she curled into a ball and hugged the pillow to her, and then she slept.

She dreamed of Niall. The dreams were chaotic, turbulent, full of swords and battlefields. She dreamed of a castle, a great dark one, and the sight of it sent shivers of dread through her. The people whispered about the castle, and about the lord who lived there. He was a ruthless, brutal warrior who slew all who dared cross him. Decent folk kept their daughters away from the castle, for otherwise the lasses lost their virtue to him, and he wed none of them.

She dreamed of him sitting sprawled before the huge fire in the great central hall, black eyes narrowed and unreadable as he watched his men drink and eat. His hair was long and thick, braided at the temples.

A saucy wench plopped herself in his lap, and in her dream Grace held her breath, afraid of what this dream Niall might do. He merely smiled at the serving wench, a slow curve of his mouth that made Grace's breath catch yet again. Then, in the way of dreams, the image shifted and moved on, and she slept more peacefully.

* * *

He felt it again, that sensation of being watched.

Niall lifted the wench from his lap with a promise of more attention when they were abed that night, but his alert gaze was moving around the hall. Who watched him, and why? He was lord of this castle and as such was accustomed to people looking to him for answers, for approval, or just to measure his mood. A lot of people looked at him, and to him, but this was different.

This was . . . watching.

There seemed nothing amiss in the hall. The air was smoky, the men loud. Laughter spilled from one bench and others turned to hear the jest. The serving wenches moved about, filling cups, fielding advances, bestowing smiles or frowns depending on how welcome was each advance. All was normal.

But still he felt that presence, the same one that had pulled him from his bed a few nights past. There was a softness that made him think it was a woman who watched him. Perhaps she found him to her liking, but she was shy. She couldn't come to him boldly as most of the wenches did when they wanted a night of hard riding. She merely watched, and yearned.

But, looking around, he could find no lass who fit that description, and he scowled in frustration. If indeed a woman watched him, he would know her identity. Perhaps she had no reason other than a lass's soft feelings, but Niall never forgot the Treasure he had sworn to protect. Any unusual occurrence heightened his alertness, and his hand unconsciously sought the blade at his belt. His black eyes narrowed as they swept the smoky hall, probing the shadows, reading men's expressions in an instant, and passing on if nothing was amiss. The women, too, were carefully judged.

Again, he found nothing unusual.

But twice now he had felt himself watched, felt that other presence. He did not think it mere imagination. Niall had fought too many battles against foes both open and unseen, and he trusted his warrior's instincts which had grown even more acute over the years.

His probing regard of the hall had been noticed, and the noise of many voices was quieting, uneasy glances sliding his way. Niall was aware of the whispered tales that had spread over the years. He was Black Niall, a warrior so fearsome he'd never been defeated in open fight, so canny he'd never been taken unawares. His own men trained with him, knew he bruised when hit, bled when cut, knew he sweated and groaned and cursed just as they did, but still . . . why was he so vigorous at an age when most men were losing their teeth and becoming graybeards? It was as if the hand of time had left him untouched. His hair remained black, his body strong, and illness didn't touch him.

He sometimes wondered, uneasily, if Valcour had damned him to immortality by appointing him Guardian of the Treasure for which so many of his brothers-in-arms had died.

He didn't like to think so. He would do his duty, uphold his vow, but he did it with bitterness. He guarded God's treasures, but God had not guarded the guardians. Niall had not prayed, had not been to mass or confession, in more than thirteen years. His belief had died on a black night in October, along with so many of his friends, his brethren. It was for them he remained on guard, for otherwise they would have died in vain.

But he did not want to spend eternity guarding the secrets of a God whom he no longer worshipped. What a bitter joke that would be!

His mouth twisted with cold amusement, and restlessly he rose from his chair. His gaze sought and found the wench who had whispered so naughtily in his ear, and with a motion of his head he directed her toward the stair, and his chamber. As always, when the blackness of spirit was upon him, the relief he sought was in a woman's body.

As soon as he'd stood, a woman had moved forward to remove his cup, and now he heard a hissing sound from her.

"What ails you, Alice?" he asked without looking around.

"Have a care with that lass," she grumbled, earning an amused glance from him.

"Why is that?" He was fond of Alice. She had worked in the castle from the time of his return, a widow who had desperately needed even the most sinister of shelters for herself and her bairns. She was roughly his age, but was now a grandmother. Having been blessed with rather stringent common sense, over the years she had gradually assumed responsibility for household matters, and he was pleased with the situation.

She settled her cap more firmly over her springy gray hair. "She says ye'll wed 'er, if she catches yer bairn in her belly."

Niall's eyes grew cold. Marriage and children were not for him, not with his life dedicated to guarding the Treasure. The women who shared his bed knew from the outset that he would not wed them, that he was interested only in bed sport, and he had always taken care that they were experienced in the ways of avoiding conception. It annoyed him that a woman, no matter how saucy or pretty, should try to trap him in such a way. With Alice's warning, however, he wouldn't let it happen.

He nodded briefly, then took himself up the stairs to rid his bedchamber of the untrustworthy wench. Before he left the hall, however, he took one last look around, hoping to espy the woman who had been watching him, whose feminine concentration he had felt.

There was nothing, but he knew she had been there. He had felt her. He would find her.

Chapter 7

There was nothing unusual about the woman who got off the bus in Chicago. No one had paid her any attention, not the agent who had sold her the ticket, not the driver, not the other passengers who sat absorbed in their own lives, their own troubles, their own reasons for being on the bus.

Her hair was blond and curly, one of those frizz jobs that didn't look good on anyone but required no maintenance beyond washing. Her clothes were clean but nondescript, the kind that could be bought at any discount store: baggy jeans, inexpensive athletic shoes, a navy blue sweatshirt. Nothing about her luggage attracted attention, either. It was a cheap nylon model, in a particularly unappealing shade of brown that the designer had tried to brighten by adding a red stripe down one side. It hadn't worked.

Maybe it was a little unusual that she'd worn sunglasses the entire trip, because, after all, the bus windows were tinted, but there was one other passenger who also wore sunglasses, so overall there was nothing about her that would make anyone look twice.

When the bus lurched to a stop at the depot in Chicago, Grace silently produced her luggage receipt and took possession of the ugly brown duffel. She would have preferred keeping the laptop with her, but people tended to notice if someone carried a computer everywhere. With that in mind, she had packed the computer in its protective case, then further buffered it in the duffel with her meager supply of clothing.

It had been a week since her world had shattered, a week exactly.

Her life then had ended, and another had begun. She didn't feel the same, didn't look the same, didn't think the same way she had before she had lost everything and been thrown into a life in the streets and on the run. The sharp paring knife rode in a scabbard on her belt, and was covered by the sweatshirt. The screwdriver she had taken from the storage building on that horrible first day was tucked into her right sock; it wasn't as good a weapon as the knife, but she had honed it against a rock until she was satisfied with its sharpness.

She had exhausted the Eau Claire library's fund of knowledge about the Templars. She had learned a lot, including the significance of the date on which the Order had been destroyed: Friday the thirteenth, giving birth to the superstition about the combination of day and date. Interesting, but not what she had wanted. She had searched in vain for any reference, in either the Templars' recorded history or in Scotland's history, to Niall of Scotland.

She had to dig deeper, and Chicago, with its vast library on things Gaelic, was a good place to start. Remaining another day in Eau Claire would have been risky, anyway. Parrish's men would have tried to pick up her trail outside Eau Claire, but when they didn't find anything they would return to the town. Any halfway competent goon would begin checking the motels, and though she'd been careful to alter her appearance by either wearing the blond wig or tucking her hair up under the baseball cap, eventually they would find her.

She felt stronger now, no longer operating in a barely controlled panic, but at the same time she was alert. She had slept, and she had forced herself to eat a peanut butter andwich at least once a day. Eating was still difficult, and her jeans were even looser now than they had been before. The belt she wore, bought at another Kmart, was a necessity. She had even washed the jeans in hot water in an effort to shrink them, but any shrinkage must have been in length instead of width, because they still hung on her. If she lost much more weight, even the belt wouldn't help. She didn't intend to spend any more of her precious store of money on new clothes, so what she already had would have to do.

She had formulated a plan. Rather than living off her cash until it was all gone, she had to have a job. There were underground jobs in Chicago, washing dishes or cleaning houses, and those suited her perfectly. No one would become concerned if one day she didn't show. On the other hand, those types of jobs would be low-paying, and while they would tide her over for now, she would soon need something better. For that, she would need to develop another identity, and back it up with documentation.

Being what she was, a researcher, that was the approach she had used to find out how to establish a new identity. In this instance, the Eau Claire library had provided her with the information she needed.

It seemed relatively simple, though it would take time. First she would need a dead person, someone who had been born about the same time she had, but who had died young enough that there wouldn't be a job history, school records, or traffic violations to follow Grace around after she assumed the girl's identity. Once she had a name, she could write to the proper department at the state capital and get a copy of the birth certificate. With the birth certificate, she could get a social security number; with that, she could get a driver's license, establish credit, become a new person.

She stored the duffel in a locker and carefully tucked the key in her front pants pocket.

Then she located a phone book and flipped through the directory until she found the listing for cemeteries. After jotting down the names, she stopped a maintenance worker and asked which cemetery was the nearest, then went to someone else, a ticket agent, and asked for directions.

Two hours later, after having ridden on five different buses, she arrived back at the bus depot.

She bought a newspaper, found a seat, put on her glasses, and began looking through the tiny, densely printed classifieds for a place to stay. She didn't want crummy and couldn't afford comfortable, so run-down was the best alternative. By comparing prices, she eliminated both ends of the scale, and that left several places that fell in the middle. Two were boardinghouses, and she put those at the top of her list. Two phone calls later, she had a place to stay and directions on how to get there, including which El train and buses to take.

The best thing about a large city, she thought as she walked toward the El station, was the intracity transportation system. The buses had made getting to the cemetery easy enough. She could have walked to the boardinghouse; a week ago the distance would have daunted her, but now five miles seemed like nothing. She could easily walk five miles in an hour and a half. But the trains and buses were cheap and fast, so why should she? Half an hour later she got off the train, walked a block just in time to get on the bus she needed, and five minutes after that was walking down the street looking at house numbers.

The boardinghouse was a square, lumpish three-story building that hadn't seen a new coat of pain in several years. A three-foot-high picket fence, sagging in places, separated the scraggly, minuscule patch of lawn from the broken sidewalk. There was no gate. Grace walked up to the door and pushed the buzzer.

"Yeah." The voice was the same one that had answered the telephone: deep and raspy, but somehow female.

"I called about the room for rent —"

"Yeah, okay," the voice interrupted brusquely. Grace waited, and heard heavy steps clomping toward the door.

Grace had put on her sunglasses again as soon as she'd finished reading the classifieds, and was deeply grateful for that protection when the door was unlocked and swung open to reveal one of the most astonishing creatures she'd ever seen. At least the woman couldn't see her gawking.

"Well, don't just stand there," the landlady said impatiently, and in silence Grace entered the house. Without another word the woman — and now Grace wasn't so certain of the gender — closed and locked the door, then clomped back the way she'd come. Grace followed, bag in hand.

The woman was easily six feet tall, rangy and loose-limbed. Her hair was bleached lemony white, and cut in short spikes. Her skin was a smooth, pale brown, like heavily creamed coffee, hinting at some exotic ancestry. A huge sunflower earring dangled from one ear, while a row of studs marched up the outer rim of the other. Her shoulders were broad and bony, her feet and hands big. Her feet looked bigger than they probably were because she was wearing hiking boots and thick socks. Her ensemble was completed by a black T-shirt with a loose yellow tank top layered over it, and tight black bicycle shorts with narrow lime-green stripes on the sides. She managed to look both ominous and festive.

"You a working girl?"

The question was fired at her as the landlady led her into an office so tiny it had to be a converted closet. There was a small, scarred wooden desk, an ancient office chair behind it, a two-drawer filing cabinet, and what looked like a kitchen chair. It was scrupulously neat, the two pens, stapler, receipt book, and telephone lined up like soldiers for inspection. The woman took a seat behind the desk.

"Not yet," Grace replied, taking off her sunglasses now that she had her reaction under control. She would have preferred leaving them on, but that would look suspicious. She sat in the other chair, and placed the bag beside her. "I just got into town, but I intend to look for a job tomorrow."

The landlady lit a long, thin cigarette and eyed Grace through the billow of blue smoke. Every finger was decorated with an ornate ring, and Grace found herself watching the movements of those big, oddly graceful hands.

Suddenly the woman snorted. "I guess not," she said shrewdly. "Honey, a working girl is a whore. Didn't think you looked the type, despite the cheap wig. No makeup, and you're wearing a wedding ring. You on the run from your old man?"

Grace looked down at her hands, and gently turned the plain gold band Ford had given her when they married. "No," she murmured.

"He's dead, huh?"

Surprised, Grace looked up.

"You ain't divorced, or you wouldn't be wearing the ring. First thing, you split from an asshole, the ring comes off." Sharp green eyes flicked over Grace's clothes. "Your clothes are too big, too; looks like you've lost some weight. Misery takes away the appetite, don't it?"

She understood, Grace realized, both terrified and comforted. In less than two minutes this strange, tough, disturbingly astute woman had sized her up and accurately read details no one else had even noticed. "Yes," she said, because some answer seemed indicated.

Whatever she saw in Grace's face, whatever deductions she drew from it, the woman abruptly seemed to make up her mind. "M'name's Harmony," she said, leaning over the desk and holding out her hand. "Harmony Johnson. More people named Johnson than Smith or Brown or Jones, you know that?"

Grace shook it; it was like shaking a man's bigger, rougher hand. "Julia Wynne," she said, using the name she'd taken from a small marker on an unkempt grave. The girl, born five years before Grace, had died just after her eleventh birthday. The marker had read: "Our Angel."

"Rooms are seventy a week," Harmony Johnson said. "They're damn clean. I don't allow no drugs, no parties, no whores. I got outta that, and I don't want it in my house. You clean up after yourself in the bathroom. I'll clean your room if you want, but that's another ten bucks a week. Most people do for themselves."

"I'll do the cleaning," Grace said.

"Thought so. You can have a hot plate, coffeemaker in your room, but no major cooking. I like to cook a big breakfast. Most of my people eat breakfast with me. How you feed yourself the rest of the time is your problem." She gave Grace another once-over. "Don't guess you're too worried about food right now, but time'll take care of that."

"Are there phones in the rooms?"

"Get a grip. Do I look like a fool?"

"No," Grace said, and had to stifle a sudden urge to laugh. Harmony Johnson looked like a lot of things, but fool wasn't on the list. "Do you mind if I have my own line installed? I do some computer work, and use a modem sometimes."

Harmony shrugged. "It's your money."

"When can I move in?"

"As soon as you pay me a deposit and haul your bag upstairs."

"Tell me, Conrad," Parrish said lazily, tipping his chair back. "How can Grace St. John, of all people, elude you for a week?" He wasn't at all pleased. Conrad had never failed him before, and though the Minneapolis police had bought the setup with a gratifying completeness and issued warrants for her arrest, no one had managed to find her. A nerd, an *ancient languages specialist,* of all people, had somehow managed to outsmart them all. "Mind, I don't give a shit about Grace, but she has the papers and I really do want them, Conrad. I really do."

Conrad's face was impassive. "She managed to empty out their bank account, so she has cash. The police figure she overrode the bank's computer system, but the bank's systems analyst hasn't determined how."

Parrish waved that aside with a languid movement of his hand. "The how doesn't matter. All that matters is finding her, and you haven't accomplished that."

Fool, Conrad thought dispassionately. The how always mattered, because when something worked once, people invariably repeated it. That was how patterns were established, and patterns were detectable.

"She had been traveling at night, but I think that's changed now. She had a bag when Paglione saw her in Eau Claire, so it follows that she has accumulated more clothing and now we have no idea what she's wearing." There were notes in his thick, brutish hand, but he didn't need to consult them. "A woman roughly answering her description bought a red wig in Eau Claire."

"A redhead should be easy to find."

"Unless it was a decoy." Conrad was of the opinion that the red wig was exactly that, and his admiration for Ms. St. John had risen sharply. She was proving to be very interesting quarry. "There haven't been any leads on a redhead. She could have stolen another wig, one the proprietor didn't know anything about. She could also have cut her hair, colored it, done any number of things to change her appearance."

"Well then, damn it, how do you intend to find her?" Parrish snapped, his patience at an end.

"Her most likely destination, after Eau Claire, would be Chicago. A big city would give her a sense of security. Even though she has money, she's cautious; she will try to save that money in case she has to run again. She'll get a job, but it will have to be off the books, because she can't use her social security number. The kind of job she will be able to get will be low-skill, low-paying. I will put men in the streets, put out the word that there is a cash reward for information on her. I will find her."

"See that you do." Parrish rose and walked to the window, indicating the interview was ended. Conrad left, his movements as noiseless as always.

The garden was looking good, Parrish thought, eyeing the prize-winning roses beneath his window. The cold snap hadn't been a severe one; the temperature had remained above freezing. The days were growing warmer as spring settled in again, perhaps for good this time. The cold had to have been a trial for poor little Grace, though she had some extra padding on her bones for warmth. How soft she had looked! A man on top of her wouldn't feel as if he were lying on a skeleton.

What a strange attraction, he mused, setting his fingertips against the cool panes. He'd always preferred sleek women, but little Gracie was so unconsciously, unaccountably sensual, despite her weight. She wasn't much overweight, just enough to look rounded.

Perhaps he should instruct Conrad to keep her alive, just for a while. One day, perhaps, long enough for him to satisfy a particular fantasy.

He smiled, thinking about it.

Chapter 8

Wearily Grace untied the apron from her waist and tossed it into the hamper. This was her sixth day on the job, as part-time dishwasher and general slave in Orel Hector's pizza and pasta restaurant. Sometimes she thought she'd never get the smell of garlic out of her hair, off her skin. The constant exposure to spicy food had, if anything, depressed her appetite even more. The workers were allowed to have anything in the restaurant for lunch, free, but so far she hadn't eaten anything. Just the thought of sitting down to a hearty pasta meal made her stomach clench.

"You comin' back tomorrow?" Orel asked as he took the cash box out of a locked drawer and opened it to pay her. There were three part-time workers in the restaurant, and none of them was on a payroll list. About a third of each day's take went into the cash box instead of being rung up on the cash register. He paid them in cash at the end of each day, and if one of them didn't show up the next day, he'd find someone else. Cut way down on the damn federal paperwork, he said.

"I'll be here," she said. It was exhausting

work, but it suited her to be part of the underground economy. Orel handed over three tens, thirty dollars for seven hours of work, but it worked out to a hundred eighty dollars for the six days she'd been working. After paying Harmony seventy dollars a week, she'd have a hundred and ten left over. Her expenses were minimal, just the bus fare to work every day, and a few more clothes. She had bought two more pairs of cheap jeans, a size smaller this time, and a couple of T-shirts. Washing dishes was hot work. The new jeans were loose, too, and growing baggier by the day.

She folded the bills and slid them into her front pocket, then retrieved her computer case from under the cabinet where she'd stored it safely away from spills and drips. She'd told Orel she was going to school nights, and everyone accepted the explanation. Her coworkers didn't ask many personal questions, content to go their own way and not get involved with anyone. She preferred it that way, too.

She left through the back door, stepping out into a littered alley. The wind wound its way even down this narrow little space, freshening the air. She inhaled deeply, thankful for a breath that didn't bring the scent of garlic with it.

Cautiously she looked both left and right, the computer case clutched tightly in one hand and her other hand on her knife. So far she hadn't had any trouble, but she was prepared.

She walked two blocks to a bus stop, where the next bus was due in about ten minutes. The late-afternoon sky was a clear, dark blue; the day was fresh and sweet, and there was a jauntiness to everyone's step even this late in the day. Spring had definitely arrived, sending the temperature into the high seventies. Grace remembered her joy in the spring as she had walked across the Murchisons' backyard — how long ago had it been? Two weeks? Three? Closer to three, she thought. It had been the twenty-seventh of April, the last day she had felt joy in life. She could see the clearness of the day, but it didn't touch her heart. Inside, everything was bleak and barren, colorless.

The bus arrived and she got on, paid her fare. The bus driver nodded to her. This was the sixth day in a row she'd gotten on at that stop, and he had learned her face. She would have to take a different bus for a while.

She got off at the Newberry Library, one of the world's foremost historical research libraries. She had waded through text after text of medieval history, in both books and computer files, looking for some mention of Niall of Scotland. So far she had learned a lot about medieval times, but hadn't turned up one iota of information on the warrior Knight. She wasn't discouraged, though, because she had barely scratched the surface of the available material.

She went straight to the appropriate aisle and picked up where she had left off the night before, selecting several books and carrying them to an isolated table. Then she put on her glasses and began skimming, page by page, looking for any mention of anyone named Niall who had been connected to the Templars.

She almost missed it. She had been reading for more than two hours and her mind had gone on automatic. The reference didn't register for a moment, and she continued down the page. Then the similarity between the names caught her attention and she reread the paragraph:

"Chosen as Guardian was a Knight proude and fierse, a Scot of Royal blude, Niel Robertsoune."

Excitement flared, and her heartbeat kicked into a faster rhythm. It had to be Niall! The names were too similar, and the reference to the Guardian was the clincher.

Had she read anything before about a Niel, and passed over it because she hadn't connected the names? She knew how erratic spelling had been; she should have paid particular attention to any name that began with an *N*. And at last she had a surname! Robertsoune, or Robertson. Quickly she began rechecking the references for any variation of Niall, such as Niel, Neil, Neal, and also for anything remotely close to Robertson.

There was nothing. There were Robertses

and Robertsons, even a couple of Neals, but nothing within the time frame she needed. Her hands trembled as she closed the book, and she had to restrain herself from pounding on the table in frustration. The wildness of her disappointment took her aback. She had been thwarted in her studies before, and taken it in stride. This fierce sense of desperation burned through her protective numbness, frightening her with its intensity. She didn't want to feel anything except rage and the unquenchable thirst for revenge, because she was afraid she would shatter if she ever began feeling again. The few times grief had managed to leak past the numbness had almost destroyed her.

But she *did* feel, she realized, had felt this intense interest in Niall of Scotland from the first moment she'd received the copies of old parchments and glanced through them. All that had happened to her since hadn't changed that, or even lessened it. If anything, her fascination grew with each day, with every page she read.

She had begun to think Niall of Scotland only a myth, though why his fictional exploits should be included in a history of the Knights Templar was something she couldn't fathom. This one mention of "Niel Robertsoune" being chosen as Guardian was the only confirmation of his existence she'd been able to find, but it was enough. He had existed, had been a real man who lived and breathed and ate and slept as all men did. Perhaps, after the Order had been destroyed, he had escaped persecution and had lived a normal life, had found happiness with a wife, had children, died an old man. The real Niall of Scotland had likely been nothing similar to the black-haired warrior who haunted her dreams, but the fantasy was one she needed emotionally, so she couldn't regret it. The dreams were proof that her inner self hadn't completely died; shreds of Grace St. John still existed deep inside her.

And Niall of Scotland had existed. Briskly, with renewed determination, she pushed the heavy reference books aside. She wouldn't find him there. As one of the notorious Knights, his life would have depended on remaining as anonymous as possible. Anything she discovered about him would be in the pages of documents to be deciphered, the exquisite photographed copies —

Copies.

Her mind stumbled to a halt for a moment, then began racing. Why did Parrish want this copy of the documents, when he could have the real McCoy? Why was he so desperate to get his hands on this copy that he would kill Ford and Bryant, and try to kill her?

Logically, there were only two explanations, both of them requiring a degree of coincidence that strained her credulity. One was that he didn't know where the originals were now, but obviously they had been recorded and photographed, and the copies sent to her. Could someone have stolen the originals, for some unfathomable reason — the same reason Parrish wanted them? If so, what about the negatives? Other copies could be made from them. The other explanation was that the originals had somehow been destroyed; accidents happened. Again, what about the film negatives?

That led her to two other possibilities. One was that the negatives had also been destroyed or stolen, and the other was that Parrish not only wanted this copy, he wanted to erase all knowledge of its contents, which would mean killing anyone who knew about it.

Her reasoning brought her full circle, back to what she had known from the beginning: Parrish meant to kill her. And the why of it was hidden in the mystery of those pages.

She had been wasting her time looking through reference books. From now on, she had to concentrate on translating the crabbed, tightly crowded text of the documents, and that was a task better accomplished in the privacy of her room at Harmony's rather than in a public library.

Quickly she returned the books to the shelves and gathered her things. By habit she carefully looked around for anyone unusual, or anyone watching her, but the people seated at the desks and tables seemed to be lost in their own studies. The Newberry attracted serious scholars more than the average high-schooler researching a term paper.

When carrying the computer, she looped the strap of the carrying case around her neck and over her shoulder, and also clutched the handle tightly in her left hand. When she walked, her right hand was always on the knife at her belt. The bus fare was in her right jeans pocket, so she never had to release the computer to fish out money.

It was almost dark when she left the library and hurried to the bus stop. That wasn't unusual; several times she had stayed much later. A cool evening breeze fanned her face as she joined the two people waiting at the corner, a plump young black woman with a round, pleasant face, who clutched the hand of a wide-eyed and energetic two-year-old. The little boy repeatedly climbed on and off the bench, not much hampered by his mother's determined grip on him. He crawled over and under and between her legs, and she merely adjusted her hold to whatever part of him she could reach. Grace thought that being a mother must be something akin to wrestling an octopus, but the young woman rode herd on her rambunctious offspring with remarkable calmness.

There was no warning, no sudden footsteps behind her. Someone slammed into her, hard, and Grace stumbled off balance. Her neck wrenched to the left as violent hands jerked at the computer case. The young woman uttered a startled scream, grabbed her child into her arms, and began running. The attacker, frustrated when the case didn't come free, uttered a foul curse on a cloud of equally foul breath. Desperately Grace tightened her grip on the handle and managed to get her feet under her, letting the man's own tugging efforts pull her upright. He cursed again and slashed a knife at her, trying to slice the strap around her neck. She twisted, protecting the strap, and cold fire burned along her forearm. She saw his eyes, narrow and vicious under a grimy fall of hair, as he jabbed the knife at her again.

In sheer reaction Grace swung the heavy case at him. Startled, he jerked back and the case caught him on the arm, jarring the knife free. It sailed through the air and clattered on the sidewalk. "Shit!" he said between clenched teeth, and turned to run.

And then fury arrived, surging through her veins like a flash flood. He hadn't even completed his turn to escape before she was on him, a foot thrust between his ankles to trip him. He yelled as he sprawled on the rough sidewalk, taking Grace down with him in a furious, punching tangle. Her hands were balled into fists and she used them, going for his eyes, his nose, his ears, any part of him that was momentarily unprotected as he tried to shove her away. Remembering the service station attendant, she tried to jab a knee into his groin, but he rolled aside. Growling in frustration, Grace grabbed his greasy hair with both hands and jerked as hard as she could. He howled with pain and struck back, punching her in the belly. Her breath exploded out of her and she gagged, momentarily paralyzed, but somehow she hung on. He hit her again, and one of her hands loosened. His fist jabbed at her face, caught her a glancing blow on the chin. The blow jarred her, made her eyes water, and he took advantage of her momentary weakness to shove free of her and lurch to his feet. Grace scrambled onto her hands and knees but he was already gone, running down the sidewalk, shoving his way past pedestrians who paid him little attention.

Groaning, Grace got to her own feet and stood swaying. The computer case still hung around her neck. The battle fury left as suddenly as it had arrived and almost unbearable fatigue dragged at her. A small crowd of about ten people had gathered, watching, and their faces swam before her like balloons. She took a deep breath, then another, then still another when the first two didn't work.

The mugger's knife still lay on the sidewalk. The handle was black, wrapped in electrician's tape, and the blade was a good six inches long. It looked much more lethal than her kitchen paring knife. She hobbled over to it, abruptly aware of bruises and scrapes she hadn't noticed during the heat of struggle. Bending over with effort, she picked it up and stared with some surprise at the red stain on the blade. Only then did she notice the blood dripping down her arm to splash scarlet dots on the sidewalk, and feel the burn of the two-inch gash that slanted across her forearm.

The wound needed stitches, she thought rather dispassionately, examining it as best she could for the welling blood. Tough. She wasn't inclined to spend two or three hundred dollars of her precious cash for emergency room care, in addition to probably being questioned by the cops. So long as she didn't get an infection, she could take care of the cut herself. Shrugging, she slipped the knife into one of the outside pockets of the case.

At least the mugger had been only that, a mugger. Probably he made a good living, or at least supported a drug habit, by snatching laptop computers. If he had been one of Parrish's men he would have sliced her throat first, then made off with the computer. But she had attracted attention, even if none of the bystanders had been inclined to help her, so the first thing she had to do now was get out of sight. The bus she had intended to take turned the corner then and stopped with a wheeze of hydraulics, but Grace didn't board it. The bus driver would be too likely to remember the passenger with the bleeding arm, and the stop where she got off, which would lead any followers that much closer to Harmony's house. Instead Grace quickly crossed the street and walked in the opposite direction.

Her arm began to ache, and blood was dripping on the computer case. Scowling, Grace pressed her right hand over the wound. She had acted with a disgusting lack of presence of mind, she thought as she strode along. She had felt so tough and well prepared because she'd had a kitchen paring knife on her belt, and instead she was so far from being street smart she hadn't even thought of the knife.

Look at me now, she thought furiously. She was walking openly down a busy sidewalk, dripping blood marking her every step. She could walk smack into a cop at any second, and that was only the most immediate danger. Any number of people were taking note of her, and Parrish was capable of putting a small army on the streets to locate her. Surely the search had moved to Chicago by now, it being the most logical place for her to hide, not to mention affording her the resources she needed to work. She had to assume the worst, and that meant she had to get off the street and change her appearance, immediately.

Just ahead of her, a couple entered a busy bar and grill. Grace barely slowed down, darting through the closing door. She stood close to them, angled so that the man's body hid her bleeding arm from the hostess, who smiled as she asked, "Smoking or non?" and plucked three menus from a stack.

"Non," replied the man. The hostess checked her seating chart, made a notation, then led them through the maze of close-crowded tables and booths. Grace spied the sign indicating the location of the rest rooms down a narrow hall, and she walked swiftly in that direction.

The ladies' room was small, dark, and empty. The decor didn't invite people to linger. The lighting was dim, and swallowed by the dark glazed tiles of the floor and walls. A pink and purple neon flamingo was poised over the upper right corner of the mirror, casting a decidedly unnatural tint on the face of anyone repairing her makeup or admiring herself. Grace did neither. Instead she pulled several paper towels out of the holder and swiftly washed her hands and arm. Blood welled from the cut as fast as the water rinsed it away.

"Damn, damn, damn," she whispered. Glancing in the mirror, she saw that the blond wig was askew. Hastily, using one hand, she removed the pins that still halfway anchored the wig in place, then snatched it from her head. Her long, matted hair tumbled down her back.

She needed the use of both hands, if only for a minute. Taking one of the folded brown paper towels, she pressed it over the bleeding wound, holding it until the paper adhered to her arm. The red stain immediately began spreading, but for the moment she wasn't dripping. She stuffed the wig into the computer case, wound her hair into a knot on top of her head, and pinned it in place. Pulling out her baseball cap, she jammed it on and pulled the bill down low over her eyes.

Using her arm made it ache even worse. The makeshift pad was soaked with blood already, and coming loose. She peeled it off and tossed it into the trash, then pressed another towel over the wound. Gritting her teeth against the pain, she stared at her pale, sickly reflection in the mirror. Essentially the wound was negligible; she wasn't likely to bleed to death, and she still had the use of her arm. Niall wouldn't even have paused for so paltry a wound, but continued the battle.

And so had she, Grace realized with a spurt of surprise. Granted, her counterattack hadn't been well thought out, but she hadn't even realized she'd been cut until the fight was over. Niall would be proud of her, after he got over his murderous rage that she'd been hurt at all —

"I'm losing it," Grace said aloud, blinking. She must have lost more blood than she had realized, to be thinking of Niall as if he were someone she actually knew, instead of an obscure medieval warrior who had been dead for hundreds of years. She would be better off figuring out how to bandage her arm, and with what.

The answer followed on the heels of the

thought. Holding the pad of towels in place with her right hand, she used her left to untie her shoe. Slipping out of it, she removed her sock, then shoved her bare foot back into the shoe. The sock had considerable stretch in the fabric. She laid the sock on the vanity top, then positioned her arm across it. Using her teeth and her free hand, she knotted the sock around her arm, pulling it as tight as possible over the pad of towels and then knotting it again for security.

The makeshift bandage wouldn't last long, but it should do to get her home. The effect was pretty noticeable, so she pulled off her other shoe and sock, and tied the remaining sock around her right arm. At least now it looked as if she'd done it for some reason other than necessity, maybe insanity, or membership in a gang. Socks around the arms weren't exactly in the same class as 'do rags, but there were a lot of crazies in Chicago.

An hour later, Grace let herself into the boardinghouse. She intended to slip quietly up the stairs, but as luck would have it she met Harmony herself in the hallway.

"That's some getup," Harmony drawled, taking in the baseball cap, the absence of the blond wig, and the socks tied around Grace's arms.

"Thanks," Grace muttered.

"Arm's bleeding," Harmony observed.

"I know." Grace started up the stairs.

"No point in running. Anybody in my house gets in trouble, I want to know what it's about, in case the cops gonna beat my door down in the middle of the night." Her green eyes narrowed, Harmony was right on Grace's heels as they climbed the stairs.

"I was mugged," Grace briefly explained. "Or rather, someone tried to mug me."

"No shit. Whadja do, scare 'im off with that wussy little knife you carry?"

"I didn't even think about it," she confessed ruefully, wondering how Harmony knew about the knife.

"Good thing. Any self-respecting mugger would've laughed, then made you eat it." Harmony waited while Grace unlocked the door, then followed her inside. After eyeing the spartan neatness of the room, the tall woman turned her attention back to Grace. "Okay, Wynne, let's see the arm."

After two weeks, Grace had accustomed herself to her pseudonym enough that she no longer hesitated at the name. Two weeks was also long enough for her to learn that Harmony Johnson considered her home her castle, over which she had a dictator's authority, and anything that went on in her house was her business.

Silently she untied the bloodstained sock. Beneath it, the pad of paper towel was completely soaked. She removed that, too, and Harmony studied the sullenly oozing cut.

"Needs stitches," she pronounced. "And when was your last tetanus shot?"

"Not quite two years ago," Grace replied after a little thought, and with some relief. She hadn't even considered tetanus. Fortunately she'd updated all her vaccinations before going with Ford on a dig in Mexico. "No stitches, though. I can't afford an emergency room."

"Sure you can't," Harmony said shrewdly. "Any street bum can see a doctor for a cut, but you can't? More likely you don't want to answer no questions. Anyway, forget about a hospital. You want, I can sew that up for you, if you don't mind not having nothing for pain."

"You can?" Grace asked, astonished.

"Sure. I useta do it for the other girls all the time. Wait here while I get my kit."

While Harmony was gone, Grace pondered her landlady's undoubtedly colorful past. She wondered how successful a streetwalker Harmony would have been, with her brusque manner, unusual height, and equally unusual looks. Today she was wearing scarlet leotards and a sleeveless scarlet T-shirt, which revealed remarkably well-muscled legs and arms. Men who frequented prostitutes were looking for sexual gratification rather than sexual attraction, but still, how many would choose a woman who was not only taller than most men, but more masculine? Grace would have thought Harmony a cross-dresser or even a transsexual, if it hadn't been for a throwaway comment she had once made about having a miscarriage when she was fifteen and never getting pregnant again. Modern surgical procedure could outwardly change someone's sex, but it couldn't retain fertility for the patient.

Awkwardly, because her left arm was really aching now and she used only her right hand, she retrieved the tangled wig and bloodstained knife from the computer case. She laid the knife on the tiny round table she used for eating, and gave the frizzy wig a shake before placing it on the bed. Remembering it was supposed to be bad luck to put a hat on a bed, she wondered wryly if a wig qualified for equal status in the superstition.

Harmony returned, carrying a bottle of whiskey, a small black box, and an aerosol can. A clean white towel was draped over her arm. She set the first three items on the table, and eyed the bloody knife before pushing it aside and placing the towel over the clear space. "Yours?" she asked, nodding toward the knife.

"I guess it is now. I knocked it out of his hand." Exhausted, Grace sank into one of the chairs and laid her left arm across the towel.

Harmony's eyebrows rose. "No shit? He musta been surprised." Taking the other chair, she opened the bottle of whiskey and shoved it toward Grace. "Take a few good swallows.

Won't stop it from hurting as bad, but you won't care as much."

Grace warily eyed the bottle. It was an expensive Scotch whiskey, but she had never drunk whiskey before and had no idea how it would sit. Given her exhaustion, and the fact she hadn't eaten since breakfast, it was likely to knock her on her butt. Shrugging, she seized the bottle and tipped it to her mouth. She could get her arm stitched while on her butt as well as she could sitting in a chair.

The smoky taste of the whiskey lay smooth and rich on her tongue, but when she swallowed, it was like swallowing fire. The liquid flame seared its way down her esophagus and into her stomach, stealing her breath along the way. Her face turned red and she began gasping and wheezing, trying to draw enough oxygen into her lungs to cough. Everything inside her was in revolt. Her eyes watered; her nose ran. She coughed violently, bent over at the waist while spasms wracked her. Finally, when she could breathe half normally again, she tilted the bottle and took another healthy swallow.

When the second bout had ended, she straightened to find Harmony watching and waiting with unruffled patience. "Not much of a drinker, are you?" she observed neutrally.

"No," Grace said, and drank again. Perhaps the nerves in her esophagus had already been burned out, or perhaps they were merely numb. For whatever reason, this time she didn't choke. The fire was spreading through her entire body, making her head swim. She broke out in a sweat. "Should I take another one?"

No smile cracked Harmony's angular face, but the corners of her green eyes crinkled in a subtle expression of amusement. "Depends on whether or not you want to be conscious."

Suspecting that she had only begun to feel the effects of the whiskey, Grace pushed the bottle aside and capped it. "Okay, I'm ready."

"Let's wait another few minutes." Harmony leaned back in the chair and crossed her long legs. "Guess the guy was after that computer you tote around like it was a baby."

Grace nodded, unaware that her head bobbed unsteadily. "Right outside the library. People saw what was happening, but no one did anything."

"Guess not. He'd already proved he meant business with the knife."

"But even after I'd knocked the knife out of his hand, and tripped him, and was punching him in the face, no one tried to help." Grace's voice rose indignantly.

Harmony blinked, and blinked again. She threw her head back and a deep, full-bodied laugh erupted from her throat. Rocking back and forth, she whooped until tears ran down her face and she was gasping for breath, much as if she had been into the whiskey bottle herself. When she could breathe, she hunched first one shoulder and then the other to dry her wet cheeks on her shirt. "Hell, girl!" she said, still giggling a little. "By that time they were probably more scared of you than they were of that stupid son of a bitch!"

Startled, Grace considered that. She was much taken by the possibility. Her face brightened. "I did good, didn't I?"

"You did good to come out of it alive," Harmony scolded, despite the grin on her face. "Girl, if you're gonna get in fights, somebody's gotta teach you *how* to fight. I would, but I ain't got time. Tell you what. I'll fix you up with this guy I know, meanest little greaser son of a bitch on God's green earth. He'll teach you how to fight dirty, and that's what you need. Somebody as little as you don't need to be doing something as dumb as fighting fair."

Maybe it was the whiskey thinking for her, but that sounded like a fine idea to Grace. "No more fighting fair," she agreed. Parrish certainly wouldn't fight fair, and neither did the street scum she would have to deal with. She needed to learn how to stay alive, by whatever means possible.

Harmony tore open another antiseptic pad and carefully washed Grace's arm, examining the cut from every angle. "Not too deep," she finally said. She opened a small brown bottle of antiseptic and poured it directly into the wound. Grace caught her breath, expecting it to burn like the whiskey, but all it did was sting a little. Then Harmony took up the aerosol can and sprayed a cold mist on the wound. "Topical analgesic," she muttered, the medical terminology somehow fitting right in with her street slang. Grace wouldn't have been surprised if her landlady had begun quoting Shakespeare, or conjugating Latin verbs. Whatever Harmony was now or had been in the past, she certainly was not ordinary.

With perfect calm she watched Harmony thread a small, curved suturing needle and bend over her arm. Delicately squeezing with her left hand, Harmony held the edges of the wound together and deftly began stitching with her right. Each puncture stung, but the pain was endurable, thanks to the whiskey and the analgesic spray. Grace's eyelids drooped as she fought the fatigue dragging at her. All she wanted was to lie down and sleep.

"There," Harmony announced, tying off the last stitch. "Keep it dry, and take some aspirin if it hurts."

Grace studied the neat row of tiny stitches, counting ten of them. "You should have been a doctor."

"Don't have the patience for dealing with nitwits." She began repacking her small first aid kit, then slid a sideways glance at Grace. "You gonna tell me why you don't want nothing to do with the cops? You kill somebody or something?"

"No," Grace said, shaking her head, which was a mistake. She waited a minute for the world to stop spinning. "No, I haven't killed anyone."

"But you're running."

It was a statement, not a question. Denying it would be a waste of her breath. Other people might be fooled, but Harmony knew too much about people who were running from something, whether the law or their past or themselves. "I'm running," she finally said, her voice soft. "And if they find me, they'll kill me."

"Who's this 'they'?"

Grace hesitated; not even the stout whiskey was enough to loosen her tongue to that extent. "The less you know about it, the safer *you'll* be," she finally said. "If anyone asks, you don't know much about me. You never saw a computer, didn't know I was working on anything. Okay?"

Harmony's eyes narrowed, a spark of anger lighting them. Grace sat very still, waiting for this newfound friend to become an ex-friend, and wondering if she would have to find a new place to live. Harmony didn't like being thwarted, and she hated, with reason, being left in the dark about anything concerning herself and the sanctity of her home. She pondered the situation in silence for a very long minute, before finally making a decision and giving one brisk nod of her lemony-white head. “Okay. I don’t like it, but okay. You don’t trust me, or anyone else, that much. Right?”

“I can’t,” Grace said softly. “It could mean your life, too, if Pa— if he even suspected you knew anything about me.”

“So you’re gonna protect me, huh? Girl, I think you got that backwards, because if I’ve ever seen a babe in the woods, you’re it. The average eight-year-old here is tougher than you are. You look like you lived your whole life in a convent or something. Know it’s not your style, but you’d make a helluva lot of money on the street, with looks like yours.”

Grace blinked, startled by the abrupt, and ridiculous, change of subject. Her, a successful prostitute? Plain, quiet, nerdy Grace St. John? She almost laughed in Harmony’s face, which would never do.

“Yeah, I know,” Harmony said, evidently reading her mind. “You got no sense of style, you don’t wear makeup. Stuff like that’s easy to change. Wear clothes that fit, instead of hanging on you like a bag. You don’t want loose clothes no way, gives people something to grab, understand? And your face looks so damn innocent it probably drives a lot of men crazy, thinking how much they’d like to be the one to teach you all the nasty stuff. Men are simple sons of bitches about stuff like that. A little makeup would throw them off, make 'em think you're not so innocent after all. Plus you got one of those pouty mouths all the models pay good money for, having fat or silicone shots in their lips. Damn idiots. And that hair of yours. Men like long hair. I guess I know why you're wearin' that tacky wig, though."

Harmony's speech was a fast-moving mix of accents and vocabulary, from Chicago street to Southern drawl, with the occasional flash of higher education. It was impossible to tell her origin, but no one listening to her for more than thirty seconds would have any doubts about her mental acuity. Sprinkled among the comments on Grace's appearance had been a nugget or two of sharp advice.

"Is the wig that noticeable?" she asked.

"Not to most men, I don't guess. But it's blond. Blond and red stand out. Get a brown wig, light brown, in a medium length and a so-so style. And get one that's better quality. It'll last longer and look more natural." Abruptly she got to her feet, first aid kit in hand, and walked to the door. "Get some sleep, girl. You look like you about to fall outta that chair."

As exhausted as she was, and with the effects of the whiskey thrown in, Grace expected sleep was all she would be able to manage. She was wrong. Several hours later, her head finally clear of alcohol but her body still heavy with fatigue, she still hadn't managed to doze. She sat propped against the headboard, her left arm dully throbbing, with the laptop balanced on her blanket-covered legs. She had tried to work, but the intricacies of ancient languages, written in an archaic penmanship style, seemed to be beyond her. Instead she logged on to her personal journal and read her past entries. She couldn't remember some of the entries, and that disturbed her. It was as if she were reading someone else's diary, about someone else's life. Was that life so completely gone? She didn't want it to be, and yet she was afraid that she couldn't survive if she held on to it.

The loving but casual references to Ford and their life together, to Bryant, almost undid her. She felt the rush of pain and hastily scrolled down, closing her mind to the memories. She reached the last entry, made April twenty-sixth, and with relief saw that the entire entry was about the intriguing documents she'd been deciphering and translating. She had typed "NIALL OF SCOTLAND" in capital letters, and followed it with "real or myth?"

She knew the answer to that. He'd been real, a man who strode boldly through history, but behind the scenes, so that few traces remained of his passing. He'd been entrusted with the enormous Treasure of the Templars, but what had he done with it? With the means at his disposal, he could have accomplished anything, toppled kings, but instead he'd vanished.

Her fingers moved over the keys. "What were you, Niall? Where did you go, what did you do? What is so special about these papers that men have died just for knowing they existed? Why can't I stop thinking about you, dreaming about you? What would you do if you were here?"

A strange question, she thought, looking at what she had typed. Why would she even think of him in modern times? Dreaming about him was at least understandable, because immersing herself in her research, trying so hard to find any mention of him, had indelibly imprinted him in her mind. Because of Ford's and Bryant's deaths, there was nothing more important to her now than finding out *why*, so naturally she dreamed about the research.

But she hadn't, she realized. She hadn't dreamed about the Templars, about ancient documents, or even about libraries or computers. She had dreamed only of Niall, her imagination assigning him a face, a form, a voice, a presence. Since the murders she hadn't dreamed much at all, as if her subconscious tried to give her a respite from the terrible reality she faced every day, but when she had dreamed it had been of Niall.

What *would* he do if he were there? He'd

been a highly trained warrior, the medieval equivalent of the modern military's special forces. Would he have run and hidden, or would he have stood his ground and fought?

Whatever was best to achieve my goal.

Her head snapped around, her heart racing. Someone had spoken, someone in the room. Her panicked gaze searched out every corner of the small room, and though her eyes told her she was alone, her instincts didn't believe it. Her body felt electrified, every nerve alert and tingling. She breathed shallowly, her head cocked as she sat very still and listened, straining to hear a faint rustle of fabric, a scrape of a shoe, an indrawn breath. Nothing. The room was silent. She was alone.

But she'd *heard* it, a deep, slightly raspy voice with a burred inflection. It hadn't been in her head, but something external.

She shivered, her skin roughening with chill bumps. Beneath her T-shirt, her nipples were tight and hard.

"Niall?" she whispered into the empty room, but there was only silence, and she felt foolish.

It had been only her imagination, after all, producing yet another manifestation of her obsession with those papers.

Still, her fingers tapped on the keys again, the words spilling out of her: "I'll learn how to fight. I can't be passive about this, I can't merely react to what others do. I have to make things happen, have to take the initiative away from Parrish. That's what you would do, Niall. It's what I will do."

Chapter 9

Parrish sipped the merlot, and gave a brief nod of appreciation. Though merlot usually wasn't to his taste, this one was unexpectedly fine, very dark and dry. Bayard "Skip" Saunders, his host, considered himself a connoisseur of wine and had gone to great lengths to impress Parrish by trotting out his best and rarest vintages. Parrish was accustomed to members of the Foundation becoming slightly giddy whenever he visited; though he would have preferred a fine champagne or a biting martini, or even a properly aged bourbon, he was publicly never less than gracious about his underlings' efforts.

Skip — a ridiculous nickname for a grown man — was one of the more wealthy and influential members of the Foundation. He also lived in Chicago, which was the sole reason for Parrish's presence. Though Conrad had been unable to find a definite trail, he was nevertheless certain Grace had made her way to Chicago, and Parrish had faith in his henchman. Skip Saunders would be able to provide support in the search, in the form of both logistics and influence. Should Grace's capture be too messy — in other words, too public — Skip would be able to whisper a few words into an ear or two and the matter would simply go away, as if it had never existed. Parrish appreciated the convenience.

What he would appreciate more, he thought idly as his gaze briefly met that of Saunders's wife, Calla, was half an hour alone with the lovely Mrs. Saunders. What a superb trophy she was, a glorious testament to the seductiveness of money and power. Wife number one, the recipient of Saunders's youthful seed and vigor and the bearer of his two exceedingly spoiled children, was unfortunately fifty and therefore no longer young enough or glamorous enough to satisfy his ego. Parrish had met the first Mrs. Saunders, when she had still been Mrs. Saunders, and had been charmed by her wit. At any dull social affair he would have much preferred to have number one beside him — but if the position were changed to *under* him, he would definitely choose the lovely Calla. Saunders was a fool. He should have kept the wonderful companion as his wife, the main course, and enjoyed Calla as a side dish. Ah, well. Men who thought with their genitals often made poor choices.

Calla was certainly tempting. Parrish's manners were too polished to allow him to stare openly at her, but nevertheless each look was thoroughly assessing. She was about five-six, willowy, impeccably dressed in a simple, midnight-blue sheath that lovingly hugged every siliconed and liposuctioned curve and provided ample bare flesh on which to display the multitude of diamonds and sapphires she wore. She was a striking woman, with warmly golden skin and big, china-blue eyes, but what interested him most was her long, straight swath of hair, which she let hang freely down her back. Smart woman. She knew her hair was a magnet for male attention, the way it lifted and swung with every graceful movement she made. It wasn't as long as Grace's, he thought dispassionately, or as dark, but still . . .

She was taller than Grace, and more slender. She probably hadn't blushed with shyness since the age of eight, and the expression in her eyes was knowing, completely lacking Grace's innocence and trust. Her mouth wasn't thin, but neither did it have the lush, unconscious sexuality of Grace's lips. Her hair, though . . . he wanted to wrap his fist in that hair, hold it tight while he used her. He would close his eyes and pretend she was shorter, softer, that the hair he gripped was as sleek and thick as dark mink.

Perhaps later, he thought, and gave her a long, cool, deliberate look he knew she wouldn't misunderstand. One elegantly arched brow lifted as she caught his intent, and her lips curved in both invitation and satisfaction. Once again she had attracted the most powerful male present, and she was obviously pleased.

That minor detail taken care of, Parrish turned his attention back to her husband. "Very good," he said, seeing that Skip was anxiously awaiting verbal approval of his choice of wine. "I don't usually care for merlot, but this is exceptional."

A flush of pleasure warmed Skip's tanned face. "There are only three bottles of that particular vintage left in the world. I have two of them," he couldn't resist adding.

"Excellent. Perhaps you should acquire the third bottle as well," Parrish suggested, and hid his perverse amusement at the knowledge that Skip would now spend an untold amount of time and money trying to do just that. The three bottles could turn to vinegar for all Parrish cared.

He clapped a friendly hand to Skip's shoulder. "I want to have a private word with you, if I may, whenever you are free from playing host."

As he'd expected, Skip immediately straightened. "We can go to my study now. Calla won't mind, will you, darling?"

"Of course not," she calmly replied, knowing her role and in truth not giving a damn where her husband was or what he did. She immediately turned away to see to the needs of her other guests, a select fifty or so of Chicago's wealthiest citizens.

Skip led the way down a wide corridor to a set of double doors which he opened inward, admitting them into a mahogany-paneled office with a huge expanse of window overlooking Lake Michigan. "Magnificent view, isn't it?" Skip asked with obvious pleasure, crossing to the window.

"Magnificent," Parrish agreed. The view was more spectacular than his view of Lake Minnetonka, but he wasn't envious. He could have had such a view, had he chosen. Instead he was well pleased with the more staid but equally moneyed Wayzata; it suited him to be slightly out of the mainstream of the larger cities, tucked away in Minnesota. His neighbors were incurious, and so long as he gave the impression of being socially and politically correct, no one ever looked beneath the surface.

The two men stepped out onto the balcony, and the brisk wind off the lake still carried a chill even though summer had truly arrived. Parrish looked both left and right to make certain they were completely alone. "We're searching for a woman, Grace St. John. She's been accused of murdering her husband." He didn't bother to explain that he himself was responsible for both the accusation and the murder. "I believe she has information we would find of vital importance, so of course I would prefer finding her before the police do."

"Of course," Skip murmured. "Anything I can do —"

"My men have the search operation in hand, but should things go wrong, I want you on hand to turn any interest away. I hope requiring your presence here won't interfere with any vacation plans you've made." Parrish said it knowing Skip and Calla were scheduled to leave shortly for a month-long stay in Europe, not that it mattered; Skip would cancel an audience with the Pope to be of service to the Foundation. Of the two, the Foundation was more powerful, though its power and influence were far less noticeable.

"No problem," Skip hastily assured him.

"Good. I'll call you if I need you."

As Parrish turned to enter the study he saw Calla standing just inside the doors, and he paused, wondering what she knew and how much she'd overheard. It would be a pity if she fell over the balcony; such a tragic accident, but accidents happened.

"Dear," Calla said to Skip as she glided onto the balcony. "I'm sorry to disturb you, but Senator Trikoris has just arrived, and you know how he is."

The senator was notorious for expecting a great deal of ass-licking in exchange for legislative favors. The Foundation was working to develop a file on the senator, one that would bring him in line so that the favors he did were for the Foundation's benefit. When that happened, the senator would be the one doing the ass-licking, and Parrish's would be the ass being licked. The senator wasn't yet aware of the future direction of his legislative efforts, and until he was, Parrish was content to let Skip keep him happy. He nodded a dismissal, and Skip hastily left.

Calla leaned against the wall, her gaze cool and brilliant and calculating as she watched him. The wind lifted the silky ends of her hair, playing with it. Out here in the night, her hair looked dark, as dark as Grace's. Perhaps he would fuck her before assisting her over the balcony, Parrish thought, and felt his body respond to the excitement of the idea.

"Yes, I know about the Foundation," Calla murmured, her gaze never wavering from his face. "Skip's a fool. He leaves paperwork lying around in his office where anyone can see it. You would be better off to get rid of him and work with me."

Parrish lifted his eyebrows. She was right; Skip was a fool, and an unforgivably careless one. He would have to be taken care of. Dear Calla wasn't a fool, however, and the problem of what to do about her was one that demanded an immediate decision.

He leaned against the balcony railing, slim and elegant in his black silk trousers and white evening coat. His debonair image was both carefully cultivated and entirely natural to him, blinding people to the cold reality that lay beneath the silk. He sensed that Calla, unlike most people, had read him correctly and knew how close she was to death. Instead of being dismayed, she was excited by the danger. Beneath the clingy midnight fabric of her dress, her nipples were erect.

"It's Skip who has the contacts, the money," he said neutrally, but he was becoming more excited, too. Grace was the only other woman who had instinctively sensed the reality of him, and she had resisted his charm. Calla made no effort to resist him, but the similarity was enough to make him hot. It wouldn't be like having Grace; Grace had an innocence, a shining incorruptibility, that would drive him to new heights in his efforts to sully her. He doubted there was any sullying in which Calla had not already indulged. But in a way Calla was a twisted, corrupted version of Grace, and he wanted her.

Calla grimaced at his statement. "He has the power, you mean, because he controls the money. But does the true power lie with the man who controls the money, or with the woman who controls the man? What I know about the movers and shakers in this city is ten times more useful than Skip's social contacts."

"You use the word *know* in the biblical sense, I presume?"

Her lips curved in a slight smile but she didn't answer the charge. "The Foundation is real power. Forget the trade unions, the political parties; they all have ties to the Foundation, don't they? No matter which party is in the White House, you have a private line to the Oval Office."

In most cases, he thought, but not all. The Foundation hadn't had good luck with the past two Republican presidents, or the Democratic one before them. Their luck had changed four years earlier, however, and he had moved swiftly to make the gains denied the Foundation for sixteen long years. He was also working hard to make certain he maintained guaranteed access for another four years, at least. Politics was boring, but necessary, at least for now. If he could get his hands on the documents Grace held, he wouldn't have to bother with manipulating politics to try and ensure a reasonable occupant of the White House; the president would be coming to him, as would all the world's ostensible leaders.

The Foundation had been poised for centuries, ready to act when the papers were found. How wonderful that the discovery had been made on *his* watch, Parrish thought, but less wonderful that a bungling fool in France had let the documents slip out of his hands. Those papers meant power. Unimaginable power. The world would be in the palm of his hand, to be manipulated as he willed. Oh, the money and the power would *technically* belong to the Foundation, to be passed on to his successor, but his to use as he wished for his lifetime. A man of limited imagination wouldn't see the possibilities, but Parrish had no such limitations.

He had no interest in holding any office, whether president or prime minister, or in waging war. War was so gauche, so much effort for so little gain. The time had passed when nations could be won; now war meant little but destruction. Real power lay in money, as Calla had observed, and whoever controlled the money controlled the world as well as the puppets who stood onstage, in the limelight, and pretended to be the ones in power.

The documents in Grace's possession led to such power, to unlimited wealth. Over the centuries legends and superstitions had formed about some magical source of power the Templars had controlled, much like the ridiculous claims about the Ark of the Covenant, but unlike some in the Foundation, Parrish secretly scoffed at the idea. If the Templars had controlled some magical power, how could they have been so easily destroyed by treachery? Obviously the only power they had possessed had been a material one, an enormous treasury that had attracted the envy of a king and caused their downfall. No, the Templars' power had been wealth, more than could be imagined. There was nothing magical about it, though to the fourteenth-century mind the sheer magnitude of the treasury must have been beyond comprehension, and thus had to be magic. They had been nothing but superstitious fools. Parrish, however, was not.

Nor was he sentimental. If Calla thought to enslave him with her considerable charm, she was doomed to disappointment.

"I'm interested in working with the Foundation," Calla said when he remained silent, his cold gaze fixed on her face. "My assets are considerably more useful than Skip's."

"No one works *with* the Foundation," Parrish corrected. "The proper term is *for.*"

"Not even you?" she delicately needled.

He shrugged. For his lifetime he *was* the Foundation, but it wasn't necessary for her to know that. It wasn't necessary to talk to her at all. As delightful as it would undoubtedly be to let her into the Foundation, to have her at his beck and call until he was bored with her, he wasn't about to let someone of her intellect and daring, as well as complete lack of scruples, get that close to the center of power. He would have to watch his back every minute.

She moistened her lips, staring at him. "Do you know what I think?" Her voice was a purr. "I think you're the center of it all. A man with your kind of power — why, you can do anything, have anything you want. And I can help you get it."

Oh, she was definitely too smart for her own good.

He reached her in three steps, smiling slightly in the semidarkness as he looked down at her. Calla stood very still, her perfectly chiseled face illuminated by the light from the study behind her. She licked her lips again, the action unconscious, feline.

"Here?" she whispered. "People with telescopes watch, you know."

He paused. If he were merely going to screw her, he wouldn't care who watched. But since she would be going for a long, vertical walk afterward, he didn't want witnesses.

Smiling, he stepped back and gestured to the door. She laughed as she walked ahead of him into the study. "Somehow I expected you to be more adventurous."

"There's a difference, my dear, between adventurous and stupid." He went to the wall switch and turned out the lights, then locked the door. Calla stood calmly waiting for him, the city lights spilling through the windows, glittering on the jewels at her ears and throat.

He took off his dinner jacket and draped it over the back of a chair, not caring to have it smeared with telltale makeup. His shirt would likely bear the marks, but it would be covered by the jacket, and he would dispose of it as soon as he returned to his own hotel. As a last precaution he took his handkerchief from the jacket and put it in his pants pocket.

Arousal coursed through him as he stood in front of her and worked the tight sheath of her skirt up about her waist. She didn't have on any underwear, but then he hadn't expected any. He lifted her onto the desk and she leaned back until she was lying flat across the polished surface. They both knew what this was, and it wasn't lovemaking. She didn't pretend to have any romantic feelings, or demand foreplay. This was power sex, a gambit involving bodies, though she hadn't yet realized the true game or that she wouldn't survive it.

He unfastened his pants and stepped between her spread thighs, entering her with a smooth thrust that had her humming with pleasure. *Good*, he thought as he began thrusting. It would be nice if she enjoyed her last time.

Calla's long hair fanned across the desk. Parrish closed his eyes and thought of Grace, of her luscious mouth. He imagined that the heat surrounding him was Grace's heat, and he pumped steadily into it. She too would die afterward, but perhaps not immediately. Perhaps he would play with her for a while.

Calla gasped, arching. The response struck him as too theatrical, and he paused to consider her. Her eyes were half closed, her head tilted back, her lips open and moist. It was a lovely picture she made, and a totally false one. Why, she was faking, damn her, pandering to his ego. She probably faked it with all her rich lovers, twisting and moaning so they thought they were great in the sack, while all the time she was smirking inside and feeling nothing but contempt because men were so easily manipulated with sex.

Not this time.

He slipped one of her shoes off, dropping it to the floor. Deliberately he reached down between their bodies and pinched her clitoris, rubbing his thumb across it in a repeated motion. She gasped again, and tried to twist away from him. Parrish dragged her back, thrusting into her to the hilt and recapturing her hardened nub. "What's the matter?" he softly taunted, his voice coming in soft pants in rhythm with his thrusts. "Don't tell me you like faking it better than actually coming. Can't you feel superior if you let yourself enjoy being fucked?"

"Bastard," she hissed at him, digging her claws into his sleeved arms. Her breath was coming faster, her eyes furious and gleaming in the darkness.

"You like the power you have over men, don't you? You like knowing you can turn them into panting beasts. Is that what makes your nipples get so hard, or do you fake that too, pinching them when no one's looking?"

The glitter of her eyes almost matched that of her jewels. "I pinch them. Did you think a *man* could turn me on? Don't be funny!"

"What does turn you on? A woman?" He

kept his rhythm steady, his thumb moving ceaselessly back and forth while he thrust. Her hostility was far more exciting than her compliance had been; if it hadn't been for her superficial resemblance to Grace, he would simply have pushed her over the railing without giving her a tumble first. But he liked her venom, her contempt; at least she wasn't faking *that.*

"That would please your ego, wouldn't it, if I were a lesbian? No wonder you couldn't make me enjoy it, I'm a man-hater! No such luck," she jeered. "I please myself, a lot better than a man can."

"Until now." He openly gloated as he felt how wet she was getting. Her breath was getting faster and faster, her nipples standing upright without being pinched. He read the signs and thrust harder and deeper, driving into her, and with a choked cry she began climaxing. Triumphant, he rode her to the end, until his own climax began boiling upward. He snatched the handkerchief out of his pocket as he jerked out of her, coming into the silk square while he stroked himself in the final pleasure.

Her features twisted with rage as she sat up. It wasn't just that he'd made her climax, but that he had pulled away from her at the last and accomplished his own pleasure without her, taunting her with the reversal of her usual role with men.

Calmly Parrish folded the handkerchief and replaced it in his pocket, to be disposed of when he could safely do so. He straightened his clothing, tucking and zipping, then assisted her off the desk. She stood silently as he restored her dress to its proper position. "Don't sulk," he advised. "It isn't becoming. You should learn, my dear, to be a better loser. And to be a better judge of the men you play your power games with, because I fear you badly misjudged the situation this time."

She glared at him, not ready to give him any sort of victory, and bent down to retrieve her shoe. Parrish stayed her with a hand under her elbow. "Not yet," he said, smiling, and clipped her under the chin with his fist.

She obligingly sagged forward, and he lifted her in his arms. She wasn't unconscious, just stunned, and she blinked owlishly at him as he swiftly carried her out onto the balcony. "I would apologize for the little bruise you'll have," he told her as he stood her up at the waist-high wall, "but really, my dear, no one will notice." Then he bent and caught her ankles, and tipped her over.

She didn't scream at all, or if she did, the sound was stifled by terror. Parrish didn't linger to watch; after all, they were fifty-six stories up, and it would take her several seconds to hit the street. He went back into the study and picked up her shoe, then returned to the balcony. Crouching, he pressed the heel of the shoe against the polished marble until the high, sharp heel snapped off. He thought about tossing the shoe over too, but someone might notice its arrival on the street several seconds after its wearer, so instead he left it lying on the marble. All that remained to do was to retrieve his jacket and rejoin the guests, and wait for the cops to arrive and tell Skip his wife had apparently taken a header off the balcony. That should take long enough for everyone to be hazy about the time he rejoined them, especially since the wine and cocktails had been freely flowing for at least an hour now.

He did regret having to soil his handkerchief.

Chapter 10

Gaelic was a bitch. Grace had spent two weeks working on the Gaelic section, and made very little headway. The language wasn't in her computer programs, so she had no electronic aid in deciphering the faint chicken scratches. Whoever had copied the originals had tried to darken the copy to bring out more detail, with little success. She could see the tattered edges of the originals on the copy, telling her that the Gaelic sections hadn't fared as well as those written in Latin. Perhaps the paper hadn't been of as good a quality, or the pages had gotten damp at some time. Not that a good, clear copy would have helped much.

She had bought a Gaelic/English dictionary, and several guides to speaking Gaelic to aid her in figuring out syntax. The problem, however, was that she hadn't been able to find any guides to Gaelic as it had been spoken in the fourteenth century. She thought she would go mad with frustration. There were only eighteen letters in the Gaelic alphabet, but the Scots and Irish had overcome that restriction by using wildly creative spelling. Add to that the archaic styles of handwriting, word usage, and no standard spelling anyway, and the effort involved in translating one sentence was twice what it would have taken her to do an entire page of Latin or Old English.

But even with all the difficulties, eventually she pieced together sentences that made sense. The Gaelic section detailed the exploits of a Highland renegade called Black Niall. Though the section's inclusion with the rest of the papers made it likely Black Niall was the same man as Niall of Scotland, Grace didn't automatically assume they were one. She had already dealt with the complication of different spellings of the same name, so it was just as possible that the spelling could be the same but refer to someone else. After all, any number of Nialls had lived in Scotland. *Her* Niall was Niall of Scotland, of royal blood; what connection would royalty have with a Highland renegade? These chronicles were different from the others; different handwriting, different paper. They could have been mixed by accident with the others, simply because of the name.

Black Niall was an entertaining rogue, though. Deciphering his exploits occupied all her free time, except for the hours she spent with Harmony's "mean little greaser son of a bitch," one Mateo Boyatzis, a delicate and deadly young man of Mexican and Polish heritage. Matty knew more dirty tricks than a political ad man, and as a favor to Harmony he had agreed to teach "Julia" a few basics of fighting to win. She had no illusions about her slowly growing skill; she was not and never would be anything approaching expert. All she hoped to do was to be able to use the advantage of surprise to protect herself and the papers.

Not that she had anything to worry about, she thought, rubbing eyes grown weary from hours of wading through incomprehensible spellings and unlikely pronunciations. Any minute now, Gaelic was going to reduce her to drooling insanity, and then she wouldn't care what happened.

To give herself a break, she put the Gaelic section aside and turned on the computer, then scrolled through until she came to a section in Old French. The papers weren't in any chronological order; putting the story together was like placing pieces of a puzzle, an ancient one in many languages.

She saw the name almost at once, so attuned to it that her eyes picked up the familiar pattern of letters almost before she'd brought the words into focus. *Black Niall.*

"Whaddaya know," she murmured, leaning forward. It looked as if Black Niall and Niall of Scotland were indeed one and the same. Why would papers written in French detail the exploits of an obscure Scots rogue, unless he wasn't so obscure after all? A Templar of royal blood, excommunicated, under the penalty of death should he ever be taken outside Scotland, and Guardian of the Treasure to boot — obscure perhaps by design, but certainly not unimportant. There had been people, perhaps remnants of the Order, who had known who and what Black Niall was, and made a point to keep track of where.

But royal? She had gone over and over the genealogical charts in the Newberry Library, and there hadn't been a Niall recorded during that era.

"Who *were* you?" she whispered, seeking that elusive wisp of contact, almost like touching the mind of a man who was centuries dead. She had never before realized how powerful her imagination could be, but she took comfort in the sense of connection. She didn't dare let anyone else too close, not even Harmony, but there were no limits with the man who lived now only in her dreams. She didn't have to be wary with him, didn't have to hide her identity, didn't have to disguise herself.

These papers were yet another account of his exploits, where he had searched out a band of raiders and destroyed them, leaving no man alive. Niall had evidently gone to a great deal of trouble to protect his stronghold, dealing swiftly and harshly with any threat. This was another sticking point: if he were royal, he would have a title, and legal claim to his stronghold. The Gaelic papers, however, called him a renegade, a man who had taken by force a remote castle in the western Highlands, and held it without title or deed, without anything except the power of his sword. Could a royal be a renegade, and if he had indeed been outcast from the family to such an extent that his name had been stricken from all records, would or could Robert the Bruce have tolerated such insolence within his own borders?

The Gaelic papers would probably be more enlightening, but her brain simply couldn't absorb any more of it that night. Putting aside the French papers, she thumbed through until she found the pages in Old English.

Again, the name almost jumped off the page at her: Black Niall, a Scots warrior so bold and ruthless he was feared throughout the Highlands. His stronghold, Creag Dhu, was never breached, except once by "a layde who entered bye wicked trickery." Grace felt a tiny spurt of amusement when she read that, for of course a woman couldn't have accomplished the seemingly impossible without using "wicked trickery."

"She fooled you, didn't she, laddie?" she murmured to Niall, almost smiling as she imagined his disbelief, his outrage at finding his castle's protection breached by a lone woman. He would have been in an absolute fury, the kind that had the castle guards hiding from him — Grace stopped her thoughts, grimacing as she realized her imagination had kicked in again. She might dream about him, he might seem so real that sometimes she thought she could turn her head and actually see him standing there, but in reality he had turned to dust a good six centuries before she'd ever been born.

Reading on, she found that Black Niall had captured the woman, so the "layde" 's trickery had gained her nothing, except his attention, and perhaps that was what she had wanted. The papers didn't indicate what he had done with her after capturing her. Bedded her, probably, Grace thought. He'd been a lusty man, ill suited for monkhood.

Another account began: "Black Niall, the MacRobert —" and Grace sat upright as all the tumblers clicked into place.

Niel Robertsoune — son of Robert, and a great warrior in an order renowned for its warriors. Niall MacRobert — again, son of Robert, and a warrior so great his stronghold was never breached, save by that unnamed enterprising lady. "A Scot of Royal blude" . . . son of Robert . . . son of *Robert the Bruce?*

Electrified, she quickly checked the dates, only to sag back in disappointment. She could only guess at Black Niall's age, since she knew neither his birthdate nor the date he had died, but he had been a grown man when the Order had been condemned in 1307. King Robert I of Scotland, the most famous Bruce, had been too young to be Black Niall's father. Quickly Grace rechecked her notes on the chronology of Scotland's royal line. Robert the Bruce's father, the Earl of Carrick, had also been named Robert.

Was Black Niall *brother* to Robert the Bruce? How? The Bruce's four brothers, Edward, Nigel, Thomas, and Alexander, had been well documented as they fought with their brother and king to push the English out of Scotland. The only way Niall could be connected, but left in obscurity, would be if he were illegitimate.

"That's it," Grace breathed, sitting back.

The ramifications, the possibilities, made sitting still impossible. She jumped up and began pacing the confines of her small room as detail after detail fell into place to complete the puzzle. A bastard half-brother, in medieval times, wouldn't have been that unusual or even that important — unless the legitimate heir happened to be aiming for a throne. Scotland had always been different from the rest of Europe in the way it looked at kinship, and while Niall's bastardy would normally have put him beyond the pale, in Scotland the crown had been up for grabs by the one who wielded the most power. The Bruce had been an undeniably powerful warrior and foe, but Niall's skills in warfare had been legendary. His very existence would have been a threat to Robert.

The wonder was that he hadn't been murdered, to remove that threat. The fact that he hadn't suggested that he had been held in some affection. Then, too, he had joined the Templars, so perhaps his ambitions had been churchly rather than political. No — remembering what she'd already read about Black Niall, he hadn't been the churchly sort at all. So why had he been a Templar? Adventure, wealth? She could see where the promise of both might have lured Black Niall to the Order, but overall his nature seemed far too fierce and earthy for him to accept the restrictions.

Whatever his reasons for becoming a Templar, his doing so had been convenient for the future King of Scotland. The Bruce wouldn't have had to worry about a monk gaining the crown, because his vows of chastity would have precluded heirs to the throne.

His chastity had ended with the destruction of the Order, Grace thought, if she had translated some of the passages correctly. The references to sexual activity hadn't been explicit, but fairly plain for all that. However Niall had honored his vows while a Templar, after the Order had been destroyed he had embraced life — and women — to the fullest. He still would not have been a threat to the throne, because as an ex-Templar he would have shunned exposure.

But it explained so much — why Niall had been able to take Creag Dhu and hold it without interference from the King, even why the Bruce had been the one European monarch who had not only not enforced the papal death sentence against the Templars, but whose country had become a sanctuary of sorts for the hunted men. Robert had refused to sign his half-brother's death sentence. It even explained why Niall had been chosen as Guardian; the Temple Masters had known his lineage, known he and the Treasure would be safer in Scotland than anywhere else in the world.

She inhaled suddenly, and the room turned dark around her as knowledge struck with the force of a blow. The Treasure. Ford and Bryant had died because these stupid papers told the location of the famed, lost Treasure of the Templars: Creag Dhu.

Money. That was what it came down to. They had died because of money, money that Parrish Sawyer wanted. Because she had the papers, he had either assumed she had already translated enough to know what they were about and also told Ford and Bryant, or he had wanted to wipe out all knowledge of them regardless.

She had thought the grief would be easier to bear if she just knew *why.*

It wasn't.

Conrad lay quietly in bed, lights off, but the city was never dark and the bland hotel walls were washed with muted, flickering colors from a plethora of neon. The latest computer list lay on the desk, put aside for now. Some things were best reserved for the night, but others had to wait for busy daylight and normal office hours. The delay didn't bother him; he was a patient man. Grace wasn't going anywhere, at least not yet. She had gone to ground somewhere in the massive urban sprawl, and she would stay there as long as she felt safe. She was a scholar, a researcher; she would research. The libraries in Chicago were very good. Yes, he was confident she would remain in Chicago for a while, and all the time he would be looking for her. She wouldn't know he was close until he was ready to pounce.

Mr. Sawyer had a small army of men out combing the streets, but Conrad didn't put any faith in that tactic. The people who operated in the underground economy weren't about to answer any questions truthfully, for one thing, and for another, Grace had proven herself capable of quite a few disguises. By now she could have shaven her head and dressed in leather, so relying on description was a waste of time.

Conrad preferred his own methods. To him it was simple: if anyone on the run remained in one place for long, he or she would have to establish an identity. For some it would be as uncomplicated as selecting a name. That worked so long as there was no need for credit, or a driver's license, or you didn't try to work in a legitimate place that demanded a social security number. In the long run it was smarter to establish a documented identity, and Grace St. John had impressed him with her intelligence.

The process was simple, but slow. To document an identity, one had to have a birth certificate. To get a birth certificate, one had to have a real name. Obviously, using a living person's name could be complicated when the two identities began colliding with each other, as would inevitably happen, so the best thing was to go to a cemetery and read tombstones. Find someone who had been born at approximately the same time as you were, within a couple of years either way, but who had died young. Sometimes the parents' names were on the tombstone, too: something along the lines of "Beloved Daughter of John and Jane Doe." Bingo, you had the information you needed to get a birth certificate.

Requests for birth certificates would go to the state capital, in this case Springfield. Getting a birth certificate was fairly easy; it was getting a full set of identification papers that would take time. Next she would have to get a social security number, and the federal government was slow. He had time to focus on the birth certificate requests.

With the Foundation's resources, gaining

access to the Illinois state computer system had taken a mere phone call. He had been surprised, however, by the volume of requests. It was amazing how many people needed to prove their existence, whether for social security claims, passport applications, or whatever. The sheer numbers involved were what was slowing him down.

He could automatically delete those requests for men, but again there were a lot of people with ambiguous names. Shelley, for instance. Male or female? And what about Lynn, or Marion, or Terry? Those people had to remain on his list until he could check them out.

Nor did he have a specific date of request, which made his task more difficult. She couldn't have made a request any sooner than the day after he had almost caught her in Eau Claire, but what if she waited a few days, a week, maybe even a couple of weeks? That uncertainty added literally hundreds of people to the list, from all over the state. He narrowed the focus to the Chicago area, but that still left hundreds because he figured at least a fourth of the state's entire population lived in the metro area.

Checking out that many people took time, and the list grew every day. Some of the people who requested birth certificates had moved in the meantime; they had to be located, and sometimes they had moved out of state. Some had gone on vacation, but until he had traced them he didn't dare eliminate them from his list. Grace could be hiding behind any of those names, even the most improbable. He would not underestimate her again.

"Girl, you look like shit," Matty said genially, uncoiling his compact, graceful body from the tattered sofa in his apartment.

"Thanks," Grace muttered. She was tired from sitting up nights trying to decipher Gaelic. Her eyes felt gritty, she had the energy of a slug, and she had burned her hand that day when she picked up a pan to wash and discovered it had just been taken from the oven. Harmony had tended the burn, scowling the entire time, and then had insisted on accompanying Grace to Matty's for another "lesson," just to make certain something else didn't happen to her.

"Just skin hangin' on a rack of bones," Harmony pronounced, still scowling. "I can't get her to eat, no matter what I cook. She's done lost ten pounds or more since she's been living in my house, which ain't exactly the best advertisement I could have."

Grace looked down at herself. She was used to Harmony's complaints that she didn't eat enough, but still she was surprised now when she really *looked* at herself, and saw her bony wrists, her body lost within the baggy folds of clothes that had once been the right size. She knew she'd lost weight, a lot of weight, that first horrible week after the murders, but she hadn't realized she was still losing weight. She was *thin,* and verging on downright skinny. She had to use a safety pin to tighten the waistband of her jeans so that they didn't slide right off. Even her underwear was too big these days, and loose panties weren't comfortable.

"I told her she don't need to be wearing those baggy clothes," Harmony continued, folding bonelessly onto the couch and crossing her long legs. "But does she listen to me? You tell her."

"Harmony's right," Matty said, frowning at Grace. "Don't give no sumbitch nothing to grab. You ain't got no size to you, Julia, and you ain't got no meanness. You'll fight if you're cornered, but the thing is, you gotta keep from gettin' cornered, 'cause then your chances go way down. Are you listenin' to me?" It wasn't like him to give a shit about anybody, but he worried about Julia. Something bad had happened to her, and she was still on the run. She didn't talk about it, but he could see it in her eyes. Hell, he was used to shootings and stabbings, drug overdoses, gang violence, little kids with big, scared, uncomprehending eyes, so he didn't know exactly what it was about Julia that got to him, but something did. Maybe it was because she looked so frail, so that sometimes he thought he could almost see right through her, or maybe it was the sadness that wrapped around her like a coat. She never smiled, and her big blue eyes just looked . . . empty. The look in her eyes made him hurt inside, and Matty was a man who made a point of not letting people close enough to him that he'd be hurt if anything happened to them. He'd failed with Julia.

"I'm listening," Grace said obediently. "I listen to Harmony, too. I just can't afford a bunch of new clothes."

"You heard of yard sales?" Harmony asked. "Take your nose outta your books once in a while and look around. People sell old jeans for four or five dollars, and usually you can get 'em for a dollar if you stand around long enough complainin' that five bucks is too much."

"I'll look," Grace promised. Yard sales. She'd never been to one in her life, but if she could get jeans in her size for a dollar, she was about to become a yard-sale fanatic. She was getting tired of holding her clothes up with safety pins, and tired of her underwear wandering around inside her jeans.

"Okay, enough of shoppin'," Matty said impatiently. "I'm tryin' to teach you how to stay alive. Pay attention here."

Matty's method of teaching didn't involve gyms or dojos, because he said fights generally didn't happen there. They happened on the streets, in houses, where people went about their business and lived their lives. A couple of times he'd taken her down to an alley for her lesson, which involved him attacking her from a variety of directions, tackling her or simply wrapping his arms around her and throwing her to the ground, and she had to get away from him. He'd shown her where to kick, where to punch, and what items commonly found in an alley could be used as a weapon, from a wooden slat to a broken bottle. He'd taught her how to carry her knife, the one she'd taken from the mugger, how to hold it and how to use it.

Matty saw weapons everywhere. In his hands, a pencil was lethal, a book could do serious damage, and a salt or pepper shaker presented a priceless opportunity. Flashlights, paperweights, matches, pillows, a sheet, a jacket — all those could be used. Such a ridiculous notion as a fair fight never entered his head. Chairs were battering rams. A baseball bat or a golf club was for beating people in the head, ice skates were for slicing them open — the possibilities were endless. Grace didn't think she would ever be able to look at a room the same way again. Before, rooms had been just . . . rooms. Now they were weapons repositories.

He fell on her without warning, wrapping his surprisingly strong arms around her and dragging her to the floor. The fall stunned her, rattled her brain, but she remembered her earlier lessons and promptly raked the sole of her shoe down his shin, and simultaneously got enough leverage with one arm to hit him under the chin with the heel of her palm. His teeth snapped together with an audible pop, and he shook his head to clear it. Grace didn't stop. She wiggled, she butted him with her head, she tried to punch him in the testicles, she gouged for his eyes.

Matty didn't just let her beat up on him, because that wouldn't teach her much, he said. She had to work to get in her licks. He deftly turned aside most of her efforts, but he'd explained to her that he was expecting her to fight and had a good idea what she'd do; a stranger wouldn't have that advantage. Still, she landed some of her attempts, enough to make him grunt occasionally, or swear when she managed to hit him in the chin again and he bit his tongue. Harmony sat on the couch and didn't exactly smile, but she looked pleased.

The effort quickly exhausted Grace. She collapsed on the floor, breathing heavily. Matty stood up and frowned down at her. "You're too weak," he pronounced. "Weaker than last week. I don't know what's eatin' at you, Julia, but you gotta eat, 'cause you ain't got no stamina." He wiped his mouth, and looked with interest at the blood that smeared his hand. "Guts, but no stamina."

Grace struggled to her feet. She truly hadn't

realized how weak she had become; she had simply attributed her fatigue to staying up late trying to decipher all the papers. Once she had enjoyed food, but now she had no interest in it; everything was tasteless, as if her taste buds had been dulled by shock and never recovered.

"I'll eat," she said simply, realizing now that she didn't have a choice. Because it was such a struggle now to work up any appetite at all, what she did eat would have to be nutritious. She had no idea how long this time of sanctuary would last; she had to be ready to leave at any time, and she had to be healthy. Suddenly she felt a little edgy; perhaps she shouldn't wait until something happened, perhaps she should leave now, and find another brief sanctuary. She had Julia Wynne's birth certificate; she had filed for a social security number, and when she got that she would be able to get a driver's license. With a driver's license she could risk driving, and not worry if a cop stopped her for speeding, or for a blown taillight. She could buy a cheap car, risk driving, go anywhere she wished whether there was a bus route there or not.

Harmony stood and stretched. "I'll start feedin' her tonight," she told Matty. "Maybe some strengthening exercises, too, whaddaya think?"

"Food first," Matty said. "Poke some meat down her throat. You gotta have the brick before you can build the wall. A nice steak, or some spaghetti and meatballs, stuff like that."

Grace tried not to gag at the mention of spaghetti. After working at Hector's, she couldn't stand the smell of garlic and tomato sauce.

"I'll think of something," Harmony promised, noticing the look of revulsion on Grace's face. She understood, because she'd once worked three months at a seafood joint down south; she still couldn't stand the smell of hush puppies frying, but thank God she'd never even caught a whiff of one in Chicago. Pissed her off when she thought about it; she'd always liked hush puppies before, and now she'd lost that pleasure.

Grace and Harmony walked down three blocks to a bus stop. Grace had developed the habit of looking all around her, and Harmony watched with approval as she checked out her surroundings. "You learning," she said. "Now, what made you so uptight all of a sudden, there at Matty's?"

Harmony was the most observant person Grace had ever met. She didn't even try to blow smoke. "I was thinking of leaving."

Harmony's eyebrows slowly climbed toward her yellow-white hair. "Was it something I said? Maybe you don't like my cooking? Or maybe something's got you scared."

"Nothing has happened to make me nervous," Grace tried to explain. "It's just . . . I don't know. Intuition, maybe."

"Then I guess you'd better be packing," Harmony said calmly. "It don't pay to go against your gut feeling." She looked up the street. "Here comes the bus."

Grace bit her lip. Though Harmony hadn't asked her to stay, and wouldn't, suddenly she felt the other woman's loneliness. They hadn't been intimates; both of them had too much to hide. But they had been friends, and Grace realized that she would miss Harmony's tough unconventionality.

"You need to stay a couple more days, if you can," Harmony continued, still watching the bus. "Let me get some food in you, build up your strength a little. And get you some clothes that fit, damn it. Plus I got a few things I can show you, too, things that might come in handy."

She could live with the edginess for a day or two, Grace thought. Anything Harmony wanted to teach her was bound to be worth the stress. "Okay. I'll stay until the weekend."

Harmony's only reaction was a brief nod, but again Grace felt her pleasure.

That night, sitting in the kitchen while Harmony worked a small miracle with a wok, Grace idly leafed through an impressive stack of newspapers. Harmony read the morning paper while sitting at the kitchen table and methodically emptying a pot of coffee, and tended to toss the paper onto an unused chair rather than into the trash. It had been so long since Grace had read a paper or listened to the news that she had no idea what was happening on a national level, and it felt strange to read the headlines and peek into an unknown past.

She had flipped through about half the stack when a grainy newsprint photograph caught her attention, and her gaze flew back to it. Suddenly she couldn't breathe, her lungs stilled in her chest, and her ears buzzed. *Parrish.* Parrish was one of the men in that photo.

Dimly she heard Harmony say something, then a hand was on the back of her neck, pushing her head down until it rested on her knees. Gradually the buzzing in her ears began to fade, and her lungs began working again. "I'm all right," she said, the words muffled against her knees.

"Izzat so? Coulda fooled me," Harmony said sarcastically, but she released Grace's neck and plucked the newspaper from her nerveless fingers. "Let's see. What did you read that made you keel over? 'Peace Talks Resume'? Don't think so. How 'bout this: 'Graft in City Hall Costs City Millions.' Makes *my* blood pressure go up, but it ain't never made me faint. Maybe it was 'Industrialist's Wife Dies.' There's even a picture of the poor grievin' husband to tweak your emotions. Yep, that looks like something would hit you hard." She slapped the paper down on the table, staring at the photo. "So, which one of these guys do you know?"

Still breathing deeply, Grace looked again at the photo. It was still a shock to see Parrish's handsome face, but now she noticed there were other people there as well. The husband, for one, his face stark with grief. Beside him stood a man who looked vaguely familiar, and a quick look at the caption beneath the photo identified them as Bayard "Skip" Saunders, wealthy industrialist, and Senator Trikoris. Three other men were in the background, Parrish among them, none of them identified by name. Parrish's expression was suitably somber, but knowing what she did about him, she didn't trust the impression he gave.

Swiftly she read the four inches of column space. Calla Saunders had apparently fallen to her death from her penthouse balcony. There was no evidence of foul play. One of Mrs. Saunders's high-heeled shoes, with the heel broken off, had been found on the balcony. Investigators surmised she had fallen off balance when the heel broke, and gone over the railing; flecks of white paint from the railing had been found on her evening dress. She had evidently been alone on the balcony.

The investigators didn't know Parrish Sawyer the way she did, Grace thought, shivering. If he was anywhere near a death scene, she doubted the death was accidental.

She had forgotten how handsome he was.

In her mind he had taken on a demonic aspect, his features shaped by the evil within, but the black-and-white photo captured his smooth, blond good looks, the chiseled face and slim, athletic body. As usual, he was impeccably attired. He looked completely civilized and cosmopolitan, a gentleman to his manicured fingertips.

His expression had been just as pleasant when he shot Ford in the head.

He was in Chicago. She checked the date on the newspaper, saw that it was almost two weeks old. Parrish was *here.* She wasn't safe, as she'd thought. Her instincts were right; it was time to leave.

"Let's see," Harmony mused when Grace didn't answer. "Wouldn't be the senator; he's all bullshit. Forget that Saunders guy; he's a complete wuss, just look at him. The other three . . . hmm . . . one looks like a cop, see the bad suit?"

Harmony was systematically, and with irritating accuracy, summing up every person in the photo. In another few seconds she would arrive unerringly at the correct conclusion. To save her the time and trouble, Grace tapped her fingernail once on Parrish's face.

"Now forget you ever saw him," she advised, her face and voice tense. "If he even thinks you might know something about me, he'll kill you."

Harmony's lashes shielded her eyes as she

studied the photo. When she finally looked up at Grace, her green gaze was hard and clear. "That man's evil," she said flatly. "You gotta get out of here."

The next two days were a flurry of activity. Grace worked furiously on translating as much of the Gaelic as possible, because she wouldn't have time to work while she was traveling. Harmony made the rounds of yard sales, and came up with some jeans that actually fit Grace, as well as some tight knit tops and a pair of sturdy hiking boots. When they were together, Harmony talked. Grace felt like Luke Skywalker listening to Yoda, but instead of imparting pearls of mystical wisdom Harmony discussed ways of losing a tail, how to travel without leaving tracks, how to get a fake driver's license and even a fake passport if she didn't have time or it was too dangerous to acquire the real thing. Harmony knew a lot about how to survive on the streets, and on the run, and that was her gift to Grace.

Her final gift was borrowing a car and driving Grace to Michigan City, Indiana, where she planned to catch a bus. Grace didn't tell Harmony her intended destination, and Harmony didn't ask; it was safer for both of them.

"Watch your back," Harmony said gruffly, hugging Grace to her. "And remember everything Matty and I showed you."

"I will," Grace said. "I do." She hugged Harmony in return, then gathered her bags and trudged into the bus station. Harmony watched the slight figure disappear inside, and blinked twice to dispel the blur from her eyes.

"God, you watch over her," she whispered, giving her orders to the Almighty, then Harmony Johnson got back into the borrowed Pontiac and drove away.

Grace watched from the window, her eyes dry despite the tight ache in her chest. She didn't know how many more good-byes she could say; maybe it would be best to stay on the go, not staying in any one place long enough to get attached to people.

But she still had a lot of work to do on the papers, and she needed a safe place in which to do it. She studied a map of the bus routes, then bought a ticket to Indianapolis. Once there, she would decide her next destination, but it had to be something totally unexpected. Parrish hadn't been in Chicago by accident, she was certain. Somehow, he'd known she was there. His men had been searching for her. She must have been utterly predictable, and soon they would have found her.

That wouldn't happen again, she promised herself. She was going to ground, in a place where they would never expect to find her, and suddenly she knew exactly where she was going. It was the one place they wouldn't think to look, the one place where she could keep tabs on Parrish and his movements: Minneapolis.

Chapter 11

The name Grace took from the cemetery in Minneapolis was Louisa Patricia Croley. This time she didn't get a birth certificate. Instead, armed with Harmony's pearls of illegal wisdom, by that afternoon she had a social security number, an address, and a driver's license. The last two were fake. The social security number was real, because it had belonged to the real Louisa Patricia Croley. Getting the number had been a snap, and she didn't need an actual card, just the number.

The next morning she was the owner of a pickup truck, a beige, rusted-out Dodge that nevertheless shifted gears smoothly and did not emit either any strange noises or telltale puffs of smoke. By paying cash, she got the owner to knock four hundred off his asking price. With the title and bill of sale in her possession, she then stood in line to get the title switched to her name — or rather, to Louisa Croley's name.

Grace was grimly satisfied as she walked back out to the truck. She had wheels now. She could leave any time she wished, and she didn't have to buy a ticket to do so, or worry about disguising herself in case the ticket agent remembered her if anyone came around asking questions. The truck meant liberation.

She rented a cheap room close to downtown, and after a little research applied for a job with the cleaning service that cleaned some of the lavish homes in Wayzata. There was no better pipeline of information than a cleaning service, because no one paid any attention to the cleaners. She knew that Parrish employed a full-time housekeeper, as did some of the other home owners on the lake, but enough of them used an outside service to make the business very lucrative. Not enough of the lucre made it down to the hands of those who did the cleaning, however, so the turnover was fairly high. She was hired immediately.

That night, in her drab little room, she lay in the lumpy bed and thought drowsily of the papers she had just finished translating. In 1321, a man named Morvan of Hay had tried to kill Black Niall, but lost his own head. His father, a clan chieftain whose lands lay to the east, had then launched the entire clan into open warfare with the renegades of Creag Dhu. Niall had been captured during one battle and locked in the Hays' dungeon, but escaped by unknown means that same night.

Niall. Grace kept her thoughts focused on him, afraid to let them wander. Being in Minneapolis was more difficult than she'd thought — not because of the danger, but because this was the city where she had lived with Ford, the city where her husband and brother were buried. She wanted desperately to go to their graves, but knew she didn't dare. Not only would it be an extremely risky move on her part, but she didn't think she could bear it. Seeing their graves would destroy her, shred the paper-thin wall she had built around her emotions. How long had it been now? Two months? Yes, two months and three days, almost to the hour. Not long enough. Not nearly long enough.

She would think of Niall instead. Concentrating on him was what kept her sane.

He was loving her.

On the periphery of her consciousness, Grace knew she was dreaming, but that awareness wasn't enough to stop the images. Always before when she had dreamed of Niall she had been an observer, but that night she was a participant.

The dream was vague, shifting, but she knew she was in bed with him. The bed was huge, piled high with furs; she would have felt lost and insignificant in such a bed, but with *him* there she was only vaguely aware of the vast expanse on which they lay. He mounted her, and the intense heat of his body startled her. Surprised, she realized they were both naked, his bare skin scorching hers. He was heavy, and the pressure of his weight almost crushed her, but it felt so wonderful to have a man on top of her again that she held him close. She had missed that so much, the weight of a man on her, the strength of a man's arms around her, his smell in her nostrils, his taste on her mouth.

She ran her hands over his back, feeling the layers of hard muscle under his taut skin. His mane of black hair was damp with sweat, his body was sheened with it. His scent was raw and hot and wild, that of a man aroused beyond control. She had caused this wildness in him and she loved it, she reveled in it, she wanted everything he could give her.

Then he entered her, and in her dream she cried out from the unbearable pleasure of it. He was so big she felt stretched, so hot she felt seared. Her body gathered and focused and tightened, and she began climaxing.

The spasms awoke her and at first she lay there awash in voluptuous sensation, breathing deeply and feeling the tremors subside. Niall must have just left her, she thought sleepily, because she could still feel in her loins the lingering throb caused by his thrusts. She wanted to curl in his arms, and she reached out her hand and touched —

Nothing.

Grace came sharply awake, her breath suddenly harsh in her lungs. She sat up, staring wildly around the dark, empty room. Horror filled her at what she had done, and she clenched her teeth against a howl of rage, of despair, of violent rejection.

No.

She hated herself, hated her stupid hungry body for letting a figment of her imagination tempt it to pleasure. How dare she dream of Niall, how dare she let the dream Niall invade her body, give her pleasure? He wasn't Ford. Only Ford had ever touched her, made love to her, explored with her the intense sexuality of her nature. She had lain naked only with Ford, loved only Ford, yet only two months after his death she dreamed of another man, a *dead* man, and found sexual pleasure in the dream.

She huddled on the bed, keening softly to herself. She had betrayed Ford. It didn't matter that she had done so only in imagination, in her subconscious. Betrayal was betrayal. It should have been Ford she'd been dreaming about, Ford who had died protecting her.

But if her dreams were of Ford . . . she would have gone insane by now. His death, Bryant's death, was a great internal wound she didn't dare touch because it was still bleeding, still too painful to bear. She had focused on studying the documents about Black Niall because that was the only way she could function, and her subconscious had thrown her a curve ball by continuing to focus on him during her sleep.

Damn her body, damn her own nature.

When she was awake it was as if her sensuality had died with Ford; she felt no desire, no frustration, no attraction. But when she slept, her body remembered, and yearned. She had loved making love, loved everything about it — the smells, the sounds, the delicious rub of his body against hers, the way he had stroked her while she arched and purred, the sweet, startling moment of entry when their bodies linked. When Ford was off on a dig and she hadn't been able to join him, she had been tormented by sexual frustration until he returned. He had always walked into the house grinning, because he knew that within five minutes they would be locked in their bedroom.

Grace locked her arms around her knees and stared at nothing. Perhaps, now that she had calmed down, she could understand how she had come to dream about Niall, but she didn't want it to happen again. She wouldn't think about the papers when she was in bed. Instead she would think about Parrish. That would be safe, because she didn't find him remotely attractive; she could see the evil beneath the beauty of his form. She would try to devise some means of revenge. She didn't just want him dead, she wanted justice, she wanted the world to know the truth about him. She wanted it known he had killed two wonderful men, and why. But if justice eluded her, she would settle for vengeance.

Finally she lay back down, half afraid to sleep again but knowing she had to try; she started work at seven in the morning, and cleaning houses was hard work. She needed to sleep, she needed to remember to eat, she needed . . . oh, God, she needed Ford, and Bryant, she needed everything to be the way it was before.

Instead she lay alone in a narrow, lumpy bed, and watched the night pass while she tried to think of some way to use the papers against Parrish.

Niall jerked himself out of sleep, cursing as he carefully rolled onto his back and pushed the bedcovers away from his straining, jutting penis, unable to tolerate even the slightest touch lest he spill his seed in the bed. He hadn't done such a thing since he was an untried lad of thirteen, not even during his eight years of sexual deprivation as a Knight.

He had dreamed of a woman, dreamed he was plowing deep into her belly. He couldn't fathom why he should be dreaming of such, when only a few hours earlier he had enjoyed a lusty encounter with Jean, a widow who had sought the safety of living within castle walls and traded her skills in the kitchen for a pallet in Creag Dhu.

He hadn't dreamed of Jean, or of any other woman he knew. But the woman in his dreams had been familiar, somehow, though in his dream they had coupled in darkness and he hadn't been able to see her face. She was small in his arms, as most women were, but there had also been a certain frailty, a slightness that made him want to take care with her. She hadn't wanted careful tenderness, however; she had been hot and wanton, clinging to him, her hunger as fierce as his. Her hips had lifted to meet him and as soon as he had entered her, groaning at the perfect, silky tightness that gloved him, her spasms of pleasure had begun. The intensity of her response to him had made him burn hotter and faster than he ever had before, and he'd been on the verge of joining her in climax when he abruptly woke to an empty bed, empty arms, and furious frustration.

He judged the hour to be near dawn, too near to seek sleep again. Scowling, he groped for flint and lit a candle, then strode to the fireplace to stir the banked embers and add a few small sticks to catch fire. The chill air washed around his naked body, but he didn't feel cold; he was hot, almost steaming from the force of his arousal. His penis was still thick and erect, aching from the loss of that tight internal clasp. He could feel her on his flesh as vividly as if he had indeed just left her body.

She had smelled . . . sweet. The memory was elusive, fleeting, but his thin nostrils flared as he instinctively tried to catch it again. Clean and sweet, not the overpowering sweetness of a flowery perfume but something light, tantalizing, and underlying it had been the exciting muskiness that signaled her arousal.

Ah, it had been a great dream, despite the frustrating aftermath. He seldom laughed, for life did not much amuse him, but his lips curved upward as he stared down at his rebellious manly parts. The dream woman had aroused him more than any real woman ever had, and he had greatly enjoyed many women. If he should ever truly lay his hands on one such as his dream woman, he would no doubt kill himself rutting on her. Even now, when he remembered how it had felt to enter her, the heat and wetness and tight, perfect fit —

The throb in his loins intensified, and his smile grew to a grin, one that none of his people had ever seen, for it was free and lighthearted, and he hadn't been that since the age of sixteen. He grinned at his own foolishness, and at remembered pleasure, real or not. He tormented himself by letting his thoughts linger on the dream, yet it was too arousing to forget.

Small tongues of flame were licking at the sticks now, so he added a larger log, and pulled his shirt on over his head. After wrapping his plaid about his hips and belting it, then draping the excess around his shoulders, he put on his thick wool stockings and shoved his feet into the soft leather boots that he preferred over the short, rough *brogaich* worn by his men. He never went unarmed, even in his own castle, so next he slipped a slender dagger into his boot, a larger one into his belt, then buckled on his sword. He had just finished when a hard knock sounded on his door.

His dark brows snapped together. It wasn't yet dawn; a knock at this hour could mean only trouble. "Come," he barked.

The door opened and Eilig Wishart, captain of the night guards, poked his ugly head inside the chamber. He looked relieved at seeing Niall already dressed.

"Raiders," he said briefly, in Scots. He was a broken man from Clan Keith, a man separated from his clan by will or by expulsion, and the Lowlanders more normally spoke Scots than Gaelic. Eilig always did so when he was excited.

"Where?"

"T' the east. 'Twill like be the Hays."

Niall grunted as he strode from the chamber. "Rouse the men," he ordered. He agreed with Eilig; over the years Huwe of Hay had come to bitterly hate the renegades of Creag Dhu, for they controlled a large area he had previously regarded as his to plunder. He had made bleating protests to the Bruce, for such a large gathering of broken men from all over Scotland could only mean trouble. Robert, during one of his midnight visits, had warned Niall to be wary of his neighbor to the east.

The warning had been unnecessary. Niall was wary of everyone.

He himself saw to having the horses readied, and invaded the kitchens to have provisions gathered for himself and the men. Big loaves of coarse bread were already baking in the ovens for the evening meal, and a huge pot of porridge was beginning to bubble over the fire.

He tore off a hunk of stale bread from yesterday's loaf, and washed it down with ale. Between bites, he gave orders. Jean and the others scurried around, gathering bags of oats and wrapping bread, cheese, and smoked fish in cloth. The women's eyes were large and frightened, but they regarded him with confidence, trusting him to see to the matter as he'd done for the past fourteen years.

When he went down into the inner bailey he found it teeming with terrified crofters who had been allowed into the castle for protection. Torches burned brightly on the turmoil, as the horses were brought around and his men descended to take their bags of food and make the many small preparations for going to war. The wounded lay where they had fallen, and others scurried around them, sometimes stepping over them. One sturdy old woman was making an effort to gather the wounded into one area so they could be cared for. Men cursed and snarled, and some women wept inconsolably for loved ones they had lost, husbands and children, and perhaps for what they had endured at the hands of the raiders. Some women were silent, closed in on themselves, their torn clothing telling the tale that their closed lips refused to speak. Children huddled close to their mothers, or stood alone and wailed.

It was war. Niall had seen its image many times, been hardened to it. That did not mean he would ignore such an attack on what was his. He strode over to the old woman who was trying to bring order to chaos, recognizing in her the hallmarks of a leader. He put his hand on her plump arm and pulled her aside. "How many hours have passed?" he asked curtly. "How many were they?"

She gaped up at the big man who towered over her, his black mane swirling about his broad shoulders, his eyes as cold and black as the gates of hell. She knew immediately who he was. "It canna ha' been more than an hour or twa. 'Twas a fair party, thirty or more."

Thirty. That was a large raiding party, for raiding was something best accomplished by stealth. In fourteen years he had never left Creag Dhu guarded by fewer than half his men-at-arms, but if he pursued and engaged that many men he would need more than his usual force.

Such a large raiding party was a challenge, an affront, that couldn't be ignored. Huwe of Hay must know that Niall would retaliate immediately, so it followed that he would have prepared for such an event. Perhaps he had even planned it deliberately, to draw Niall and most of his men away from the castle.

Niall beckoned to Artair, who left his horse with a lad and obeyed the summons immediately. The two men walked a little away from the noise and chaos. Artair was the only other former Templar left at Creag Dhu, a solitary and devout man who had never lost faith even when the Grand Master had gone to his fiery death seven years before. Artair was forty-eight and gray-haired, but his shoulders were still straight and, like Niall, he trained every day with the men. He'd forgotten none of the battle strategies they had learned in the Order.

"I suspect this to be a ruse to draw most of the men away from the castle," Niall said quietly. His mouth was a grim, thin line, his eyes narrowed and cold. "The Hay will likely attack as soon as he thinks us well away. I canna think he's close enough to watch, nor do I think the clumsy oaf that canny. I will take fifteen with me; the others will remain here, under your command. Be watchful."

Artair nodded, but his gaze was worried. "Only fifteen? I heard the woman say thirty —"

"Aye, but we've had the training of these lads, have we not? Two to one are not fair odds, for we've still the advantage."

Artair smiled wryly. The Hay clansmen

would be fighting against unknowing, unsworn Templars, for Niall, with his help, had trained them well. Most Scots roared into battle with little thought other than to slash or stab whoever was in front of them, but the clanless men at Creag Dhu attacked with a discipline that would have done a Roman legion proud. They had been taught strategy and technique, had it hammered into them by the most fearsome warrior in Christendom, if they but knew it. They knew only that since he had appeared in the Highlands none had defeated Black Niall, and they were proud to serve under him. All their clan loyalty, their sense of kinship and belonging, had been transferred to him, and they would unhesitatingly fight to the death for him.

Satisfied that Creag Dhu was well defended, Niall chose fifteen of his men and led them out of the gates, then rode hard into the dawn. He pushed both man and beast hard to overtake the raiders, for he suspected their intent was to lead him as far away from Creag Dhu as possible. His face was grim and hard as he rode. The Hay clansmen had made a fatal mistake by committing their thieving, raping, and murdering on land Niall considered his own. He had taken Creag Dhu, fortified it, remade it for his purposes; the Treasure was safe there, and no one was going to take it from him.

Huwe was a fool, but a dangerous one. He

was a blustering bull of a man, quick to take offense and too stubborn to admit when he was outmatched. Niall was a soldier by both nature and training, and despised the heedlessness that cost unnecessary clan lives. Though he usually tried not to cause such an uproar in the Highlands that Robert would be called upon to intervene, for he knew it would mean trouble for his brother when he refused to oust the renegades and broken men from Creag Dhu, Niall's patience was at an end. By threatening Creag Dhu, the Hay now threatened the Treasure — and he would die because of his foolishness.

A good horse could make the difference between victory and defeat, and Niall had made a point over the years of providing the best mounts possible for his men. By stopping only to water the sturdy beasts and allow them a moment's rest, he overtook the raiders at midmorning.

The raiders were in the middle of a glen, laden with the goods they had stolen and driving a straggling herd of stolen kine before them. The morning sun glittered on the mist that still hung overhead like a veil. There was no place for them to take shelter, and when Niall and his men first thundered out of the wood toward them the raiders milled about in a moment of panicked confusion.

The old granny had guessed aright, Niall saw; the enemy numbered more than forty, making the odds close to three to one, but almost half the forty were on foot. His teeth bared in a savage grin. Seeing the relatively small number of pursuers, the raiders would no doubt turn to meet them — a move they would have leisure to regret for only a short time.

As he had expected, there was a flurry of shouts and the company gathered, then charged across the glen, shouting and waving a variety of weapons, claymores and axes and hammers, even a scythe.

"Hold," Niall said. "Let them come to us."

His men ranged on either side of him, spreading out so that they weren't clumped together and thus couldn't be flanked. They held, the horses stamping restlessly and tossing their heads, while the screaming attackers poured across the misty, sun-dappled glen.

But a good three hundred yards had separated the two groups, and three hundred yards is a long way for a weary man to charge, especially when he has been about the tiring business of raiding all night and has not slept, and has been traveling hard to evade pursuers. Those on foot soon slowed, and some stopped altogether. Those who pushed stubbornly on were no longer shouting, no longer borne onward by battle fever.

So the host of horsemen who charged ahead of the stragglers barely outnumbered Niall and his men. Niall's gaze targeted a bullish young man who rode in front, his wild tangle of sandy hair flying behind him. That would be Morvan, the Hay's ill-tempered, brutish elder son, and the spit of his father. Morvan's small, mean eyes were likewise locked on Niall.

Niall raised his sword. The claymore was, for most men, a two-handed weapon, but his strength and size gave him the power to swing the six-foot blade one-handed, freeing his left hand for yet another blade, or a Lochaber axe. Seizing the reins with his teeth, he took up an axe. His well-trained horse quivered beneath him, muscles bunching. When Morvan and his men were a mere thirty yards away, Niall and his men charged.

The impact was swift and staggering. Once he had fought with shield and armor, a hundred pounds of mail weighing him down, but now Niall fought free and wild and savage, his eyes burning with a fierce light as he blocked a sword with his axe and then went in under the man's defenses with his own sword, spitting him. He always fought silently, without the yells and grunts of other men, instinctively sensing the next attack while he was still dealing with the present one.

Before his sword was free he turned, swinging the axe up to block another blow. Metal clanged as a sword struck the axe head, and the force of it jarred his arm. One powerful leg pressed and his horse turned, bringing him around to face this new challenge. Morvan of

Hay pressed forward, using all his considerable weight in an effort to unhorse Niall.

Niall shifted his horse back, away from Morvan's weight. With a curse the younger man straightened, his yellowed teeth bared as he drew back the claymore for another attack. *"Dìolain!"* Morvan hissed.

Niall didn't even blink at being called a bastard. He simply swung his own sword to parry, then buried his axe in the oaf's head, cleaving it almost in two. With a jerk he freed his weapon and turned for another adversary, but there was none. His men had worked as efficiently as he, and the Hay clansmen who had been mounted were no longer astride their horses, but lay sprawled in the indignity of death, limbs exposed, their blood turning the sweet earth to mud. The familiar stench of blood and waste marked their death.

Niall's black gaze swept over his men. Two were wounded, one seriously. "Clennan," he said sharply, drawing the attention of the man who had taken a wound in the thigh. "Care for Leod." Then he and his thirteen remaining men charged to meet the Hay clansmen who were on foot.

It was a rout, for a man on horseback had an enormous advantage over one afoot. The animals themselves were weapons, their steel-shod hooves and massive weight simply crushing those who could not move out of the way. Niall vaulted from his horse's back, the blood lust singing through him as he swung sword and axe, twisting, parrying, thrusting. He was a dark blade of death, unutterably graceful as he moved in his lethal dance. Five men fell before him, one beheaded by a massive sweep of the claymore, and Niall did not even feel the shock in his sword arm as the blade sliced through bone.

The carnage lasted two minutes, no more. Then quiet fell across the glen, the clash of swords replaced by an occasional moan. Swiftly Niall took stock, not expecting his men to have escaped unscathed. Young Odar was dead, lying sprawled beneath the body of a Hay clansman. His clear blue eyes stared sightlessly upward. Sim had taken a sword cut in the side and was cursing luridly as he tried to stanch the flow of blood. Niall judged him well enough to ride. Goraidh, however, was unconscious, his forehead bloody. All suffered from small cuts and bruises, himself included, but those wounds were as nothing. With two wounded in the first attack, he had ten healthy men remaining, and two would have to stay behind to help with the wounded and herding the cattle back to Creag Dhu.

"Muir and Crannog, remain with Sim and Clennan to help with the wounded, and the cattle." The two he had named did not look pleased at having to remain behind, but knew it was necessary.

They could not ride as hard as they had

before, for the horses were tired. Niall kept them to a steady pace, his warrior's heart beating fierce and wild in his chest as he rode to another fight. The wind lifted his long hair, drying the sweat of battle. His thighs were clamped to the powerful animal beneath him, heat meeting heat, flesh against flesh. The thick wool plaid kilted about his waist gave him a freedom that braies and hose and hot sheepskin undergarment had denied him, and he exulted in his unfettered wildness.

He had easily cast aside the physical accoutrements of the Knights, let his hair grow long, shaved his beard, discarded the hated sheepskin. Though he had become one of them, there had always been a place in his soul that yearned for Scotland, for the wildness and freedom, the mountains and mists, the sheer lustiness of youth. The life of warfare offered by the Knights had appealed to him, and as he had grown older he had learned what they did and accepted the burden, the sheer faith, but still Scotland had lived within him.

He was home, and though he reveled in his physical freedom he was bound now by a far heavier burden, one that ruled his life far more rigidly than before. Why had Valcour chosen him, an unwilling though faithful Knight? Had Valcour suspected how easily and eagerly he would rejoin his former land and life, giving no hint that he'd once been a Templar and thereby better protecting the Treasure? Had

Valcour guessed the secret relief with which Niall had accepted his freedom from all his vows, save one? But that one was the greatest of all, and the most bitter, for it served to protect those who had destroyed the Order.

Why could not Artair have been chosen? Of necessity he had shaved his beard and grown his hair, for to do otherwise would have been courting death, but other than that he held still to the vows he had taken, to chastity and service. Artair never doubted, never cursed God for what had happened, never turned from the faith to which he had sworn. If he had hated, at first, he had long since found peace and released his hatred, finding solace in prayer and war. Artair was a good soldier, a good companion.

He would not have been a good Guardian.

Niall had not forgiven either the Church or God. He hated, he doubted, he cursed himself and Valcour and his own vow, but in the end he always came back to the same truth: he was the Guardian. Valcour had chosen well.

To protect the Treasure, Niall rode to face Huwe of Hay, well aware that a blood feud had started that day and determined that most of the blood would leak from Hay clansmen. Huwe wanted war? Very well, then, there would be war.

Part Two

Niall

Chapter 12

"Fear-gleidhidh," Grace muttered to herself, moving the words around on the computer screen and trying to make sense of the sentence. *Fear-gleidhidh* meant "guardian"; she was familiar enough with *that* word to recognize it at a glance. Over the past several months she'd spent so much time with these blasted Gaelic papers that she'd learned to recognize a lot of the nouns, though sometimes the spelling threw her off. Even with the help of a two-hundred-dollar set of tapes that promised to teach her how to speak Gaelic, and which she'd bought in a useless hope that it would help clarify the murky medieval Gaelic syntax, it could still take hours to translate a few sentences.

But what on earth did *cunhachd* mean? Running her finger down the page of the Gaelic/English dictionary, she couldn't find any such word. Could it be *cunbhalach,* which meant "steady," or *cunbhalachd,* which was "judgment"? No, it wouldn't be the first, for if she was reading it correctly the sentence was "The Guardian has the Cunhachd." The capitalization didn't necessarily mean anything, but the sentence certainly wouldn't be "The Guardian has the Steady."

"The Guardian has the Judgment"? Grace rearranged the words on the screen once again, wondering if she had misread the verb or tangled the syntax for what seemed like the millionth time. Without the benefit of classes, it was taking her more time to learn Gaelic than any other language she had studied. She was getting better at it, though.

She rechecked the paper, bending close and using her magnifying glass to study the faded letters. No, the verb was definitely "has." *Cunhachd* was the stumbling block. She turned her attention to it, and noticed that the *n* was smeared. Could it be an *m* instead? Returning to the dictionary, she looked up *cumhachd,* and a surge of triumph went through her. *Cumhachd* meant "power."

"The Guardian has the Power."

She raked her hands through her hair, lifting the long strands and letting them sift through her fingers. What were some synonyms for *power? Authority, right, might, will.* All of those would fit, yet each differed somewhat in meaning. If she interpreted the sentence literally, then what power did the Guardian have? Power over the Treasure, absolute control of it? Money was power, as the old saying went, but the chronicles had also said that the Treasure was "greater than gold." It followed, then, that though there had likely been a monetary treasury, that wasn't the Treasure referred to so reverentially.

So what had the Treasure been, and what sort of power had the Guardian wielded because of it? If Black Niall had been the possessor of such mighty power, why had he spent his life as a renegade in the remote western Highlands? How had a Templar, supposedly a religious man, become a man as renowned for his sexual appetite as he was for his skill with a claymore?

Two more hours of work still left her in the dark. The Treasure was either "a knowing of God's will," something that was certainly ambiguous enough, or "proof of God's will," which was equally unenlightening. It possessed the power to "bow kings and nations before it," and "vanquish evil."

She read aloud the words on the screen. "The Guardian shall pass — or travel, or walk — beyond the bounds of time, or season — in the way of Our Lord Jesus Christ, to do His battle with the Serpent." That sounded as if the Guardian would emulate Jesus's struggle with Satan, which hardly translated into any great power, but rather an effort to live an honorable, blameless life — something difficult enough, and from what she'd read about Black Niall he hadn't even *tried.*

So what was the Treasure, and what was the Power? Religious myth? Parrish evidently believed the gold was real; on the surface that was motive enough, yet she kept coming back to the Treasure that was greater than gold, and wondering if more than wealth was involved. If so, what? No Templar had ever betrayed the secret of the Treasure, though some of them had been hideously tortured. Perhaps most of them hadn't known anything to tell, but certainly the Grand Master had known, and he had gone to the stake with the secret untold. Instead he had cursed the King of France and the Pope, and within a year both Philip and Clement had died, giving credence to the superstition of the time that the Templars had been in league with the devil.

Slowly Grace paraphrased the unwieldy sentence. "The Guardian shall walk beyond time to vanquish evil." Sometimes putting the words in a more modern context helped her see through the lapsed centuries to find the most logical translation. She tried again. "The Guardian shall pass the season in battle against evil." What season? The years following the destruction of the Order? Was the Guardian supposed to fight Philip and Clement on behalf of the Order? If so, Black Niall had instead fought his skirmishes in bed and in the mountains and moors of Scotland.

It didn't make sense, and she was too tired to keep at it. Grace saved the file, then turned off the computer. In six months she had translated all the tales of Black Niall's battles and conquests, the Latin and French and English, but parts of the Gaelic still defeated her. Come to that, some of the Latin didn't make sense, because for some reason a *diet* had been included. What did a carefully regulated consumption of salt have to do with a history of the Templars? And why was the amount of water they drank based on their weight? But there it was, right in the middle of a long passage on the duties of a Guardian: *Victus Rationem Temporis,* the diet of time, or for time.

She paused in the act of removing her sweatshirt. Time. What was this about time, that it cropped up in both Latin and Gaelic? Come to think of it, there had been something similar in the French documents. Swiftly she returned to the rickety table she used as a desk, flipping through the documents until she found the page she sought. "He shall be unbound by the chains of time."

Walking beyond time. Unbound by the chains of time. Diet for time. There was a common thread here, but she couldn't make sense of it. They had all been fixated on time, but was it in a metaphorical sense, or a conceptual thing? And what did time have to do with the Templars?

Well, it wasn't a puzzle she was going to solve by worrying at it; she would have to complete her translations, a project she could see the end of now. Another three weeks, perhaps a month, and she would have the Gaelic section completed. Gaelic was so difficult she'd saved it for last and she couldn't be certain of her translation, but she'd done the best she could. Whether it would tell her anything beyond the supposed location of the Templars' gold remained to be seen.

After undressing for bed, she neatly placed the computer and all her papers in the computer case, and set it within easy reach beside the bed. If she had to leave abruptly, she didn't want to waste time gathering everything together.

She turned out the light and lay on the narrow, lumpy bed, staring out the dingy window at the softly falling snow. The seasons had changed, summer giving way to fall, color dulling into the monochromatic shades of winter. It had been eight months since her old life had ended. She survived, but she couldn't say that she lived.

Her heart felt as bleak and stark as the winter. Her hatred for Parrish kept the pain at bay, untouched and undiminished. She knew it was there, knew she would someday lose control over it, but she would pay that price when the time came.

She blessed Harmony every day. She had a passport in Louisa Croley's name, in case she had to get out of the country in a hurry. After obtaining that, she had left Louisa behind and taken another name, as well as another job. Marjorie Flynn had existed for two months, then she'd moved on and become Paulette Bottoms. Another low-paying job, another cheap room. The Minneapolis–St. Paul area was large enough that she could lose herself in it, never meeting anyone she knew from before, so she had no difficulty in changing names. She made no friends, on Harmony's advice. She saved every penny she could and had amassed almost four thousand dollars, counting what she'd had left after buying the truck. She would never again be as helpless as she'd been after the murders.

Not that she ever *could* be, even without the assets of cash and transportation. Part of her helplessness had been her own total lack of knowledge about survival on the streets, and she was no longer ignorant. Her face was a cool, expressionless mask, and she walked with an alertness, a readiness, that told seasoned street predators she wouldn't be easy prey. At night, alone, she practiced the moves Mateo had taught her, and she carefully arranged her grim little rooms to provide the maximum in protection and opportunity for herself.

She was never unarmed. She had bought a cheap revolver and kept it with her, but she also had the knife in its sheath, tucked out of sight under her shirt. She had a sharpened screwdriver in her boot, a hatpin threaded in her shirt cuff, a pencil in her pocket. Finding a place to practice her nonexistent marksmanship hadn't been easy; she'd had to drive far out into the country, but she had achieved, if not true skill, at least a degree of efficiency and familiarity with the weapon, so she could carry it with some confidence.

She doubted anyone from her former life would recognize her now, even if she came face-to-face with a friend. Her long, thick hair was let down only in the privacy of her room; she wore a cheap, light brown wig to work, and at other times she twisted her hair into a knot on top of her head and covered it with a baseball cap. She was thin, weighing barely a hundred pounds, her cheekbones prominent over hollow cheeks. She had managed not to lose any more weight, but she had to make a deliberate effort to eat, and she exercised faithfully to stay strong. She wore tight jeans and sturdy black boots, and a fur-lined denim jacket as protection against the frigid Minnesota winter. On Harmony's excellent advice she'd bought some cheap cosmetics and learned how to use mascara, blusher, and lipstick so she didn't look as if she were fresh out of a convent.

A couple of men had hit on her, but a blank, frozen expression and a terse "No" were enough to turn them away. She couldn't imagine even having a cup of coffee with a man. Only in her dreams did her sexuality reawaken, and she couldn't control that. Black Niall was so firmly in her thoughts, preoccupied her so many hours of the day, that she had found it impossible to shut him out of her subconscious. He was there, living in her dreams, fighting and loving, grim and beautiful and terrifyingly male, and so lethal she sometimes woke shivering with fear. She never dreamed that he threatened *her,* but the Black Niall of her imagination was not a man one crossed with impunity.

She felt alive, painfully so, when she dreamed of him. She couldn't preserve the vast emptiness that protected her when she was awake; she ached, and yearned, and trembled at his touch. Only twice more had she dreamed of actual lovemaking, but both times had been shattering.

It was a mistake to remember those dreams now, when she was trying to sleep. She knew that, and turned restlessly on her side. She was all but inviting a recurrence. But the dreams of lovemaking were more welcome than the dreams of battle, which had been occurring incessantly for the past four months. He hacked and slashed his way through her sleep, wading through blood and body parts, the images so intense she could hear the clang of swords striking together, see the men slip and stumble, hear them grunt with effort, hear the screams of pain and watch their faces distort in death throes. Given a choice between carnage and sex, she would definitely choose sex, were it not for the guilt that haunted her afterward.

After an hour of lying there she sighed, resigning herself to a sleepless night. She was tired but her brain refused to stop working, going over and over the papers, thinking about Niall, trying to piece together some feasible means of revenge against Parrish. She had hoped to find something in the papers to use against him, but if she'd been thinking straight she would have realized there couldn't be anything incriminating about him in papers that were almost seven hundred years old. The papers fascinated her so much that she hadn't been able to see past her own obsession. No, if she could manage any sort of revenge against Parrish it would have to be something much more straightforward, like killing him herself.

She got out of bed and turned on the light, her eyes stark, her soft mouth set in a grim line. Over the past eight months she had learned she could fight to protect herself, perhaps even kill in self-defense, but she didn't know if she could kill in cold blood. She paced back and forth, hugging her arms around her to ward off the night chill. Could she kill Parrish? Could she walk up, stick the revolver to his head, and pull the trigger?

She closed her eyes, but the vision that came to mind wasn't of herself shooting Parrish, but of the utter disregard, almost boredom, with which he had shot Ford and Bryant. She saw the sudden blankness on Ford's face, the bonelessness of his body as he slumped over.

Her teeth clenched, her hands knotted into fists. Oh, yes, she could kill Parrish.

Why didn't she just do it, then?

She had driven by his house a few times when she'd been working for the cleaning service; she had never seen him or his car, but then she hadn't expected to. If he were at home, his car would be in the garage, and Parrish wasn't the type of man who enjoyed gardening. She knew nothing of his schedule, hadn't spent her days watching his house in order to follow him. She had taken self-protective measures, but in reality she had done nothing to avenge her family. Instead she had concentrated on the papers, persuaded herself that there could be something useful in them, *deluded* herself so she could merely mark time and lose herself in the translations.

But self-delusion was at an end. She needed either to do something about Parrish or to go away quietly and spend the rest of her life grieving and hiding.

All right. She would do it. She would track Parrish down, and kill him.

Grace felt the weight of the decision settle on her. She didn't have the stuff of which killers were made, and she knew it. On the other hand, she hadn't sought any of this; Parrish had begun the dance. The Old Testament said, "Thou shalt not kill," but it also said, "An eye for an eye." Perhaps she was rationalizing, but she took that to mean that once a murder was committed, society or the wronged family had a right to put an end to the murderer's existence.

No matter. Tomorrow she would begin tracking him down like the animal he was.

Morning, however, brought a new reality: she had to work. She couldn't spend all day sitting in some hidden place and watching Parrish's house. Her old truck would be out of place, and very noticeable, in any case. Physically watching for him, following him, seizing an opportunity, simply wasn't feasible. She had to know in advance where he would be, and be there before him.

For all she knew, he wasn't even in town. During the winter he often took long vacations in warmer climes, staying away for as long as a month at a stretch.

There was only one way to find out. During her lunch break with another cleaning service, she stopped at a fast-food joint and used a pay phone to call the Foundation.

Her fingers moved without volition, punching in the familiar numbers. It wasn't until the first ring buzzed in her ear that she realized what she was doing, and her heart thumped wildly in her chest. Before she could slam down the receiver the flat, impersonal voice of the receptionist answered. "Amaranthine Potere Foundation. How may I direct your call?"

Grace swallowed. "Is Mr. Sawyer in the office today?"

"One moment."

"No, don't ring —" she started to say, but the line had already clicked and another ring was sounding. She took a deep breath and prepared to ask the question again of Parrish's secretary; she would need to disguise her voice a little, because Annalise had once been fairly familiar with —

"Parrish Sawyer."

The smooth, cultured tones stunned her, panicked her. She froze in place, her mind going blank at actually hearing that hated voice again.

"Hello?" he said, more sharply.

Grace gasped.

"Is this an obscene call?" he asked, sounding both bored and annoyed. "I really don't —" Then he stopped, and she could hear his own breathing for a few endless seconds. "Gracie," he said, purring her name. "How nice of you to call."

She felt wrapped in ice, a coldness that had nothing to do with the fifteen-degree weather. She couldn't speak, couldn't move, could only clench the receiver with white, bloodless fingers.

"Can't you speak, darling? I want to talk to you, clear up this dreadful misunderstanding. You know I wouldn't let anything happen to you. There's always been something between us, but I didn't realize how potent it was until you ran away. Let me help you, darling. I'll take care of everything."

He was a wonderful liar, she thought dimly. His warm, seductive voice oozed sympathy, trustworthiness; if she hadn't *seen* him commit the murders, she would have believed every word out of his mouth.

"Gracie," he said, cajoling, whispering. "Tell me where to meet you. I'll take you away, just the two of us, to someplace safe. You won't have to worry about anything."

He *wasn't* lying. It was lust she heard in his voice. Horrified, sickened, she finally managed to hang up the phone and blindly made her way back to the truck. She felt filthy, as if he'd actually touched her.

My God, how could he have the utter gall, how could he possibly think she would let him touch her? But there wasn't any *letting* involved, she realized. She started the truck and drove carefully away, not doing anything to attract attention, but her heart was beating so rapidly she felt faint. He didn't know for certain she'd seen him that night, so he'd taken the chance that she hadn't and tried to talk her into coming to him. She had never had any doubts he would kill her; now she knew he would rape her first.

Wispy snowflakes drifted across her windshield, just a few at first, but by the time she got to the next house on her list the snow was coming down fast enough to begin collecting on the hood of the truck. This was one of her least favorite houses to clean; Mrs. Eriksson was always there, carefully watching every move Grace made as though she expected her to walk off with a television or something. But she didn't chatter, as some people did, and today Grace was grateful for the silence. She moved in a daze through the cleaning, her mind spinning while she carefully mopped and dusted and vacuumed.

Mrs. Eriksson dumped a load of clothing on the sofa. "My bridge club is coming over tonight and I have to bake a cake; it would help me a lot if you'd fold the laundry while I start the baking."

The woman was tireless in trying to get the cleaning service to perform extra, unpaid tasks. Grace made a show of looking at her watch. "I'm sorry," she said politely. "I have to be at another house in half an hour. I have just enough time to finish your floors." It was a lie; today was a light day for her, and she had only one more house to do, at four o'clock. But Mrs. Eriksson was probably lying about the bridge club, too, and perhaps even about the cake.

"You're very uncooperative," the woman said sharply. "You've refused my requests before, and I'm thinking of changing services. If your attitude doesn't change, I'm going to have to speak to your supervisor."

"I'm sure she'll be happy to schedule laundry services for you."

"Why should I use her service for that, when you've been so unsatisfactory in everything else?"

"She can assign someone else, if you like." Grace didn't look up, but stuffed her dusting cloth back into the canvas bag in which she carried all her cleaning products, then deftly plugged in the vacuum cleaner and turned it on. The noise drowned out anything Mrs. Eriksson might have said, and Grace industriously shoved the machine back and forth across the carpet. The service owner had Mrs. Eriksson's number; she might assign someone else to clean the house, but Mrs. Eriksson still wouldn't get her laundry folded or her dishes washed unless she paid for it.

Mrs. Eriksson sat down on the sofa and began folding clothes, snapping the garments and glaring all the while, but Grace's mind immediately went back to Parrish.

Everything inside her recoiled in revulsion. She couldn't even imagine the horror of being in his hands. He wouldn't have to kill her, because she would go mad if he touched her, her mind would shut down completely.

How had he known? How had he guessed it was her on the phone? What kind of feral instincts did he have that had led him so swiftly and unerringly to her identity? More important, had he immediately phoned the

Minneapolis police and told them she was in the area?

Parrish did place an immediate phone call, but it was to Conrad instead of the police department. "Ms. St. John just called my office," he said smoothly, pleasure and exhilaration in his voice. "Doubtless she only wanted to know if I am here, and she would have expected Annalise to answer the phone. Get to our source with the phone company immediately and find out where that call came from." He glanced at his Rolex. "The call came in to me at twelve twenty-three."

He hung up without waiting for Conrad's reply, if he had intended to make one. Parrish leaned back in his massive leather chair, breathing hard from the excitement pouring like water through him. Grace! After six damnably frustrating months, in which she had seemed simply to disappear from Chicago, who would have thought she would make contact herself?

Conrad was sure he'd found where she'd been working in Chicago, at an Italian dump where most of the employees were paid under the table. The woman had been thinner but she had sometimes carried a small case, had kept to herself, and had a blond, frizzy hairdo. The blond frizz job had also been reported involved in a peculiar altercation outside the Newberry Library. The Newberry happened to be one of the foremost research libraries in the country, something Grace would know, and a resource she would need. Parrish knew by that she was working on the papers, and Grace was very good at her work. She would have a very good idea of why he wanted the papers.

But then she'd vanished again, simply not returning to the restaurant, and no one there had known where she lived. Conrad had checked the bus lines, the trains, airlines, but no one had noticed a woman with frizzy blond hair carrying a computer case. She had disappeared, and not even Conrad had been able to find a trace of her.

Where was she now? In Minneapolis, or hiding in some backwater? Why had she called? She hadn't said anything but he was almost positive, just from that one tiny betraying gasp, that she was the caller.

Soon he would know, if not her present location, at least where she'd been when she made the call. The police had to have a court order to access those kinds of records at the phone company, but he wasn't hindered by their ridiculous regulations. Conrad would at least know where to begin searching for her, and his pride was at stake now; he was still smarting from letting a little nobody like Grace St. John escape from him.

Why would she want to know if he was in the office? He laughed softly to himself. Was little Grace planning some sort of revenge? What did she think she could do, walk into his office and point a pistol at him? She knew the security of the building, knew she wouldn't get past the lobby.

Perhaps he should let her, though, draw her to him. He could overpower her easily enough, and then he'd have her.

He could work late; the building would be deserted, and she would feel more confident. He could arrange for the guards to be looking conveniently the other way, but not make it so easy that she became suspicious. He would wait by the door for her, ready to disarm her of whatever weapon she carried; he wouldn't want to give her an opportunity for a lucky shot.

Perhaps he wouldn't wait for a more comfortable, convenient place in which to take her. Perhaps he would have her right on the desk, stretched across the glassy surface. She would struggle and kick and he would soothe her, whisper to her, and kiss her astonishingly carnal mouth. She would feel so soft beneath him, so helpless.

He was fully aroused, almost panting. Once wouldn't be enough, he knew that now. He wanted to come in her mouth, and he wanted to feel her come. He wanted to hear her cry out his name in pleasure.

Then he would kill her. What a waste, but it had to be done.

* * *

"She called from a pay phone at a McDonald's in Roseville," Conrad reported. "No one noticed her, but the only other calls received around that time originated from legitimate contacts."

"Roseville." Parrish considered the location. It was a suburb just northeast of downtown. "Do you have men watching the place in case she returns?"

"Yes." Conrad had taken care of that detail immediately. People were generally creatures of habit, adhering to the same routine for months, years. Grace had shown herself to be unusually unpredictable, but he couldn't afford to assume she would immediately take off for parts unknown. If she remained in the city, sooner or later she would at least pass by that McDonald's — if not today, then tomorrow. If not tomorrow, then perhaps on this same day next week. He was a patient man; he would wait.

"So she came back here," Parrish mused. "Gutsy of her, don't you think? I never would have expected it. Do you think she's going to try to kill me?"

"Yes," Conrad said impassively. Otherwise, there was no logical reason for her to return to Minneapolis. The danger was too great.

"Perhaps we should let her try." Parrish smiled, his eyes bright with anticipation. "Let her come to us, Conrad. We'll be ready."

Chapter 13

"Niall, I dreamed about you again last night. For once, you weren't either fighting or having sex, just sitting quietly in front of a fire, cleaning your sword. You looked — not sad, but grim, as if you carried a burden that would break most men. What were you thinking about? What makes you so alone? Do you think about the Templars, all the friends who died, or is there something else that made you so hard? Do you resent being a renegade, when your brother is a king?"

Grace lifted her hands from the keys, disturbed by what she had just typed. Dreaming about him was one thing, writing to him was another. It was unsettling, the way she felt as if she were truly communicating with him, as if he would read her words and reply. She knew the constant stress of the past eight months had taken a toll on her, but she hoped she hadn't totally flipped out.

She had tried to resume writing in her electronic journal, but somehow her brain refused to seize on the everyday detail that she had recorded before. For one thing, she had no routine life, and without a routine there couldn't be anything *un*routine. She would stare at the empty screen, her fingers poised over the keys, but in the end she had no comment to make about the day. She had no appointments to keep, no news to share, no one to share it with in any case. She went through the days silent and numb, coming alive only with hatred for Parrish or when she was translating the papers.

But however illusory Niall was, he was far more vivid than anything else in the grayness of her life. He *seemed* real, as if he were just on the other side of the door, unseen but undeniably there. His myth, his history, was her one bit of color. Through him, she still lived, still felt the hot rush of vitality and passion. She could talk to him as she would never again be able to talk to anyone living. The division between before and now was too deep, too drastic; there was too little left of the shy, bookish, rather innocent woman she had been. In her own way, she was as unreal as Niall.

She felt her aloneness all the way to the bone. Not loneliness; she didn't pine for company, for a sympathetic ear, for gossip and chatter and laughter. She was alone in a way she'd never before imagined, as solitary as if she were an astronaut come untethered from the mother ship, drifting unnoticed in an emptiness so vast it was beyond comprehension. She had found a whisper of companionship with Harmony Johnson, but remaining would have been too dangerous to Harmony, and during the six months she'd been back in Minneapolis she hadn't truly talked with anyone. She woke up alone, she worked in mental if not physical isolation, and she went to sleep alone. *Alone.* What a desolate, empty word.

In her dream, Niall had been alone. Alone inside, as she was. He could be surrounded by people and still be alone, because there was something untouchable in him, something no one else even knew existed. The golden glow of the fire had outlined the hard, pure lines of his face, shadowed the deep-set eyes and high cheekbones. His movements had been deft as he saw to the cleaning and repair of his weapon, his long fingers tracing over the razor edge to find any chips that dulled its effectiveness. His manner had been absorbed, deliberate, remote.

Once his head had lifted and he sat very still, as if listening for or to something that hadn't registered in the dream. Black mane flowing over his broad shoulders, his black eyes narrowed, he had been the picture of animal alertness, on guard and wary. No threat had materialized and gradually he had relaxed, but she had the impression of a man who could never truly ease his vigilance. He was the Guardian.

She had wanted to touch his shoulder, and sit silently beside him by the fire while he tended his tools of war, giving him the comfort of her warmth and presence so that he knew he wasn't alone after all — and perhaps, in doing so, she too would find comfort and companionship. But in this dream she had been locked into the role of observer, unable to go closer, and in the end she had awakened without touching him.

"If I were with you . . ."

Startled, she stared at what she had typed. The words hadn't been consciously planned; her fingers had simply moved on the keyboard and they had appeared. Suddenly frightened, she closed the file on her journal. Her hands were shaking. *She had to stop thinking of Niall as if he were alive.* The fixation on him was too vivid, too powerful. At first concentrating on him had seemed reasonable, a way of keeping herself sane, but what if it were having the opposite effect and she was losing herself in fantasy? After reading her journal entries, any psychiatrist would be forgiven for thinking she had lost contact with reality.

But reality was seeing her husband and brother murdered, crouching in a cold rain too terrified to cross a street, going hungry and being cold, sleeping in storage buildings and fighting off attackers. Reality was freezing in horror at the sound of Parrish's voice. What did she have left except the escape she found in her dreams?

She looked at the stack of documents, at the

pages and pages of notes she had scribbled. "I have work," she murmured, and the sound of her own voice was reassuringly normal. She might feel as if she were coming apart at the seams, but she still had the work. It had saved her for eight months and would continue to save her for a few days yet, though that damn Gaelic had nearly defeated her.

Just another week or two of work, and then the tales of the Knights Templar and the Guardian, of Black Niall, would be ended. When she wasn't spending hours struggling with the translations every night before bed, the dreams of him would stop.

Unexpected desolation swamped her at the thought. Without Niall, the spark that made her feel alive, even if only in her dreams, would be extinguished. There would be no more translations, because she was too well known by sight in her field to get a job with another archaeological foundation, even under an assumed name. There would be no more intriguing puzzles, not that any other work she had done had come close to fascinating her as much as did Niall and the Templars.

She would have nothing but vengeance. The need for it burned inside her, but she sensed that beyond vengeance there was nothing but bleak, gray nothingness, assuming she survived. She would be on the run for the rest of her life, her identity gone, nothing to look forward to, and never knowing the joy of having Ford's children and growing old with him, cradling their grandchildren, perhaps watching Bryant succumb at last to love and matrimony.

Being insane was better.

She pulled the Gaelic papers to her, opened the Gaelic/English dictionary, and picked up her pen.

As usual, she was drawn almost immediately into the magic of the papers, the sense of reading something enormously compelling and important.

"Mankind shall not know the True Power," she read some minutes later. "The Cup and the Winding Cloth shall blind them to the sun, the Throne and Banner denied, but the True Power shall be used by the Guardian in the Lord's stead, to pass through the Veil of Time and protect the Treasure from Evil.

"None save the Treasure can defeat Evil, and none save the Guardian shall use the Power."

It read like a Bible passage, but she was certain nothing like this had ever been in the Bible. The Cup . . . that could refer to the Chalice, and the Winding Cloth could well be the shroud in which Jesus had been wrapped after the crucifixion. The Shroud of Turin was supposed to be Jesus's shroud, but it was surrounded by controversy; there were references to its existence long before the fourteenth century, which was when carbon dating had placed its origin. Of course, the earlier references could have been to another shroud, perhaps the real one . . . which did nothing to explain how a fourteenth-century forger could have created a cloth bearing an impregnable negative image of a crucified man, five centuries before photography had been invented.

"The Cup and the Winding Cloth shall blind them to the sun," she read again. If the Chalice still existed, it had never been found. But perhaps the arguments about the validity of the shroud did indeed blind people to the true nature of faith; they were so busy making points and counterpoints that the argument became the focus and they couldn't see the whole picture.

The Templars were irrevocably connected to the shroud. They had battled the Moors and won Jerusalem for the Crusaders for a time, and themselves occupied the Temple on the Mount for longer than that. During their occupation, they had determinedly excavated as much of the Temple as possible, perhaps finding many artifacts dating back to the early years of the Temple, to the very beginning of Judaism. What treasures indeed had they found . . . what Treasure?

One of the charges against the Templars was that they had worshipped false gods, for in every chapel the Templars had built after occupying the Temple on the Mount, there had been the face of a man, a stern, strong-boned face — the same face that had been revealed centuries later on the Shroud of Turin.

It followed that they had unearthed the shroud; it also followed that its location in the Temple gave it validity. But what else had they found? The "Cup" and the "Winding Cloth" were listed, as well as the "Throne" and the "Banner," but the "True Power" was something else, something so far left undescribed.

"The Guardian shall defend the world from the Foundation of Evil."

Grace sighed at the continued ambiguity. The Foundation of Evil was obviously Satan, but why hadn't the writer simply said so? Evidently even medieval scribes had been afflicted by wordiness.

Just the word *Foundation* made her think of better days, with Ford and Bryant delicately and happily sifting mounds of dirt through screens, looking for the smallest shard of pottery; or sitting on the ground whisking a small brush over a half-buried bone. The three of them had loved their work, and the Amaranthine Potere Foundation had been one of the few places in the world where an archaeologist could be permanently employed. Independently funded, the Foundation hadn't concentrated just on the hugely important digs, but on the smaller ones that would provide detail rather than drama. Bryant had once said that the Foundation seemed determined to leave no dirt in the world unsifted.

Grace stiffened, her pupils contracting with shock. Potere . . . Power. *Amaranthine Potere* Foundation, the Foundation of Unending Power.

Why hadn't she made the connection before? Languages and translations were her field of expertise. She should have seen it, should have realized —

It was a stretch, a real stretch. It was ridiculous. A huge foundation committed to unearthing the Templar Treasure? The money spent would surely far exceed the worth of any gold found.

"The Treasure's worth is greater than gold," she whispered. Not money, then; the documents had made that plain. Power. The Templars had possessed some mysterious power, had dedicated their lives to protecting it.

She got up and paced, mentally feeling her way through the puzzle. Was it possible the Foundation existed to *prevent* people from learning about the Power, whatever it was? Could Parrish, in some twisted way, think he had to kill everyone who learned of the papers in order to keep the Power secret? Was he acting as Guardian?

No, she could drive a truck through the holes in that theory. For one thing, the Foundation hadn't had anything to guard. The papers had disappeared centuries before and anyone who knew anything about archaeology could not have reasonably expected the documents would survive. Paper deteriorated rapidly; that was why there were relatively few original documents left from even two centuries before, much less almost seven.

No, forget about any mystic power, any great struggle between right and wrong. She was tired, and fatigue was fogging her brain. The most likely motive was money, pure and simple. Parrish must have reason to believe the Templars' Treasure was enormous beyond belief, and as director of the Foundation he could expend any amount of effort he wanted in finding it. He must have devised some way of appropriating the gold for his own use. The Foundation was probably exactly what it seemed, an archaeological foundation, without any sinister motive behind its existence. Parrish was the villain, not the Foundation itself.

But the Foundation had been founded in 1802, and named "Unending Power," long before Parrish's arrival on earth.

Where had the funding come from, all these decades? Who had originally founded Amaranthine Potere? How was it sustained now? As far as she knew, there hadn't been any fund-raisers.

She did know that the Foundation had a very sophisticated computer system, far more sophisticated than she might have expected an archaeological foundation to have; after all, why should a list of contributors, assuming there was one, be either secret or sensitive? The Foundation was supposed to be non-profit; presumably donations would be tax-deductible, so any list of contributors would be public anyway.

It would be nice if she could get into the system, just to see what she could find.

Doing so would require a hacker's skills, though, and she wasn't that good.

Kristian Sieber was.

As soon as the idea registered she discarded it. Not only was it dangerous to let anyone know where she was, but to involve Kris again was dangerous to him.

What could she possibly learn, anyway? A list of contributors, that's all. That wouldn't help her. It would be nice if she could learn Parrish's schedule . . .

She bit her lip. No. She wasn't going to call Kris.

Grace sat down and forced herself to return to the documents. After a moment, she was engrossed again.

There had always come a time, while she was studying a language, when suddenly her brain seemed to "get" it. She would struggle with syntax and verbs for months, then the accumulated knowledge and familiarity would reach critical mass, the synapses would connect, and presto! From one moment to the next she would pass from struggling to *reading,* the language opening up to her as if the letters had rearranged themselves from gibberish into real words.

Three minutes after she sat down, the old language synapses connected.

"The Guardian holds the Knowledge to bring down the Mother Church, and he Shall hold it Close, for the Power of our Lord God is Greater than the thought of Man, and so he Shall serve our Lord God all his days.

"To this End Shall he Journey through Time, his body Prepared by food and drink, and the Years shall be as nothing to him. Be it a Thousand years, yea, still he Shall go forth to Battle the Foundation of Evil, for he alone may wield the Power."

Journey through time? Grace blinked at the words. What was the Guardian supposed to be, a time traveler? She hadn't realized that bit of silliness had existed for so long. Medieval scholars hadn't even been able to grasp the concept of a round earth; they had still pictured dragons lurking around the edges, waiting to devour anyone foolish enough to fall off.

But evidently the Templars had not only believed it, they had devised a special diet to prepare the body for the trip. What else could the Diet of Time be?

Curiously, she pulled out the sheet on which she had translated the diet. At first glance, or second or third, there wasn't anything magical about it. First one precisely calculated one's weight by sitting in a barrel of water; ingenious of them, using water displacement as a measure. Then, according to one's weight, there was a formula for working out how much salt, calf's liver, and various other foods one must consume, and exactly how much water to drink.

It was a diet rich in sodium, iron, and all the trace minerals, she noted. Not a bad diet, except for the liver; that would be hell on a time traveler's cholesterol level.

She kept that page in her hand, and returned to the Gaelic documents.

"His body Prepared, he will then by striking Steel to Stone find the Spark of Lightning that will Carry him to the Chosen Time."

Grace almost choked. "What were you idiots trying to do?" she blurted, staring at the page. "Electrocute yourselves?" They had deliberately flooded their bodies with iron and water, then worked up some source of electricity. Who had been the guinea pigs for this experiment, and had anyone survived?

The rest of the page was mathematical formulas. Evidently, they had thought to control the number of years traveled by the amount of water drunk and the force of electricity applied. Interesting concept, but what had they known about electricity, much less controlling it?

She turned to the next page, and her blood ran cold.

"And the Evil one shall be called Parrish."

"Oh, my God," she whispered.

"Kris, this is Grace."

There was silence on the end of the line, then he said explosively, "Grace!"

"Shh," she cautioned. Nervously she twisted the steel cord of the pay phone, wondering once again if she had any right to involve Kris in this mess. She had been up most of the night, reading and rereading the documents, trying to apply common sense to the situation, but finally coming to the conclusion that extraordinary events called for extraordinary actions. Nothing about her life in the past eight months had been ordinary. Perhaps she would find something in the Foundation's computers, perhaps not, but she couldn't afford to leave any avenue unexplored.

"It's okay. Mom and Dad are in Florida. Where are you? Are you okay?"

"I'm fine," she said automatically. *Fine* was a relative term. She wasn't dead, she wasn't injured, she wasn't hungry. Physically, she supposed she was fine; emotionally was another story. "Did you have any trouble . . . after talking to me that time? Did Parrish or any of his men question you?"

"Maybe. I don't know," he said. "A detective came to the house that day, but he wasn't the one I'd talked to before. He showed me a badge, y'know, but how would I know if it looked the way it should? He asked me a lot of questions I'd already answered, and I stuck to the story. I'd worked on your modem, showed you a program I was working on, you paid me and left. That was all. You didn't mention anything about your work."

She breathed a sigh of relief. The "detective" could have been legitimate, and could also have been one of Parrish's men rechecking Kris's story. Kristian had pulled it off, protected by his computer wonk persona. No one meeting him would think him involved in anything beyond bytes and programs.

"Where are you?" he asked again.

"It's safer for you if you don't know."

"Yeah, well, so what?" He sounded older than before, tougher and more assured. "I know you didn't do it, so if you need help, all you have to do is ask."

His unquestioning faith hit her so hard that it was a moment before she could speak past the knot that formed in her throat.

"You'll be breaking the law if you help me." She felt compelled to warn him, because her conscience was still nagging at her for calling.

"I know," he said calmly. "I broke the law by not telling them everything I knew about that night, and I broke the law when I got into the bank's computers so you could get your money out. What's one more felony between friends?"

She took a deep breath. "All right. Is there

any way you can get into the Foundation's computer system without setting off any alarms?"

"Sure," he said, completely confident. "I told you, there's always a back door. All I have to do is find it. But if it's a closed system, I'll have to go on-site to get in. Any problem there?"

Grace took a deep breath, trying to remember what she'd seen of the computer system the times she'd been in the Foundation's offices, which actually hadn't been that often. "I think it's a closed system."

"Are we going to do some midnight breaking and entering?" He sounded eager; Kris was a true hacker, willing to go to any lengths to perform his illegal art.

"No." Harmony hadn't given her any advice on getting into a secured professional building without setting off its alarm system, but she had given her some pointers about hiding in plain sight. "We'll go in during the day, as part of the maintenance crew. I don't know how we'll get onto the floor without being seen, but we'll think of something."

"I keep telling you," Kris said. "There's always a back door."

Chapter 14

When Niall rode in from patrol, Sim met him with a worried expression. "Artair and Tearlach havena returned from hunting," he reported.

Niall looked at the darkening sky. The short winter day was fading fast, and the lowering gray clouds promised more snow. The wind whipped at his hair, blowing it across his face, and impatiently he tossed it back as he jumped from the horse.

"Bring Cinnteach," he ordered. The gelding was as steady as his name, and had the stamina of two horses.

"Done." Sim nodded to a stable lad approaching with the big bay. "I've had the other lads make ready, should ye want them also."

"Only you and Iver," Niall said. The two men were Creag Dhu's best archers, save himself. Perhaps he was foolhardy to take only two with him, but he was always mindful of leaving the castle well protected. Winter had cooled the Hay's raging blood feud with Creag Dhu; over a month had passed without attack. Still, Artair and Tearlach were both accomplished hunters, and could read the weather well; if naught was amiss, they would have returned by now.

Artair and Tearlach had gone out with the dawn, intent on a *fiadh,* a deer, whose tracks they had cut in the snow twice before, but the wily beast had escaped each time. Tearlach had slowed with age but was still the castle's best tracker. Artair had a gift for silence, Tearlach one for patience; they worked well together. Niall suspected Artair liked to hunt in winter because the wild, empty, snow-dusted mountains somehow reminded him of a cathedral, vaulted and holy. Creag Dhu had a chapel but no priest, for holy men sought safer duty than being confessor to wild renegades, and the chapel had long stood empty. Niall preferred no reminder of the Church or God, but Artair deeply felt the absence and sought his sanctuary in nature. He had thought it safe enough to replenish the castle's larder.

Niall rode out again five minutes later, having taken only enough time to wolf down a bit of bread and meat, and drink a cup of hot ale. The cold snapped at his face, but he was warm enough in wool and fur.

They rode in a slow circle about the castle, picking up Artair's and Tearlach's tracks where they went into the wood. The tracks were plain enough in the snow, and were easily followed.

Niall's head lifted, his nostrils flaring and his mouth grim as he surveyed the stark black and white wood. The snow deadened sound, so that they were surrounded by a silence unbroken except by the noise of their own passing, and that was slight enough. He sensed trouble, and there was a prickling between his shoulder blades.

"Ware," he said softly, and Sim and Iver moved apart from him, spreading out so that an ambush would be less likely to trap all three of them, and also that they might better use the cover available to them.

The day's patrolling had not revealed the tracks of either man or Highland pony coming onto Creag Dhu land, but if the Hay were determined enough, and sly enough, he could have sent in his men a day or more before the snow, and had them wait for their best opportunity. Given a small cave, Highlanders could easily survive the cold and snow in relative comfort. Hiding their mounts would be more difficult, and not even the Hay was stupid enough to send out his men afoot. They would also need running water.

"If any Hays are aboot, they'll be hard by the burn." He kept his voice low, but pitched it so both Sim and Iver could hear. They both nodded, their eyes moving restlessly, not pausing on any detail for more than a split second.

But Niall didn't sense any presence in the wood, despite his feeling of danger. He knew well when someone watched him, for he'd felt it often enough these past months. At times the eyes on him belonged to a Hay; other times, he knew it was *she,* the woman, the spirit. He didn't know why she watched or what she wanted, but ofttimes he could feel her gaze on him as he fought, feel her anxiety at his danger and her relief when he emerged victorious, and unscathed. Be damned if that wasn't less unsettling than sensing her near while he was abed with, and most like atop, a warm, willing woman. He was growing more and more irritable with her; if he ever got his hands on the wench, he'd be tempted to throttle her.

She watched him at the most inconvenient times, but now he rode through the darkening wood alone. Snowflakes swirled downward, brushing his face with their icy kiss. He could barely make out the tracks in the snow.

Cinnteach's ears pricked forward, and Niall held up a warning hand, slowing their approach. Naught moved before them, but the wind brought a scent, faint and unmistakable. Sim's mount shifted restlessly, tossing his head.

Niall dismounted, his right hand closing around the hilt of his sword. His acute senses felt the sudden brush of a gaze upon him, as definite as a touch, and he whirled to the side just as his ears caught the singing whisper of an arrow and sharp metal bit into his left shoulder with solid force.

He went down on his knee behind cover of

a large tree. Looking around, he saw both Sim and Iver also behind cover, their faces grim as they watched him. He signaled that he was all right and motioned for them to change positions, moving out and forward to catch the intruders between them.

His shoulder burned like seven hells, but he had taken the precaution of wearing a silk undertunic, something he insisted all his men do. An arrow couldn't pierce silk, something all Templars knew. The most damage from an arrow didn't occur on entry, but when it was removed. If one was wearing silk, the fabric went into the wound and twisted around the arrowhead, preventing debris from entering the wound and causing infection, and also allowing the arrow to be safely removed by covering the barbs.

He reached inside his shirt, grasped the silk around the arrow, and jerked. The weapon popped free of his flesh, though not without effort. He ground his teeth against the pain; silk might lessen the severity of an arrow wound, but he reflected that it still wasn't pleasant. Fresh blood streamed down his shoulder, wetting his shirt.

Pain had always made him angry. His eyes narrowed until they were nothing more than midnight slits as he slid to the ground and crawled forward behind a fallen log. Every move jarred his shoulder and he became even angrier.

The snow was falling faster, almost obliterating what little light remained. Both Sim and Iver were in position now, waiting for a target, but nothing moved. Niall dug his fingers under the snow, searching for a cone or rock. A pebble would suffice, for a subtle noise would be more effective than a great crashing.

Ah, there; a cone, mushy with wet and rot. Without rising from behind the log he tossed the cone in the direction from whence the arrow had come and it landed with a soft scraping noise, as if a careless shoulder had brushed against a snow-laden branch and caused it to spill its burden.

An archer rose swiftly from behind a rock, bow drawn, hunter's eyes locked on the target area. That singing whisper came again, and Iver's arrow pierced the archer's neck. His nerveless fingers released the bow tension and the arrow sank into the dirt before him. Eyes widened, teetering on tiptoe, he clawed at his throat. A choked, gurgling sound issued from his mouth, followed by a rush of blood, and he collapsed in the snow.

From the other side Sim released an arrow. He had no definite target so he sent it flying into a thick bush capable of providing concealment. His guess was correct, because a cry of pain split the cold air.

Niall took advantage of the distraction to move yet again, sliding behind another tree, much closer than he had been when caught by the arrow. His white teeth gleamed as he tilted back his head and loosed a bloodcurdling roar. He erupted from his cover like a lion springing for its prey. Four men sprang from concealment, startled by the bloody apparition that was suddenly upon them, huge sword flashing. One man managed to get his own sword up and metal rang against metal, but he went down under Niall's greater weight.

Sim and Iver each loosed one more arrow, then sprang forward screaming their own cries. Niall thrust his dagger up under his man's ribs and slashed sideways until he hit bone. The man arched and convulsed and Niall swung away from him, dropping to one knee under the rushing attack of a second foe and jabbing upward with the bloody dagger. The sharp metal sliced into the soft belly and Niall held the dagger steady while the man's momentum hurled him forward, eviscerating himself with his own motion.

Niall surged to his feet, but Sim and Iver had taken down their own men and only the three of them remained standing, panting softly, wisps of steam rising from their heads.

"Yer shoulder?" Iver asked, nodding at the wound.

" 'Tis minor enough." That was true, but it burned like hell for all that. Niall strode furiously to reclaim his horse. He was certain now that he'd not find Artair and Tearlach alive.

The Hay clansmen had planned well, skulking close and hiding until they could ambush those fewer in number than they, the whoreson cowards.

He found his men a minute later. Artair lay on his back, his blue eyes open and empty as he stared sightlessly upward. Niall dismounted and knelt beside his old friend, touching his face, lifting his hand. He was already cold, his limbs stiffening. The arrow had entered his heart.

He had not suffered, Niall thought, drawing Artair's plaid up to cover his face. His expression was almost peaceful, as if he'd at last quit a life in which he had no place.

"Adieu, mon ami," he whispered. French was the language in which he had been schooled as a Templar, and it was in that tongue he bid good-bye to his last friend from that time. They were all gone now, all the Knights who had sought sanctuary at Creag Dhu. Some had died on the battlefield for Scotland, some had died natural deaths, others lived on in quiet places. Some had taken wives, had children; some still held to their vows. But they were Knights no longer; only he remained in service to the Order. It had been so for fourteen years, and yet so long as Artair had been with him he had felt the kinship. Now there was no one left at Creag Dhu who had even a glimmer of understanding.

"Tearlach lives," Sim said, pressing his

tough, blunt fingers deep into the wounded man's neck. Surveying the amount of blood on the snowy ground, he shook his shaggy head. "He's near bled out, though. He'll no last 'til morn."

Niall stood and lifted Artair's body over his shoulder. "Perhaps," he said. "But if he dies, 'twill be among friends."

He sat alone in his chamber that night, unable to sleep, drinking raw spirits that burned down his throat. He was drunk, but the raw ale had done nothing to lift his mood. His shoulder throbbed; it had been rinsed with the same ale he drank, and bound with a poultice to draw out any putrefaction. He was hot with fever, but he didn't fear it; the fever had come soon after each wound he'd ever received, and he had noted that he seemed to heal faster than those whose fevers came on later. The wound had been clean, the ale fierce; in two days, he'd scarce feel a twinge in the shoulder.

The heat from the fireplace washed his bare shoulders and back. His plaid was draped about his hips, but except for that he was naked.

He stared across the chamber at nothing, his expression grim. Damn the Hays; if he had to wipe out the entire clan, rid the Highlands of their stinking presence, he would have vengeance for Artair. The time would come soon enough, when winter lifted its icy hand from the mountains.

But for now he was drunk, feverish, and alone with his thoughts. There was no one watching, no one near, when he needed to feel her with him.

He closed his eyes, aching inside with the loneliness. For all his life he had been forced to hide parts of himself from the world. Always his kinship with the Bruce had been hidden, even before the Bruce was king. Later, with the Knights, he had been forced to deny his own nature, though he had gone to sleep every night with his arms and loins aching with need. Now he could give free rein to his lusts, but he must hold secret his years as a Knight, though those eight years had done much to shape him into the man he was now. Even from Robert, who knew all those things, he must conceal his true role as Guardian, and the cursed vow that ruled his life.

Only with *her* was there nothing to hide. Whoever and whatever she was, he sensed that she knew him as no one else had ever done, knew his body bone-deep and his mind even when he slept. When he took her in his arms, when she came to him in the dark silence of the night, she knew all of the man he was and still she clung to him, offering her body and herself.

Niall inhaled through his teeth as lust hit him hard. He wanted her, but not in a dream. He wanted her real and warm under his hands, her sweet scent fresh in his nostrils as he took her.

He could almost feel her, his longing was so sharp. His hands curled into fists, trying to capture the sensation of her silky skin under his palms.

The fever and ale and longing combined, and suddenly she was there, her hands sliding lightly over his bare shoulders. He felt her concern as she touched the pad covering his wound, but her concern wasn't what he wanted. Fiercely he caught her to him, and held her on his lap while he stripped away the small scraps of clothing that were all she wore. He couldn't quite see her face, but she was here and that was all that mattered. He put his hand on her cool belly, warming her with his touch, feeling the muscles beneath contract as she drew in her breath. Her small nipples beaded, as he had known they would. She responded to his slightest touch; he knew that if he slid his fingers between her legs to the delicate opening hidden there, he would find it wet, ready for him.

Instead he smoothed his hand up to her breasts, cupping them, rubbing his thumb over her nipples, then bending his dark head to take the tightened buds in his mouth and gently suck. She shivered in his arms, trying to press closer to him. Such lovely, plump little things her breasts were, small and delightfully round, so delicate and sensitive he knew it would pain her if he handled them roughly as some women liked. She was more finely made than any woman he had ever known, both fragile and strong, her skin like translucent silk.

He couldn't wait any longer. He needed her too much. Swiftly he turned her, laying her back on the bench. He shoved his plaid aside and straddled the bench, spreading her thighs open and moving between them. He watched as he entered her, his thick shaft too large, too brutish, for the soft flesh that stretched under his pressure, but she took him, her back arching, her cries those of pleasure. He gritted his teeth as the tightness of her sheath enveloped him and he crouched over her, thrusting long and slow and deep, almost delirious with fever and drink and the sensations boiling through him, but needing her so much he couldn't stop. Her arms curled around his neck and he felt her passion matching his, her need as great as his, her acceptance of everything he was; and he knew he wasn't alone anymore —

But he was.

His eyes opened and the fantasy shattered. He sat there, breathing hard as he silently cursed her. Damn her for taunting him like this, tantalizing him with a whisper of her presence, then disappearing when he needed her most. His aloneness crashed down on him and he hunched his shoulders against the burden. His head dropped down on his chest and he closed his eyes, trying to regain her presence, but it was gone as if she had never been there at all.

"So where are ye now, lass?" he murmured.

Grace bolted out of bed, grabbing for the pistol. Someone had spoken right beside her, the voice almost in her ear. She stood with her back against the wall and the pistol locked in a two-handed grip, swinging from point to point in search of a target, but nothing was there. The room was empty, dark, lit only by the streetlights filtering through the drawn curtains.

She sagged back, gasping. A dream. Only a dream, and for once not of Niall — or was it? The voice that had jerked her awake had been deep, burred, and she'd heard the word *lass*.

Yes. Niall. She closed her eyes, breathing deep and slow in an effort to calm her racing heart. After a few moments she was more relaxed, but far from drowsy, and she mentally replayed that voice in her ear.

Deep, whiskey-rough, burred. Not the smooth voice of a practiced seducer, but that of a man used to command: completely self-assured, determined. And yet he'd asked, very quietly, "So where are ye now, lass?" as if he truly needed her —

Grace's eyes opened again, widening. She had been dreaming, after all; she remembered a snippet now, of Black Niall sitting quietly before a fire. But something was different, as if it wasn't her dream at all, something outside herself that had drawn her in.

More and more of the dream unfolded itself. She saw him alone, half naked, with only his plaid draped loosely about his hips. He had evidently been injured, for a rough bandage was wrapped about his left shoulder, the linen pale against his olive-toned skin. Fear licked at her and she wanted to go to him, assure herself he was all right.

A metal cup was in his hand. He was drinking, staring at nothing, his expression somber. His loneliness, his absolute *aloneness,* made her ache inside. Then he closed his eyes and abruptly she was there, in his arms, lying naked on his lap while he fondled and sucked gently at her breasts.

Grace trembled at the memory that wasn't quite a memory, was more than a memory. Somehow she was lying on the bench and he was crouched over her, his face tense as he thrust again and again. The pleasure rose beating inside her, and she reached up to twine her arms around his strong neck, almost weeping with joy.

And then, nothing. He was gone, the dream ended, with only his murmured, "So where are ye now, lass?" echoing in her mind, as if she should have been there, tending his wound, offering him the comfort women have always offered warriors.

She felt a wrench of regret that she hadn't been there.

The image of him was sharp and clear in her mind. He sat with his back to the fire and the golden light had glistened on his bare shoulders, broad and powerful with muscle, and a halo limned his long black hair. Equally black hair spread across his chest, and a thin, silky line of it ran down his washboard stomach to the small, taut circle of his navel. His long legs were thick with muscle, the most powerful legs she had ever seen on a human, the delineation of his musculature built on the rock-solid strength produced by a lifetime of swordplay and battle, of controlling a huge stallion with the strength in his thighs, wearing more than a hundred pounds of armor and actually fighting in it. His was the body of a warrior, honed into a weapon, a tool.

But he was still just a man, she thought with aching tenderness. He bled, he ached, he sat alone and got drunk and grumpily wondered why some woman wasn't dancing attendance on him. It was her imagination that made her dream he'd been speaking only to her.

If he had been . . . if she were actually with him . . . She would get him to lie down in bed, make him more comfortable. He was probably a bit feverish; a cold cloth on his brow would make him feel better. She didn't doubt, however, that he would be a terrible patient. Instead of resting he would insist she lie down with him, and soon his hands would be roaming under her shirt —

"*Damn* it!" Grace moaned, pressing her hands to her eyes. Her breath was coming soft and fast, and she felt warm, liquid. Her nipples were tight and erect, pushing against the thin fabric of her T-shirt. It was bad enough that she sometimes had erotic dreams about him, but it was a far worse betrayal of Ford that she daydreamed about Black Niall, too.

The pistol was still in her hand, cold against her temple. Carefully she replaced it and thought about getting back into bed, but she was wide awake. She glanced at the clock. Why, it wasn't even eleven o'clock yet; she'd been asleep less than an hour. Long enough, however, for Niall to take over her subconscious.

For eight months she had been dead inside, and she wanted to remain that way. There hadn't been any laughter, any sunshine, any appreciation of a deep blue sky or the drama of a storm. It was safer that way, easier; if she hadn't been numb, she couldn't have survived. She didn't want any sign of returning life because it would only weaken her. In eight months she hadn't yet been able to weep, even tears held at bay by the bleak ice surrounding her. Niall was a crack in that wall of ice; one day it would collapse, and so would she.

She couldn't afford the weakness he represented. She had to hurry with those damn

Gaelic papers, get them finished and out of her mind so Black Niall would cease to plague her. If she could get some measure of revenge against Parrish, perhaps her mind would ease and she could begin to heal, and her subconscious would then no longer need to cling to the dream image.

Well, sleep was definitely out of the question. Groaning, knowing she needed to rest because tomorrow she and Kris planned to break into the Foundation's computer system; instead she turned on a light. Her mind was racing; until she calmed, she might as well use the time to work.

She didn't bother getting out the laptop, just took her notepad and the remaining Gaelic papers and curled up in the room's one armchair, a cracked vinyl job she had made more comfortable by throwing a sheet over it. She could still hear the creaking and crackling of the vinyl, but at least now the chair didn't stick to her.

She picked up a page and groaned. More mathematical formulas, though, thank God, they were in Latin. Her brows rose in surprise. This was the first time two languages had been mixed in one section. The handwriting was different, too, heavier, plainer. She scribbled the formulas on her notepad, translating them into English. "For twenty years, the proportion of water to weight shall be . . ." On and on it went, giving the precise fractions for, supposedly, targeting the year to which one wanted to travel. Also included was the voltage of energy required, or at least she thought that was what it was; they hadn't had any knowledge of electricity other than watching lightning bolts, so what exactly had they been measuring? Energy, yes, but what kind?

Still, she copied it all down, yawning as she did so. It was like copying down a complicated recipe, though not half as interesting. If anything was going to put her to sleep, this would do it.

She began reading aloud to herself, droning the words.

" 'For DCLXXV years' — let's see, *D* is five hundred years, the *C* is after it so that adds another hundred, *L* is fifty, the two *X*'s after it add ten years each, and then a *V*, which is five. Six hundred and seventy-five years. Getting pretty precise there, aren't you?" she muttered to the long-ago writer.

Absently, she subtracted six hundred seventy-five from 1997, just to see what year a current time traveler would end up in, using this exact formula: 1322. "A wonderful year," she said, yawning. "I remember it well." What a coincidence; 1322 would have been in Black Niall's time.

She turned the page, ready for more math. She blinked at the words, wondering if she was sleepier than she had thought, or perhaps had somehow gotten a sheet that didn't belong mixed up with the Gaelic papers.

She read the words again, and chills ran over her entire body. "No," she said softly. "It's impossible."

But there it was, in Gaelic, and in the same heavy hand that had written the mathematical formulas:

"Require ye proof? In the Year of Our Lord 1945, the Guardian slew the German beast, and so came Grace to Creag Dhu. — Niall MacRobert, y. 1322."

She became aware she was panting, and a shudder wracked her. The page swam before her eyes, the words blurring. The term *German* hadn't existed in the thirteen hundreds.

How could someone who lived in the fourteenth century have knowledge of something that happened in the twentieth? It was impossible — unless the formula truly worked.

Unless they had known how to travel through time.

Chapter 15

Kris didn't recognize her. They had arranged to meet outside a supermarket late the next afternoon, and Grace had arrived more than an hour early so she could watch for anything suspicious. She hated not feeling able to trust Kris completely, but there was too much at stake for her to take anything for granted.

She watched Kris arrive in his beloved '66 Chevelle, the engine rumbling with a muscular cough that had a couple of middle-aged men throwing envious glances his way. Poor Kris. He wanted female attention, but instead his car was attracting the male variety. At least he'd done some additional work on the Chevelle since she had last seen it; it was actually painted now, a bright fire-engine red.

He parked at the end of a lane and waited. There hadn't been any suspicious, repetitious traffic during the hour Grace had been watching, but still she waited. After fifteen more minutes had passed she slid out of the truck and crunched across the thin layer of snow that had fallen on the parking lot since she arrived. It was still snowing lightly, lacy flakes swirling and dancing in the wind. She went up to the Chevelle and tapped on the window.

Kris rolled the window down a couple of inches. "Yeah, what is it?" he asked, a little impatiently.

"Hi, Kris," she said, and his eyes widened with shock.

He scrambled out of the car, slipping a little and grabbing the door to right himself. "My God," he mumbled. "My God."

"It's a wig," she said. She wore a blond one, plus a baseball cap and sunglasses. Add losing more than thirty pounds, and no one who had known her before would have recognized her.

Kris's stupefied gaze started at her booted feet, went up her tight jeans, took in the denim jacket, and ended once again on her face. His mouth opened, but no sound came out. The tip of his nose turned red. "My God," he said again. Abruptly he lunged at her and wrapped both arms around her, holding her tight and rocking her back and forth. Grace's nerves had been on edge for too long; her first instinct, barely restrained, was to kick his feet out from under him. But then he made a strangled sound, his shoulders shook, and she realized he was crying.

"Shh," she said gently, putting her own arms around him. "It's all right." It felt odd to let someone touch her, and to touch someone in return. She had gone so long without physical contact that she felt both awkward and starved.

"I've been so scared," he said into her baseball cap, his voice shaking. "Not knowing if you were okay, if you had a place to stay —"

"Sometimes yes, sometimes no," she said, patting his back. "The first week was the worst. Do you think we can get in the car? I don't want to attract attention."

"What? Oh! Sure." He trudged around the car to open the passenger door for her, a courtesy that touched her. He was still thin and gangly, his glasses still slid toward the end of his nose, but in several small ways she could see the advance of maturity. His shoulders looked a tad heavier, his voice had lost some of its boyishness, even his stubble was a little thicker. Manhood would suit him a lot better than boyhood; when other men his age were fighting middle-age spread, Kris would still be lean.

He slid under the wheel and slammed the door, then turned to survey her. His eyes were still wet, but now he shook his head in wonderment. "I wouldn't have known you," he admitted in awe. "You — you're *tiny.*"

"Thin," she corrected. "I'm as tall as I always was. Taller," she said, pointing at the inch-and-a-half heels of her boots.

"Cool," he said, eyeing them and blinking hard. He glanced at his own feet, and she thought he might soon become a boot man. There was nothing like boots to give a man attitude. Or a woman, come to that; she definitely walked with more authority when she wore the boots.

Then he looked back at her face, and she saw his lower lip wobble again. "You look tired," he blurted.

"I couldn't sleep last night." That was the unvarnished truth. She hadn't been able to close her eyes after reading that little note from Black Niall. Every time she thought of it she felt her spine prickle, and chills would roughen her skin. But after the initial shock, it wasn't the bit about 1945 that was so eerie, it was the phrase "and so came Grace to Creag Dhu." Surely he meant a state of grace, but it felt so — personal, somehow, something written specifically to her. She felt as if he were inviting her to use the formula, to step through the layers of time energy. His calculations had been very specific, for exactly six hundred seventy-five years; back to the year 1322, the year the message had been written.

Kris reached out and took her gloved hand, squeezed it. "Where have you been?"

"On the move. I haven't stayed in one place for long."

"The police —"

"It isn't the police I worry about so much as Parrish's men. At least the police aren't actively hunting me, not after this length of time. Sure, they'll follow a lead, but that's about it. Parrish's men nearly caught me once."

"It's so weird," he said, shaking his head. "Do you still think it's because of those papers you had?"

"I *know* it was." She stared out the window, which was fogging up from their breathing. "I translated them. I know exactly why he wants them."

Kris clenched his hands into fists, staring at her delicate profile. He wanted to take her somewhere and feed her, he wanted to tuck a blanket around her, he wanted — he wanted to punch something. She looked so frail. Yeah, that was it. Frail.

Grace had always been a special person to him; he'd known her most of his life, had a crush on her since he was seventeen. She had always been so nice to him, treating him as an equal when most adults didn't. Grace was a genuinely good person, smart and kind, and her mouth, oh her mouth made him feel all hot and dizzy-headed. He'd dreamed of kissing her but never worked up the nerve. It was lousy of him, but when she had called the day before, he had thought again of kissing her, and even thought that it would be okay now because Ford was dead. But looking at her he knew it wasn't okay, might never be okay. She was quiet and sad and distant, and that mouth didn't look as if it ever smiled.

He pulled himself away from his thoughts and reached into the backseat to grab a computer printout. "Here," he said, placing it on her lap. He might not ever kiss her, but he would do what he could to help her. "It's a blueprint of the building where the Foundation is headquartered."

Grace pulled off her sunglasses and put them on the dash. "Where did you get this?" she asked in surprise, flipping through the pages.

"Well, it's a fairly new building," he explained. "A copy of the plans are on file with the city planners, I guess in case of emergencies and stuff."

She gave him a sideways glance. "So you went to city hall and got a copy?"

"Not exactly. I got it out of their computers," he said blithely.

"Without setting off any alarms, I hope."

"Oh, please," he scoffed. "It was a joke."

There was no point in scolding him about it; after all, she was asking him to commit a much more serious crime than computer hacking. "Getting into the Foundation's computers won't be as easy," she warned.

"No, but I've already got it figured out. Your idea about the maintenance crew was great. We steal a couple of the uniforms, waltz right in. But all we need is to get into the building, we don't need to actually get into the Foundation's offices. Look," he said, pointing to the blueprint. "Here is the service elevator. We take it to the floor below, then use this access panel in the ceiling to get to the electronic panel. I tap into a line, pull up a file list, and we go from there."

"What about alarms?"

"Well, it's a self-contained system, so they don't have to worry about anyone hacking in; certain files may be security-coded, but not the system itself. My job is to get the coded files."

He made it sound so easy, but she didn't expect the Foundation's files to be as vulnerable as the city's. Parrish was too smart, too wily, and he had too much to hide. "There has to be a list of the passwords for any coded files, but it could be anywhere. Parrish may keep it in his house, or there could be a safe in the offices where it would be kept. Either way, we won't be able to get it."

He shook his head, grinning. "You'd be surprised how many people keep a list of passwords in their desk. It's worth a look, anyway, once we're certain everyone has gone home."

"I have some ideas about the passwords," she said. "We'll try those first." She shuddered at the idea of going into the empty offices and finding they weren't empty after all, but that Parrish had worked late. Hearing his voice on the telephone had been bad enough; she didn't think she could bear actually seeing him. Still, if it became necessary to break into his private office, she would do it. Kris would be willing, but she wasn't willing to let him; she had already involved him enough.

"Okay," he said, practically twitching in his enthusiasm. "Let's go."

"Now?"

"Why not?"

Why not, indeed. There was no reason to wait, not if they could manage to liberate a couple of uniforms from the maintenance service. "Do you have your laptop?" she asked.

"In the backseat."

She shrugged. "Then we might as well give it a try. We'll go in my truck."

"Why?" He looked a bit affronted at her reluctance to travel in the Chevelle.

"This car is a little noticeable," she pointed out, her tone dry.

A grin broke across his face. "Yeah, it is, isn't it?" he said, giving the dash a fond pat. "Okay." He got the laptop out of the backseat and took the keys from the ignition. Grace grabbed her sunglasses. They got out and locked the doors, and they trudged across the slippery parking lot to her pickup.

They were silent as Grace drove. She tried to come up with some feasible plan for getting the maintenance uniforms, but none occurred to her. And there was still security at the building after office hours; perhaps the maintenance service had a key to the rear service door, perhaps not. After cleaning houses for six months, she knew some people without thought turned over a spare key to the cleaning service so they wouldn't be inconvenienced by having to be at home when their houses were cleaned. Grace was always amazed at their lack of caution. Still, it happened. Unless Parrish owned the entire building, the chances were fifty-fifty the maintenance crew could enter without ringing for a guard. If Parrish owned the building, no way; he wouldn't care if the crew had to wait, or that a guard had to trudge from wherever he was in the building to let them in. He wouldn't even consider their inconvenience in the security scheme.

With what she had learned in the past eight months, Grace had to admit he was right. If you had something worth protecting, you protected it, and you didn't compromise security by fretting about whether or not the maintenance crew had to wait a couple of minutes. Of course, a sophisticated system would use closed-circuit cameras to identify the crew, and the door would be opened by remote control —

Cameras.

She drew in her breath with a hiss. "We're going about this all wrong."

"We are?" Kris asked blankly. "What do you mean?"

"There may be security cameras at the maintenance entrance. How are we going to waltz up to the truck and search it for extra uniforms?"

He rubbed his chin, his long, skinny fingers rasping over his beard stubble as he went into his thinking mode. "Let's see . . . okay. First thing, you let me out a block away and I'll check it out. If there *are* cameras, then we have to find out if they're closed-circuit and are being monitored, or if they're just the kind that tapes so someone can watch the tape after a crime has already been committed."

"Either way, if there are cameras, that means you need a disguise too," Grace said firmly.

He looked taken with that idea, and her heart ached at his youth.

"You'll have to take off your glasses," she decided. "I'll wear them instead. And we'll beef you up by stuffing towels in your uniform."

He looked doubtful. "I won't be able to see," he objected. "And neither will you."

That made sense. One of them had to be able to navigate. She plucked her sunglasses out of her pocket and handed them to him. "Pop the lenses." She had paid fifty cents for them at a yard sale, so she didn't hesitate to ruin them.

Kris obediently popped out the plastic lenses, and gave the frames back to her. Grace slid them on, and glanced at herself in the rearview mirror. At close range it was fairly obvious there was no glass in the frames, but a security camera wouldn't detect it.

"We really should have scouted this out and maybe taken the time to buy our own maintenance uniforms," she said, shrugging. "But it might work anyway."

It worked.

Kris came jogging back to the truck, his face red from both excitement and exposure to the cold. He climbed in, gasping, and his glasses immediately fogged up. He snatched them off and absently held them in front of the heat vent while he gave her a myopically triumphant smile. "There's a camera," he reported breathlessly. "But it isn't closed-circuit."

"How do you know?"

"I checked it out."

"Kris!"

"No problem. It's in a corner, aimed at the maintenance door. I slipped around the side of the building and stayed out of its range. I didn't see any cable wires running from the camera into the building. And even better —" He paused, grinning at her.

"*What?*" she demanded impatiently when he let the pause drag out, and he laughed delightedly.

"The door is propped open!"

It was obvious Parrish and the Foundation didn't own the building, Grace thought.

"It's the kind of door that locks every time it closes," Kris explained. "I guess the maintenance crew gets tired of having to unlock it every time, so they dragged one of those rubber-backed mats over the threshold, and it keeps the door from completely closing."

Oh, the simple, elegant ingenuity of people trying to get out of a little inconvenience. With that one act, they had negated the building's security.

"We still need uniforms."

He grinned triumphantly at her. "There's a big van parked there. I checked it out. The front doors are locked, and there's a steel screen separating the cab from the back of the van, I guess so they can leave the back doors open and not have to worry about the van being stolen. Anyway, there's lots of stuff in the back, and some dirty coveralls." He slid his glasses into place. "What more do we need?"

What more, indeed?

The camera outside the service door wasn't closed-circuit. The one in the hallway was.

Parrish watched as two more maintenance people entered the building. His eyebrows had lifted a fraction when the first crew had propped open the door. For now it suited his purposes to let it remain open, to give Grace an easy access should she take the bait, but as soon as he had her he would make certain the owners of the building found a new maintenance service. Of course, the Foundation's offices had far more stringent security measures, but that didn't excuse the sloppiness of the present crew.

These two latest arrivals carried tool boxes, and wore tool belts strapped over their shapeless coveralls. One was a skinny woman, wearing an unattractive baseball cap over her unattractive frizzy hair. Oversized glasses dominated her face. The man was tall, pudgy, clumsy. He wore gloves and a weird fur hat with ear flaps, and he didn't seem to know where he was going. The woman led the way as they trudged down the short hall to the service elevator.

He wasn't interested in them. He watched carefully for the little mouse he hoped would nibble at his bait. Perhaps she wouldn't come; if she had seen him do the shooting, she wouldn't want to be anywhere near him, unless of course she planned to shoot him in revenge, but he was certain Grace wasn't a woman who could kill. He could recognize the killer instinct in certain people; Conrad, for instance. Grace didn't have it.

On the other hand, she had surprised him and everyone else by being able to elude both the cops and his best men for more than eight months. She had proven herself to be unusually resourceful. If she hadn't called the Foundation, no one would have had any idea she was back in Minneapolis. Shocking mistake. But then, felons often tripped themselves up by returning to the scene of their crime, perhaps to gloat at their own cleverness.

But Grace had called the Foundation, himself specifically, and since she hadn't spoken, the only reason would have been to find out if he was in town. Now that she knew he was, what would she do? Show up at his house to talk to him? She could have talked on the phone, unless she suddenly panicked at the thought of giving away her whereabouts.

So had she seen him or not? Did she want to talk or shoot? Perverse of him, but he rather hoped it was the latter. The thought of Grace with a gun in her hand was strangely exciting. She would never get to use it, of course, but he didn't want her weepy and weak in his arms; he wanted her furious, fighting, so that his victory was all the sweeter when, as with Calla, his skill overrode her anger. His little interlude with Calla had been unusually satisfying; surely with Grace his pleasure would be even more intense.

Would she come or not? The service door was conveniently propped open, but perhaps she would try to enter during the day, when she could more easily mix with the flow of people coming and going.

He waited patiently.

"Here we are," Kris whispered excitedly as he opened the access panel in the ceiling of the Foundation's main computer room. It was quiet, dim, with only the hum of electronics breaking the silence.

It had taken them an hour to work their way into place. Nothing was ever as easy as it looked on paper. First they had had to dodge the real maintenance crew, finally climbing seventeen flights of stairs instead of using the service elevator. After locating the access panel to the overhead heating ducts, they climbed onto a high stool and managed to hoist themselves inside, putting the panel back in place so no one would know they were there. Then, using a flashlight taken from her glove box, they navigated the miles of ductwork only to find they had to go into the Foundation's offices after all. They located the computer room and listened for a while, but the room seemed empty. Carefully they removed the ceiling access panel.

Kris leaned his head and shoulders out of the opening and looked around. "There aren't any cameras," he whispered. "But there's a window in the door, so we'll need to sit where anyone passing by can't see us."

"If we happen to be climbing in or out when someone walks by, we're sunk," Grace said. It couldn't be helped, though; they had no access through any of the doors, so it had to be the ceiling.

Kris braced his arms on each side of the opening and slowly lowered himself through it until he was hanging by his fingers. The ceilings were standard eight feet, for easy heating; with his arms outstretched, he had little more than a foot to drop. He landed quietly on the tile floor, then turned for Grace to hand down the laptop. With that safely stored, he held up his arms for her as she swung down from the ceiling, catching her around the waist and carefully setting her on the floor.

He looked swiftly around, sizing up the setup. This was his milieu, and his thin face glowed with eagerness. "Sit over there, behind that desk," he said, pointing. "Let me get this hooked up and I'll join you." As he spoke he was busy removing cords and wires from a terminal, and rehooking them to his laptop. That done, he repositioned some operating manuals to block any view of their heads, which would be sticking up above the edge of the desk.

He flopped down beside her and drew his long legs up, cradling the laptop between them. He fingered a switch and the powerful little machine began to hum and make discreet little chirps as it booted up. They had been crossing their fingers on this, because Kris used the Windows 95 operating system; if the Foundation used DOS, he wouldn't be able to use his laptop. Instead he would have to sit at a monitor, and given the window in the door that would be risky. But the Foundation used the same operating system, and the menu flashed on the screen.

"Okay, let's see the files," he murmured, rubbing his fingertip across the little mouse tucked in the middle of the keyboard and directing the cursor to the correct icon. He clicked once, and the screen filled with file names.

He scrolled down while they looked for something interesting. "Let's look at the financial statement and tax returns," she said, and he pulled up those files. They were incredibly complicated; they didn't have time to decipher everything, so he copied the files onto a floppy and returned to the list.

"Donor list," Grace directed, and he copied that file too.

There was little else that looked interesting; they looked into the payroll file, and Grace gasped at what Parrish was paid. Millions. The Foundation paid him *millions* every year. Just for directing the Foundation? She was certain the Foundation could find an able overseer for much less money, if that was all that was needed.

"Nothing much here," Kris said after an hour of pulling up individual files and checking their contents. "What were those ideas you had on passwords? Let's try a few of them and see what happens."

"Treasure," she directed, and he gave her a sharp glance as he obediently typed in the word and clicked on "Retrieve."

File Not Found.

"Temple."

File Not Found.

"Knight."

File Not Found.

"Templar."

"You mean those bad-ass monks you were

reading about at my house that night?" Kris asked, typing the word.

"The very same."

File Not Found.

"Damn," she breathed. She was running out of likely passwords. "Guardian."

File Not Found.

"Niall . . . Pope . . . Temple Treasure. Whose bright idea was it to allow unlimited space in naming files? Let's see . . . he's egotistical enough to name a file after himself. Try Parrish and Sawyer."

File Not Found popped up on the screen after every entry. Kris had been silent except for asking her how to spell Niall.

"Power," she suggested.

He typed. "Nope."

"Shroud . . . Turin . . . Covenant . . . Ark."

He shook his head after each entry. "Nope."

Grace rubbed the back of her neck. The Ark of the Covenant had been way out in left field anyway. She had only thought of it because of the Indiana Jones movie, where the Nazis had been trying to find the Ark and conquer the world. There had been a seed of truth in the movie, because Hitler had indeed been obsessed with acquiring ancient religious artifacts.

"In the Year of Our Lord 1945, the Guardian slew the German beast, and so came Grace to Creag Dhu."

She remembered the entry, and once again chills roughened her skin. Creag Dhu couldn't be the password, because the location of the Treasure was what Parrish didn't know. "Hitler," she suggested.

Again Kris gave her a startled look, but he typed in the name.

The screen filled with words.

She sat back, stunned. It couldn't be. She hadn't even considered a connection, despite the document's warnings about the Foundation of Evil.

"My God," Kris whispered. Hastily he shoved another floppy into the disk drive and copied the file without taking time to read it. Only when the file was copied and the disk safely stored did he slowly scroll downward.

"They really think they can rule the world if they find this so-called treasure," he whispered. What they were reading was nothing less than a manifesto, a declaration of intent. "The papers you have supposedly give the location of it, right? And he's actually killed Ford and Bryant just because they *knew* about the papers?" Outrage and disbelief warred in his tone.

She looked at him. Her gaze was glassy from shock. "They do," she said dazedly. "Give the location, that is."

"Holy shit," he whispered. Then his eyes widened and he looked nervously at the screen. "I guess I shouldn't say that, huh?"

A door closed in the hallway.

They froze. After a split second, Kris hurriedly pulled the lid down so the computer was almost closed, to hide the glow of the screen. There was only a whisper of sound outside the door; whoever it was moved very quietly. But the footsteps moved on without pause, and after a moment came the sound of another door closing in the hallway.

"We gotta get out of here," Kris muttered. "You got any more ideas on passwords?"

She shook her head. He swiftly exited the file, backed out of the program, and shut off the laptop. Within a minute he had reconnected the other terminal and replaced the manuals in their original position.

He crawled over to the door and poked his head up just enough to peer out the window, checking in both directions. "It's clear," he whispered, standing up and hurriedly crossing the room.

Grace dragged a chair beneath the access panel and climbed onto the seat. First she stowed the laptop and the disks in the duct, then she levered herself through the hole. Kris assisted with a boost from beneath.

She turned to reach down and grab the collar of his coveralls, half dragging him through the hole. They were both panting as they replaced the access panel and switched on the flashlight. In silence they retraced their path, both of them thinking about what they had read.

* * *

"She isn't coming tonight," Parrish told Conrad, disappointment evident in his tone. "It's midnight; she wouldn't expect me to work this late."

Conrad didn't reply. He watched the screen as two of the maintenance crew came down the hallway and left by the propped-open door. They appeared to be hurrying, and the woman was carrying some kind of satchel.

She was small, and had frizzy blond hair. The angle of the camera wasn't good, but something about her jawline was familiar.

A growl rumbled in his throat, and Parrish lifted questioning eyebrows. "That was her!" Conrad said, already running when he hit the door.

Parrish was right behind him when he burst out the service door and ran down the short alley to the street. He looked both ways, but the sidewalks were empty. A car went by; the driver was a suited young black man, probably a junior executive who had been burning the midnight oil.

A block or so away, an engine coughed to life. Conrad ran down the sidewalk toward the sound, his shoes slipping on the snowy sidewalk. His breath fogged in the frigid air. He reached the corner in time to see a set of taillights disappear around another corner.

"Did you see her?" Parrish gasped, coming

to a stop beside him. "What kind of car was it?"

"I couldn't tell," Conrad said. "But the woman was Grace St. John. She was carrying a small satchel, perhaps a computer case."

"Computer!" Parrish felt his blood pressure rise. "God damn it, the bitch has been in our files!" He and Conrad hurried back to the office, shivering as the cold bit through their clothes. She wouldn't have been able to get into his password files, but it infuriated him that she had slipped past his guard, that she had been so close all that time and he hadn't known it. Damn the little bitch, how did she do it?

"Who was her friend, I wonder?" Who could she have found to help her? She wouldn't contact people who had known her before, because she couldn't be certain their first phone call wouldn't be to the police. It had to have been someone she had met afterward.

"Perhaps that is why we couldn't find her," Conrad suggested. "We have been looking for a woman alone, instead of a couple."

The idea infuriated Parrish. He ground his teeth as they walked swiftly to the computer room and he opened the door. Everything looked normal, except for a chair that was out of place.

Conrad pointed at the ceiling. Directly over the chair, a panel was slightly out of place.

"Find her," Parrish said in an almost soundless whisper. She had been there, so close; she had taunted him, coming there with another man. He didn't know yet if she had actually found anything of use in his computer system, but just the fact that she had dared invade it made him shake with rage. "Find both of them. And kill them."

Chapter 16

Grace's second sleepless night in a row made her eyesight blur, but she couldn't stop reading parts of the Hitler file over and over, couldn't get it out of her mind even when she laid it aside. She kept coming back to it, rereading it to assure herself she hadn't imagined any of it.

The Foundation had been founded in 1802 by a strange assortment of men; Napoleon Bonaparte had been one of the original members, perhaps the most important one and the moving force behind the forming of the organization. Certainly he had been the only one at that time who had ambitions to conquer the world. A grandiose scheme, on the surface of things, but not so unexpected when the entire picture was seen.

The Hitler file gave a different and disturbing look at well-known history. In 1799, Napoleon invaded Turkish Syria, advancing as far as the fortress of Acre. He hadn't managed to take the fortress, which the Templars had built in 1240, but perhaps he had heard something there, or found something. It was after he returned from Acre that his ambition had become full-blown; he had immediately made himself dictator of France, and then Emperor. He conquered Spain, Italy, Switzerland, Holland, Poland, attacked Russia and Austria.

Perhaps a lot of men wanted to rule the world, but few, luckily, really tried to do it or even thought they could. Napoleon had thought it possible; his intention was plainly stated in the Hitler file. He had launched an all-out search for the lost Templar Treasure, certain that when he found it he would be unstoppable, for it was promised in the papers: he who controls the Power controls the world. What was the Power? Not gold, but certainly something tangible, such as the Ark of the Covenant. Whatever it was, the Foundation believed it controlled unimaginable power, and for almost two centuries the Foundation had devoted all its resources to finding the Treasure.

There were three distinct levels within the Foundation. At the lower level were the employees, paper pushers or hired muscle. The center tier was made up of "contributors," people who were members of the Foundation and who contributed large amounts of money to it, whether by choice or coercion. From what she read, coercion was most common. At the top level were relatively few names; she recognized most of them. Napoleon. Stalin. Hitler. Two American presidents. A Middle East dictator. A French general. A British prime minister. A famous labor leader. Tycoons, both male and female. One name particularly surprised her, for he was an extremely wealthy man known for his humanitarian works. And Parrish Sawyer. His name seemed minor compared to the fame of the others, but they hadn't been famous at the beginning of their careers, either. The presence of his name on the list was a testament to his ruthlessness.

The power to rule the world. The concept was far more ridiculous now than it had been no more than fifty years before. How could any one person, or Foundation, rule the entire world? But when she looked at it in terms of national power and influence, something most nations lacked, it was indeed possible to control the world by controlling key nations. A political takeover wouldn't even be necessary, so long as the politicians obeyed the money men. Media, banking, commerce — take control of those three elements, and one did indeed control the world. World rule wasn't measured in terms of military conquest, but in economic ones.

To rule the world was a strange ambition, reasonable only to the megalomaniac personality. What was unusual was that so many of these men had joined the Foundation, for by their very personalities each would have thought himself smarter or greater than all the others. But each one had been drawn in, and in his way served the Foundation while he thought he was serving himself.

The Foundation of Evil.

Hitler and Stalin had been overtly evil, their twisted, conscienceless psyches exposed to world view. Most of the others on the list appeared, or had appeared, normal, but she knew from Parrish's example how misleading appearances could be. All of these people had pursued unlimited power and ambition, their actions guided by the Foundation. Did they use the Foundation, or did the Foundation use them?

What was the nature of evil? What face did it wear? Was the capability to do evil in every person, and like any seed it flourished in some places but not in others? Or did the impetus for evil come from without? Was evil itself a separate entity, or nothing more than a result?

Was the Foundation evil because evil people served it, or was it evil in and of itself? Had the Foundation existed, in some other guise, far longer than a mere two centuries?

When had the Guardian been created? Had the Templars created the post, or served it? Had the Order been destroyed by the servants of the Foundation? Certainly the motives of Philip IV and Clement V were suspect, greed and jealousy and a thirst for power.

Evil.

In the silence of predawn, exhausted beyond sleep, Grace paced and thought, wondering if sleep deprivation was making her crazy or if she was indeed battling nothing less than Satan.

Just when she would decide she was definitely crazy, she would remember the Gaelic papers. "The Evil one shall be called Parrish." And "In the Year of Our Lord 1945, the Guardian slew the German beast." The words had been written more than six hundred years before the event actually happened, and were accompanied by a recipe for time travel. The papers were either masterpieces of prophecy, or the Templars had known the secret of time travel.

Perhaps that was the Power the Foundation sought. Time travel! The possibilities were endless. One could zip around in history and make enormous profits by using prior knowledge. What if someone made a large bet against enormous odds that the *Titanic* would sink, or invested heavily in munitions manufacturing before the onset of World War II? Why, just knowing who would win the World Series would make someone rich beyond belief. The possibilities were endless: take out life insurance policies on someone who would soon die, lotteries, horse races, political elections.

On the other hand, it seemed the Guardian had used time travel to protect the Power, so she was still in the dark.

Finally dawn lightened the sky, and she watched it through her dingy window. A sane person would call in sick and try to get some sleep, but instead she showered and drank a pot of coffee. She felt strangely restless, and it wasn't caffeine jumpiness. Instead there was a growing sense of urgency, as if she should be doing something but she didn't know what.

Perhaps it was time to pack up and move on, find another job, another room. She had been Paulette Bottoms for a couple of months now, as long as she had kept any identity. Her instincts had kept her alive this long, so she saw no reason to ignore them now.

She hadn't made the mistake of accumulating a lot of possessions. A few clothes, the truck, the revolver. The coffeemaker was a two-dollar yard-sale find. It took her exactly ten minutes to have everything she owned packed and loaded in the truck. The room was paid for through Saturday, so she dropped the key in the super's mailbox and walked away.

The day was Friday. She would work, collect her pay that afternoon, and quit; that would be the end of Paulette Bottoms. She would pick another name, find another room, get another job. Perhaps she would even leave Minneapolis. She had come back because it seemed the best hiding place, under Parrish's nose, and with a fierce need for vengeance. She had never managed to come up with a reasonable plan, but neither had she devoted herself to it; instead she had concentrated all her energies on translating the papers. That task was finished. With Kris's help, she now knew more than she'd ever imagined about the Foundation. She didn't know yet what she could do with the information, but she felt she should leave and she could barely control the urge to get in the truck and drive until she couldn't stay awake any longer.

Leave Minneapolis. The realization eased through her, bringing a sense of relief. Yes, that's what she should do. Get away from Parrish, from the memories that always hovered at the edge of her control, threatening to crush her if she ever relaxed her guard. She didn't know yet what she was going to do with the information she had, but she wanted to get away from the snow and cold, from the short winter days. She would drive south, and not stop until she found warmth and sunshine.

All she had to do was this one day of work. Clean a few houses, collect her pay, and then she would get on I-35 and head due south.

Paglione sipped on the last of the coffee in his thermos. Winter stakeouts were the worst. You had to drink coffee to stay warm, and then you had to piss all the time. Took two people to do a decent stakeout, because one of you was always off somewhere taking a leak.

At least staking out a McDonald's wasn't so bad. He could always get something to eat, more coffee, and there was a toilet handy. He had been there three days, though, and he was getting damn tired of Big Macs. Maybe he'd try those chicken things next time —

A car pulled in beside him, interrupting him, and he glanced over. The shape of Conrad's head was instantly recognizable. Despite his years of working amicably with the man, Paglione always felt a little uneasy when he first saw Conrad each time, as if he had somehow forgotten exactly how cold and ruthless he was. Paglione had known stone killers before; he had killed a few people himself. But Conrad was different. Paglione could never guess what went on behind those emotionless eyes. Conrad didn't panic, and he didn't give up. He was like a machine, never tiring, wired to pick up on details everyone else missed. Of all the people Paglione knew, and that included Mr. Sawyer himself, Conrad was the only one he truly feared.

On a rush of cold air Conrad slid into the passenger seat. He wore an expensive wool overcoat that failed to impart any stylishness to his stocky frame.

"Glad you're here," Paglione said. "I been drinking coffee all day and I gotta piss. You want me to get you something while I'm in there?"

"No. Has anyone used the pay phone?"

"A couple of people. I wrote down their descriptions." Paglione took a small notebook off the dash and laid it beside Conrad, then heaved the door open and hurried across the parking lot to the restaurant.

The car windows were beginning to fog. Without looking away from the pay phone, Conrad leaned over and turned the ignition key to start the engine. He picked up the notebook but didn't begin reading it. That would wait until Paglione returned. Reading was too distracting; before you knew it an entire minute could pass, and a lot can happen in a minute.

He was still annoyed with himself. Grace had probably still been in the computer room when he walked by; he had glanced in and seen nothing out of the ordinary. But when he and Parrish had gone back, Conrad had noticed immediately that a stack of manuals had been moved.

So close. He could have gotten her then, and all this would be over.

She had changed. He discounted what was obviously a wig. He no longer looked for any particular length or color of hair, because that was too easily changed. She had lost a lot of weight; when they watched the film again, trying to get some clues to the identity of her companion, Parrish had remarked disappointedly on how thin she was now.

But the biggest change wasn't even the weight loss; it was how she walked. He had watched a lot of clips on her over the months, and he knew her walk as well as he knew his own. She had strolled instead of strode, and there had been something completely feminine in the subtle sway of her hips. Even he could see the sensuality that had Parrish so obsessed. But she had walked like an innocent, with no street awareness, her balance that of someone completely at ease and off guard.

That innocence was gone. Now she walked purposefully, her slight weight balanced on each foot so she could move immediately in any direction. Her head had been up, her attitude alert. Her shoulders were squared, the muscles prepared to swivel. Sometime during her eight months on the run, Grace St. John had gotten street smart, and learned how to fight.

He regretted her lost innocence. She hadn't been insipidly sweet; she was too witty, too sharp. But she had been radiant; that was the quality that had come through in the videotapes he had watched. Both husband and brother had adored her, and she had passionately loved them in return. Parrish had compulsively watched over and over one tape made at Christmas, when her husband had pulled her down on his lap and thoroughly kissed her, and been thoroughly kissed in return. There had been a lot of laughter and teasing in those tapes. The little family had been happy.

A lot could happen in eight months on the

run. She could have been beaten, robbed, raped. He didn't like to think of her being brutalized, but he was realistic. Parrish wanted to use her before he killed her, drag her soul in the dirt, humiliate her, and Conrad strongly disapproved. She deserved more respect than that.

Paglione trudged back to the car, carrying a paper sack. He slid behind the wheel and the greasy aroma of french fries and chicken filled the car. He opened the plastic lid on the coffee cup and set it on the dash, then dug out his fries and little cardboard container of poultry pieces.

Now that Paglione had returned, Conrad opened the notebook. Six people had used the pay phone. A black woman at 7:16. A teenage boy, about fourteen, had used it at 9:24, when he should have been in school. An elderly man had approached, fumbled with some change, then left without making a call. An Asian-American male driving an electric utilities truck had placed a call at 10:47. Two young men had arrived at 12:02 and camped on the phone for almost an hour. Damn! When Grace called before, it had been during the lunch hour, so if she had needed to make another call those two idiots would have forced her to go elsewhere.

"Melker's watching the drive-through," Paglione said. "Bayne's inside. Melker's been bitching because he don't know what kind of car to look for. Just look for frizzy blond hair, I told him."

Conrad sighed softly. If he had been a step faster, he would have seen more than a split-second flash of taillights, almost more of a reflection than the actual lights. Not that she would necessarily be in the same vehicle; it could belong to her companion. The important thing was that she was no longer dependent on public transportation, making her much harder to track.

But he was patient. She had been here before. She would be here again.

Grace finished her last house early, a little after two. She stopped by the cramped little office of the cleaning service and collected her pay, and told the owner she wouldn't be back. Personnel turned over so regularly that her departure didn't elicit more than a grunt.

She needed to call Kris; he would go crazy with worry if she disappeared without a word. She regretted leaving him behind once again. His company, his friendship, had been like a warm cocoon; actual conversation was rare in her life now, but for a brief time she had been able to talk to Kris, and not feel so isolated.

She pulled into the McDonald's parking lot to use the pay phone, but someone was already using it. She didn't stop, but swung the steering wheel to go around the cars lined up for the drive-through window. One of the cars in line abruptly pulled out in front of her and she slammed on the brakes to keep from rear-ending it. Her computer case was on the seat beside her, and the abrupt stop sent it pitching off the seat. The zippered section was open and several pages of her notes came out, scattering on the floorboard.

"Damn it," she muttered, pulling to the side. Computers weren't delicate, but neither were they meant to be tossed around, either. The case was padded, but still —

She leaned over and picked up the case, but some of the scattered papers had slid under the seat and, with her possessions stacked in the way, she couldn't reach that far. Swearing again, she left the truck running and got out, walking around to the passenger side.

She opened the door and began gathering the papers. She had just reached for one on which she plainly saw the words "Creag Dhu" when a gust of wind swirled into the truck and sent the sheet flying over her head. She whirled to catch it, and saw the man almost on her.

She didn't stop to think. Instantly she dropped to the ground, lashing out with a booted foot and catching him solidly on the kneecap. His leg went out from under him as if he'd been shot, and he fell on his face.

Grace rolled away from him, coming to her feet and swinging herself into the cab of the truck. Another man was suddenly there, a man with a simian head and cold, expressionless eyes. She tried to slam the door and he knocked it open, his heavyset body crowding into the opening. Grace heaved herself back but one meaty hand closed around her ankle, inexorably drawing her forward. She kicked at his face. He jerked his head back, and seized her other ankle.

The knife hissed as she drew it out of the scabbard, the blade glinting as she jackknifed to a sitting position and slashed at his hands. She held the knife the way Mateo had shown her, palm down, blade jutting outward so that the attack came from her midsection and was much harder to block than a wide, sweeping slash. The knife sliced across the back of one hand and he jerked back, releasing one ankle.

The first man was slowly climbing to his feet, groaning and favoring his knee, but within seconds he would be able to help. She could hear someone running, a third attacker hurrying to the truck. She wouldn't be able to fight off three at once, or even two.

Oh, God, the one holding her ankle was as strong as a bull. He pulled her forward, ignoring the pain in his cut hand, blocking her efforts to kick him. The pistol was stuck under her stack of clothing, easily reached if she were in the driver's seat, but now she was lying on top of it.

She threw the knife. He saw the blade coming at his face and no training in the world was strong enough to override the instinct to duck. He threw himself to the side, but even so he retained his grip on her ankle, pulling her partially out of the truck. Desperately she scrabbled under the pile of clothing, her hand striking the pistol and knocking it away. She grabbed again, and this time found it.

She bolted up, both hands folded around the butt, firing as soon as the barrel was clear of her own feet. She heard the shots but they sounded far away, muffled. In slow motion she saw the gorilla-man flinch, then falter. She heard the strange wet thud of a bullet hitting human flesh. She saw the eyes flicker with both surprise and annoyance, as if he shouldn't have let himself underestimate her.

But he didn't let go of her ankle. He set his teeth and pulled.

"I'll kill you," she said, her voice barely audible. She held the barrel centered between his eyes. Her hands were steady. She began taking out the slack in the trigger, and the hammer moved back, poising for the strike.

Their eyes met, and he saw his death in hers. She saw a cold, dark intelligence in his, an awareness that went beyond the moment, as if he knew her down to her soul. There was a flash of acknowledgment, then his hand loosened and he slumped to the ground.

The man she had kicked in the knee began to back away, his hands held up to indicate he was unarmed. She didn't believe that for a minute.

She jerked her head around to locate the third man, and heard the driver's door opening behind her. She threw herself on her back, held the pistol over her head, and shot through the door. Sitting up again, she shot at the first man as he pulled his pistol from under his jacket. She missed, but he dived for cover.

She had two shots left; she couldn't keep shooting back and forth, she had to make them count. She clambered over her jumbled possessions and settled behind the steering wheel, and jerked the transmission into gear as she jammed her foot onto the gas pedal. The old truck shuddered as it leaped forward, tires slipping on the icy patches in the parking lot. The third man's face appeared in the window beside her as he grabbed for the door handle. She shoved the pistol at the window and he ducked, letting go of the door. The truck shook as the first man jumped up on the rear bumper, trying to climb into the bed.

Grace jerked the steering wheel hard to the right, then to the left. It was like playing crack the whip, except the stakes were a lot higher. His feet slipped off the bumper but he managed to hold on. Watching in the rearview mirror, she barreled out through the parking lot entrance into the path of a car turning in. A horn blared, she jerked the wheel again, and the man lost his grip on the tailgate. He went rolling across the parking lot, and fetched up hard against the rear tire of a parked car.

The passenger door still swung open, but she couldn't take the time to stop and close it. Stepping on the gas, she took a hard left at the first corner, then a right at the next one. The door slammed itself.

She tried to think what she should do. They had a description of the truck, and probably the tag number as well. The truck was registered under Louisa Croley's name, the same name that was on her passport and her driver's license. She should ditch the truck, steal a car somewhere, and get as far from Minneapolis as she could. The police would be looking for her within minutes; a shoot-out at a McDonald's was bound to attract attention.

But she didn't ditch the truck. She didn't take the time to drive to a mall and look for a car with the keys left in it, though Harmony had assured her there were at least two fools shopping at any mall at any given time. Instead she hit 36 and drove west until she got to I-35. Then she got on the southbound lane and headed for Iowa.

"A mysterious shoot-out at a McDonald's in Roseville has police puzzled," the talking head earnestly announced. "Witnesses say several shots were fired, and at least six people were involved, with two seriously injured. But by the time police arrived, all those involved had vanished, including the wounded. Witnesses said one person, perhaps a woman, was driving a brown pickup truck. By law, all doctors and hospitals are required to report all gunshot wounds to police, but thus far no one has requested treatment."

Parrish paced back and forth, furious. Conrad sat silently on the sofa, his shoulder bound and his arm supported by a sling. A doctor who belonged to the Foundation had removed the bullet, which luckily had struck his collarbone instead of tearing through the complicated system of cartilage and ligaments in his shoulder. His collarbone was cracked, and the insistent throb seemed to pound through his entire body, but he had refused any pain medication. The cut on his hand, though it had required eight stitches, was minimal.

"Four men couldn't catch one woman," Parrish said, seething. "Bayne didn't even know anything was going on until it was too late for him to help. I'm very disappointed in the quality of your men, Conrad, and in you. She caught you with your pants down, and now she's gone to ground again. With all the people we have in this city, no one has seen her. She's one inexperienced woman; how in hell can she keep getting away from me?" He roared the last sentence, his face flushed dark red, his neck corded with rage.

Conrad sat silently. He didn't make excuses, but as soon as he was able, he would personally take care of Melker. As soon as he spotted her, the fool had run up to the truck without waiting for the others to get in place. If they had all come at her at once, taken her by surprise, she wouldn't have escaped. Instead Melker had tried to take her by himself, and she'd kicked the hell out of him.

Conrad was deeply annoyed at himself, too; he should have expected her to have armed herself by this time, but instead he had allowed himself to be caught off guard, first by the knife, then by that unwavering pistol. She hadn't hesitated, hadn't panicked. She had said, "I'll kill you," and the warning was sincere. She would have done it. In that moment, looking deep into her pure blue eyes, he saw the strength none of them had suspected.

He could have held on. She would have killed him, but the delay, and the hindrance of his body dragging on her, would likely have resulted in her capture. He had chosen to let go and pretend to lose consciousness, to save himself. He didn't want to die, he had too much left undone. He didn't want anyone except himself to capture Grace St. John, and he wanted to be alone when he did it. Parrish would never know what happened to her. To that end, though he had noted her license plate number, Conrad kept it to himself.

Rather than get involved in a tedious police investigation, they had all gotten into their cars and left. Despite his pain and blood loss, Conrad had managed to drive to a secure place and arrange for medical care. Parrish was in a rage, not yet paying attention to the sheet of paper Paglione had picked up in the parking lot, the paper that had blown out of Grace's truck.

The paper lay on the table. Conrad hadn't yet looked at it, but his gaze kept going to it. After all these months, searching for both Grace and the papers, a sheet had virtually fallen into their hands. How important could one sheet be, out of all those papers? But it drew him, and he couldn't stop glancing at it in a mixture of dread and anticipation.

At last Parrish noticed that his temper tantrum was being mostly ignored. He followed Conrad's look and stalked over to snatch up the sheet of paper. "What's this?"

"Paglione picked it up," Conrad said. "It blew out of her truck."

"It's some notes she's made," Parrish said, his tone growing thoughtful. He walked over to the desk and sat down, turning on the lamp. "I don't know this language. 'C-u-n-b-h-a-l-a-c-h' means 'steady,' *'c-u-n-b-h-a-l-a-c-h-d'* means 'judgment.' I'm so glad to know that. This is gibberish. It must be a code that's in the papers. *'Creag Dhu'* — this doesn't have any interpretation beside it. Then there's 'fear,' and beside it *'gleidhidh.'* This looks like Welch without all the *y's* and *w's.*"

Conrad didn't comment, but the feeling of dread was growing stronger. He stared at the paper, hearing his heartbeat pounding in his ears, throbbing in his shoulder. Perhaps he had lost more blood than he had thought, and was about to lose consciousness for real.

Parrish lapsed into silence, his head bent over the paper. He was an educated, sophisticated man, well traveled. He had seen this language before.

"It's Gaelic," he said after a moment, his tone soft. "It isn't a code. *Dhu* means 'black,' and I think *creag* means 'rock,' or 'rocky.' Black rock." He stood abruptly, his eyes narrow and intent. "Get some rest, Conrad. I'll have this translated. Grace's little slip may be just the break I've been needing."

Chapter 17

One of her pages of notes had blown out. Grace couldn't stop thinking about it, her insides clenched tight with dread. She had made a dreadful mistake.

She drove carefully through the snow-dusted Iowa night, well aware she was long past exhaustion and operating on sheer instinct. She needed to sleep, but she couldn't make herself stop. She felt driven, somehow, and so she drove.

She had lost one of the sheets. It was just a sheet of her notes, not one of the document sheets, but still she clearly remembered seeing "Creag Dhu" on it as she reached for it. What were the odds against one of those men picking it up? Not very good. They had to know they weren't just after her, but some papers as well.

She had given Parrish the location of the Treasure; all he had to do was figure out what it was. She had to assume he would. After all, the Foundation's business was archaeology. Parrish had access to any number of old maps, files, cross-references. He would learn Creag Dhu had been a fourteenth-century castle, and with a little effort he would be able to pinpoint its location. He could throw the Foundation's enormous resources into excavating the site — and he would find the Treasure.

Her fault. Her fault. The words drummed ceaselessly through her head. She had failed Ford and Bryant, letting Parrish attain the knowledge for which he had killed them.

She had failed Niall.

She should have done something, should have shot both the other men if necessary, and chased down that errant sheet. But all she had been thinking about had been escape, survival; she hadn't remembered the paper until she was already in Iowa.

She had actually shot a man. All of Matty's advice had worked, and she had functioned well enough to *do* something, instead of simply flailing in terror and hoping for a lucky blow. Eight months ago she wouldn't have had any idea how to use a pistol, and would have been horrified at the thought of doing so; this afternoon she had used both knife and pistol. Thinking of the moment when she had pulled the trigger, Grace wondered numbly if she was still the same person at all.

But what good had all of it done? She was alive, yes, but still she had failed Niall. She had failed to protect the papers. Parrish had won, through her own negligence.

Eaten alive by guilt, sick in the aftermath of battlefield adrenaline, it was almost ten when she thought of Kris. Swearing softly to herself at her lack of consideration, she began looking for an exit occupied by people and equipped with a pay phone. Perhaps she simply hadn't been paying attention, but it seemed as if most of the exits were nothing more than lonely intersections, access to empty roads leading off into empty night.

She must not have been paying attention. There was a brightly lit truck stop at the next exit. She pulled into the crowded parking lot, her truck dwarfed by the huge tractor-trailer rigs that sat idling, their motors rumbling like enormous sleeping beasts. She decided she might as well gas up while she was there, so she pulled up to one of the islands and stood shivering in the icy wind as the tank filled. At least the cold woke her up; she had sunk almost into a stupor, her eyes half closed, hypnotized by the endless zipper of stripes between twin banks of dirty snow, where the snowplows had cleared the highway.

It had started snowing again, she realized, seeing the white flakes blowing through the bright vapor lights of the truck stop. She couldn't go much farther; she was too exhausted to battle snow too. She paid the attendant for the gas, then got in the truck and moved it to the restaurant.

The warmth inside went right through her, making her shudder with relief. Truckers sat at a long counter, or in pairs in the booths that lined the wall. A jukebox played some rollicking honky-tonk song, and a cloud of blue cigarette smoke hovered against the ceiling. There was a tiny hallway to the left, decorated with an arrow and a sign that said "Rest Rooms," and two pay phones were crowded into it. One of the phones was in use by an enormous bearded fellow whose gut strained his thermal-knit shirt. He looked like a cross between Paul Bunyan and a Hell's Angel, but when she neared she heard him say, "I'll call you tomorrow, honey. Love you."

Grace squeezed past him and dug change out of her pocket. A quarter bought her a dial tone. She punched in the numbers, then waited until a recorded voice told her how much more change to feed the beast.

Kris answered immediately, his voice anxious.

She turned her back on the big guy, and lowered her voice. "I'm okay," she said, not giving her name. "But they almost caught me this afternoon, and I had to leave. I just wanted you to know. Is everything okay on your end?"

"Yeah." She could hear him gulp. "Are you hurt, or anything?"

"No, I'm fine."

"That was you, wasn't it?" His voice shook. "That shooting at the McDonald's. They said — on television — a woman in a brown truck. I knew it was you."

"Yes."

"The police don't know what happened. All those men vanished before the cops got there."

Grace blinked. That was surprising news. She had expected the cops to be hot on her trail, too. Evidently Parrish didn't want the cops to catch her, preferring to do so himself. She didn't know why; she had seen about half the city's muckety-mucks on the donor list, so she had no doubt he could pull enough strings to get the papers out of the evidence room, or whatever they called it. He could also have her killed in her cell, and she would be just one more jail violence statistic.

The implication was startling. Parrish wanted her alive, and he wanted her as *his* prisoner. A wave of revulsion swept her at the thought, but she didn't analyze it.

"I have to go now," she told Kris. "I just wanted you to know I'm okay, and tell you how much I appreciate what you did."

"Grace —" His voice cracked on her name. "Take care. Stay alive." He paused, and his next words came out quiet and strained. "I love you."

The simple words almost shattered her. She had been too alone; too many months had passed since she had heard them. She gripped the receiver so tightly her knuckles turned white, and the plastic creaked under the strain.

She couldn't blow off his youthful devotion as an adolescent crush; he deserved more respect than that. "Thank you," she whispered.

"I love you, too. You're a wonderful person." Then she gently hung up, and pressed her forehead against the wall.

Beside her, the trucker was saying his own good-byes, more "I love yous" and "I'll be carefuls." He hung up and glanced at her.

A meaty paw patted her shoulder with surprising delicacy. "Don't cry, little bit," he said comfortingly. "You'll get used to it. How long you been on the road?"

He thought she was a truck driver. Amazement chased away all other emotion. Did she *look* like a truck driver? Her, the poster girl for academia?

She looked down. He wore boots; she wore boots. He had on jeans; she had on jeans. Baseball caps topped their heads.

She looked like a truck driver.

She was so tired she was giddy, and nothing seemed quite real. For the first time in eight months, her lips quivered with amusement. She didn't laugh, but she was astonished at the impulse. Quelling it, she cleared her throat and looked up at Paul Bunyan. "Eight months. I've been driving for eight months."

He gave her another pat. "Well, give it a little more time. It's tough, being away from your family so much, but the freight has to move and somebody's gonna get paid for hauling it. Might as well be us, huh?"

"Might as well," she echoed. She nodded to him and escaped out to her truck. She hoped he didn't see her driving off in an ordinary pickup, instead of one of the snoozing behemoths; she didn't want to destroy his illusions about her.

The snow was falling faster, and more trucks were leaving the interstate, rumbling up the exit ramp to take overnight refuge at the truck stop. There was a small, ratty-looking motel next door, and its "Vacancy" sign was lit. Grace decided not to chance driving any farther, and to take a room before the new arrivals got them all.

The room was just as ratty-looking as the exterior. The carpet was worn and stained, the walls were brown, the bedspreads were brown, the lavatory bowl was brown — and it wasn't supposed to be. But the heating unit worked, and so did everything in the bathroom; good enough.

She stuck the pistol in the waistband of her jeans and dragged out the computer case, and a change of clothes for the next day. If the rest of her clothes weren't safe in the truck overnight, well, she hoped the thief was small enough to wear them, because she didn't have the energy to cart everything inside.

She undressed, then reloaded the pistol. Her hands trembled, and she fumbled the bullets. She thrust the gun under her pillow, then climbed into the lumpy bed and was unconscious even before her head hit the pillow.

She dreamed.

* * *

"And so came Grace to Creag Dhu."

Niall wrote the words, the pen scratching across the page. He signed it, dated it, then turned to face her. "Aye, lass, that will bring ye to me." His intent black gaze moved over her, starting at her feet and lingering at hips and breasts before reaching her face. She drew a deep breath, knowing what that look meant. He was the most intensely sexual man she had ever met, and the challenge of that burning appetite only fed her own sensuality. She could feel her body readying itself for him, growing warm, softening, her nipples standing upright and her cheeks flushing. Excited desire began coiling deep in her belly.

He knew it, saw it. His hard mouth took on a sensual curve and he dropped the quill onto the table, turning on the high wooden stool to face her. He held out his hand. "Dinna wait near seven hundred bluidy years," he said softly. "I want ye *now*."

Grace took the five steps that carried her to him, her hands lifting to sift through the thick black silk of his hair. He bent his head, and his mouth covered hers. No one else kissed like Niall, she thought dazedly. His taste was as potent as fiery whisky, his kiss was both dominating and seductive, taking what he wanted but giving pleasure in return.

His big hand covered her breast, his thumb rubbing gently over her extended nipple. Her hands clenched in his hair and she crowded closer to him, shivering.

They had already made love so many times he knew exactly how aroused she was, knew there was no need for love play. With a soothing murmur he pulled up both her skirts and his kilt, and lifted her astride him as he sat propped on the high stool. Their loins came together with ease, and she gave a little whimper of relief as his thick erection slipped up into her. Niall gasped, his teeth set, then he gathered her close and they clung together, their need deeper and sharper than physical desire.

'Twas *her.* Niall awoke, fiercely aroused and aching, but grimly triumphant. This time he had seen her face, this damned wench who tormented his sleep, who watched him from hidden places. He sat up in bed and thrust both hands through his hair, pushing it out of his face as he tried to firm his memories of the dream.

He had been sitting on a stool at a high table, writing something, while she stood off to the side. He couldn't remember what he had said, he just remembered looking at her, and the wench looking back at him, and lust abruptly burning through him. He held out his hand to her and she came to him, into his arms, and he had not even carried her to bed but taken her there, lifting her skirts and hoisting her onto his shaft. She was like liquid fire, flowing over him, lovely blue eyes closed and her face tilted back, exalted, as she pleasured him and he pleasured her.

She felt fragile in his arms, her body tender, her skin silky. She had a great swath of dark hair hanging down her back, thick and sleek, and her eyes were as pure a blue as a Highland lake under a clear summer sky. Her face . . . a chill ran over him. Her face looked like an angel's, solemn and slightly distant, as if she had some greater purpose. Her brow was clear and white, her delicate jawline slightly squared, and her mouth . . . "Ah, weel, perhaps not an angel after all," he said aloud, relieved. That mouth put him in mind of a number of things, all of them very carnal.

Still and all, there was something about her that made him uneasy, and Niall was a man who trusted his instincts. He snorted to himself. Aye, and so he should be uneasy, for she was likely a witch; how else could she watch him without being seen, and slip into his dreams whenever she wished? Witch or no, should she ever appear in the flesh he would be glad to give her the measure of his shaft in truth as well as dream, but he would not trust her.

She had to have some purpose for watching him; perhaps she had somehow learned of the Treasure.

It would be her ill fortune if that was what

she sought, for he was sworn to guard the Treasure against all threat, be that threat from male or female. He had yet to kill a woman for it, but her sex would not save her. If she came for the Treasure, though he ached at the necessity, she would have to die.

Grace slept past the eleven o'clock check-out, awakening only when the maid pounded on the door. She stumbled to her feet, told the maid to come back later, and fell back into bed. She woke for good at three, groggy from so much sleep.

She stood in the shower for a long time, alternating hot and cold water in an effort to dispel the mental fog. She felt physically rested but mentally tired, as if her brain hadn't shut down all night. She had dreamed endlessly, it seemed, her mind going over the short, violent scene in the McDonald's parking lot, replaying it like a loop of film. Time after time she saw herself reach for the sheet of paper, saw "Creag Dhu" on it. She would feel the wind coming, know what was going to happen, and over and over she grabbed for the paper but every time it sailed out of her grasp, straight into Parrish's hands. He had looked at it, smiled, and said, "Why, thank you, Grace." Then he pointed a pistol at her and fired, and the dream would start all over again.

She had also dreamed of Niall, of making love with him. His black gaze had pierced straight through her, as if he knew she had failed to protect the precious papers given to her. But he had held out his hand to her, demanding she come to him, and she had gone.

"Come to me," he had said. "Now."

A violent shudder wracked her, starting at her feet and moving upward until her entire body shook. Her knees gave out and she leaned against the shower wall, her mouth open and little whimpers coming from it. She couldn't stop shaking, couldn't control the sensation of flying apart. Some external force pulled at her, tore at her, compelled her. Her eyes dilated and the dingy shower walls suddenly looked very bright, as if they were glowing.

Come to me. Travel the years, six hundred and seventy-five of them. I have given you the knowledge. Come to me.

The voice boomed inside her head, and yet it was from without. It was Niall speaking, but the voice that was low and devastatingly sexual in her dreams now sternly demanded, *Come to me.*

The glow began to fade, and the quaking in her muscles gradually weakened until she was standing upright and steady. Cold water pelted down on her and hastily she shut it off, grabbing a thin towel to wrap around her head. She used another to roughly dry herself. God, she was freezing! How long had she been standing like a dope, hallucinating, under the cold water? She had almost given herself hypothermia.

But she hadn't been hallucinating. She knew it. It had been real. There really was a Power; she had felt it from the first moment she had seen those old documents. That was why she had been driven to keep translating them, lugging both them and the laptop around when doing so had been a lot of trouble. She had protected them when common sense should have led her to abandon both.

Everything that had happened in the past eight months had led her inexorably to this moment, standing naked and cold in a dingy little shower in a truck-stop motel somewhere in Iowa, facing an unbelievable but suddenly crystal-clear conclusion.

If it were possible, she had to travel through time. Parrish had the sheet; perhaps that was preordained, and there was nothing she could have done about it. But now that he knew, she had to prevent him from getting the Treasure, and the only way to do that was to force Niall to hide it somewhere else. Or perhaps — silly thought, because she wasn't made of heroic material, but still — just perhaps, she was meant to find the Treasure, and use the Power to destroy the Foundation.

She had to go to Creag Dhu — six hundred and seventy-five years ago.

Chapter 18

Spring came softly to the Highlands. It was May, and the mountains were carpeted with green. The cool, misty days could suddenly give way to bright sunshine and air so clear it hurt her eyes to see it. From somewhere would come a fragment of sound, the faint echo of a bagpipe, and the haunting sound made her soul weep.

It had taken her four months to get here. At first she had simply kept on driving, going south, angling toward the east. The seasons changed as she drove, winter loosening its grip more and more the farther south she went, and it was in Tennessee, in mid-February, that she saw the first flower blooming. It seemed like such a miracle, in the form of a cheerful yellow jonquil, that she stopped driving then, and rested, and planned.

An early spring, the locals said, after a mild winter. The jonquils were blooming a couple of weeks earlier than usual. The winter hadn't been mild in Minnesota, but eight hundred miles farther south put her in a different climate, a different world.

She had quickly realized she couldn't do this

alone, and there was only one person she could think of to call.

Harmony had listened silently to Grace's request to travel with her to Scotland for an unspecified length of time.

"Scotland," she finally said. "They don't still paint their faces blue, do they?"

"Only in movies."

"I don't have no passport."

"That's easy to get, if you have your birth certificate."

"You said you need my help doin' something. Reckon you can bring yourself to tell me exactly what it is I'd be doin'?"

"If you go," Grace said.

"I'll think about it. Call me in a couple of days."

Grace gave her three days, then called again. "Okay," Harmony said. "If I go, would I be doin' anything illegal?"

"No. I don't think." Given that she had to expect the unexpected, Grace couldn't swear that she would stay on the side of the law.

"Dangerous?"

"Yes."

Harmony sighed. "Well, hell," she drawled. "You do make it hard to resist, don't you? How long would I be gone? I got my house to look after, you know."

"I don't know. A couple of days, a couple of weeks. I'll pay all your expenses —"

"I'll pay my own way, if I go. That way, if

I get pissed, I won't feel beholden to stay." She was silent for a moment, and Grace could hear her tapping her nails on the phone. "I got one more question."

"Okay."

"What's your real name?"

Grace hesitated. It felt strange to say her own name. The only time she had heard it spoken in months was when Kris had said it. She had gone by so many names that sometimes she felt as if she had no identity. "Grace," she said softly. "Grace St. John. But I'll be traveling under the name Louisa Croley; that's the name on my passport and driver's license."

"Grace." Harmony sighed. "Shit. If you'd lied to me, I coulda said no."

Finding where Creag Dhu had stood took some time. Grace and Harmony had been in Edinburgh more than a week before Grace managed to track down the name, and then it was in such a remote section of the western Highlands that it was almost inaccessible. While Grace researched, Harmony did Edinburgh. She toured the castle, she toured Holyrood House, she took day trips to St. Andrews and Perth. It wasn't until Grace actually found Creag Dhu that she told Harmony what she was going to do. Harmony laughed in her face, but when Grace quietly went about her preparations, Harmony sighed and pitched in. She didn't laugh when she heard about Ford and Bryant.

When she had everything gathered, Grace rented a car and they drove to a small Highland village five miles from where Creag Dhu had supposedly stood. The only accommodation in the village was a small bed-and-breakfast, which they took, but the local tavern was a hotbed of gossip. Harmony could stand elbow-to-elbow with hard-drinking Scotsmen and hold her own with them, whether it was beer or whisky, and as a reward they answered all her questions. Aye, a fancy American had arrived some two months ago, bent on digging up a great pile of rock. A storm had delayed him a bit, turning the ground to mud and making getting to the site a bit difficult, but the weather had since turned fair and word was he was making a great deal of progress.

"It won't take him long to find it," Grace said when Harmony reported back to her. "I can't wait any longer; I have to go."

"You talk like this is a guaranteed trip," Harmony said irritably. "Like as not all you're gonna do is give your ass a major shock."

"Maybe," Grace replied. During her own more reasonable moments, she knew that was exactly what was likely to happen. But then she would think of the documents and the things she had read, and the dreams, the sense of compulsion, and she knew she had to try no matter how crazy it sounded.

She hadn't had any dreams since arriving in Scotland. Everything felt so strange, as if a veil were hanging between her and everyone else. Nothing quite touched her, not fear or anger or even the more mundane things such as hunger. An essential part of her was already gone, turned away from this time. She knew she was going, and she had prepared as thoroughly as she could.

They set out just after lunch the next day, driving as far as possible, then they got out and walked. Storm clouds hovered to the west, out over the ocean, and the mountain shadows were purple under a gaudy blue and golden sky.

Grace had carefully considered the logistics. The documents had given the formula for time, but not for location. She decided that location didn't change; where she was when she went back would be where she arrived. Standing in the middle of Creag Dhu's ruins would have been perfect, but she hadn't dared go close enough even to see it. She had to settle for getting as close as possible, then walking the rest of the way to the castle when she arrived in that time.

The narrow road they had chosen was little more than a path, and it gave out while they were still some three miles from the ruins. Gathering Grace's things, the two women left the car and walked higher into the mountains.

The air was sweet and fresh, a bird's cry high and lonely. Grace could already feel something tugging at her, a quiet anticipation, a need.

"Why don't we just shoot the son of a bitch?" Harmony suggested suddenly, lifting her lemon-white head into the wind. Her nostrils flared, her pale green eyes narrowed. She looked like some exotic goddess of war, ready to slay her enemies. "It's easier, neater, and a hell of a lot more likely to get the job done."

"Because it isn't just Parrish, it's the Foundation. Even if we kill him, another will take his place." She had finally reached that conclusion, and found a measure of peace in it. She would love simply to kill Parrish and be done with it, claim her vengeance, walk away. She couldn't do it. *The Foundation of Evil* . . . she couldn't let the Foundation get control of the Treasure.

She spotted the place where she wanted to be, and pointed it out to Harmony. The nest of rocks was almost at the peak of the mountain. Carefully they climbed up, their feet alternately sinking into damp sod and slipping on loose rock. When they reached their goal, they stood quietly looking at the empty glen below, at the mist blowing in from the ocean. The Creag Dhu site wasn't visible; it lay beyond the next mountain. The local folk said it was a bed of black rock, jutting against the ocean. Grace tried to picture it in her mind, but even though she had seen numerous archaeological sites, the image that formed was of the great castle when it was whole, looming dark against an angry gray sea.

"Are you sure you have everything?" Harmony asked, placing her bundle on the ground and quickly arranging the items.

"I'm sure." She had made a list while still in the States, and had begun making her preparations even then. According to the instructions, she had altered her diet more than a week ago, tailoring it to the specifications. She bent down and attached the electrodes to her ankles, taping them in place.

She sensed that her detachment worried Harmony. "I'm all right," she said in answer to an unvoiced concern. "If this doesn't work — well, it just won't work. I'll get a shock, but it won't be enough to kill me."

"You hope," Harmony snarled, her irritation growing.

"If it *does* work — I don't know if any of this stuff will go with me, or if I'll suddenly appear there stark naked. If it doesn't go, carry it back to the village and do what you want with it."

"Sure. I've always wanted a velvet dress that's three sizes too little and a foot too short."

"I'm leaving the laptop anyway. I've deleted all my notes from the hard disk, but my journal is still on there. I've put everything down. If anything happens to me and I don't make it back . . ." She shrugged. "At least there will be a record of what happened."

"How long am I supposed to wait?" Harmony asked furiously.

"I don't know. I'll leave that up to you."

"Damn it, Grace!" Harmony turned on her, face red with fury, but she bit back her angry words and merely shook her head. "I can't reach you, can I? In your head, you're already there."

"I know you don't understand it. I don't, either." The wind plastered her gown to her form and lifted her hair, streaming it behind her. The glen stretched below her but she didn't see it, her eyes looking beyond. "It's been a year since Ford and Bryant were murdered. I haven't been able to cry for them yet. It's as if I don't deserve to, because I haven't done anything to avenge them."

"You haven't had time to cry." Harmony's voice was rough. "You've been busy just stayin' alive."

"I haven't been to their graves. I was back in Minneapolis for six months, and I didn't look for their graves. I didn't put flowers on them."

"Damn good thing. From what you've told me, this Parrish bastard would have men watching the cemetery. They'da nailed you for sure."

"Maybe. But I couldn't have gone even if I

had known it was safe. Not yet. Maybe when I get back."

After that, there didn't seem to be anything left to say. Harmony hugged her, green eyes wet, then walked quickly away.

Grace sat down on the rocks and opened the laptop, turning it on. She logged into her journal and tried to gather her thoughts. It was useless; they darted about like swallows. Finally she stopped trying and simply began typing.

"May 17th — Revenge takes over your life. I never realized this before, but then I've never hated before. One moment my life was ordinary and secure, happy — and the next moment everything was gone. My husband, my brother . . . I lost them both.

"Odd how things change, how in the blink of an eye one's life goes from the ordinary — even mundane — to a nightmare landscape of horror, disbelief, and almost crippling grief. No, I haven't cried. I've held the grief locked inside me, a wound that can't heal, because I don't dare let it out. I have to concentrate on what must be done, rather than allow myself the luxury of mourning those I've lost. If I falter, if I let my guard down even the slightest, then I'll be dead too.

"My life feels as if it belongs to someone else. Something is wrong, discordant, but what: before — or now? It's as if the two halves don't match, that one or the other simply isn't my life. Sometimes I can't feel any connection at all with the woman I was, before that night.

"Before, I was a wife.

"Now, I'm a widow.

"I had a family, small but familiar, and achingly dear. Gone.

"I had a career, one of those obscure, intellectually challenging jobs in which I could, and did, lose myself in dusty old parchment and precious, unknown little books, where I mentally wandered in the past for so long that Ford sometimes teased me about having been born in the wrong century.

"That too is gone.

"Now I have to run, to hide, or I too will be killed. I've spent the months scurrying from hole to hole like a rat, lugging around some stolen manuscripts and ancient translations. I've learned how to change my appearance, how to get a fake ID, how to steal a car if necessary. I eat occasionally, though not well. Ford wouldn't recognize me. My husband wouldn't know me! But I can't let myself think about that.

"How did I come to this?

"A rhetorical question. I know how it happened. I watched it happen. I saw Parrish kill them both.

"There was no transition between before and now, no time to adjust. I went from respectable to fugitive in the space of a few shattering minutes. From wife to widow, from sister to survivor, from normal to . . . this.

"Only hatred keeps me going.

"It's a hate so strong and hot and pure that sometimes I feel incandescent with it. Can hate purify? Can it burn out all the little obstacles that might keep you from acting on it? I think it can. I think mine has. I want Parrish to pay for what he's done to my life, pay for the deaths of those I love. I want him to die. But I don't want Ford and Bryant to have died for nothing, so I have to go after the Foundation too, not just Parrish.

"I don't know how long it will take me to reach my destination. I don't know if I can do it in time (a bad pun) or if I'll die in the effort. All I can do is try, because hate, and revenge, are all I have left.

"I must find Black Niall."

She stopped typing, staring at the words on the screen. When she was in college she had kept a paper journal, with a butter-soft leather cover. Ford had given it to her the first Christmas after they started dating. She had intended it to be a record of her work, her thoughts on it, how the research and translations were going; instead it had become a diary of her private life, and when she switched to a laptop computer the habit had carried over to the electronic page.

In the journal she had recorded her flight from Parrish Sawyer. In it, too, was the only relief she had from the grief she kept bottled inside, for only there had she mourned Ford and Bryant. She had also chronicled her deepening fascination, and her warring senses of disbelief and awe, with what she had discovered in the old manuscripts for which Parrish had killed. She had wanted to dismiss them, but she couldn't; there were too many details that tied together, too many coincidences for them to be mere coincidences after all. Certainly Parrish didn't dismiss the secrets contained in the documents. And in the end, she too had believed.

Carefully she closed the file and turned off the laptop, setting it safely aside. She didn't know if any of the articles she had gathered would make the trip with her, or if she would arrive there — or was it *when* — without anything, even a stitch of clothing. She hadn't been joking about being stark naked.

She didn't know anything for certain, not even if the whole damn procedure would work. If it didn't, at least only Harmony would be a witness to what a colossal fool she made of herself. And if it didn't work, she would find some other way to stop Parrish and the Foundation. But if it did —

She took a deep breath. She had everything ready. She had checked and rechecked her figures, then checked them again. She had found the correct mineral surroundings, the rocks, for better conductivity. She had drunk the correct amount of water, calculated according to her weight and the time she needed to travel, so much that she felt bloated. She had eaten the correct things, subtly altering her body chemistry. She had prepared herself mentally, rehearsing what she would do, the sequence in which she would do it. Even the weather was cooperating, with the offshore storm advancing nearer and nearer, so that the air was crisp and crackling with electricity. The storm wasn't needed, but its presence seemed like a blessing.

It was time.

Grace picked up the big, rough burlap bag she had sewn herself, and hugged it to her chest. She and Harmony had also handmade the heavy, old-fashioned garments she wore, though neither of them was particularly skillful at sewing. At least early-fourteenth-century fashions had been simple. She wore a plain cotton gown, with long sleeves and a scoop neck, not formfitting at all. Over it was another gown, a sleeveless one, of good, soft wool. The undergown was called a kirtle, the overgown a surcoat. In the bag was a heavy velvet surcoat, should she need to convey a bit of status. A length of wool was folded in the bag, to be used as a shawl should she need it.

She had taken the precaution of buying a pair of handmade moccasins while she was in Tennessee, and the soft leather molded to her feet. She wore long white stockings, secured with old-fashioned ribbon garters which she tied above her knees. She wore no bra or panties, for there hadn't been any such thing as underwear back then. There were no elastic bands or garment tags to make anyone suspicious. Her long hair was secured in a single thick braid, in the style she had worn a long time ago — before. She covered her head with a thick cotton scarf, tying the ends behind her neck.

The only thing she carried in the way of money was a few pieces of jewelry, the earrings and wedding band set she had been wearing when it all happened. There was nothing about her appearance, she hoped, that would be glaringly out of place. What she carried in the burlap bag would be enough to get her burned for witchcraft if she were caught.

The storm was growing closer, thunder echoing like a brass gong. *Now or never,* she thought. She had to hurry so Harmony could collect the laptop; rain wouldn't do it any good.

Carefully she placed her foot on the pressure switch she had rigged, holding her weight just short of tripping it. She could feel the electrodes where she had taped them to her ankles, and wondered how they had managed this in the days before electrodes and batteries existed.

Closing her eyes, she began breathing deeply, slowly, and forced herself to focus on Black Niall. She had done all the right things so she should go back exactly six hundred seventy-five years, but she felt as if she needed a target. He was the only target she had, this man who had lived almost seven hundred years before. There were no portraits of him, not even a crude drawing such as had been common back then, for her to bring to mind. All she could do was concentrate on *him,* the man, the essence of him.

She knew him. Oh, she knew him. He had haunted her for months, owning her waking mind while she struggled to decipher the ancient documents, then invading her dreams with images so vivid that sometimes she woke herself talking to him in her sleep, and always — always — she felt as if he'd just *been* there. He had made love to her in her dreams, tormenting her with her subconscious's sensuality. Black Niall had in some ways been her savior, for he had given her hope. The force of his personality, of the bigger-than-life man he had been, had reached out to her across the span of seven centuries. He drew her, somehow, and kept her from sinking into the tar pit of despair. There were times, during these past months, when he had been more real than the world around her.

His image began to fill her mind, forming against the darkness of her closed eyelids: a man as vivid as the lightning, as forceful as the thunder. Dimly she was aware that it was dangerous to focus on her imaginary picture of him, rather than on facts, but she couldn't change her mind to a blank screen. She could feel him, drawing closer. He was there, he was *there* . . .

Breathe, deep and slow. Draw the air in one nostril, circle it around, expel it out the other nostril. Complete the circle, again and again. Breathe. Breathe . . .

She saw his eyes, black and piercing, burning through the fog of time until it was as if he glared straight into her eyes. She saw the high, thin blade of his nose, the thick mane of his black hair as it swung against his muscled shoulders, the small braids that hung on each side of his face in ancient Gaelic fashion.

She saw his mouth open as he roared a command. She faintly perceived around him the din and horror of battle, but he was the only clear figure. She saw the glint of a weak, watery sun on his sword blade as he swung the massive weapon with one powerful arm. The other arm wielded a fearsome axe, rather than a shield, and both weapons were stained with blood as he hacked and parried, felling one foe after another.

In. Out. The air circled around and around inside her, drawing ever smaller, tighter, her mind fastening ever more firmly on the man who was her target. The spiral began to shrink, hugging around her, creating a sense of suction, and she knew she was almost ready to go.

Niall! Black Niall!

Mentally she called to him, screaming his name, her yearning so fierce and intense that it ached in every cell of her body. There was a sensation of being compressed, condensed, concentrated. In her mind she saw his head jerk around in surprise, as if he heard the distant echo of her cry, and then his image too began condensing, tugging on her, pulling her down into a pit of darkness. She fastened on the pure beacon of his essence, like a pilot surely guiding an airplane down on a beacon of radio waves. With her last remnant of consciousness she let her foot relax on the pressure switch, and the world exploded in a flash of blinding heat and light.

Chapter 19

Grace lay on her side in the cool grass. She felt dazed, bruised. Around her she heard a confusion of noises but they came from a great distance, and she couldn't quite tell what any of them were. Her mind, lingering between times, struggled to grasp any detail of existence. She felt as if she were waking up from anesthesia, aware first of external details but with no clue of who or where she was. Then details began seeping back; first was a vague "Oh, yeah, I'm Grace" moment of self-recognition. After a moment, or an hour, she wondered drowsily if the procedure had worked or if she had merely succeeded in shocking her ass, as Harmony had phrased it.

She became aware of various aches, as if she had been beaten, or had rolled down a hill.

The noise was steadily growing louder. The din became annoying, and she struggled to open her eyes, to gain control of her body so she could sit up and tell whoever was yelling like that to shut up. Then the smell hit her, and she gagged.

That involuntary reaction seemed to complete the transition from unconsciousness to complete awareness. The noise exploded into a roar, a horrifying din of what seemed like hundreds of men yelling in battle, screaming in pain. The discordant clash of metal against metal hurt her ears. Horses thudded the ground with steel-shod hooves, neighing shrilly. And the smell was an unholy combination of hot, fresh blood, urine, and emptied bowels.

She sat up, then gasped and hurled herself to the side as two dirty, long-haired, plaid-wrapped Scotsmen clashed almost on top of her. A bloodstained blade swiped through the air, barely missing her.

Dear God. She had landed in the middle of a battle.

Her breath caught. She had seen Black Niall in a battle, focused on him, and the procedure carried her directly to the place in her mind.

He was *here.* Somewhere. An almost painful excitement seized her insides.

Clutching her bag, she scrambled farther away from the clash of bodies. She stumbled over something soft and heavy and pitched hard onto her back. Winded, she sat up and saw that her legs were draped over a bloody dead man. A shriek caught in her throat, hung there unvoiced. Instead she hastily jerked herself away and came to her feet, swaying unsteadily as she swiveled her head, trying to orient herself.

They were in the glen, just below the rocks

where she had gone through the procedure. The scene was madness, some men on horseback but most afoot, running, attacking, pivoting, slashing. Panic seized her; she couldn't see Black Niall anywhere, couldn't find a big man with a flowing mane of black hair, who effortlessly swung a huge sword with one hand. God, oh God, was he lying somewhere in the middle of this carnage, his own blood adding to the red flow?

Reality asserted itself with a thud. Despite her dreams and imaginings, she had no idea what he really looked like. The Guardian wouldn't glow like an archangel with a fiery sword; he would look just like everyone else. He could have been one of the grimy combatants who had almost stepped on her and she wouldn't have known him.

So how was she to find him? Climb the hill and scream "Black Niall!" at the top of her lungs?

"Niall Dhu! Niall Dhu!"

She heard the screaming, the sudden roar from one end of the battlefield, and all the seething bodies seemed to surge in that direction. Grace backed up, climbing a little way up the hill so she could have a better view.

"Niall Dhu!"

She started, the hoarsely screamed words suddenly making sense. *Dhu* meant "black." They were yelling his name.

Blood drained from her head. Had he fallen

under a sword? She stumbled forward, her feet slipping in the red mud created by many feet churning a blood-soaked ground, driven by an insane need to reach his side. He couldn't be dead. No. Not Niall. He was invincible, the most fearsome warrior in Christendom.

The surge abruptly reversed, coming back to her. Grace halted, transfixed by the sight of all those screaming, dirty, long-haired men, bare legs flashing as they ran toward her. Hard reality slapped her. She was in the middle of a fourteenth-century battle, and if any of these men got their hands on her she would likely be raped and killed.

She turned and ran.

It was like waving a cape at a bull. They were already in a blood lust, and a collective roar burst from a hundred throats when they saw her. Grace pulled up her skirts and hurdled bodies, the bag she clutched in one hand banging heavily against her legs. She struggled to draw breath but panic clutched her throat, squeezing, threatening to cut off her breathing altogether.

The ground shook under a horse's thundering impact and a beefy, bloodstained arm swept around her. Grace shrieked as the world abruptly whirled off kilter and she was jerked into the air, flailing, to land heavily across a stinking, wool-covered lap. The man roared with laughter, roughly fondled her rump, then kneed the horse around. He yelled something, his tone obviously gloating, but she couldn't understand anything he said except "Niall Dhu."

Helpless, upside-down over a horse, all she could do was hang on to the bag and hope against hope that the ruffian who had captured her was Niall himself. She had caught a glimpse of a beefy face with a dirty beard, a dreadful disappointment compared to her dreams, but if he were Niall at least that would save her the trouble of hunting him down.

She didn't think she was that lucky.

The bastard was in high spirits, laughing and yelling as he rode. Others on horseback were around them, but most of the men were afoot. There was a great deal of activity in a group just out of her limited view, more yelling and laughter.

The man holding her put his hand between her legs, roughly feeling her through her skirts. Fury swept over Grace in an abrupt, unthinking tide, and swift as a snake she turned her head and sank her teeth into his bare, dirty calf. He roared in surprised pain and jerked on the reins. The horse half reared, neighing, and its hooves hit the ground again with a bone-jarring thud, jerking her teeth out of the man's leg. She gagged at the taste, and nausea overwhelmed her. She began to heave, and vomited over his foot.

Laughter rose around them, men pointing and howling with glee. Her captor seized her and furiously jerked her upright, his fetid breath hitting her full in the face as he roared at her. She couldn't understand a word he said, but his breath made her gag again. Hastily he pushed her off the horse and she sprawled in the dirt, landing with the bag under her stomach and knocking the air out of her.

She was jerked upright, held there while she swayed and gasped for breath, and a rope was tied around her waist. The beefy man tied the other end around his own waist and kicked his heels to the horse's sides, and she had to walk or be dragged. She walked, wheezing, desperately clutching her bag in both hands.

She expected the bag to be taken from her at any moment, but the men evidently didn't see any need to carry anything extra when she could do it. She wasn't going anywhere, and they could relieve her of her possessions whenever they reached their destination.

At least now she could look around. She didn't know if it was morning or afternoon, so she had no way of telling in what direction they were traveling. Not north or south, though, because the sun was behind them. If it was morning, they were traveling west; if afternoon, they were going east.

Behind her, a group of men were carrying a long bundle, completely wrapped and tied in a motley collection of dirty plaids. The bundle heaved occasionally, and was rewarded by a thump from one or more of the men. She looked around and one of the men met her gaze, grinning to display a few remaining teeth, the rest rotted to mere stumps. "Niall Dhu," he said proudly, indicating the bundle.

Aghast, she stopped walking, and was jerked forward when the slack was taken out of the rope. Niall! She looked over her shoulder at the bundle, struggling to make sense of the situation. These couldn't be his men, or they wouldn't be hitting him. Obviously he had been captured, and his own men hadn't been able to pursue for fear he would be killed.

Her mind buzzed with possibilities. He might be ransomed, or his captors might take pleasure in torturing and killing him. If he were held for ransom, he would likely be well taken care of; she thought she remembered reading that medieval Scots had practiced kidnapping as a fairly normal means of income, which of course would work only so long as the captive was returned unharmed. If killing them had been routine, obviously no one would have been willing to pay their hard-earned gold to no avail. The Scots were too practical for that.

But if they intended to kill him . . .

She had to find some way to help him. The problem was that she was a captive herself, and whenever they reached their destination she was likely to find herself in much more dire straits than she was in now. She was a captured woman, vulnerable, nothing more than a piece of meat to these men. Grace knew she was facing rape, probably multiple rapes, unless she could come up with some miraculous plan. Fear chilled her, but she forced it away. She was here. She had actually traveled through time. The circumstances weren't good, but she had found Black Niall almost immediately. Whatever happened later, she had to keep her mind focused on her objective. If necessary, she would endure. She would survive.

She was *here.* The amazement of it suddenly pushed out all other concerns, and her head swiveled from left to right, trying to take everything in. Her heart pounded in her chest. There was nothing really different to see; odd how little the Highlands had changed. Even in the twentieth century they were still mostly deserted, as if time had passed them by. The craggy mountains looked the same, perhaps a bit rougher, with patches of mist clinging to them.

She looked around her at the men, curiously examining their faces. Even under tangled thatches of dirty, uncombed hair, and sometimes an equally dirty, untidy beard, they looked so identifiably Scottish. She saw a long, thin nose here, high slanted cheekbones there, over there a cheerfully round cheek.

The men weren't in a good mood, despite their success in capturing Black Niall. Their losses had been heavy, and none of them had escaped completely unscathed. They laughed whenever one of them punched Niall, but the laughter was mean.

They talked among themselves, but she couldn't understand them. Learning to read Gaelic was a far cry from speaking it, and she doubted any of them could read even if they were inclined to let her write notes to communicate.

The bearded beast who had captured her looked around and scowled at her, and snapped something in Gaelic. Grace started to shrug her shoulders, but a risky plan popped into her head. She didn't give herself time to think about it. She found herself smiling and saying, "I'm sorry, I can't understand you," in the softest, sweetest voice she possessed.

His eyes popped wide open. The men around her gave her startled looks. Until then they had probably thought she was one of Black Niall's crofters, perhaps his woman or belonging to one of his men, but when she spoke in a foreign language they all realized she wasn't what they had assumed.

The beast's small, piggy eyes roamed over her clothes, and for the first time he noticed she wasn't wearing the rough, shapeless clothing of a crofter. He reined his horse to a stop and said something else. Everyone was watching her now. Even the bundle that held Black Niall had stopped wriggling. Grace didn't stop, but walked up beside the horse and gave the beast, the mounted one, another smile. She hadn't smiled in so long that the movement of her face felt strange, but if the beast noticed how false it was his stupefied expression didn't change.

"You stink as if you haven't bathed in your entire life," Grace said pleasantly. "And your breath would knock this horse down if he got a good whiff of it. But you seem to be the leader of this war party, so if being nice to you will protect me from them, I'll take my chances with just one man instead of a crowd any day of the week." She accompanied this with the sweetest smile she could manage, and held her arms up to him.

He was so startled that he automatically leaned down and lifted her onto the horse in front of him. The beast was strong as an ox, she thought, daintily settling herself in a proper position and arranging her skirts. She tried not to breathe through her nose so she wouldn't smell either his body stench or his breath, but she didn't let herself flinch. She acted as if it were her right to ride instead of walk, gave him a regal nod, and said, "Thank you."

They were all gaping at her, and they began gabbling excitedly among themselves, pointing at her clothes. She hadn't realized what good quality her plain cotton and wool garments were, until she compared them to the rough-woven fabric the men wore.

The beast lifted her hand, fingering her rings, and Grace held her breath. She expected him to tear them off her fingers, but instead he grunted and turned her hand over to look at her palm. She looked down, and saw the difference in their hands. His was thick and beefy, callused, the ragged nails black with encrusted dirt. In contrast her hand was soft and pale, the skin smooth, her nails well shaped. Her hands didn't look as if she did any physical labor; in this age, that meant she was at least nobility. She could almost see the ponderous thoughts forming in his brain. She was foreign, and wealthy, and of value to someone somewhere. Perhaps he didn't intend to ransom Black Niall, but here was a little godsend who could add considerable weight to his purse.

He prodded her bag and said something. Guessing he wanted to know what was in the bag, Grace obligingly opened it. The men crowded close, craning their necks in curiosity. She took out one of the books she had brought, flipping the pages to show him the paper and words, then shoving it back into the bag. She hoped no one would be very interested in it, because books didn't exist yet. Priests and monks did illuminated manuscripts, but the printing press wouldn't be invented for another hundred years or so.

The beast wasn't interested in the book,

waving his beefy hand in dismissal. She pulled out the velvet surcoat, just enough to let him see the fabric. He murmured in pleasure, rubbing his dirty hand over the plush texture, and grinned in anticipation of riches. Next she showed him a larger book, hoping he wouldn't want her to flip the pages in it too, because this book had photographs. He grunted, shaking his head, and she shoved it back into the bag.

She had brought several books, chosen with care. There were also several kinds of drugs in the bag, but she didn't want to display the pills. She had gotten prescriptions for them and gone through customs without any problem, but the beast would either eat them or scatter them on the ground. So she pulled out another book, and he looked impatient. He probably wanted to see something he recognized as valuable.

Perplexed, she pulled out the length of wool. Again, he fingered the fine weave, then shoved it aside. She pulled out another book. He said something rude, causing the men to laugh. She shrugged, and brought out still another one, hoping that would allay any suspicions he might have about the weight of the bag, should he investigate.

Abruptly he decided to do just that, grabbing the bag and shoving his hand inside. Grace held her breath. The pills were carefully rolled in a handkerchief, then placed in a small wooden box to keep them from getting crushed, and the box secured in a pocket she had sewn into the inside of the bag.

He didn't notice the pocket or the box. His searching fingers found the Swiss Army knife, and he pulled it out with a triumphant expression that swiftly changed to puzzlement as he stared at it. With all the blades and utensils folded in, it didn't look like much. She didn't want to lose the knife, but if he figured out the blades she knew she would. She drew a quick breath and reached for the knife.

He drew it back, scowling. Grace made her expression impatient. She untied the scarf from her head and unbound her hair, letting it fall free. He blinked at the long, thick mass. She reached for the knife again and this time he let her have it. She closed her hand around it so the blades didn't show, and turned it so he could see the head of the small tweezers. Delicately she plucked it out, and he blinked in astonishment. She held the tweezers in the palm of her hand, letting him look at it, then she quickly gathered her hair and began rolling it up around the knife, forming an oblong bun. When the roll was tight against her nape, she stuck the tweezers into her hair to secure it, and gave the beast a beatific smile.

He looked at her, then at her hair. He blinked again. Then he evidently decided ladies' hairstyles were beyond him, and turned his attention back to the bag.

Next he found a small penlight, luckily the kind that came on when the top was twisted instead of one with a button. Grace sighed, pulled the tweezers out of her hair, and started to unroll the bun, but he got the idea and dropped the penlight back into the bag without examining it very closely. He missed the book of matches, but it had probably gotten stuck between the pages of one of the books.

Next he found an extra pair of stockings, rolled into a ball. To her relief, she didn't have to put them in her hair. He found her comb, and exclaimed over how well made it was. She had searched for a wooden one that wouldn't cause comment, then carefully scratched off the maker's name. The comb was one thing he really could have used, but he dropped it back into the bag without further interest. A few more halfhearted pawings, and he decided she didn't have any valuables hidden from him. He gathered the horse's reins, and with a click of his tongue and a touch of his heels they rode on, with her held carefully in front of him like a queen — a queen with a Swiss Army knife rolled up in her hair.

Chapter 20

The grimy group of men and their two captives reached a castle just before nightfall. The setting sun had given Grace their direction of travel, and she had carefully noted what landmarks she could. Luckily, they seemed to be traveling due east, so if — when — she managed to free Niall and they escaped, she knew they should go due west.

The castle was surprisingly small, little more than a keep with a great hall added, and in ill repair at that. Grace was ushered into the dark, smelly interior, but at least she walked on her own. She watched, trying to hide her anxiety, as Niall was carried in. The bundle had stopped squirming a couple of hours before, and she wondered if they had inadvertently smothered him. Evidently the same thought occurred to the beast, because he shouted something and one of the four men carrying Niall cuffed him on the side of the head. A muffled growl reassured them, and Grace.

Securing Niall was much more important than dealing with her, at least for the moment. A smoky torch was fetched, and Niall was carried down a narrow, winding stone staircase, deep into the bowels of the castle. Grace trailed along because she didn't know what else to do, and the dirty, sullen women who had watched her arrival didn't seem welcoming. Besides, she needed to know where Niall would be held.

The dungeon was creepy. It was dank and dark, with moisture oozing from the slimy stone walls. The air was noticeably colder. There were three cells dug into the earth, each of them secured by an enormous wooden door. There weren't any grilles in the door; the prisoners in this dungeon would live in total darkness, cold and damp, and likely die of pneumonia within a week or two.

The beast cut the ropes that bound the plaids about Black Niall; he and his men all stood with weapons ready, should Niall try to escape. Grace stood on tiptoe, her eyes wide as she tried to get a glimpse of the man who had haunted her for so long. Her movement drew the beast's attention and he scowled at her. He barked an order, and one of the men reluctantly took her arm and forced her to the stairs. She tried to resist, slow him down, but he wasn't happy to be missing the fun and he literally hauled her up the stairs, wrenching her arm in the process. Below, yells burst from male throats and she twisted her head, trying to see, but she was already too far up the curving stairs. There was a crash, and curses, and the sounds of a scuffle, feet scraping on stone and the thud of fists into flesh.

She flinched, wondering if they intended to beat him to death. Her guard jerked at her arm, scowling at her. She gave him a frustrated glare. Yelling at him wouldn't do any good, because no one understood her.

They reached the great hall and he shoved her toward another flight of stairs, this one curving upward into the keep. This staircase was just as dark and narrow. Grace glanced down and saw the sullen faces watching her.

The guard paused in front of a crude wooden door, opened it, and shoved her inside. Immediately she whirled but he closed the door in her face, with a snarled order that she took to mean "Stay there!"

There was no keyhole in the door and the bar was positioned on this side of the door, meaning she wasn't locked in, but when she laid her ear against the wood she heard the guard settling himself on the other side.

She turned and looked at her jail. The room was small and dark, lit by a single smoking torch whose light didn't quite reach all the corners of the room despite its lack of size. The only window was a narrow slit, cut so an arrow could be shot from it at any angle. The floor was covered with rushes gone black and smelly with age, and the only furniture was a roughly made bed that was about the size of a modern double, a single chair, and a wobbly table. A small chest sat against the far wall, and a single candle stood on the table. There was a fireplace, but no fire. A leather bottle stood on the table beside the candle, and a single metal cup.

Grace took advantage of her privacy, which she was sure was only temporary. Unless she missed her guess, this was the beast's bedchamber. Hastily she removed the tweezers from her hair, which had held up remarkably well, and unrolled the knife. After replacing the tweezers in their slot, she thrust the knife inside her stocking and retied the garter, determined to keep the combination weapon and tool with her from now on.

Taking the small wooden box from its pocket inside the burlap bag, she opened it and removed the handkerchief, carefully unrolling it so she didn't lose any of the precious pills. She had brought a full course of antibiotics, and prescriptions of painkillers and Seconals, in addition to picking up some over-the-counter stuff in Edinburgh. The Seconals were an impulse, an effort to cover all bases; it was strange that they would be the first drug she would need to use.

The reddish capsules were hundred-milligram doses, enough to put someone to sleep. What she had to figure out was the delivery system, because she couldn't hand one to the beast and say, "Here, take this."

She looked at the leather bottle, thinking.

Alcohol intensified the effects of Seconal; what wasn't a lethal dose of the drug could become lethal if the user also drank. She didn't want to kill the beast, just knock him out. Two or three pills were enough to put someone to sleep; the pharmacist had carefully told her that she shouldn't take more than one, because she didn't weigh very much.

The beast was a heavy man, not very tall but she guessed his weight at two hundred pounds. She picked out three capsules, and returned her drug stash to the burlap bag.

She opened the leather bottle and sniffed the contents. Her eyes watered at the smell of raw, strong ale. He wouldn't notice anything wrong with the taste if she dissolved the entire thirty capsules in his cup.

Three should do the trick, however. Carefully she pulled the capsules apart, pouring the powder into the battered metal cup. Then she poured a little ale into the cup and swished the liquid around until the powder dissolved. She peered into the cup. The color of the ale looked a little cloudy, but in this light he wasn't likely to notice.

Then, forcing herself to calm and patience, Grace sat down in the chair with the cup in her hand.

She waited a long time. The noise that drifted up made her think there was a revelry going on downstairs. She was hungry, but she wasn't anxious to join them. If someone thought to send food, fine. If not, she had been hungry before.

She grew drowsy. The flickering torch was as sedative as watching a fire in a fireplace, and gave off enough warmth that she wasn't cold. She thought of Niall, and knew that he was neither warm nor comfortable enough to sleep. He would be hungry, too; if they hadn't fed her, they certainly hadn't fed him. That was assuming he was even still alive, but she didn't think they had killed him yet. If the beast intended to kill him, he would want to gloat a bit first. He struck her as that kind of man.

Finally she heard voices outside the door. She didn't jump up, but continued sitting relaxed in the chair, or at least as relaxed as she could be on something as hard as rock. The door opened and the beast came in, his shaggy head lowered and his small, mean eyes bright with anticipation. He looked at the cup, at the open bottle of ale on the table, and his lips spread in a big grin, displaying terrible teeth and remnants of the dinner he had eaten.

Grace yawned and leisurely came to her feet. She pretended to sip the ale, then looked at him and raised the cup in a silent question, nodding at the bottle. He rumbled what she took to be agreement, and she filled the cup, then passed it to him.

He downed the ale in two gulps, then wiped the back of his hand across his wet mouth. His eyes never left her, and lust burned hotly in them.

She fought the impulse to gag even as relief filled her. Dear Lord, how long would it take the Seconals to work? He had eaten, which would slow the effect, but from the look of him he had also had a good deal to drink. She had to stall for time, anything that would keep him from assaulting her now.

Genius struck, and she made an eating gesture, her brows lifted, and then she rubbed her stomach to indicate hunger. He scowled, but went to the door and bellowed something, she hoped a call for food. Evidently he didn't intend to starve her, but had merely forgotten.

He stomped to the chair and sat down, and poured himself another cup of ale. Grace smiled at him, pointed to herself, and said, "Grace St. John."

"Eh?"

At least she understood that sound, she thought in relief. She said again, "Grace St. John," then she pointed at him and waited.

He caught on now. He thumped his bull-like chest. "Huwe dhe Hay."

"Huwe," she repeated. She tried another smile. "Well, Huwe, I don't wish you any harm, but I hope the Seconal knocks you flat on your butt. I know you have big plans for tonight, but so do I, and you aren't included. As soon as everyone is asleep, I'm going to see what kind of damage you and your goons have done to you-know-who, and then I'm going to get him out of here."

Huwe listened to her speech with growing impatience, and he cut her short with an impatient wave of his hand. Then he spouted something involved at her. She made a helpless gesture, spreading her hands and shaking her head.

A brief thud sounded at the door and it swung open. A plump, slatternly woman with wiry dark hair came in, carrying a small platter on which rested a thick piece of coarse bread and a hunk of cheese. She set the platter down with a thunk, glaring at Grace all the while. Either no one here liked outsiders on principle, or the woman had a thing for Huwe, which gave her a new appreciation of the old saying that power was an aphrodisiac.

The woman left, and Grace pinched off a piece of bread. She sauntered around the room, nibbling daintily at the bread and making an occasional comment to Huwe. His gaze still followed her, but after ten or fifteen minutes she noticed he was blinking owlishly. She continued to pace, her manner completely relaxed, returning to the table to taste a tiny bit of the cheese. It wasn't bad.

Huwe's eyelids were drooping heavily. Grace walked over to the narrow window and stood still, looking out at the night while she pretended still to eat. In the shadows as she was, as drugged as Huwe was, he likely couldn't tell her hand was empty.

The night was bright with starlight, and a soft mist was gathering in the glens. Grace quietly watched, listening for Huwe's snores, but the inaction gnawed at her. She felt — she felt as if her body couldn't contain the force of her blood, pounding through her veins. She felt excited, anxious, burning with energy. The constant wariness with which she had lived the past year, the sense of doom hovering over her, was gone. Parrish couldn't reach her here. There were very real dangers she might face but still she felt oddly light, as if a weight had been lifted from her.

She felt alive.

The realization shocked her. She had become so accustomed to the numb bleakness inside her that she hadn't even noticed its absence. Until today, all she had felt for a year had been fear and rage and hate, punctuated by moments of a pain so sharp the numbness had been welcome. But today she had felt excitement, and interest; she had even smiled like mad at Huwe — *Huwe!* The smiles were totally false, but they were more than she had managed in a year.

She was really here. She ached in every muscle, she felt sore inside, but she was here and Black Niall was just two floors below her. They were both captives, he was likely wounded, by their captors' fists if not their swords and daggers, but she could feel his presence like an energy field, making her fingertips tingle.

A soft rumble reached her ears. She looked over at the table, where Huwe was slumped across the surface, his head pillowed on one outstretched arm.

She tiptoed over to the table and moved the bottle to a safer location. A swipe of his arm would have dislodged it, and perhaps awakened him, though she thought likely not even a cannon would do the job tonight. She wasn't going to take the chance.

She had no idea of the time, so she gingerly sat down on the bed and forced herself to wait. The ale would have flowed freely that evening; the men would be tired and sore from the battle earlier, and the ale would ease their aches. They would sleep early that night, and deeply.

Still she waited, until she was in danger of falling asleep herself. When she jerked herself to attention for the second time, she knew she had to go now.

She picked up her bag and walked silently to the door. She eased the door open, peering through the crack to see if a guard stood outside. Empty darkness greeted her, lightened only by a dim glow from down below.

She slipped out of the chamber and eased down the stairs. Men slept in the great hall, snoring lumps rolled in their plaids. She didn't tiptoe; she walked quietly, as if she had a right to be there. Anyone who woke and saw her in the dim light might think her nothing more than a serving wench, but if she were sneaking about, her furtiveness would rouse suspicions. Harmony had told her that: "Walk as if you have a right to the entire sidewalk, and the bad dudes will leave you alone."

A big iron candlestick was set on a table, the thick candle burned half down. Grace picked it up in case there was no light below; she didn't want to use her penlight and try to explain it to Niall, at least not yet.

The staircase to the dungeon was at the back of the great hall, hidden behind a door so dark she almost didn't see it. She set both candlestick and bag on the floor, and eased the door open by increments, taking care the leather hinges didn't creak. A light came from below; there would be a guard, then, for a prisoner wouldn't need light.

She eased her body into the opening, holding the door while she retrieved both bag and candlestick. She didn't need the candle, but she did need a weapon. She blew out the candle and pinched the wick with spit-dampened fingers, then removed the candle from the spike atop the stick and placed it in the bag. Carefully setting the bag down on the top step, she took a deep breath, then another, and silently prayed.

The stone wall of the dungeon was cold and damp against her back as Grace eased down the narrow, uneven steps. There was no railing, and the flicker of the torch below didn't penetrate up the inky, curving stairs. She had to feel her way down, wishing for the candle after all, but it would have alerted the guard to her presence.

The weight of the heavy iron candlestick pulled at her arm. When she was halfway down the curve of steps she could see the single guard, sitting below on a crude bench with his back resting against the wall, a rough skin of wine at his elbow. Good; if she were lucky, he had drunk himself into a stupor. Even if he had a Scotsman's hard head for spirits, at least the liquor would have slowed his reflexes. She hoped he was asleep because given where he was sitting, she would have to approach him almost head-on. The light was poor and she could hide the candlestick against her leg, but if he stood up it would be much more difficult for her to hit him hard enough to knock him out. She was so sore and battered from the trip through time that she didn't trust her strength; better if she could simply lift the heavy candlestick and swing it downward, letting gravity aid her.

Grace cautiously edged her foot forward, searching for the edge of each step while trying not to scrape her shoe against the stone. The air was cold, and fetid; the smell assaulted her nose, making it wrinkle in disgust. The odor was composed of unmistakable human waste, but beneath that lay the sharper, more unpleasant odors of blood, and fear, and the sour sweat of pain. Men had been tortured, and died, in these foul depths that never saw the sun.

It was up to her to make certain Black Niall didn't join their ranks.

She had a guilty thought: was it her fault he had been captured? Common sense told her that was ridiculous; it was impossible for Niall to have heard her mental call to him. She couldn't have caused a split second of inattention that could have resulted in his capture. She hadn't actually seen what had happened, anyway, so it was silly to feel guilty. But then, her very presence here was evidence that the impossible was possible, so she couldn't say for certain that Niall hadn't heard her call him.

She didn't know how much time she had. Huwe of Hay would sleep until late morning, under the double influence of alcohol and Seconal. Given how much he had drunk, she only hoped she hadn't overdosed him. Crude and disgusting as he was, she didn't want to kill him. But she was heartily grateful she had brought those drugs; without the Seconal, she could never have escaped from Huwe at all, much less avoided being raped.

Her searching foot found no more steps. The floor was nothing more than hard-packed dirt, uneven and treacherous. She stood still for a moment, taking deep, silent breaths as she tried to steady her nerves. The guard still sat slumped on the bench, his head nodded forward onto his chest. Was he truly asleep, or drunk, or merely playing possum? As careful as she had been, had he still heard some betraying rustle, and was now trying to lure her closer?

It didn't matter; she didn't have any choice. Even if his capture wasn't her fault, she couldn't leave Black Niall here for Huwe to kill. Niall was the Guardian, the only person alive who knew both the secrets and the location of the Templars' Treasure. Unless she could find the Treasure herself, she needed his knowledge, his cooperation, to prevent Parrish from getting his hands on the Treasure. She wanted Parrish stopped, and she wanted Parrish dead; for that, she needed Black Niall alive.

She considered the guard. If he were awake and merely being crafty, then she would arouse less suspicion by approaching him directly, as if she had nothing to hide. Harmony's theory, again. Moreover, if he saw her, he wouldn't expect any threat from a woman. Her heart thumped wildly in her chest, and for a moment black spots swam before her eyes. Panic made her stomach lurch, and she thought she might throw up. Desperately she sucked in more air, fighting back both nausea and weakness. She refused to let herself falter now, after all she had already been through.

Cold sweat broke out on her body, trickled

down her spine. Grace forced her feet to move, to take easy, measured strides that carried her across the rough floor as if she had nothing at all to hide. The torchlight danced and swayed, as if under the spell of some unheard music, casting huge, wavering shadows on the damp stone walls. The guard didn't move.

Ten feet. Five. Then she stood directly in front of the guard, so close she could smell the stench of his unwashed body, sharp and sour. Grace swallowed, and steeled herself for the blow she had to deliver. She sent up a quick prayer that she wouldn't cause him any lasting damage, and used both aching arms to raise the heavy candlestick high.

Her clothing rustled with her movements. He stirred, opening bleary eyes and peering up at her. His mouth gaped open. Grace swung downward, and the massive iron candlestick crashed against the side of his head with a solid thud that made her cringe. Anything he might have said, any alarm he might have given, dissolved into a grunt as he slid sideways, his eyes closing once more.

Blood trickled down the side of his head, matting in his filthy hair. Looking down at him she saw that he was younger than she had thought, surely not much more than twenty. His grimy cheeks still held a certain childish curve. Tears stung her eyes, but she turned sharply away, need shouldering aside regret.

Of the three cells, only one was barred. "Niall!" she whispered urgently as she grasped the massive bar. How was she best to communicate with him? Today had taught her that Gaelic wasn't a possibility. He was a Templar, though; he would almost certainly speak French. She felt capable in either Old English or Old French, but Latin hadn't changed at all since his time, so that was the language she chose.

"I have come to free you," she said softly as she struggled with the bar. My God, it was heavy! It was like wrestling with a tree trunk, six feet long and a good ten inches wide. Her hands slipped on the wood, and a splinter dug deep into her little finger. Grace bit off an involuntary cry of pain as she jerked her hand back.

"Are you hurt?"

The question was voiced in a deep, calm, softly burred voice, and came very clear to her ears as if he stood close against the other side of the door. Hearing it, Grace froze, her eyes closing as she struggled once more with tears and an electrifying surge of emotion that threatened to overwhelm her. It was really Black Niall, and oh, *God,* he sounded just as he had in her dreams. That voice was like thunder and velvet, capable of a roar that would freeze his enemies or a warm purr that would melt a woman into his arms.

"Only . . . only a little," she managed to say,

her voice shaking. She struggled to remember the correct words. "A splinter . . . the bar is very heavy, and it slipped."

"Are you alone?" Concern was there now. "The bar is too big for a mere woman."

"I can do it!" she said fiercely. Mere? *Mere?* What did he know? She had survived on the run for a year; she had managed to get here, against all odds, and moreover she was the one on the *free* side of the door. Anger mixed with exhilaration, surging through her veins, making her feel as if she would burst through her skin. She wanted to scream, she wanted to hit something, she wanted to dance. Instead she turned her attention back to the bar.

Abandoning any attempt to lift it with her hands, she bent her knees and lodged her shoulder under it, driving upward with all the strength in her back and legs.

The weight of the bar bit into her shoulder, nearly drove her downward again. Gritting her teeth, Grace braced her legs and strained. She could feel blood rush to her face, feel her heart and lungs labor. Her knees wobbled. Damn it, she *wouldn't* let this stupid piece of wood defeat her, not after all she had already gone through!

A growl of refusal burst past her lips and she summoned every ounce of strength in her aching body, gathering it for one final effort. Her thigh muscles screamed in pain, her back burned. Desperately she shoved upward, forcing her legs to straighten, and one end of the bar slowly rose inch by inch. It teetered for a moment and she shoved again, and the bar began sliding down through the other bracket. The rough wood scraped her cheek, snagged her clothes. Using both hands, ignoring the need for quiet, she shoved the bar forward until it was free of the right bracket.

Instead of continuing its slide through the other bracket, the heavy bar slowed, its weight tipping it back toward her. Grace scrambled out of the way as one end hit the dirt floor with a reverberating thud. The bar stood braced there, one end on the floor and the other balanced against the second bracket.

She stood still, breathing hard, trembling in every muscle, but triumph roared through her, fierce and sweet. Heat radiated from her, banishing the cold as if she stood close to a fire, and she couldn't feel any pain in her injured hand. She felt invigorated, invincible, and her breasts rose tight and aroused beneath her clothing.

"Open the door," she invited, the words coming out breathlessly despite her efforts to steady her voice. Then she couldn't resist a taunt: "If you can."

A low laugh came to her ears, and slowly the massive door began to open, pushing the huge bar before it. Grace took a step back, her gaze fastened hungrily on the black space yawning open between the door and the frame, waiting for her first glimpse of Black Niall in the flesh.

He came through the door as casually as if he were on vacation, but there was nothing casual in the black gaze that swept over the unconscious guard and then leaped to her, raking her from head to foot in a single suspicious, encompassing look. His vitality seared her like a blast, an almost palpable force, and she felt the blood drain from her face.

He could have stepped straight from her dreams.

He was there, just as he had been in the images that had plagued her for endless nights, as he had been when his essence had pulled her across nigh seven centuries. Slowly, like a lover's hand drifting over the face of a beloved, barely touching as if too strong a contact would destroy the spell, her gaze traced his features.

Yes, it was he. She knew him well, his face memorized in countless dreams. The broad, clear forehead; the eyes, as black as night, as old as sin. The thin, high-bridged Celtic nose, and chiseled cheekbones; the firm and unsmiling lips, the uncompromising chin and jaw. He was big. Mercy, she hadn't realized how big he was, but he stood more than a foot taller than she, at least six-four. His long black hair swung past his shoulders, shoulders that were at least a two-foot span of solid muscle. The hair at his temples was secured in a thin braid on each side of his face.

His shirt and plaid were dirty, and dark with dried blood. Bruises mottled his face; one eye was swollen almost shut. But for all that, he was strong and vital, impervious to the cold that was making her shiver, or at least she told herself it was the cold. He was wilder than she could have imagined, and yet he was exactly as she had dreamed. The reality of him was like a blow, and she swayed.

He looked around, his face hard and set, every muscle poised for action. "You are alone?" he asked again, evidently doubting that she had managed the bar by herself.

"Yes," she whispered.

No enemies rushed from the inky shadows, no alarm was raised. Slowly he returned his gaze to her, and with the torch behind her outlining her form she knew he could see how violently she was trembling.

"Frail but valiant," he murmured, coming closer. Despite herself, she would have shrunk back, but he moved with the deceptive speed of an attacking tiger. One hard arm passed around her waist, both supporting and capturing her, drawing her against him. "No, don't fear me, sweetings. Who are you? No relation of Huwe's, I'll wager, not with such a pretty face — and a command of Latin."

"N-no," she stammered. The contact with him was going to her head, making her feel giddy. Oh, God. His voice had taken on a deep, unmistakable note. Her stomach clenched in panic. She lifted her right hand to brace against his chest; the touch jammed the splinter deeper into her finger, and she flinched from the sudden pain.

Instantly he caught her hand, hard fingers wrapping gently around it and turning it toward the light. Her stomach clenched again at the contrast of her hand lying in that callused palm. Like Huwe's, his hand was dirty from the battle he'd fought that day, but that was the only resemblance between the two men. Black Niall's big hand was lean and powerful, the long fingers well shaped, the nails tended. For all the obvious strength in that hand, it cradled her much smaller one as delicately as if he held a baby bird.

She glanced at the small, burning wound on her hand. The long, jagged splinter had entered her finger lengthwise, and the end protruded just above the bend of the first knuckle. He made a softly sympathetic sound, almost a croon, and lifted her hand to his mouth. With delicate precision he caught the end of the splinter in his animal-white teeth, and steadily drew it out. Grace flinched again at the pain, sucking in a hissing breath and rising on tiptoe against him, but he held her hand steady in his powerful grip. He spat the splinter out, then sucked hard at the sullenly bleeding wound. She felt his tongue flicking against her skin, laving her hurt, and a moan that had nothing to do with pain slipped from her lips.

That black gaze moved back to her face, so close to his now, and his eyes grew heavy-lidded as he sensed how it was with her. His thin nostrils flared like a stallion's, drawing in her female scent. And then his expression changed, shifting into furious recognition.

"You!" He spat the word as if it were an epithet. His hands bit into her shoulders as he whirled her toward the light. She hadn't put her hair back up after removing the knife, and he sank one hand deep into the heavy mass, lifting it as if to measure its length. His olive-toned face was savage.

"M-me?" she squeaked ungrammatically, in English. She caught herself and returned to Latin. "I?"

"Who are you?" he asked again, and this time the question was hard with barely contained fury. "It was you, screaming my name, who distracted me today and caused me to be captured. You have watched me for months, never showing your face until you invaded my dreams. Are you a spy, a witch?"

Grace went white, staring at him in horrified dismay. He had felt her dreams, shared them with her? *Oh, no.* She felt a fiery blush begin to heat her cheeks. Then she jerked as his last words registered. "No! I'm not a spy, or a witch!"

"Then why have you watched me?" he asked grimly, releasing her to cross swiftly to the unconscious guard. He looked briefly at the young man's bleeding head, then at the iron candlestick lying beside him, before taking both sword and dagger as if he felt the need to be armed in her presence. The dagger disappeared inside his soft leather boot, and he turned to face her, eyes narrowed and watchful. "How have you come to my bed so often I know the very smell of you? How came you to be with Huwe today? I heard your voice, I know you were there."

"They c-captured me, too." The unsteadiness of her voice annoyed her, and she took a deep, irritated breath. She was mortified that he had shared those erotic dreams with her; she didn't know how it had happened, but everything about this went beyond the normal and there was nothing she could do about it.

"A likely tale. You hardly bear the look of mistreatment."

"Huwe intended to ransom me, I think."

"That would not keep him from rutting on you, sweetings."

She blushed again, unable to control the heat in her cheeks, but it seemed as much in response to the rather biting endearment than to his crude words. "No. *I* kept him from that."

"How did you accomplish that feat? A spell?"

"I am not a witch! I gave him a drink that made him sleep. He was drunk, anyway."

"And all the others?"

"They are all asleep from drink. They think you safely locked away, and that your men will not dare attack while they have you."

"No, but they will be nearby." He didn't seem as angry now, though his gaze was still hard when he looked at her. "You have not yet answered my question. Who are you?"

"Grace St. John." She said it in English, because she didn't know the specific Latin applications.

He repeated her name as she had said it, slowly duplicating the pronunciation, his tongue sure on the syllables with the deftness of someone who spoke several languages. Then he stepped closer to her, the sword still in his hand, so close that his big body blotted out the light of the flickering torch. "And how have you watched me?"

"I haven't." She made a helpless gesture. "I dreamed."

"Ah. More dreams." He was still angry, she could feel it, but his voice had taken on that low, seductive note again, making her shiver as she fought the pull of it. "In your dreams, sweetings, was I inside you?" he whispered, moving even closer, his left arm sliding about her waist and slowly, inexorably, pulling her against him. "Were you beneath me in my bed, did I ride you hard?"

Grace struggled to breathe. Her lungs weren't working properly, only drawing in fast, shallow breaths. She braced her hands against his chest, feeling the incredible heat of his body through his rough linen shirt. She felt hot, too, restless and panicky, her skin almost painfully sensitive.

His gaze was sharp and hot, startlingly aware. His lips parted slightly, his own breathing coming a little too fast as the hard arm around her waist urged her even closer, closer, until her breasts touched him. "I'm a fool," he murmured, this time in Scots, but somehow she understood him. "I've no time for more, but I'll at least have the taste of ye."

He lifted her, turning to pin her against one of the cell doors. His big, iron-muscled body ground against her from shoulder to knee, and her breath snagged at the fullness of his arousal. Instantly he took advantage of her parted lips and set his mouth to hers. His kiss was ravaging, not in force but in effect. Her blood surged wildly in response, and her body instinctively molded to him. His taste was hot, tart and uncivilized, shatteringly familiar. He used his tongue with soul-searing skill, demanding her response, then deepening his advantage when she helplessly gave it. His hands moved over her body, cupping her breasts, her bottom, moving her against him. His long fingers slipped between her legs, feeling her through her gown. Grace had a second of warning, an almost painful inner tightening, and frantically she pushed against him but it was too late. Sensation splintered into a thousand piercing shards, and with a hoarse cry she arched into him.

She felt his surprise as his mouth muffled her cry, then he gathered her tighter while her climax pulsed through her, those devilishly knowledgeable fingers gently rubbing to give her a full measure of satisfaction. The spasms finally slowed, diminishing to tremors, and she sank weakly against him.

She jerked her mouth from his and pressed her head hard against his shoulder, her face hot with mortification. She had never been so embarrassed and humiliated in her life. Reaching climax in a dream was unsettling enough, but to do it in front of him, with no more stimulation than a kiss and a bold caress — she burned with shame.

"Lass," he said, his voice low and husky, almost a whisper. His lips pressed briefly to the exposed curve of her neck, the touch hot and tender. His breath came in soft, short pants as he let her slide to her feet, all down the length of his body.

She would have kept her head down but he cupped her chin, lifting her face so he could see it. His thumb swept over the soft bloom of her mouth. His own lips were swollen and shiny, his eyes narrow with lust. "A pity I must go," he whispered in Scots. "Ye burn a man to a fair crisp, but I'd turn to ash wi' a smile on my face." He bent and brushed her mouth with his, then patted her bottom and set her away from him.

Shaking, Grace leaned against the door, her mind a blank and her knees like water. He moved so fast that he had already reached the stairs before realization sank into her brain. She struggled upright, her eyes wide. "No, wait!" she cried. "Take me with you!"

He didn't even pause, his powerful legs taking the stairs two at a time. He tossed her a grin. "I give you thanks for my liberty, but gratitude doesn't make me a fool," he said, returning to Latin, and he disappeared upward into the darkness.

Oh, damn! She didn't dare call out again. She launched herself after him but her legs were still shaking, and she barely had the strength to climb the stairs. There was no sign of him when she emerged from the dungeon.

She couldn't sound an alarm, for after all she didn't want him recaptured. Nor did she herself dare to remain. She collected her bag and tiptoed toward the kitchen, thinking that the most likely avenue of his escape. If there were a guard there, Niall would have taken care of him. She had to get out of this grimy hold and find him again. He wasn't a hero, damn him, no knight in shining armor. He was just a man, though bigger than most, more bold and vital. He was arrogant and rude, and he was her only hope.

Chapter 21

Grace was a little gratified to realize she had guessed right. Outside the kitchens she found a guard's body, slumped on the ground in the boneless attitude of death. There was an uproar in the stables, torches being lit, men running and cursing. Niall must have stolen a horse and escaped through the postern gate. There was no chance of her stealing a horse now, and the keep was coming awake behind her. She dodged into a small storeroom, little more than a shed built against the side of the keep. It was evidently the granary, for the dusty smell of oats made her stifle a sneeze.

She heard rustlings in the oats that made her grit her teeth. Where there was grain, there were rats. She was acutely aware of the vulnerability of her legs beneath the long skirts. What she wouldn't give for her jeans and boots!

But she stood grimly still, even when the noisy search discovered the guard's body just outside her hiding place. Even though she couldn't understand the words, she could grasp their anger and agitation. Their chieftain couldn't be roused; the dungeon guard was injured, perhaps dead; both captives were gone, though only one horse was missing. She only hoped they would assume she was with Niall, that somehow they had simply failed to see her, because otherwise they would begin a thorough search of the keep.

Damn Niall, she thought violently. Why couldn't he have taken her with him? Even if he refused to take her to Creag Dhu, he could at least have gotten her away from Huwe. Gratitude didn't make him a fool, indeed!

The uproar eventually died down. They couldn't pursue Niall in the dark, and without Huwe they weren't inclined to take action anyway. She waited, rustling her feet whenever the munching rats seemed to get too close, sending them squealing and scurrying. She would never forgive Niall for this.

At least security would be lax, now that their prisoner was gone. The Hay stronghold wasn't very strong anyway, from what she had seen. There had once been a wall around it, but it hadn't been maintained and the mortar had crumbled, leaving big gaps. Unfortunately, someone would still be watching the horses.

His tough luck, she thought when she finally crept out of her hiding place. She didn't know the time, so she didn't dare wait much longer. Dawn could come at any time, and with it her only opportunity to escape.

A soft mist was falling, not much more than a heavy fog. Her heart sank. That was probably why they hadn't pursued Niall, because they couldn't see in this pea soup. Unfortunately, she didn't have any choice, even though she didn't know where she was. She had carefully noted the direction from which they had come the day before, but the fog greatly increased her chances of getting totally turned around.

She walked quietly into the stable. A guard snoozed against a pile of hay, a small candle with a protective globe over it guttering by his side. What was she supposed to bash *him* with? She looked around and spied a rough pitchfork, its handle made of a sturdy length of wood. She picked it up, gripped it like a bat, and gave it a healthy swing. The wood swatted him in the side of his head and he jerked once, then fell heavily limp.

"I'm going to go to hell," she whispered into the night. That made two innocent men she had knocked in the head tonight, and for all she knew she had killed both of them. Severe head injuries in medieval times likely resulted in death. If Niall had taken her with him, hitting this last guard wouldn't have been necessary.

She bit her lip, looking at the curious equine heads surveying her. She knew how to ride, because it was a convenient skill to have when out on a dig, but she wasn't an expert and in any case hadn't been on a horse in more than two years, except for being held in front of

Huwe on his horse yesterday, and that didn't count.

"Pick a horse, any horse," she muttered to herself. Geldings were always less fractious than stallions or even mares, but in the darkness she couldn't tell anything about her available choices except their size. She settled on a brown horse that was neither the largest nor the smallest, hoping that moderation was the key to success.

The horse stood quietly as she saddled it, and followed obediently when she led it to a keg. She stepped up on the keg, then mounted the horse. After tying her bag securely to the saddle, she clicked her tongue to the animal and carefully rode it out of the stable. Behind her, she heard a quiet groan as the guard began reviving. She was glad he wasn't dead, but that meant she had only a minute or so to get away before the alarm was raised.

She rode the horse at a walk to one of the gaps in the wall, and let it pick its own way over the tumbled rock. In the dark and the fog, the run-down keep was soon out of sight.

The safest course would be to find a place to hide, and wait until dawn when both she and the horse would be able to see. But if she remained close by, that increased the chances the Hays would recapture her and she doubted she would escape abuse so easily again.

When she saw Black Niall again, she was going to throttle him, even if she had to climb on a stool to do it.

She clicked to the horse and nudged it with her heels, but she let it pick its way at its own cautious speed. She could barely see past the horse's nose, so it seemed wiser to trust the animal's instincts; it at least had its feet on the ground. Still, she hoped sunrise wasn't several hours away.

To be fair to Niall, she hadn't tried to explain herself or her presence. Part of her reticence was pure caution, because as Guardian his duty was to protect the Treasure from all threats, including herself. If he discovered she knew the procedure for time travel, he might feel it necessary to kill her. If she could get the Treasure herself, without his assistance, she preferred to do so. If she found she needed him, then would be the time to confess.

But all the logical reasons for remaining quiet weren't what had kept her from telling him. She had simply been too shocked, first by the embarrassing discovery that he had shared the dreams with her and then by the way she had humiliated herself in his arms. She had been hard put even to speak, much less launch into a detailed explanation.

Her cheeks burned again as she remembered what had happened, and she lifted her face to the chilly mist.

She had been agitated from the moment she had arrived back in time, nervous, excited. She hadn't thought that agitation could so swiftly convert into sexual response, but it had. It was as if her body had been numb for a year, but something had happened to her during the time transition and now she felt everything too much.

Niall had fascinated her from the moment she had first read his name. She had spent so much time concentrating on him, dreaming about him, it was no wonder all her senses had been so acutely focused on him. All those hours she had been so aware of his actual presence that it had been difficult for her to think of anything else, her skin hypersensitive, prickly. She should have recognized the sexual charge underlying her jitters, but she hadn't. While she had accepted and rationalized the sexual aspect of her dreams, it hadn't occurred to her the physical attraction would be as strong in reality.

It wasn't. It was stronger.

She had been unfaithful to Ford in every way except the actual act, but she couldn't find any solace in that detail. If circumstances had been different, if they had been alone in a safe place, she had no doubt Niall would have had her. But now that she recognized her weakness, she could safeguard against giving in to it. She must never let Niall so much as kiss her again.

But as she rode through the night, she was uncomfortably aware that if Niall wished to kiss her or do anything else to her, her defenses were very weak indeed.

Creag Dhu was a massive stone castle, the rock from which it was built as dark as a stormy sky. Unlike the Hay keep it was in excellent repair, with thick stone walls surrounding four huge towers. The big main entrance was guarded by two sets of gates twenty feet apart, and the men who guarded it looked healthy, well clothed and armed, and well trained. Everyone who entered was stopped and questioned, and no carts or bundles went through those gates without being thoroughly inspected.

Grace knew she should have expected as much, given Niall's military background, but when she looked at Creag Dhu she felt overwhelmed by the task she had set herself. Just getting in looked impossible; how on earth would she manage searching it?

She had to stay hidden, because a stranger would be immediately noticed. The castle was busy, having attracted its own small village as people moved closer to safety, but everyone would know everyone else. She was hungry, and tired from having ridden for two days. She had wandered off course in the fog, and a journey that shouldn't have taken an entire day had instead taken two.

At least the horse was content, because there was plenty of grass and water.

The animal was a gelding, blessed with a

calm and forgiving nature. If it hadn't been, Grace was certain she never would have survived. She ached from head to foot, and her bottom was so sore she didn't think she would be able to climb back into the saddle even if Huwe of Hay suddenly appeared in front of her.

She had tethered the horse in a copse of forest, while she assessed the situation, which wasn't promising. Perhaps she should just walk up to the gates and ask to see him. He might not be pleased, but she *had* freed him from the dungeon; if she told him she was hungry, could he turn her away?

Of course he could, she thought. He was the Guardian. He wouldn't let anything as paltry as gratitude stand in the way of his duty.

She had to think of some way to get inside the castle.

She couldn't smuggle herself inside by hiding in any of the carts she saw going in; all the carts were searched, even when the guards obviously knew the owner and they chatted genially together while the goods or produce were inspected. She didn't even speak the language, so when they asked questions she wouldn't be able to answer. She could try speaking Old English, but that wouldn't win her any friends here in Scotland; the two countries had been at war for years. She could understand most of the Scots dialect, but speaking it was useless because the parts of it she understood were English, so she wouldn't gain anything.

Even if she did manage to get into Creag Dhu, what then? The castle inhabitants would certainly know one another far better than they knew the village folk, so there wouldn't be any way she could escape notice by mingling with the crowd. Exploring the castle would take time; she needed to be able to come and go without being questioned. Grimly she arrived back at one inescapable conclusion: even if she got into the castle, she would need Niall's permission to stay.

She decided to face one problem at a time, and found herself back at the beginning: how to get into Creag Dhu?

She began making her way back to the horse, stumbling over rocks and roots, catching her skirts on bushes and twigs and having to jerk them free. She was becoming more and more irritated with the nuisance of a long gown. To tell the truth, she was irritated with everything, but at least her ill humor had distracted her from the humiliation of what had happened with Niall.

By the time she reached the horse, she was sweating from the effort of fighting her way through brambles and bushes. The wool surcoat, which felt good on cold nights, now suffocated her. Irritably she stripped it off and tossed it over the saddle, sighing in relief as air seeped through the lighter cotton kirtle.

She loosened the laces that held the neckline and sleeves tight, pulling the neckline completely open and then pushing up the sleeves as far as she could, which was only to the middle of her forearms. Under the scarf, her hair was wet with sweat. Off came the scarf, and she unwound the heavy knot of her hair, running her fingers through it and letting fresh air reach her scalp. She had expected Scotland to be uniformly chilly even in May, but that wasn't the case today.

There was no way she was putting that heavy wool gown back on, and the velvet one would be just as hot. Grace looked down, checking the kirtle for modesty. She was dismayed to find it failed miserably, unless she didn't mind any casual observer being able to see both her nipples and the darkness of her pubic hair. Inspiration struck, and she shook out the big scarf, then tied it around her waist so that it draped strategically over both front and back. Then she bloused the kirtle out from the waist so the fullness gave her a bit of modesty up top, too. Satisfied with her effort, she stuffed the dirty wool surcoat in the bag and remounted the horse. She hadn't solved any of her problems, but at least now she was comfortable.

Five minutes later, as she watched a group of five women trudge along the rutted road, obviously heading to Creag Dhu, inspiration struck again.

The business of the women wasn't in any doubt. Their skirts were hiked up farther than any Grace had seen since arriving, and their bodices were pulled low. They hadn't bothered with long-sleeved, high-necked kirtles; their undergarments were short-sleeved and loose. No kerchiefs covered their heads, and though their hair was for the most part unkempt, as Grace watched they began finger-combing the tangles, pulling strands over their shoulders to curl flirtatiously around their breasts. They pinched their cheeks and bit their lips, and there was a good deal of laughter and obviously naughty observations.

Whores, or at least loose women, on their way to the castle for a night of recreation or commerce, or both. And Grace now looked remarkably like them, with her scanty clothing and loose hair. She kneed the horse into a walk, approaching the group from an angle.

"Good afternoon," she said pleasantly when she neared, trying to alter her accent so the "good" sounded like "guid." No help for it; she would have to speak Old English, which was at least close enough to Scots for her to be largely understood.

The whores watched her suspiciously, no hint of welcome in their faces.

"My man left me," she said baldly. "I've no coins, no food for two days, and I have no place to sleep."

An overblown redhead who had seen better

days looked her up and down. "Aye?" she said in a tone that clearly meant, "So what?"

"If you are going to the castle, could I go with you? A night's work would bring me a coin or two, and at least food for my belly."

"Ye have yer beast," the redhead pointed out, nodding at the horse. A horse was a valuable animal, worth more than all their possessions put together. They weren't likely to have any sympathy for her so long as she possessed him.

Grace thought quickly. "You can have him," she promised, "if you will take me with you."

The five women put their heads together, and a swarm of Gaelic buzzed around her ears. Finally the redhead held up her hand and nodded to Grace. " 'Tis a bargain." She waited expectantly, and Grace climbed down from the horse, not without a great deal of relief. Her bottom was so sore after two days of riding that she was much happier walking. She untied her bag from the saddle, and presented the reins to the redhead, who looked triumphantly around at her friends.

They resumed their trek up the road. As they trudged around a bend and the castle came into sight, the redhead said, "What's yer name?"

"Grace."

"I am Wynda." She nodded in turn at the four other women. "Nairne, Coira, Sile, and Eilidh." Introductions accomplished, they completed the walk to the castle.

Both guards stepped forward to meet them, stubbled cheeks stretched in huge grins. A great deal of giggling, pinching, and butt patting went on, then both guards looked questioningly at Grace. Evidently the other five were well known by the men-at-arms.

"Grace," Wynda said in reply to their questions. "She's a Sassenach hoor."

The guard took the bag from Grace and opened it, thrusting his big hand within. He pawed through the articles of clothing and pulled out a book, looking at it in puzzlement. Grace was too tired and hungry to do anything but stand there. Wynda repeated Grace's tale of her man leaving her behind. Perhaps it was the explanation, Grace's lack of anxiety, or that the bag obviously held no weapons, but with a shrug the guard handed the bag back to her. He called out to the guards on the other side of the double gate, and the six women walked through.

She was in. Her heart began pounding with excitement, the rush of adrenaline dispelling her fatigue.

Wynda proudly led her horse to the stable, while the others made their way toward the barracks. Grace fell behind them, slowing her steps until they were well ahead of her. They were chatting, laughing, paying her no mind. Calmly she changed direction, looking around with interest.

The inner ward was neat and busy, people going about the daily business involved in running a castle. To the left were the stables and barracks, to the right a training ground where a number of men, stripped to the waist, practiced their swordplay. She could see a well-shaped head with long black hair, towering over all the others, and quickly she looked away as if he might feel her gaze.

Black Niall was there, so she wanted to go in a different direction. Now that she was inside she could see that in addition to the four tall towers which stood at each corner, there were two smaller inner towers, one on each end of the center great hall. The entire thing was huge; she couldn't begin to guess how many rooms the castle contained.

She walked into the great hall, and a wave of dizziness swept over her. The hall was just as she had seen it in her dreams. She knew where Niall sat, and exactly where the kitchens were. The smell of roasting meat filled the air, and she wondered if her dizziness was caused by hunger.

Men and women alike were looking at her strangely, and she ducked her head, walking quickly toward the kitchens. Perhaps she could beg a piece of bread; if not, perhaps she could steal it. She had already stolen a horse, so why worry about bread? She doubted either was as serious a sin as the rash of head bashing in which she had recently indulged.

Her appearance in the kitchen went unnoticed for a few moments, largely because there were so many people bustling about, chopping and stirring and pounding. A young boy slowly cranked a spit on which turned what looked like an entire pig. Fat dripped sizzling into the fire, sending out a wonderful smell to mingle with the yeasty scent of baking bread.

Finally a buxom woman spotted her, and snapped out a question in Gaelic. "I've come a very long way," Grace said. "I've had no food for over two days —"

"Sassenach!" the cook spat in disgust, and made a shooing motion with the cloth tied around her waist.

Evidently being thought an Englishwoman was more to her discredit than being dressed like a whore. Grace shook her head and said, "French." Then she abruptly turned white as another wave of dizziness hit her, and she swayed, reaching out to the wall to support herself.

The dizziness was all too real. Gasping, Grace bent over from the waist, trying not to faint. The need for food was becoming more pressing by the minute.

Perhaps it was the reassurance that she wasn't English, but supporting arms were suddenly around her, leading her to a bench. The buxom woman pressed a piece of bread into her shaking hand, and poured ale into a shallow bowl for her to drink. Slowly Grace chewed on the bread, which was of much better quality than that she'd had at the Hay keep. She didn't dare take more than a few sips of the ale, not after being so long without food.

The work went on around her, though the buxom woman kept looking in her direction, perhaps assessing the return of color to her face. After a bit, when the bread stayed down, another piece was placed before her, along with some cheese and a few slivers of cold pork. Feeling stronger now, Grace ate as greedily as good manners allowed, and drank more ale.

The cook clucked her tongue approvingly and put even more meat and bread in front of her. "Ye're scarce as thick as a strae, lass. Ha' a bit more. Ye'll need yer strength tonight."

Grace tried, but she was full. After a few more bites she sighed, replete, and smiled at the woman. "Thank you. I was very hungry."

"Ye're welcome. Go on wi' ye, now." Charity served, the woman made shooing motions with her cloth again, and Grace went.

Her first priority now was to find a secure hiding place, at least until she decided what to do. When everyone's attention seemed to be elsewhere, she dodged into a curtained alcove and gingerly sat down on the floor, prepared to wait.

She leaned her head back against the cold stone wall. What had she gotten herself into? Coming back had seemed reasonable when she was still in her own time, but in the three days since her arrival she had accomplished exactly nothing toward her goal. What had seemed fairly simple — find the Treasure and return to her own time — had taken on gargantuan proportions.

Now that she had seen the size of the castle, she knew it would take days, weeks, to search it thoroughly. She certainly couldn't stay hidden the entire time. Unless she enlisted Niall's help, which didn't seem a viable alternative, she needed an excuse to stay in the castle. To do that, she had to have Niall's permission.

She had to face him again. She didn't look forward to it, but she had done more difficult things than this during the past year. What was humiliation, after all, compared to seeing her husband and brother murdered, to being hunted like an animal?

She was very tired. Now that she had eaten, she was so sleepy she couldn't keep her eyes open. She hauled the heavy burlap bag around behind her back and reclined in a more comfortable position, her head pillowed on books and clothing. She slept within minutes.

After declining enthusiastic offers of company from both Jean and Fenella, a lusty serving wench, Niall climbed the stairs that curved along the outside wall of the tower, leading to his private chamber. He was in a foul mood. He ached for a woman, but not one with

Fenella's overripe charms. Not even Jean tempted him, and over the months she had become his favorite, if not only, bedmate.

"Damn the witch!" He swore viciously as he slammed the door to his bedchamber. He strode to the table and lifted the bottle of wine that sat there, then thumped it down unpoured. He didn't want wine; he'd had wine when he supped. What he wanted was what he had left to Huwe's untender mercies.

Witch or spy, still he should have taken her with him. At least then he wouldn't feel this gnawing discontent, this sharp-clawed lust that refused to be slaked on other women's bodies.

The feel of her was still in his arms, along his body. No woman in his life had ever responded as she had, so swiftly and completely, her body pulsing to his touch as if she had been made for him alone. It had been like holding fire, delicate fire, and he wanted it again. He wanted more. He wanted to push deep into her and hold himself there while she spasmed around him, arms and legs clinging, hips pumping.

He groaned aloud. He had done so in his dreams, *their* dreams, but when at last he'd had his hands on her, like a fool he had left her behind. He had been so angry to find her with the Hays that all he could think was that she was somehow in league with them, and had spied on him apurpose. His sense of betrayal had made him furious with her.

Later, when he had found his men and was well away from the Hay keep, logic had returned. She wasn't a Hay; one look at her had told him that. He should have discovered why she was there, who she was, where she was from. She had said her name was Grace St. John, a name he didn't like repeating even in his own mind. It was somehow mocking, a reminder of the faith he had lost. Her clothing had been uncommonly fine, her accent strange. She spoke Latin; that alone was so unusual it raised an internal alarm. Why would a woman speak the language of the Church?

The hour had grown late while he sat downstairs, trying to work up a bit of interest in any of the women available to him, but he wasn't inclined to sleep. He paced around the chamber, thinking of clear blue eyes and a swath of shiny dark hair. She had smelled as sweet as in his dream, and her mouth . . . he closed his eyes, whispering a strained profanity under his breath as he helplessly imagined her mouth sliding down his body, closing over his shaft, and his entire body jerked in reaction.

Furiously he threw off his clothes. He was fully erect, aching. All he had to do was open the door and call for one of the women, or two, and he could ease the ache. He didn't open the door. Instead he paced, and he wondered what had happened to her. She had helped him escape, after all; had anyone seen her? He had initially thought his escape a trap, to what end he couldn't imagine since Huwe could have killed him at any time anyway, but perhaps he had overlooked something. But nothing had happened, and he had soon found his men. What had happened to her? Had she suffered for aiding him? Huwe wasn't gentle with women at the best of times; if he knew the lass had released Niall, he would kill her.

Even if no one had seen her aid him, by now Huwe would have taken her to his filthy bed, used her harshly. Niall ground his teeth. The thought of that delicate, fine-skinned body lying beneath Huwe enraged him. He would take his men and ride on the Hay keep, take her from that pigsty, care for her, gently bring her to trust and respond to him again —

The door began to creak slowly open. Niall whirled, automatically grabbing his sword, the woman forgotten as he balanced his weight on his bare feet and began the lethal swing of the blade.

Pure blue eyes peeked around the door. They flared wide in alarm as she saw the naked warrior and the shining blade whistling toward her, but she didn't scream. Instead she ducked, dropping to the floor, and at the last split second Niall deflected his aim so that the blade bit deep into the edge of the door just above where her head had been.

Cursing viciously in every language he knew, Niall worked the blade free of the wood and leaned down, gripping her arm and dragging her on her bottom into the bedchamber. She gasped, and then somehow she turned in his grasp, her legs whipping out. One dainty foot hooked behind his ankle, the other foot kicked hard at his knee, and he went down on his back. His body reacted even before he landed, flowing into the momentum, tucking, rolling, and with a lithe backward flip he came to his feet in a perfectly balanced crouch, sword in his hand.

She was still sitting on the floor, glaring at him, her skirts above her knees. He glowered down at her in silence for a moment, then with very deliberate movements walked to the table and laid the sword on it. Calmly he wrapped his plaid about his hips and turned back to face her.

She hadn't moved. Her gaze jerked up to his, and with primitive satisfaction he realized where she had been looking.

"If ye wished to see my arse, lass, ye had only to ask," he said rather mildly, considering he was so furious with her for nearly causing him to kill her that his hands ached to give her a good shaking. He approached her, reaching over her head to slam the door and flip the bar into place, then he leaned down and hauled her to her feet, standing her before him. "Now. How in hell did ye get here?"

"I stole a horse and rode," she replied, lifting her chin.

His brows lifted. "So ye speak English as well as Latin. What other accomplishments have ye?"

"French," she said readily enough. "And Greek."

"Then we may converse in any of four languages," he observed in French, as if to test her. "Given that, there should be no misunderstandings between us."

"No, there should not," she said in the same language.

He reverted to English. "Then perhaps you will tell me now how you evaded my guards and come to be in my castle, in my bedchamber."

She squared her shoulders, facing him as steadily as if he weren't more than a foot taller and easily twice her weight. "I freed you from Huwe's dungeon," she stated. "I am alone, and have no home. I came to ask you for shelter."

"Ah." His voice was soft. "You've told me the why, but what I asked was the how."

"I came in with the whores, and hid."

His teeth ground together. "And no one saw you? Asked your cause for being here?"

"I told you, I came with the whores. My cause seemed obvious enough, given the way I'm dressed." With her hand she indicated the thin cotton garment she wore, laces loosened, the shadow of her small nipples dark against the fabric. Her hair flowed sleekly down her back, hanging below her hips.

For all the provocation of her dress, no one with eyes should have mistaken her for a whore. She had none of the look about her; her skin was too fine, her hands soft and pampered. Nor was there any vulgarity in her speech or her manner. Remembering her searing response to him, he thought she was a woman who had been well loved, not well used. But that night in the dungeon her eyes had been fierce with excitement, her awareness of him plain on her face. Tonight she was guarded, wary, despite the way she had looked at his nakedness.

There were depths and shadows in her eyes that made him wonder what she had left unsaid. A simple request for shelter? No. She had watched him for months, caused his capture, then conveniently rescued him from the dungeon. There must be a deeper purpose behind her actions, and he knew he could not risk trusting her.

His loins throbbed. He wanted to toss her onto the bed and sink himself into her. He wanted it with a ferocity that knotted his gut. He knew what it was like, knew how she felt beneath him, how she moaned with that little catch in her throat as he slowly pushed all his swollen length into her. He knew it with his mind; he wanted to know it with his flesh.

But because he wanted her so violently, he didn't dare relax his own guard.

He unbarred the door and opened it, bellowing Sim's name, then stood watching her while the castle came awake and running feet thundered up the stairs. Sim arrived gasping, clutching his sword, and behind him were ten more men.

"Aye?" Sim fought for breath, relieved at seeing Niall standing there unhurt and apparently unalarmed.

Niall opened the door wider, allowing them to see the woman standing in the middle of his bedchamber. "Put her in a bedchamber and post two guards at the door. If ye canna keep her out, perhaps ye can keep her in."

Sim gawked at her. "Wha— ?" Then he recovered and grabbed her arm.

"Mind her feet," Niall advised, stepping aside so Sim could lead her from the chamber. She went easily enough, though she gave him a long, quiet look over her shoulder. The guards thrust her into the small chamber next to his and locked her in, then two of them took up position on each side of the door.

The chamber was dark and chilly. The only light was a thin sliver of starlight coming through the narrow, cross-cut window. Grace fumbled around, searching for a candle and flint, but found nothing. If she had kept her bag with her she could have struck a match and briefly surveyed her surroundings, but she had thought it safer to leave the bag hidden.

The room was unfurnished. There weren't even rushes on the stone floor. Her skin roughened with chill bumps, and she hugged her arms.

Abruptly the door was opened, banging against the wall. One of the guards thrust a burning candle into one hand and a thick plaid into the other. Without a word he closed the door again, and she heard the massive key turning in the lock.

She dropped the plaid onto the floor and carefully shielded the flickering candle with her hand as she set it down. She looked around. The room was small, empty, but she had already discerned that.

At least she had light, and a plaid to keep her warm. She was in Creag Dhu. Sighing, she wrapped herself in the plaid and lay down on the hard floor. Things could have been worse.

Chapter 22

Grace woke the next morning to the sound of the key grating in the lock. She sat up in her plaid nest, pushing her hair out of her face. She had merely dozed for most of the night, until fatigue had finally taken its toll and toward dawn she had finally slept. Niall stood in the doorway watching her, his face expressionless, and she rose creaking to her feet. She was stiff and sore in every muscle but her legs in particular didn't want to cooperate.

"Come wi' me," he said, holding out his hand, and she limped to the door. She reflected that if he had only said those same words the night in Huwe's dungeon, she wouldn't now be aching all over.

He led her to his chamber, ushering her inside with a big, warm hand on the small of her back. A fire leaped merrily in the big fireplace, dispelling the early-morning chill. A large round wooden tub had been placed before the fire, and steam rose gently from the water that filled it.

"For you," he said, indicating the tub. "For all ye knocked my feet from under me last night, I saw ye moved with care. Ye've a sore arse, I suspect."

She took a deep breath, staring at that wonderful hot water. "I do."

"Then get ye in the water, lass, afore it cools."

He reached out and untied the scarf from about her waist. Grace slapped his hand, backing away. "I can undress myself," she said warily. "But I won't do it with you in the room."

Those expressive black brows rose. "Ye saw me naked," he pointed out. "And it isna as if there's no been any intimacy between us."

She flushed. Having a sword swung at her head the night before had distracted her from the embarrassment she expected to feel, but now he'd been kind enough to remind her. "That was a mistake," she said evenly. "It won't happen again."

"I'm no of the same opinion," he said softly, his gaze sliding down her body. Remembering how thin the kirtle was, she turned away from him, her blush growing hotter. He chuckled, and though she didn't hear him approach he was suddenly right behind her, so close she could feel his heat. With one fingertip he lightly stroked the side of her neck, the tender underside of her jaw.

"I'll give ye privacy to bathe," he murmured. "Then Alice will bring your porridge, and we'll talk."

Grace shivered as he left the room. The first two things sounded wonderful; the last terrified her. Talk? Seduction had been in his voice, in the small touches, the way he had stood so close to her. For whatever reason he hadn't tried to take her to bed last night — anger, surprise, suspicion — this morning he had evidently decided that reason no longer held sway.

He wanted her. The thought made her knees watery as she quickly undressed and slid into the hot water, moaning aloud as the heat soaked into her sore muscles. Underlying all his suspicious questions was that sharp animal awareness between them, forged during months of shared dreaming. He had been fully aroused during that devastating kiss. He had the same memories she did, of those dreams. Just as she knew how it was to lie beneath him, he knew how it was to mount her. Yin and yang, she knew the inward thrust that stretched her around his erection, he knew the hot, moist inner slide and clasping. She knew the hardness of his hands; he, the softness of her breasts.

How could she resist that? For Ford's sake, how could she not?

She distracted herself by vigorously washing, first her hair and then the rest of herself. Just as she finished, the door opened and a sturdy gray-haired woman came in, carrying a wooden platter on which rested a covered bowl, a spoon, and a cup.

"Such hair!" she exclaimed, hurrying to the table and setting the platter on it. Lifting a heavy ewer, she came to the side of the tub. "My name is Alice; I manage the household for Lord Niall. Stand up, then, lass, and I'll pour the clean water o'er ye."

Grace felt her face heat again, but she stood up out of the protective water. Alice poured the water over her head, rinsing away the last of the soap. She was given a sheet of linen with which to dry herself, and another, smaller one to wrap about her head.

Alice made a clicking sound with her tongue. "Ye need meat on yer bones, lass. I'll keep ye fed, now ye're here. Sit ye down, now, and eat while the parritch is hot."

Wrapped in the linen cloth, Grace sat down on the bench and dipped the spoon into the porridge. It tasted nothing like the oatmeal she had eaten before, being rich with butter and milk, and having a salty taste. She ate all of it, and drank the water in the cup. "That was wonderful." She sighed. After a year's absence, her appetite seemed to be making a reappearance.

Alice had sat quietly while Grace ate, but now she bustled into action. Soon Grace found herself dressed in a soft linen smock, looser than the cotton kirtle and with short sleeves, and then a plain brown overdress was dropped over her head.

Clean stockings were provided, and ill-fitting leather shoes that had been made to fit either foot. Her hand-sewn moccasins were set aside to be cleaned. Then Alice set to work on Grace's hair, sitting her down on the bench before the fire and slowly drawing a wooden comb through the wet strands. "What's yer name, lass?" she asked comfortably.

"Grace." The motion of the comb in her hair was soothing. Grace's eyelids drooped almost shut.

"Ye've lovely hair, so thick and shiny and smooth. Takes a bit to dry, though, aye?"

"I braid it while it's still wet, sometimes," she said in answer.

The door opened behind her, and she recognized the booted footsteps. "I'll finish, Alice," Niall said, taking the comb from her hand. Alice took the wet linens and the platter with her when she left.

"Turn," Niall said, and Grace swiveled on the bench, turning her other side to the fire. He was as skilled as Alice with the comb, sliding his muscular forearm under her hair and lifting it, letting the heat of the fire dry it more evenly.

Her heartbeat had speeded when he entered. Though she sat quietly while he combed her hair, the sedative effect had vanished. Instead that feeling of being hypersensitive had seized her again, tightening her skin, sending twinges through her nerve endings.

Panic began to tighten her stomach. She had been braced for a full-scale seduction. This subtle gentling was far more dangerous to her resolve.

"Ye asked for food yesterday, in the kitchens," Niall said conversationally. "Ye were weak wi' hunger, having not eaten for two days, ye said. Then ye vanished, and no one saw ye for hours, until ye came into my chamber. Where were ye?"

"I told you last night," she said, her tone as even and without heat as his. "I hid, and I fell asleep."

"Where did ye hide?"

"In an alcove." She turned her head to glance at him over her shoulder. "Or did you think I turned myself into a bat and perched in your belfry?"

"Creag Dhu doesna have a belfry," he said in amusement. "Tell me where ye've been for two days, if ye left Hay Keep hard on my heels. Why did ye come here? Creag Dhu is for broken men and outlaws, not lovely lasses with hands soft as a bairn's."

"I couldn't escape right away," Grace explained. "I had to hide in the granary for several hours, until everyone slept again. I stole a horse, but there was fog . . . I got lost." She turned around again, this time to glare at him. "If you hadn't left me behind, I wouldn't have gotten lost."

"Sit still," he commanded, turning her back.

"Ye'll pull your hair." The comb resumed its strokes through her hair. "As for why I didna bring ye with me, the reason is the question I just asked, and ye didna answer. Why did ye come *here?* Last night ye said for food, and shelter, but when ye got here ye didna even try to ask those things of me."

She was silent, searching for a plausible answer. She couldn't say because of the dreams, because for the most part they had been so blatantly sexual in nature, and yet she had rebuffed him not an hour ago.

"Also," he continued softly, "there was other shelter, closer than two days' ride, if that is truly what ye wanted. And once ye were here, all ye had to do was ask for me, instead of tricking your way into the castle. If ye thought I would refuse ye, lass, then your insistence on coming here is no verra logical. I still have the same question. Why Creag Dhu?"

He was relentless, and he hadn't missed any of the holes in her logic. She hadn't come to this time expecting everyone to be ignorant barbarians, easily outwitted, but still she was dismayed by the sophisticated nature of his reasoning. Niall wasn't at the disadvantage here; she was, tripped up by her own actions. He was right; simply approaching the gates and asking for him would have been far less suspicious.

She bowed her head, looking at her hands

twisting together in her lap. She fingered her wedding ring, and for once deliberately tried to bring up Ford's image in her mind. She needed him now, sitting here before the fire with Black Niall's hands gentle in her hair. But it was difficult to concentrate, and she couldn't pull the details together.

"I was too embarrassed," she blurted.

The comb paused. "Were ye, now?" The deep voice was little more than a murmur. He slid his hand around her neck, under her hair, and she jumped in surprise. He crooned something soothing in Gaelic, and his thumb began to rub the nape of her neck. "Because I gave ye pleasure, in the dungeon? I'll admit to a bit of surprise, but then I greatly enjoyed it. A man likes for a lass to shiver and moan in his arms."

She shivered now, in response to both the memory and the caress of his thumb on her neck. He moved his hand just a little, so that he rubbed and massaged the cords that joined neck and shoulder, and she bit back a moan. Desire pooled deep in her belly, between her legs, and her breasts tightened. It was a dangerous man who knew the sensitivity of a woman's neck, where a caress was like a bolt of lightning through her body. A touch on her breast was more intimate — but a touch on her neck was more seductive. Niall knew well what he was doing.

She tried to control her breathing, which

was coming in short, erratic spurts. "I haven't — I mean, there's been only . . . we had just met!"

He laughed, the soft sound totally male and self-confident. "That isna true. Ye've been in my bed many times."

She gathered herself, tried to inject a note of firmness into her tone. "Those were dreams, not reality."

"Were they not? When I wake wi' my seed spurting from me, it feels verra damn real to me." The words were full of masculine wryness.

Her breath caught on a surge of yearning so abrupt and intense it felt like pain. She wanted to feel him come inside her, wanted to feel that powerful body surge and convulse while she held him close, wanted to watch his face.

"Ye like that thought, do ye? Your wee nipples ha' gone as hard as berries."

She wasn't the only one aroused; she could hear it in the slight thickening of his accent. She closed her eyes and for a moment the only sound was that of their breathing, fast and erratic.

The comb was tossed aside and he stepped over the bench to stand in front of her. His hands slid down her arms, lifting her to her feet. She stared at the pulse throbbing in the base of his strong throat.

"Come lie wi' me on the bed," he murmured, rubbing her back now, each caress subtly urging her closer and closer to him. Her nipples tingled in anticipation. Closer . . . their bodies touched, and she swallowed a gasp.

"No — I . . ." Her disjointed refusal trailed off, lost as his arms closed around her, lifted her on her toes to bring them together more firmly.

"I willna hurt ye." His breath was hot on her ear as he nibbled the lobe, and licked the small hollow beneath.

She knew he likely would, though not deliberately. She had seen him naked, though she had tried not to dwell on it; she had *felt* him in their dreams. His size wasn't limited to his height. To her dismay, the thought of such intimate discomfort wasn't the deterrent she would have preferred.

Her hands were flattened against his chest, and she had to clench them into fists to keep them from sliding around his neck. Even that small a surrender would be the one step too far, because they were both trembling. Amazed, she felt the quivering of that strong body, the result of fierce need tightly leashed.

"Lass . . ." His mouth slid across the underside of her jaw, planting small kisses as it went. His hands knew no boundaries; they cupped her bottom, lifting her to even closer contact. His erection pushed hard against the juncture of her thighs.

Ford.

In despair Grace wrenched herself away and

fled to the other side of the table, a flimsy barrier he could dispose of with one flick of his hand if he chose, but she knew he wouldn't force her. Seduce her, yes, with his devastatingly successful technique of alternating subtlety with boldness. He wasn't a man who found force either desirable or necessary.

He was very still, watching her from beneath heavy lids.

She clenched her hands together, turning her wedding ring around and around, using the small symbol to remind her of both loyalty and betrayal. The ring was so loose now she worried about losing it, and had developed the habit of checking to make certain it was still there.

He was waiting.

"I'm a widow," she said, forcing out the word. Her throat constricted, and she swallowed. "My husband is the only man I've ever —" She stopped, and couldn't say more. She didn't need to.

"Did ye love him, then?"

She swallowed again at his swift understanding. "Yes, I do." The words were almost inaudible.

He walked around the table. She stood her ground, though she wanted to flee. Niall cupped her face, a hint of a smile on his firmly molded lips, understanding in his dark eyes. " 'Tis new to ye, wanting another man. Ye think it a betrayal of him that yer body, which has known only him, should quicken against mine."

"It is," she whispered.

"And yet ye came here, knowing how it is between us. Your body is ready. Your mind needs a bit more time." He leaned down and kissed her forehead. "I'll not force ye, lass, but I'll no leave ye for long in an empty bed. Ye'll learn my kisses, and my touch, while your thoughts settle."

She thought he would kiss her then. Her lips parted in anticipation of the pressure, the taste, the wildness. Instead he dropped his hand and strolled to the door, his tall, muscular body as graceful as a dancer's. "I would like to think you came to Creag Dhu because of me, and what we both want." He spoke now in precise English, the easy burr of his Scots accent gone. "But gratitude did not make me a fool, nor does lust. Until I know your true reason for being here, you'll not be allowed freedom within my castle. Someone will be with you at all times during the day, and at night you will be locked in either your chamber —" He paused, black eyes glittering. "Or mine."

Chapter 23

It was impossible to do any searching at all. Alice was with her every moment of the day, except when she used the garderobe. Rather than intensify Niall's suspicions, Grace willingly followed in Alice's busy footsteps, listening to the chatter and increasing her understanding of both the Scots dialect and a little of Gaelic, as her mind began to associate pronunciation of a few words with the spelling she knew.

The advantage of being with Alice was that the woman's duties carried her all over the castle. Without having to sneak about, Grace quickly became familiar with the different rooms. She tried to think where the most secure hiding place for the Treasure would be; Creag Dhu had a dungeon, much larger than the one at Hay Keep, but the dungeon was such an obvious choice she doubted it would be correct. Nevertheless she would have liked to inspect it, but could hardly ask Alice for a tour.

The wine cellar was an interesting possibility, dark and cool, with casks and racks that could conceal a hiding place. "Are there any hidden tunnels?" she asked Alice. "A way to escape if the castle is under attack?"

"Aye," Alice said readily enough. "There's a passage leads to the sea, should it be needed, but my thinking is that 'tis safer in the castle than without. Lord Niall has built the best defenses in Scotland," she boasted. "We could withstand a siege for a year or more."

As she followed Alice about, Grace was struck by how natural everything seemed. Of course, she had the advantage of her education in medieval languages and culture so that she was at least technically familiar with much about the normal lifestyle, but not even when she first awoke was she disoriented. It was as if her mind had neatly slotted itself into the time. Why, yes, of course meat was salted for preservation, and milk had to be churned, and herbs had to be scattered on the floor rushes to keep them sweet-smelling. Her taste buds had adjusted immediately to the plain fare, accepting that there was little seasoning to be had. When Alice sat her down with a needle and a linen sheet that needed mending, Grace didn't even think of how easy it would be to go to a department store and simply buy new sheets instead of mending the old ones. Instead she took pains to make tiny, even stitches.

She had made a mistake in her clothing, she realized. Cotton wouldn't make an appearance in Europe for quite some time, and velvet was reserved for royalty. No wonder Huwe had been impressed by her velvet gown! He had probably thought her a foreign princess, and anticipated a huge ransom for her return. Luckily her cotton kirtle was unbleached and the finish wasn't shiny, so at least it didn't look rich. Since Grace obviously wasn't a Scot, her strange clothing hadn't elicited any suspicion from Alice, who had taken the garment to be washed, or from the woman who washed it. She would keep the velvet surcoat hidden, though. She wanted to check her hiding place and make certain the bag was still safely tucked away, but she reasoned that if it had been found she would have heard, and it was more likely to remain hidden if she didn't attract attention to the area.

Niall trained with his men all day, or hunted, or patrolled the area around the castle. If he returned for a noon meal, Grace didn't see him. She heard the clash of swords in the courtyard but didn't go to watch. The sight of his muscled body, sweaty and half naked, would not help shore her resolve.

She hadn't known lust could be so powerful, so consuming. Even though Alice kept her busy, her thoughts went time and again to that expert, devilishly knowing touch on her neck, to his kiss, the silky brush of his long hair against her face. He was so wonderfully barbaric and untamed, yet astonishingly well educated and sophisticated. She managed in his time with prior knowledge and training; she suspected he would manage as well in hers without those benefits, by the sheer determination of his character and the force of his intellect.

She tried to think of Ford, but he seemed so far away. A year had passed, a year in which she had had none of his things to touch and hold and weep over. She hadn't dared let herself think of him too much, and now when she needed to she couldn't quite capture his face, or the quality of his voice.

It had been easier before she came back, as if the distance of time was a veil that blurred her other life now, making it seem like a dream. *This* was real, *now* was real. Niall was all too real, too vital and dominating. Everyone in the castle bowed to his wishes, obeyed his slightest command.

The men returned for the evening meal, disturbing the efficient peace of the castle with their boisterous, chaotic masculinity. There were shouts, curses, rumbling voices, the clang of swords and shields, the stomping of feet and excited barking of dogs, the sharp muskiness of male sweat. When Niall appeared all eyes went to him; he looked around and located Grace immediately, nodding his head toward the table where he sat.

She hesitated, and Alice gave her a nudge. "He wants ye to sit wi' him," the older woman said, stating the obvious. "Best do as he says."

Grace hadn't had any thought of disobeying, only a reluctance to be so close to him again. She wanted to, too much, and there was where the danger lay. With slow steps she walked across the great hall to where the head table was set. Niall stood beside his chair, waiting for her.

He had either dunked his head in a barrel of water or taken time to bathe, for his long hair was wet and sleeked back. His simple linen shirt was clean, his plaid belted about his lean waist. A knife was thrust into his belt, and another into his right boot. The huge claymore was slung in a scabbard over his back; he removed that, hanging it on the back of his chair. Even here, in his own hall, he kept his fearsome weapons to hand.

Looking around, Grace saw that all the men did. Niall had called them broken men and outlaws; they were hard men who had lived hard lives, yet they chose to be governed by Niall. They were the castoffs of clans all over Scotland, but here they had formed their own clan, with Niall the unelected but undisputed chieftain, and he had transformed them into a prime fighting unit with pride and discipline. These men would willingly die for him.

A smaller chair had been placed beside Niall's. Those were the only two chairs there; everyone else sat on benches. Grace was burningly aware of all the curious glances coming her way, especially from the men. The women of the household had gotten accustomed to her during the day; some of *their* glances were hostile.

Niall cupped her elbow as he seated her, his hand very warm on her bare arm. "Ye asked Alice about the escape tunnel," he said, his tone mild, his eyes sharp.

Grace blinked in amazement. She had been by Alice's side almost every minute of the day; she was certain Niall had had no opportunity to speak to her since the morning. "Yes, I did," she admitted without pause. "But how did you know?"

"I was displeased that ye managed to enter Creag Dhu on false pretenses, and no one questioned ye or even saw ye for the rest of the day. Nothing ye do now goes unobserved." He leaned back in his chair as the meal was set before him, roasted pork, turnips, fresh bread, cheese, and stewed apples. Taking the knife from his belt, he carved several slices of tender ham from the haunch and placed them on the trencher set on the table between him and Grace.

"Have ye a knife?" he asked Grace.

She thought of the Swiss Army knife in the bag she had hidden, and shook her head. Niall drew the smaller dagger from his boot and surveyed it, then thrust it back into his boot. "I dinna think I trust ye with something so wicked sharp. I'll cut your meat for ye."

"I wouldn't stab you," she said, shocked.

One eyebrow lifted. "No? When first I met ye, ye were with the Hays."

"You know I was captured! You could hear what they were saying."

"It could have been arranged, aye? I was half smothered with plaids, as ye remember; I couldna see anything. Ye might have been captured, or ye might have been with them from the start. Ye released me from the dungeon, then followed me here to Creag Dhu, knowing I wouldna cast ye out. Now ye've asked about the tunnel. Do ye plan to tell the Hays, and let them into my castle to murder us in our beds?"

Furious, Grace turned on him. "Huwe already had you at his mercy. Why would he scheme to help you escape, when he could kill you and be done with it?"

"As to why, if Huwe wanted only to kill me then, aye, he could ha' done it then. But he wants Creag Dhu as well, and he kens well he couldna take it from without. To take the castle, he must find a way inside." Expertly he cut a small piece of meat and offered it to her.

She ignored it. "I only asked about a tunnel because I was curious. I didn't even ask where it is, as you should know since you've obviously had my every word reported to you!"

Niall eyed her flushed face, and saw that her eyes had gone as dark as a stormy sea. "And will continue to do so," he said. He offered the meat again. “Eat, lass. A good wind would blow ye away.”

Grace took the meat with her fingers and neatly popped it into her mouth, then deliberately turned her head from him to watch the others. He paid no attention to her ire or her efforts to ignore him. He fed himself and her, alternating between the two of them, and patiently holding each bite until she took it. She could see people watching them, and good manners prompted her not to make a public scene.

His consideration undermined her efforts to remain angry. He didn’t try to force her to talk, didn’t belabor his point; having made it, he was content. She knew now how closely she was watched, which had been his intention.

His leg pressed against hers. Instantly she moved away, then glanced at him to see if the contact had been deliberate. It was. He was watching her, his gaze steady. He took a drink of spiced wine, then put the cup in her hand so she too could drink. “Do ye remember a time,” he said in a low voice, “when I was sitting on a stool, and ye came to me, and I lifted ye astride —”

Her hand shook, and she hastily set the cup down before she spilled the wine. She didn’t reply, but the hot color in her cheeks gave him his answer.

“How can it be?” he wondered.

She shook her head, and whispered, "I don't know."

"At times I wasna asleep, and still I could feel ye watching me." He lifted her hand, holding it in his palm and tracing his fingertip over the slender bones that fanned in the back of her hand.

"Sometimes when I was awake, I thought I heard you speaking." She couldn't look at him as she made the confession. The words felt torn out of her, a reluctant acknowledgment of the awareness between them that had tormented her for months, and tempted her now. It would be so easy to turn her hand in his, lace their fingers together. He would know what she wanted. He wouldn't ask any questions, simply lead her up the stairs to his chamber.

She stared at the saltcellar. She had once had this unspoken intimacy with Ford; they had known each other so well that a lot of times words hadn't been needed. When he died, she thought that wonder, that sense of belonging, had died with him and she would never know it again. How could it be duplicated? They had forged that mutual knowledge during years of dating and marriage, of making love, of quiet talks in the darkness as they lay together, of working and laughing and worrying, of *living* together.

She couldn't feel it now, with Niall. Her imagination was working overtime again, making her think the link was there when it couldn't be. From the moment he had walked out of that dungeon cell until now, the total time she had spent with him was less than two hours. He couldn't possibly know what she wanted, nor could she predict what he would do.

"All ye have to do is take my hand," he murmured, watching her, drawing her gaze. "My bed is big, and warm, and ye won't be alone."

A chill ran over her, and her eyes went blank with shock. No. It wasn't possible.

"Such big, sad eyes. What do ye see, lass, when ye look through me as if I'm not here, when ye go away in your mind? Does Huwe hold someone ye love, a child perhaps? Does he force ye to do his bidding?"

Her throat felt tight. "No," she managed. "I have no one, and I'm not in league with Huwe."

An expression passed over his face, tightening his flesh over the chiseled bone structure, giving him a remote, austere expression as old as the one in his eyes. So must the ancient saints have looked, stripped down to the essentials of character by the burdens they had borne. "Tell me," he said. "And I will aid ye."

How matter-of-fact he was about assuming yet another responsibility! His friends had been tortured and burned to death, he was excommunicated and under a death sentence should he venture outside Scotland; as a young man he had been made Guardian of the Treasure, his entire life dedicated to and dominated by the burden he had accepted. He had created a disciplined fighting force out of loners and misfits and outlaws, then extended his protection to the crofters and villagers living around Creag Dhu. The burdens he had accepted onto those broad shoulders would have crushed most men, but not even knowing how he could help her, he offered to assume responsibility for her, too. Her throat tightened even more, this time with unshed tears. Silently she shook her head.

He sighed as he stood, lifting her to her feet too. "Ye will tell me," he assured her, walking with her to the stairs. At a nod from him, two men rose from their benches and followed. "Ye will tell me, willingly or no. Ye'll come to my bed, too, and lie soft and yielding beneath me. I'm a verra patient man, lass, but never forget I hold all the power here."

Her mouth went dry. Was that a warning that he suspected she knew about the Treasure and wanted to find it? Her heart hammered painfully against her breastbone. She was struggling with him on both a personal and an impersonal plane, and uncannily he sensed it. Viewing him as a man, she desired him with a ferocity that terrified her; seeing him as the Guardian, she feared him. Defeat on either level could destroy her.

He opened the door to the small chamber where she had been locked the night before, and ushered her inside. She paused in surprise. Sometime during the day a small bed, not much more than a cot, had been moved into the chamber. A small fire crackled in the hearth, dispelling the chill, and two thick candles appeared to have been lit only moments before, for the tallow was only now beginning to melt down the columns. To her relief there was also a chamber pot, and a small basin and ewer of water.

"Thank you," she said, turning to him. The small chamber felt almost luxurious to her after some of the places she had slept in this past year.

"I dinna intend to freeze ye to death," he replied, his brows quirking in amusement. He smoothed his hand up her arm. "I like ye warm and tender."

He kissed her, his arms folding around her and molding her to his body. Grace gripped his biceps, concentrating on holding tight to her self-control even though she could feel the foundation of resolve crumbling beneath her. He slanted his firm mouth so that it fit perfectly to the soft contours of her lips, and despite her best intentions her mouth parted under the pressure. His tongue gently penetrated, cajoling rather than demanding.

Desire clawed at her, hot and sharp. She jerked her mouth from his and buried her face against his chest, breathing hard. The question of loyalty to Ford aside, how could she even consider making love with Niall? She intended to be in this time only for as long as it took her to find the Treasure and discover if she could somehow use the mysterious Power herself, to stop Parrish and the Foundation. If she could, she would steal the Treasure and return to her own time, leaving Niall behind.

Success or failure, she would not be staying. Any relationship she had with Niall would only be casual — God, she thought, could making love with Niall ever be considered *casual?* — and even were the circumstances different she wasn't a woman who had casual affairs. Perhaps he would be content with only sex, but she knew she wouldn't be; for her, making love was a commitment, something she couldn't make.

He cradled her so carefully in his arms, rocking slightly back and forth as he stroked her back, that she wanted to weep. She had never met a man like him before, and never would again; he was extraordinary in any century. Just for a moment she gave in to temptation and slid her hands around him, flattening her palms on his back and absorbing the vital heat and power of his body. His muscles subtly flexed with every breath he took, and his heart beat strong and steady under her ear.

"When a woman has been wed," he said low, into her hair, "she becomes accustomed to her man in bed beside her at night, and if aught happens to him, she loses not only her husband but that comfort of no being alone in the dark. I offer ye that, lass. I'll hold ye close against the dark and the chill, give ye the comfort of my body."

She almost groaned aloud against him, aching from temptation. To sleep with his arms around her, to wake and be able to reach out and touch him, stroke his hairy chest, slide her hand down the flatness of his belly, hold his penis while he slept and feel it soft in her hand — how had he known the way she hungered for that, for the intimacy that went beyond sex? He was in her mind again, reading her with uncanny accuracy.

"No," she whispered, and knew that she wanted to say yes.

His lips brushed her forehead. "I wish ye a good night, then. If ye decide ye need comforting in the night, ye've only to knock on the door, and the guards will bring ye to me."

When he was gone, Grace pressed her shaking hands to her lips. She was walking a tightrope between passion and danger, but the knowledge didn't lessen the need. If she gave in to him, would that incline him toward a greater indulgence than he would normally show, if he discovered her true aim?

No, it would not. She knew from the documents that Black Niall was ruthless in his protection of the Treasure. Perhaps he had merely meant he held all the authority here, but he had said "power," and that could be a warning. Being a woman, and moreover a woman he wanted to bed, wouldn't protect her if he should discover she was after the Treasure. He would kill her, and she knew it.

Chapter 24

The next day dawned cool and rainy, the mountaintops to the east lost in mist. There was no hot bath waiting for Grace that morning, only a basin of cold water and a hasty scrubbing in front of the fire. Breakfast was porridge again, and then Alice swept her up in another whirlwind of activity. Then men trained in the courtyard despite the rain — "Lord Niall says trouble doesna wait for a fair day," Alice explained — and clotted the rushes with mud when they all tromped in, soaking wet and grousing.

Alice warmed them up from the inside with *colcannon,* a cabbage stew, and the men occupied themselves with games of dice, flirting with the serving women, sharpening their swords and daggers, and swapping tales that grew both louder and taller. Not all the men were there; Niall and ten others patrolled around Creag Dhu.

The rain dripped monotonously, and the dark gray sky made torches necessary for light. Grace yawned, thinking that a rainy day was better suited for napping in front of a fire than anything else. She wasn't the only one yawning; a few of the men sought the darker corners and nodded off. Others' thoughts turned to bed for a different reason. Grace saw hairy masculine arms wrapping about plump waists here and there, and soon there were noticeably fewer women going about their work.

They were all startled by the shouts from the gate, the sudden alarm. Sim had Alice on his knee, teasingly pinching her bottom and trying to cajole her away from her work; he jumped upright at the shouts, dumping Alice on the floor. His hand closed over his sword and he was running before his plaid had settled around his knees.

Alice scrambled up and ran to the huge ten-foot-high double doors that opened into the great hall. Her heart in her throat, Grace ran too. Niall was outside the safety of the gates; had something happened to him?

The scene was chaotic, confusing. A crowd of people rushed toward the gates, yelling in alarm, their heads covered against the pelting rain. Behind them was the sullen red glow of burning huts. "The Hay!" they howled. "The Hay!" Men surged on horseback, waving axes and swords.

"Open the gates!" Sim yelled.

Men roughly pushed Alice and Grace aside as they rushed to their posts in a well-ordered drill, some going to the top of the walls with their crossbows, some to the stable to get the horses, others falling in behind Sim.

Grace ran into the courtyard, heedless of the rain. The Hays were attacking, and Niall was somewhere outside. Had he and his men been attacked by a much larger force? Her chest clenched, panic welling. No. *No!* She couldn't bear it again, couldn't lose —

Alice grabbed her arm, jerking her around. "Come inside! Arrows —"

The gates were open, the pounding crowd only yards away. Grace gave them an agonized look as Alice dragged her toward the doors, and her gaze fell on the beefy man who ran in front of all the others, his plaid pulled over his head. She saw him grin suddenly, saw his rotted teeth, and she jerked away from Alice, running forward as she screamed, "Close the gates! It's a trick!"

Sim's head jerked around and he gaped at her, then her words sank in and he spun back toward the gates. "Close the gates!" he roared, rushing forward. The guards began pushing the massive doors closed but it was too late. The Hays poured into the narrow gatehouse, shoving the gates open. Swords and axes were pulled from beneath plaids, and the "victims" attacked.

"Run!" Alice screamed, pulling on Grace's arm again and hauling her back inside the great hall. Women were screaming and rushing about, excited dogs barking and leaping about their feet, getting in the way. "The doors!" Alice gasped, and she and Grace turned to throw their weight against them, closing them so the massive bar could be dropped in place. Alice outweighed Grace by fifty pounds or more, and she got the right door closed first, then darted over to aid Grace. They almost made it.

Heavy bodies thudded against the doors, bursting them wide, and the fighting spilled into the hall. The impact knocked Grace to the floor. Alice ducked under a slashing blade and grabbed Grace again, bodily lifting her and shoving her down the hallway toward the kitchens. "Run!" she screamed again, and Grace lifted her skirts and ran.

From in front of them came thundering feet and the rattle of metal. Grace skidded to a halt just outside the larder. "They're in here, too!" she yelled, trying to reverse her direction. Then the door to the larder slammed open and Niall came through it at a dead run, claymore in hand, black hair flying around his head and his eyes like murder. He was followed by the ten men who had been on patrol with him.

Grace flattened herself against the wall to keep from being smashed to the floor. Niall didn't even glance at her as he ran past but he barked to Alice, "Get to safety!" Then with a roar he ran into the hall and threw himself into the battle, pushing Hays back a few steps with the sheer force of his size and the swing of his blade. Screaming, his men followed him.

"Come!" Alice screamed to make herself heard over the din of battle, and she dashed into the kitchen without looking behind her.

Grace started to follow, then looked at the larder. That had to be the secret passageway, for otherwise how could Niall and his men have gotten back into the castle? She hesitated only a second, and plunged into the cool, dark room. There was a small store of candles just inside the door and she grabbed one, her hands shaking as she took up the stone and flint lying beside the candles and struck a spark to light the candle. When the small flame flickered to life, she hastily shut the larder door and looked around.

A whole section of the back wall had been swung open. Blackness yawned beyond the opening.

Her breath came in quick spurts as she approached the open section. This might lead to the Treasure's hiding place; it might not. But this was the first time she had been alone to search, and in the chaos of battle it would be some time before she was missed. She thought of Niall hurling himself into the fight with terrifying abandon and she bit her bottom lip until blood welled. He might be hurt, even killed —

And there was nothing she could do.

Here was her chance, likely her only chance, to accomplish what she had come to Creag Dhu for.

The deafening roar of battle was only slightly muffled in here. Men screamed, in fury and in agony, sword clashed on sword, wood splintered. She had come into this time in the middle of a battle; perhaps she was meant to leave during one, too.

Niall. Her heart whispered the name, and her hands shook, making the candle flame dance. Then she thought of Ford and closed her eyes, trying to see his face. The only image that came to mind was the last one, his eyes blank in death as he toppled over.

A wordless sound of pain vibrated in her throat, and she stepped through the opening.

The air was immediately colder, danker, and had a faint smell of salt water. Steep, narrow stairs plunged straight down into complete darkness. She took them cautiously, guarding her candle so the flame didn't go out.

Everyone knew of the secret passage, she thought. Was it likely Niall would hide the Treasure there?

But where there was one passageway, perhaps there were others.

She reached the bottom of the stairway and found herself in a narrow, rock-lined tunnel. The smell of the sea was stronger there, and she could hear the muted thunder of crashing waves. The passageway was a short one, then, leading straight out to the rocky shoreline.

Her supposition was right. Though she moved slowly, she reached the end of the tunnel within two minutes. A jumble of boulders before her almost completely filled the opening, so that only a sliver of gray, rain-washed light filtered through.

No Treasure there.

She retraced her steps, and began to climb the treacherous stairs. She held the candle in her right hand and put her left against the wall to steady herself. She had never had claustrophobia, but the inky darkness seemed to clutch at her feet, trying to pull her down. She shivered and moved closer to the wall, and her fingers slid over a section of rock that jutted out a quarter inch from the other stones.

She stopped, lifting the candle higher to enlarge the pool of light. She could hear her own breath eerily echo as she examined the section that was out of alignment. Could there be a secret passage within a secret passage?

She pressed around the edges of the rock, feeling foolish but doing it anyway. Nothing happened. She held the candle nearer to see if there was a minute seam in the mortar, or if she was wasting her time.

The mortar was cracked, but when she examined the rock around that particular section she found hairline cracks in that mortar, too. There were no hinges that she could see, no way of opening the door — if it was a door.

Archaeology and translations had taught her to approach the unknown logically. If this were a hidden door, there had to be an easy way to open it, easy because a method that took a lot of time or trouble would increase one's chances of being discovered in the act of opening it. A hidden door would be silent and fast.

The easiest method would be to put an opening mechanism behind one of the other stones, but given the steepness and narrowness of the steps, it stood to reason almost anyone going up or down them would put a balancing hand against the wall, making it too likely a hidden door would be opened by accident.

She climbed a few steps and surveyed the section of rock from above. Yes, a rectangular section definitely jutted out a fraction of an inch. Where could a mechanism be hidden? It had to be someplace accessible, easily reached.

Easily reached. Grace's eyes widened. In this time, she was of average height for a woman, with most of the men she had seen in the range of five-five to five-eight, with very few taller than five-ten. Sim was a large man, perhaps reaching six feet; only Niall was taller. Niall was six-foot-four. He could reach higher than anyone else in the castle.

She looked up. If this was a door, and there was a mechanism to open it hidden behind one of these rocks, logically it would be behind one of the higher rocks, one that only Niall could comfortably reach.

She stretched on tiptoe, pressing every rock she could reach. The rectangular section remained stubbornly stationary and rocklike. There was a flat stone that looked promising, being slightly smoother than those surrounding it, but it was half a foot out of her reach. She climbed another step and leaned to the side, balancing precariously on the edge of the step as she stretched, her fingers scrabbling on the rock, trying to pull herself just a fraction of an inch farther. She almost lost her balance and quickly flattened herself against the wall, gasping in fright. A fall down these steps would break her neck. Cautiously she lifted herself on her toes again, perched on the very edge of the step. Her extended fingers couldn't quite brush the edge of the rock.

Swearing in frustration under her breath, Grace sat down on the step and removed her left shoe. Once more she stood on tiptoe, stretching outward, and she slapped her shoe against the flat rock.

Silently the rectangular section slid inward, leaving a black hole in the wall.

Holding the candle before her, she leaned in, not setting a foot inside that hole until she knew what was in there.

The blackness was Stygian, swallowing the feeble light of her small candle. She could see a solid stone floor, and nothing else, not even walls.

She stepped inside, squeezing past the stone door. She waited, ready to throw herself back through the opening if the door began to close on its own, but it remained reassuringly open. Probably there was another mechanism on this side of the wall that one had to press to close the door, which she had no intention of doing.

Warily she moved forward a few feet, and made out a wall three or four yards in front of her. She turned to her left, squinting her eyes at a darker patch. She went closer, and saw that it was another door, this one made of a very dark wood, and the bar that lay through the brackets was attached like a lever on one end so it could be lifted up and swung over to unbar the door, but not removed.

A breeze from somewhere made her candle flicker, and she quickly cupped her hand around the flame to steady it. She glanced over her shoulder at the opening in the wall, but the breeze didn't seem to be coming from there. It was coming from the direction of that dark, closed door, which didn't make sense. The air must be coming in through the rock opening and swirling around the antechamber, confusing her.

Grace approached the door and tried to lift the bar, but though it was a small bar compared to the massive ones in other parts of Creag Dhu, it was heavier than it looked and she couldn't manage it with one hand. She set the candle on the floor, and seized the lever with both hands. By bracing her weight below the bar and shoving, she slowly inched it upward. The pivoting connection was smooth, but the action was incredibly difficult for so slender a bar. There was a definite mechanical click when she forced the bar straight up, and it locked in the upright position.

The door itself swung silently inward, and more stairs yawned at her feet, a stone wall on one side and black emptiness on the other. The breeze was more pronounced now, and the candle flickered wildly, almost going out. Grace crouched and cupped her hands around the flame again until it steadied, picked up the candle, and stood with one hand still held in front of it.

How much time had passed? she wondered as she went down the stairs into nothingness. Had the battle ended? Was Niall unhurt? The compulsion to turn around and return to the upper reaches of the castle stopped her with one foot poised to take another step downward. *Niall,* she thought in despair, terrified for him. He was a fearsome warrior; she had seen him fighting in skirmishes and in pitched battles, and understood why his name had struck terror into the hearts of his foes, but still he was human. He bled if cut, he bruised if struck. He could be overwhelmed, as he had been when Huwe's men had captured him.

There was nothing she could do to affect the outcome of the battle overhead. If she found the Treasure, then according to the documents for which Parrish was so willing to kill, she could affect the outcome of events in her own time. Her choice was simple, but more difficult than she had ever imagined. She had been in this time less than a week; how could Niall have so quickly become important to her?

Because she had known him much longer than a week, her inner soul whispered. She had known him for a year, through the documents given into her safekeeping, and she had been fascinated, obsessed, beguiled by him even before her world had been destroyed by two bullets. If she hadn't been so anxious to have her modem repaired so she could access files and learn more about Niall, she would have been at home when Parrish and his men came, and she too would be dead now.

She wanted to go back. Instead she went forward, step by cautious step.

"Ahhhhh!" Mouth open, screaming, Huwe rushed at Niall, claymore held over his head with both hands. For a split-second Niall jerked his attention away from the Hay clansman on the other end of his sword; Huwe was behind him, the other in front, and he had only one more second in which to keep Huwe from splitting him from gullet to arse. He ducked under the swinging sword of the Hay clansman, grabbed him by the arm, and slung him into Huwe's path. Huwe's great sword was already arcing down and it bit deep into his clansman's shoulder and neck. A great spray of blood drenched his clothes, but Huwe kept coming, his small eyes mad with rage.

"Bastard!" he howled. "Bastard!" He lifted the sword again and brought it whistling down, intent on separating Niall's head from his shoulders.

Niall parried the blow with his axe, the force of it numbing his arm. He went in low with his own sword but Huwe was more nimble than he expected, jerking away from the long blade. "Ye kilt my son," he roared. "Ye bastard, I'll have yer head!"

Niall didn't waste his breath on speech; aye, he had killed Morvan, and would again had he the opportunity. He was filled with a cold, merciless rage, that the Hay filth had dared invade Creag Dhu, his home. Not only was the Treasure endangered, but Grace; he remembered the terror plain on her face as he raced by her, and he knew the fate that would befall her, and all the women of Creag Dhu, if he and his men failed to repel the invaders.

He would not allow that to happen.

He seized the offensive, attacking with silent ferocity, the steel of his sword clanging as it met Huwe's. He advanced steadily, axe and sword swinging, driving Huwe before them. A Hay clansman ran screaming at him from the left and he hurled the axe, burying it in the man's chest. The man gave a strange gurgle and dropped like a stone, his heart stilled by the massive blade that had cleaved it in two.

Niall had only the sword now, but he hadn't dared let the man engage him. He gripped the hilt with both hands to better balance himself, holding the weight centered with his body. Huwe rushed forward, heartened by Niall's loss of the axe. Niall parried the downward arc of Huwe's sword, steel sliding along steel with a hissing sound, disengaging, slashing in from his left and burying the blade deep in Huwe's right side, in the kidney. Huwe jerked, his face turning gray. His sword clattered to the floor. He rose on his toes, convulsing as his body reacted to the massiveness of the injury. Niall jerked his blade free and struck again, straight into the heart, a death stroke.

A howl rose above the roar of battle as Huwe's clansmen saw their chieftain slain. Disconcerted for a moment, it was a moment that cost them dearly, for Niall's men took swift advantage, their training bringing the struggle to a swift finish.

Niall leaned on his bloody sword, panting. Slowly he surveyed the ruin of his great hall, noting which of his men lay sprawled in death. There was a moment of eerie silence; then moans began to rise, the sobs and curses of wounded men. Here and there he saw a tangle of longer skirts, gently rounded limbs, and he knew some of the women had not found safety.

What of Grace? She had been with Alice, fleeing to the kitchens.

Sim slowly walked toward him, his face so covered with gore Niall almost didn't recognize him. The big man limped, his entire left hip wet with blood. "What do we do with the Hays who live?" he asked.

Niall's first impulse was to kill them all, but he stilled it. 'Twould cause Robert difficulty if he destroyed the clan. There were Hay women and children, too; they would need what men survived. The clan would not recover for many years from Huwe's stubborn stupidity. "Turn them out," he said.

The women were creeping from their hiding places. There were tears, of both joy and sorrow, as they identified both the survivors and the dead, and then as women do they set about restoring order, tending to the wounded, laying out the dead, bringing drink for those who wanted it, sweeping out the bloodstained rushes. Alice took charge, her manner brisk and capable, though her cheeks were still pale with fright.

Niall's black gaze darted from one woman to another, searching for a dainty form, a long, thick fall of hair. He listened, but could not catch that voice with its strange accent, the emphasis on all the wrong syllables. "Alice!" he called. "Where's the lass?"

Alice had no doubt which lass he meant. She looked around in puzzlement, but reached the same conclusion as had he. Grace was not there.

"She didna follow me," Alice said slowly. "But she was there behind me when ye came from the larder. Perhaps she hid there." She paused. "The lass saved us, gave us warning. She recognized Huwe."

So she had not been in league with Huwe. The thought brought him relief, but another worry sent him striding rapidly from the great hall. Inside the escape passage was yet another passage, one that he had sworn to protect with his life. There was something mysterious about the lass, something she kept hidden. What if she were the most serious threat to the Treasure he had yet encountered? Could he keep his vow, if it meant killing her?

Cold sweat beaded on his brow as he took a candle and ducked into the escape passage. Halfway down the long, narrow stairs an area of the wall was even darker, as if a hole had been knocked in the stone. Niall felt his heart still, his skin going cold with dread. Then rage came, saving rage.

Silently he took his bloody sword and followed her.

The stairs ended. Grace lifted the candle but couldn't see anything except cold stone walls, made of the same dark rock as the rest of the castle. It was very cold down there, and she began shivering. An odd pulse hummed through the air, not a sound but a sensation, brushing against her skin.

Her skin prickled, but not from the cold.

Slowly she paced around the walls, looking for any indication of a door. Blank stone was all that met her searching fingers.

The subtle pulsing was mildly disorienting. She must be below sea level, and what she felt was the force of waves battering against the rock.

Beneath the stairs was a deeper darkness. Her heart pounding in her throat, Grace stepped forward, and the frail light of her candle illuminated another opening, a black hole leading where?

The pulsing was stronger. She could feel it on her face. It was coming from the dark opening.

She stopped, the small hairs on the back of her neck lifting. Dear God, what was *in* there?

She could do this, she told herself. For Ford, and for Bryant, she could do anything. She had proven that to herself time and again during this past year of hell.

Bone-aching cold seeped from the stone straight through the thin soles of her shoes, crept beneath her skirts to curl its icy fingers around her legs. She had to act quickly, before the dangerous cold began to sap her strength. Her small candle wouldn't last much longer, and she didn't want to be caught down there without light. Calmer now, driven by necessity, she moved toward the black hole in the wall.

It engulfed her as soon as she stepped

through, the darkness, the sensation of trembling on the edge of something.

Was that warmth she felt?

She went deeper, her candle fluttering madly. The light picked out the dim shape of what looked like a large chair . . . a throne? . . . carved with lions. A tattered banner, the sort carried into battle and woven with fire in the strands, hung over the throne and in it golden lion eyes shimmered in the candle's light. Beside the throne was something else, something she couldn't quite see, and she took another step forward.

"Ah, lass." The deep voice was low, regretful, controlled. It came from no more than a few feet behind her. "I dinna want to kill ye."

The fine hairs on her body lifted in sheer terror, and for a moment Grace felt herself sway as the blood left her head.

Blood. She could smell it now, hot and metallic. The blood of battle was on him, the fierceness of it singing through his veins, intensifying the rage she could feel blasting from him in waves.

He was going to kill her. She could feel his intent, the cold resolve that had guarded the Treasure all these years. Underlying that, however, was his barely restrained rage at . . . what? Her trickery? How close she had come to succeeding? It was the rage she felt most, a fire burning beneath ice, and it ignited her own rage.

She couldn't let him kill her. If she died now, then Parrish would win. There would be no vengeance for Ford, for Bryant; their courage in death would have been in vain. She would die knowing she had failed them, and that, more than anything, was unbearable.

Niall's hand closed on her shoulder, turning her, his fingers gripping like iron. Grace dropped the candle and it rolled away, its fragile flame glinting on the sword in his hand, wavering, almost extinguishing before flaring to renewed life. She turned into his grip, stepping closer, whirling. Warrior that he was, he began reacting even before she could complete the move, turning his hip to the side to catch the brunt of her knee. But it wasn't her knee she used, it was her elbow. She jabbed it hard into his midsection, aiming for his solar plexus. The impact with his hard stomach jarred her arm all the way to her shoulder. She missed her target but the force was enough to make him grunt and bend forward a little, his grip on her shoulder loosening for a fraction of a second.

It was enough. She jerked backward, wrenching herself from his grasp. His fingers caught in the cloth of her bodice and a seam gave, the ripping sound almost unbearably loud in this deep, silent sepulcher. The fabric tore loose and she stumbled at the sudden release, going down almost to her knees before literally throwing herself back to her feet, panic lending her strength. She pulled her skirts high and raced into the darkness beyond the candlelight, instinct guiding her to the stairs.

Her chances of outdistancing him were slim, and getting out of the castle even more unlikely. Still, she had to try. The soles of her shoes slipped on the stones and she banged into the wall, hard. The light of the candle behind her was no more than a faint glimmer, of no use in finding her way, but now she had the wall for guidance. She put one hand on it and ran.

She tripped on the bottom stair and fell, hard. Instantly she bounded up, knowing he was right behind her, *feeling* his presence even though she couldn't see him, couldn't hear him over the thunder of her own heartbeat, the harsh gasps of her breathing. He was close, that terrible bloody sword in his powerful hand, his rage pulsing through him.

Grace ran up the stairs, hurling herself upward into the inky darkness. If she missed one step she would plunge off the side, down onto the stone floor, maiming if not killing herself outright. If she faltered, he would be on her. There was certain death behind her, possible death waiting at every step. She could do nothing but throw herself forward, hoping she had that one extra step on him that would allow her to gain the top of the stairs and bar the door before he could reach it.

Just one extra step. She had barely been able

to move the bar, but she would manage, somehow. If she could get the bar in place, she would make it. Niall would hack his way through but that would take time, time enough that she could flee the castle. One step.

No. She couldn't flee, not now, not when she was so close. She would have to hide . . . and return.

There were no more stairs. She staggered off balance when her lifted foot came down hard on a level surface. She reached desperately for the door.

And she heard him, heard his breath, felt it hot on her neck.

No time for the door.

Her scrabbling hands had barely closed on the frame when his weight hit her in the back, overwhelming her, driving her forward and down and crushing her beneath him.

Grace put out her hands to break her fall but still landed heavily. Stunned, she lay helplessly beneath him, her cheek ground into the grit covering the cold stone floor. He was so heavy she could barely breathe, and so big that he surrounded her, his heat burning her back, scorching through her clothing. His hot breath stirred her hair. She inhaled his pungent scent, the hot, mingled odors of sweat and blood and man, primitive and dangerous. The smell of him filled her, warming her within as his body warmed her without.

Caught. Captured. This was the end, then.

He could snap her neck with one hand, and perhaps he would, for she could feel the great rage seething within him. She was down, and helpless. He would kill her now.

He didn't move, didn't lift his heavy weight from her.

She couldn't see him; the darkness was almost total. Far away there seemed to be some lessening of the darkness, perhaps a torch set in a sconce on the outer stairs, but it was too dim to be of use. He didn't speak. All she could do was feel him, his body stretched on top of hers, his iron-muscled limbs controlling her. She could feel his chest move with his controlled breathing, feel the strong thudding of his heartbeat against her back. He wasn't even winded, damn him. She wanted to scream at him, claw at him in her own frustrated rage, but all she could do was press her face against the icy stone and wait.

The silence grew as they lay there, and then she felt the prod of his stiffened penis against her buttocks, the slow and deliberate movement of his legs, pushing between hers.

Grace's breath stopped.

She had known great emotions; she had thrilled to love, been devastated by grief, ridden the sharp blade of hatred. The riptide of lust that seized her body now went beyond the force of even those things, smashing through her barriers as if they had never existed, sweeping everything away in the sudden, blindingly intense need for him that overtook her. She had known she was weak where he was concerned; the first time he kissed her, her lonely, yearning flesh had exploded into climax at his touch. He aroused her as no other man ever had, ever could, aroused her to a response so overwhelming she couldn't control it.

He wasn't Ford . . . *he wasn't Ford!* How could she want him so much, this big, violent man who held the key to her desperate quest in his powerful hands? He was sworn to protect the Treasure, he had killed in its defense, and he would kill her . . . afterward. For now, lying there on the cold stone floor in the darkness, there was only the sound of his breathing, and hers, coming faster and harsher as his rage transmuted itself into lust.

A low moan slipped past her lips, a husky, helpless sound of want. *Yes. Oh, God, yes.* Even if he killed her afterward, before she died she wanted to feel him within her, absorb his driving force, cool this insane, inexorable fever that burned in her flesh for him.

Her hips lifted the scant inch they could, instinctively pushing upward against him, grinding her buttocks harder against his rigid shaft. Just that, a slight movement at best, but it sent shards of pleasure spearing through her. Her breasts hardened in painful need of his touch, her loins moistened and clenched, aching with desire and frustration and emptiness.

"Damn you," she whispered into the silence, almost weeping. Damn him for being a man like no other, for being hard and ruthless, for being more dominant in the flesh than she could have ever imagined. Other men paled beside him; he was too vital, the force of his personality and the strength of his sword arm smashing any resistance to his will. And damn herself, for how could she resist him, when he had only to touch her and her weak, traitorous body instantly began preparing itself to yield to him?

"Damn me, then, if ye must," he murmured against her hair, accepting her despair. Subtle, instinctive bastard that he was, he knew she was his for the taking now, all resistance gone, and he moved to claim her willing flesh.

He slid her skirts up, bunching the fabric on her back, and the cold air washed over her bare legs and bottom. Her skirts were still caught under the pressure of his knees, anchoring her in place. Grace quivered, fear and desire twisting sharply together until she couldn't separate them. The coarse wool of his kilted plaid scratched the tender backs of her thighs. His hand moved between them, pulling his plaid up and to the side, and his naked flesh was suddenly against her own, thighs to thighs, groin to buttocks. His heat was startling, almost unbearable, as if she touched fire.

He slid his right arm under her, curving

around her belly, and lifted her up and back, onto her knees, raising her hips and positioning her for him. Grace squeezed her eyelids tightly shut as she struggled with the abrupt, startling exposure and vulnerability of her sex. His rigid penis stabbed at her soft folds but he wasn't trying to enter her, not yet. Her loins pulsed, throbbing as she waited in paralyzed agony for the thrust that would carry him deep inside her, and at last this terrible need would be eased.

His sustaining arm slipped from around her but she maintained her position, on her knees with her bottom lifted. Her fingers scraped against the icy stone, trying to sink into it. Why was he waiting? Why didn't he just do it, before she went mad?

He touched her then, his warm palm shaping itself over the curves of her buttocks, learning her. His hand slid between her legs and he cupped her sex, his hard fingers opening the closed, secretive folds. He searched out her small, exquisitely firm nub, pushing back the protective hood of flesh and exposing her to the rasp of his callused fingertips. A soft cry exploded from her, and her hips writhed. Oh, God, another touch and she would explode, just as she had before. But he didn't give her that touch. Those damnably knowing fingers withdrew after the brief caress, dragging through her swollen folds to find and stroke the entrance to her body. He circled her soft opening with one finger, spreading her moisture but not probing inside her even though he had to feel the convulsive clench of her loins. He touched between her buttocks, exploring, and murmured a soft reassurance when her entire body jolted in shock.

He bent forward, his entire body covering hers, his weight supported on his left elbow and forearm. "Lay your head on my arm, lass," he whispered, and blindly she did so, pressing her forehead against the hard muscles of his forearm, her right hand entwining and clinging to his while her left hand curled around the iron swell of his biceps, anchoring herself against what she knew was to come. With his free hand he guided his jutting penis to her prepared opening, and slowly pressed within.

Grace couldn't prevent her sudden intake of breath, her involuntary whimper of feminine distress. She had known he was big; she had seen him naked. But until she felt him pushing into her, her body hadn't known the true measure of him. He was thick, and hot, and so hard she felt bruised by the inexorable advance of his shaft into her. He wasn't brutal, just relentless. Her hips undulated, instinctively trying to ease her clasp of him as inch by slow inch he completed his penetration.

Her fingers dug into his biceps, and she pressed her forehead harder against his arm. Surely she couldn't take any more; he was too big, he was hurting her, and helpless little cries broke from her throat. But he continued to push, and her hips rocked back and forth, adjusting, taking. Then he was in her to the hilt, seated hard, his pubic hair coarse against her bottom, his heavy testicles swaying between her spread legs and brushing against the burning nub he had exposed.

He moved carefully within her, just a little, the sensation setting off tiny explosions in her nerve endings. "Here?" he asked softly, his deep voice rustling against her ear. "Or . . . *here?*" He moved again, his swollen shaft nudging a place inside her she hadn't known existed, and her wild, helpless cry gave him his answer.

Slowly he began moving, a subtle flexing of his hips that wasn't a thrust at all, but instead a tenderly ruthless internal stroking of that place deep inside her. Grace cried out again, her entire body clenching under the lash of a pleasure so intense she couldn't bear it. She shuddered convulsively, her loins shivering around the thick intrusion of his penis. Oh, God, she had climaxed before with less arousal than this, but somehow she couldn't quite reach that blessed relief. This was exquisite torment, paralyzing pleasure, and she couldn't fight it. She couldn't pump her hips faster to gain her peak, for his body too completely controlled hers. All she could do was quiver just short of fulfillment, each slow rub of his cock taking her almost there, but not quite. Low, rhythmic cries wrenched from her with each inward movement he made, and her arousal grew even more intense, until she thought she would faint. She heard herself pleading with him, wild, disjointed words of need. "Niall — please! More — *do it!* Please . . . I can't — no!"

"No?" he panted softly in her ear, his voice low and raw. The next incremental movement tore a groan from him. "Ye'll bear it, lass, for I say ye must."

"I can't," she said again, moaning. She tried to move, tried to end this delicious torture, but he locked his right arm around her hips and held her still for yet another deep stroking. She strained against that warm, iron-muscled band, knowing it was useless, that his strength was far greater than her own. In this sensual battle she was helpless to take anything except what he gave her, her body too slight and delicate to resist being overwhelmed by a man who was a foot taller than she, and who had spent his life either in battle or training for battle, so that he was stronger than anyone she had ever known before.

Tiny red sparks exploded behind her closed eyelids. Her heart thundered, reverberating against her rib cage. She couldn't drag in enough air; her lungs strained, her entire body strained, and with a thin cry of despair, of pleasure taken beyond bearing, she turned her face into the crook of his arm and wildly sank her teeth into the bulge of his biceps. She heard his answering growl, and his big body flexed, a guttural sound rattling in his throat as his control shattered.

Like a stallion he set his teeth into the curve of her neck and shoulder, gripping the sensitive cord that ran there, and his hips plunged. She screamed, electrified by the primitive bite, the sudden hard thrust, and everything in her body gathered, concentrating, pushing, clamping down until she broke apart in cataclysmic upheaval. The sensual fury that seized her was so intense she was only dimly aware of the power of his own convulsions as he pumped violently into her, and the contractions went on and on, deep and hard, gripping him, shattering her.

The silence afterward was like death, black and complete.

Perhaps she lost consciousness; she didn't know. Reality returned in bits and pieces, first the awareness of the cold, gritty stone floor beneath her, and the heat of his body above her. His arm was wet, from her bites and her tears. There was the smell of sex, sharp and musky, added to the other scents of man and battle. The cord in her neck throbbed, an echo of pleasure like the lingering pulse in her loins. She felt the wetness of his semen. He was still inside her, not as large or as hard as before, but still firm, still *there.* Her vagina contracted in a sated, gentle caress and he grunted, shifting a bit upon her as he dealt with his own final wave of orgasm.

Perhaps he would kill her now. The thought formed out of the nothingness of exhaustion. So be it. She couldn't fight him, couldn't even move.

Slowly he withdrew from her body, taking away his support, his warmth, leaving her sprawled half naked and exposed on the floor. She could hear the hard rush of his breathing, the scrape of steel as he picked up his sword, and she waited to feel the cold bite of death.

Then he picked her up too, standing her upright for the barest second before he dipped and set his left shoulder to her belly, then stood with her draped like a limp bundle of rags over that broad shelf. At least her skirts had fallen into their proper position, she thought vaguely, so that her bottom wasn't exposed as he carried her to . . . where?

He strode through the darkness, his step sure and strong as he effortlessly carried her on one shoulder and his huge sword in his other hand, climbing steps as easily as if he hadn't just fought a battle and then emptied his body's seed into her in a shatteringly intense coupling.

He was still furious. Not just angry, but raging. She could feel the force of it inside him, controlled but unabated, and she knew their personal battle wasn't over.

Chapter 25

Grace let her eyes close, unable to deal with anything right then, unable even to worry. She felt disconnected, drifting apart from reality. Her world had just been shattered, again, and she couldn't quite accept what had just happened between them.

She had never before made love *without* love; she had slept only with Ford, known only his touch, and known that when he took her it was with love. With Niall, what was there? Lust, definitely. Lust beyond measure, beyond comprehension. Desperation on her part, rage on his. And yet he had forced from her a response deeper and far more powerful than any of the joyous loving she had felt with Ford. She hated him for that, hated him for taking something that should have been Ford's, but which she hadn't known was within her for the giving.

Lights danced beyond her closed eyelids, and the icy cold of the hidden passageway changed to the greater warmth of the castle.

"Alice!" Niall called, his deep voice like thunder. "Bring hot water."

"Is the lass hurt, then?" asked Alice, her tone startled.

"Nay," he curtly replied, then he was going up more steps. After a moment she heard a door creak on its leather hinges as it was opened, then closed again with a thud. A few more steps and he stopped and dragged her off his shoulder, holding her briefly while she found her balance. Startled, she opened her eyes, swaying a bit as he moved away from her.

They were in his chamber. She looked around as if she had never seen it before, for she couldn't grasp why he had brought her there. She looked at the sturdy table, and the carved, massive chair that sat to one side of the fireplace, in which a fire was springing to life as Niall bent and struck a spark to it. On the other side was a bench, large and heavy. A big wooden trunk occupied the space at the end of the bed . . . the bed. It was at least four feet high, and looked to be seven feet square. A huge bed, more than large enough for the man who slept there. It was piled high with furs and rugs, and looked as if she would sink out of sight in it.

The fire grew, chasing the shadows to the farthest reaches of the chamber, sending its waves of heat out to flow over her chilled body. She looked out the narrow window and saw that night had fallen while she had been below. The castle was quiet, the intruders repelled or killed, repairs and recovery going on in the hush that follows a battle.

Niall unbuckled his sword belt and dropped it across the bench; the sword he kept in his hand, however, as he took a piece of straw and stuck it in the fire, then used the flaming twig to light the tall tallow candles on the table. Grace stood where he had deposited her, afraid to move lest he wield that wicked, bloodstained blade against her.

In the flickering mellow light of fire and candle she could see now the signs of battle on him, see the dark patches of dried blood. His shirt was splattered with it, there were dark splotches on his kilt, and smeared on the leather of his boots. The blood of many others adorned him, this warrior, and she wondered if hers would soon join the stains. His black hair swung about his shoulders, freed from even the small braids that were usually at his temples.

Without glancing at her he sat down on the bench and took an oiled rag to the stained surface of his sword, meticulously cleaning it, inspecting the edges for ragged chips. He would sharpen it himself, as she had seen him do before in her dreams, not trusting the weapon to anyone else's care.

The sword restored to its previous gleam, he laid it on the table. Then he stood and began to strip.

The bloody shirt had been pulled off over his head and dropped on the floor when Alice softly knocked on the door, and at his growled permission she entered with a pitcher of steaming water, and cloths for washing. As she set the water and cloths on the table beside the sword, Alice cast a curious glance at Grace, who stood white-faced and silent.

Alice picked up Niall's bloody shirt. "Will ye be wantin' food, and wine?" she asked.

"Nay," he said, then changed his mind. "Aye, bring bread and cheese, and wine."

Alice left with another furtive glance at Grace. It hadn't happened to Lord Niall before, but mayhap the strange lass was less willing than others, and he thought to soften her resistance with wine. He was angry. Alice knew his mood, knew he was in a rare rage, and it was centered on the young woman whose eyes made one want to weep.

Niall moved to the table and poured some water into the washbowl. Wetting one of the cloths, he scrubbed it over his face and shoulders. By the time his chest and arms were clean, Alice was back with the wine and food, curiosity having given her feet wings. He denied her the opportunity for observation, however, by going to the door and opening it only enough to take the platter, then closing the door and dropping the heavy bar in its brackets.

Now he stripped completely, removing his boots and stockings, dropping his plaid. Splendidly naked, he stood in front of the fire and washed himself clean of the grime and blood and sweat of battle. He gave Grace no more attention than if she were part of the furniture, unconcernedly washing his armpits, his muscled legs, his genitals.

She had been blessedly numb, but this last act brought reality intruding again, making her sharply aware of his body and hers, of the aches from fight and flight, of the throbbing tenderness deep inside and the stickiness between her thighs as his semen dried on her skin.

Firelight played across his powerful muscles. She stared as if mesmerized at the gleam of his shoulders, the flat ridges of his stomach, the round hard buttocks, the long, brawny muscles of thigh and calf. Black hair grew in a thick patch on his chest, around his genitals, and to a much lesser extent decorated his forearms and lower legs. Sheer perfection. She had never before seen a man so acutely male, his body as God had surely meant His creation to be formed. The beauty of bone and muscle and sinew, honed by a lifetime of work and battle, made her weak.

Warmth began to pool deep in her belly as she stared at him, and in despair she recognized the return of sexual desire. This unreasoning need felt like the deepest betrayal of all Ford had meant to her but she couldn't stop it and, it seemed, couldn't sate it. How could she possibly want him again, so soon after that soul-searing upheaval of body and mind? But she did. She wanted to know it again, take him within her, milk him with the internal caress of her body. Even when he came to her covered in the blood of battle, she wanted him. Should he take up that sword now, and take her life from her, she would die with her flesh aching for him.

Her gaze dropped to his groin. His testicles swung heavy against his thighs, evidence of his recent climax, but her heart jolted in her chest when she saw his penis jutting out, thick and erect. She remembered the tales she had read, the whispers she had heard since coming there, of how he could ride a woman all night long when a hungry mood was upon him, of how he sometimes required two women before his appetite was slaked. Suddenly she knew that his moods weren't hungry, they were savage. She could see it in him now, feel it pulsating beneath his skin. He gave no outward sign of it, except for his erection, but she felt the rage that still burned in him and manifested itself in the stiffness of his cock — a rage that somehow didn't feel as if it were directed at her.

He poured the bowl of red-stained water into the chamber pot, then refilled the bowl with fresh water. He looked at her for the first time since carrying her into the chamber, and the expression in his black eyes made her shudder with both dread and anticipation.

"Remove your clothing," he said quietly,

but she heard the underlying iron. If she didn't undress voluntarily, he would perform the service for her.

She obeyed in silence, removing shoes and stockings, her bare toes curling with nervousness. Next came the overgown, then the kirtle. As that garment dropped to the floor, she stood in complete nakedness. Twentieth-century clothing revealed more, she thought irrelevantly, but it provided much more protection. A man had to deal with hooks and snaps and zippers, had to peel off layers of formfitting clothing before he could get to a woman's private parts. Medieval clothing, all-covering as it was, offered a woman little protection. All a man had to do was lift a woman's skirts and he could take her. The Scots had simplified matters even further, for a man had only to do the same to his own garments.

He looked at her, leisurely inspecting her breasts, the narrow curve of her waist, the dark curls at her pubis, her trembling legs. Then he held out his hand and said, "Come," and those trembling legs moved, carrying her to him.

He dipped a clean cloth in the warm water and began cleaning her as gently as a mother would a babe. He bathed the grime from her face, the smears of blood from her skinned palms and knees. His callused hands were careful with her, easing over the dark bruises forming under her pale skin. He knelt down and parted her legs, steadying her with a warm palm on her bottom as he gently wiped the cloth between her thighs, washing away his dried semen. Her thighs quivered, and she gasped for breath. The cloth felt raspy on her oversensitive flesh as he moved it along and between her folds. He even covered his fingers with the cloth and washed inside her, gently probing. He was very slow, very thorough with his washing, and the warmth in her belly grew into a fire. Her hips arched, seeking. Without a word he tossed the cloth aside, leaned forward, and set his mouth on her.

He knew exactly how to handle her, how to drive her insane. He sucked at her clitoris, drawing it forth, then licked it until she writhed and could barely stand up. All the while his long fingers probed, sliding into her, withdrawing, circling her tender opening. Then he kissed her, holding her hips with his iron hands and arching her forward while his tongue moved in and out of her, and helplessly she gave in to her exploding senses.

She went boneless, collapsing over him. He lifted her and sat down in the chair, and she lay limply across his lap, unable even to lift her head.

With his free hand he reached to pour the wine, holding the goblet to her lips, and she sipped. He drank after her, the expression in his black eyes shielded by his lashes. Grace relaxed against his chest, feeling warm and hollowed out, and oddly reassured. He might have taken her while still planning to kill her, but she doubted he would have pleasured her the way he just had if he intended to kill her afterward. It wasn't just his manner of pleasing her, but the fact that he'd done it at all; executioners generally weren't concerned with their victims' pleasure.

The heat of the fire licked over her bare body, chasing away the last of the chill. His thighs were hard and warm under her bottom, his shoulder a wonderful resting place for her head. He fed her bits of bread and cheese, feeding himself, too, and held the goblet to her mouth again. Again she drank, more deeply this time. When he raised the goblet to his mouth again he turned it so that he drank from where her lips had been, and the subtly erotic action squeezed at her heart.

"I have to tell you —" She stumbled into speech, not at all certain what she would say, but he pressed the back of his knuckles to her mouth.

"Nay. We'll not speak of it tonight. In the morn will be time enough." His voice was low and quiet, his Scots accent gone. He spoke now in the precise, measured tones of the Guardian. "For now — I like the taste of you, and I mean to have more of it." He leaned over and set the goblet on the floor, and then he kissed her as he had not since the night she had freed him from the Hay's dungeon, as he had not even during those other kisses they had shared. The kiss was wild and deep and she put both hands in his hair and held him, almost moaning with delight and arousal. He could make a fortune with his kisses, she thought dimly. What woman wouldn't give her gold to experience such sweet, wild mastery, such play of lips and tongue, such a blend of teasing and promising and authority? He kissed like an angel, or perhaps it was the devil, for surely an angel wouldn't know such carnal delights.

Swiftly he carried her to the bed and placed her on it, then joined her there, his broad shoulders blotting out the light as he came up over her. Panting, Grace opened her legs and took him between them, gripping his hips with her thighs even as she pushed hard on his shoulders. Willingly he rolled onto his back, and Grace sat astride him, gripping his penis in both hands and lowering herself onto it.

The penetration was just as shocking, just as full. She braced her hands on his belly and pressed her hips down, taking all of him. Her breath shuddered between her lips. God, oh God, she felt frenzied, unable to get enough of him. Her body had been starved for a man's hardness, the hunger shoved into her subconscious where it could surface only in her sleep, and now that hunger was released in an ungovernable flood. She rode him hard, and he squeezed her breasts, and she came again.

And still it wasn't enough.

He hadn't climaxed, he was still iron-hard within her. The hunger built again even before she had the energy to deal with it. Lying on his chest, his hands moving comfortingly over her bottom, stroking her back, she felt her inner muscles tighten around him.

He laughed, the sound rough and male, his white teeth gleaming in the golden firelight. She sat up, the motion pushing him deep inside her once more. She rode him hard again and this time he came before she did, his powerful body arching between her thighs, his hands gripping her hips and grinding her down on him. Wet with his spurting seed, she climaxed again.

They dozed a bit, with her lying on top of him and one of his hands threaded through her hair. Grace woke to find the fire still warmly blazing, so she knew not much time had passed. He slept, his penis soft. She slithered down his body and took him in her mouth, feeling him wake, feeling him grow hard. And then she mounted him again.

The hours blurred together. He gave his body generously, letting her do as she would with him. He gritted his teeth and fought his own climax, not letting himself reach pleasure again so he would remain hard until she was sated. She didn't know if the frenzy would ever stop, if her body, so long denied, would ever tire of her almost intoxicated enjoyment of his body. She stroked every inch of him, her hands shaking with delight at the textures of his skin. She kissed his jaw, his ears, his wonderful mouth. At the last, when finally she was exhausted and emptied out and at peace, she tormented him by taking him deep in her mouth. Knowing how he fought to control himself, she swirled her tongue around his shaft and sucked at the swollen head, and with a strained, hoarse sound he bolted upright, lifting her away from him and tumbling her onto her back.

He mounted her, pushing her thighs wide. "You've put me to hard use tonight," he whispered, sliding into her. "Now 'tis my time."

He should have been beyond control, but she discovered that wasn't so. When he climaxed again, he should have been beyond arousal, but that wasn't true either. His use of her was as devastatingly thorough as hers had been of him, and the sensations blended together. His thrusts hammered deep in her belly, over and over, and she held him when he shuddered and convulsed. The fire burned down, the candle guttered, and in the darkness he did things to her she had never imagined she would let a man do, but instead she reveled in his raw sexuality.

And in the darkness, finally, quiet came.

She lay against him, her head pillowed on his shoulder, her body heavy and limp. His hand covered her breast, his thumb absently stroking her velvety nipple. She inhaled his scent, the musky, unique smell of him, and she realized she could no longer recall how Ford had smelled.

Agony rushed out of the darkness, and she had no defenses left. It boiled out of her, deep and wrenching, sharp claws shredding her insides. A guttural cry ripped out of her throat. Niall's arms closed hard around her, and she came apart.

She didn't know how long she wept. Endlessly, unceasingly. The grief had been kept bottled up too long and now there was no holding it back. She cried in deep, wrenching sobs, her entire body shaking. She cried until her chest hurt and her eyes were swollen almost shut, until her throat was raw and the sounds she made sounded like an animal's.

He held her through it all, not letting her go even when she fought him, kicking and scratching. She raged silently against the two senseless deaths that had devastated her, against the terror and fury of the past year. She pounded Niall's chest with her fists until he caught them and held them, rolling over on top of her and using his weight to control her.

She began gagging, and he swiftly dragged her to the chamber pot and held her while she vomited. Then he gave her more wine and carried her back to bed, and held her until she could cry no more.

Dawn's faint gray light was creeping through the narrow window. "You loved him," Niall said quietly, smoothing her tangled hair away from her hot, grief-ravaged face. "You have not wept for him before, have you?"

"No." Her voice was a croak. The sound shocked her. "I couldn't."

The wine was warm in her belly, and her mind was fuzzy from both alcohol and fatigue. His hands were on her body, her breasts and thighs and loins, ensuring she acknowledged his claim on her even as he comforted her. She was so sore from the night's excesses that she flinched when he entered her again, but she didn't resist. He pressed deep, nudging her womb, and held himself deep and still until all the tension eased from her muscles and she lay limply beneath him, breathing deeply.

He didn't climax, didn't even thrust, just maintained the link. After a time he maneuvered them onto their sides, and put his hand on her bottom to keep her anchored to him.

Grace put her hand on his face, her fingers tracing the slope of his brow, the high curve of his cheekbone. "I know who you are," she said numbly, all emotion exhausted except for the uneroded joy of touching him. "I know what you are, Guardian. I came from the year nineteen ninety-seven to find the Treasure, and use it to destroy the man who killed my husband and my brother."

Chapter 26

Niall sat at the table, quietly looking at the books Grace had brought. Thinking to convince him she was telling the truth, she had told him where her sack was hidden and he had fetched it, but she realized now he hadn't required proof. He looked at the books out of curiosity, and for knowledge, not for confirmation.

He rapidly absorbed the changes in the language, saying once, "I knew the rhythm of your speech was odd, even though you spoke English." Another time: "So there are other lands across the ocean. I have always wondered."

He wasn't shocked, he wasn't disbelieving. He was highly educated; he spoke seven languages, and he dealt daily with the fantastic. But he was unnervingly calm, and it was destroying what little of her nerves were left.

"These papers you translated," he finally said, turning to face her. "You say I wrote part of them?"

"Yes. You signed your name, and dated them. Thirteen twenty-two."

"I have not written any papers," he said.

"But I saw them —"

"Perhaps you are the cause of their existence."

She digested that, and bit her lip. "You mean they wouldn't have been written if I hadn't come back? But I came back *because* of what you wrote!"

A bitter smile touched his lips. "I have hated God for what He allowed to happen to my brethren," he said calmly, "but I cannot doubt His existence. How could I, when I guard His power on earth? Who knows what the hand of God does?" He shrugged. "I have ceased trying to understand Him, I only do my duty."

"You hate God?" Stunned, she could only stare at him.

"How could I not? I did not want to be a Knight; I was forced into the Order. I have a talent for killing," he said in unflinching acceptance of his skill. "I became the Knights' best warrior. I learned the secrets we protected — in service of God! — and He allowed His servants to be butchered in defense of those secrets. No Knight betrayed his greater oath, not one talked even with the flames of the stake licking up his legs, devouring his entrails. They suffered and died, and He let it happen. Perhaps He directed it, to destroy those who knew. Only I am left, and fool that I am, I have kept my oath all these years, because my last oath was not to God but to my friends who died for Him."

His tone was unemotional, his eyes remote. Grace wanted to go to him but somehow she couldn't, he was too distant.

"Look at me," he said. "I have thirty-nine years. I should be growing old, but my hair remains black and my teeth stay in my head. I never sicken, and if I am wounded I quickly heal. He has cursed me to guard His damned Treasure even after I should be dead."

"No," she said softly. "You're just a healthy man." She could reassure him on this, for she was all too piercingly aware of his humanity, his mortality. "In my time, people easily live into their seventies and eighties, sometimes even over a hundred. I'm thirty-one."

His brows lifted and he looked a little surprised. He surveyed her, noting her smooth, clear skin and lack of wrinkles, her shiny hair. "You look a mere girl."

She didn't want to think of her looks, with her eyes red and swollen from her emotional storm, her face drawn with fatigue from the long night of nothing less than debauchery. She sat down on the bench, wanting to be close to him even if she didn't dare touch him.

"Tell me of this Foundation," he ordered.

She told him what she knew. She had already choked out the details of what had happened to her, how Ford and Bryant had died, and why. He listened, his long fingers drumming on the table.

"I wonder how they discovered the Treasure's existence," he murmured at one point.

"An archaeological discovery, probably," Grace said. She hesitated. "This Power — what exactly is it?"

"It is God's power," he said. "With it, all things are possible."

"But power isn't something you can leave in a chest and take it out when you need it! God can't store His power in the basement of a Scottish castle and —"

He shook his head. "Nay, 'tis not that. Though He could, if He wished. The Knights understood that, the fact that mortal man cannot understand God, that we must not say a thing is impossible, because all things are possible to Him, and our understanding too paltry. God is not limited by our imagination or our small minds. The Church makes rules and says they come from God, but they come only from man and his attempt to interpret God."

Believing God was so powerful, how indeed could he not hate Him? Grace wondered. Niall had long since reached the conclusion that God had deliberately destroyed the Templars, for had He wished to save them they would still be flourishing.

"But why would He want to destroy the Order?" she whispered, and Niall's black eyes flashed.

"To protect the Church," he said tiredly. "Flawed as it is, still the good outweighs the bad. The Church gives the framework of civilization, lass. Rules. Limits."

"How were the Knights a threat to the Church?"

He stood and walked away from her to the window, where he looked out over the wild and beautiful land he ruled. "We knew."

"Knew what?"

"Everything."

She waited, and the minutes passed. Without looking at her he said, "Did you note I never called you by name? Your name! Grace-Saint-John. I want you until I think I shall burn alive, but your name eats at me. There is no state of grace, there is only one of ignorance."

She hadn't noticed, but now she felt a pang, as if he had rejected her. Perhaps he had; he hadn't touched her since her confession. "What did you know?" she whispered.

"They found it all in the Temple, in Jerusalem. The Lion Throne, that great barbaric throne on which are carved both Yahweh and Ashara, god and goddess, male and female. They were two, and they were one; the ancient Israelites worshipped them both. Then the priests deliberately destroyed all the altars built to Ashara, and tried to erase knowledge of her. Yahweh became Jehovah, the one God."

"Yes, I know," she said. Archaeology had uncovered all that, eliciting a storm of conjecture among the scholars of ancient Jewish history.

"There were other things," he said. "The Cup. 'Tis a plain thing, and despite the quest for the Holy Grail it gives no powers. The Banner. The army it flies over is never defeated, its firebirds rising again and again from the ashes. It plainly depicts the same lions of the Throne, though legend has it that it isn't that old, and that only the Knights had it." He sighed softly. "And there is the Cloth."

Her mouth went dry. "The Shroud?"

He made an impatient gesture. "So it would be called, but that is false."

"Then what is it?"

"The cloth in which Jesus was wrapped when he was taken from the cross," Niall explained.

"Then it is the Shroud. He was entombed in it."

Niall's eyes were blacker than she had ever seen them before, looking through her. His mouth had a bitter line. "No, not a shroud, because he lived. He was God's son in spirit and the cross could not defeat him. The Church built itself around the preposterous tales of the resurrection even though its own writings plainly state he did not die, and afterward the truth could not be told without destroying the Church. So we remained silent to protect the Church, to serve God — and He destroyed us in return.

"His face." The words were pulled out of him, taut with fury. "We had his face from the Cloth. We revered it, because he was proof of God's power. Jesus lived! God reached down and saved him, because his duty was fulfilled, and then he left in an explosion of light and heat. We found the record of it! *We know how!* But when our duty was fulfilled, He broke us, He destroyed us. And still . . . still I serve."

Grace couldn't speak. Her lips tingled, and she realized she had stopped breathing. The explosion of heat and light . . . she had felt something like that, when she had come back —

"We knew the *how* didn't matter. The method He used did not matter; we trusted Him, worshipped Him. Others wouldn't understand, though, with their small minds and rigid superstitions. They try to limit God to their own understanding, their own imaginations. They would have turned from the Church. *We* didn't."

The bitterness spewed out of him, his lips drawn back in a snarl. She swallowed her fear, and crossed to the window to stand beside him. She didn't dare touch him, though, not when his anger was like a force field blasting from him. "But you're doing it, Niall. Trying to fit His reasons and methods into your own understanding." She paused, trying to work through her thoughts. She believed in basic goodness and when it came down to it she believed in God, sensed a higher power, a deeper meaning, but she was no theologian. "I think . . . I don't believe God causes all things to happen. I think He gives us the freedom to be either good or bad, because if there is no choice then our actions have no worth, and no blame. I think when people do bad things it's because they have chosen to do so, and we should blame them, not God."

"Why did He not stop Philip? Why did He not strike Clement dead? He could have, but instead He let them act."

"He let them choose, and they'll be judged by their actions."

"Then I'll meet them in hell."

"Oh, Niall." She did touch him now, leaning her head against his arm. She felt overwhelmed with tenderness for him, and admiration. "You won't go to hell. How could you? Even with all your pain and anger you've kept your oath, and served God. Don't you think your service is more valuable to Him than the service of those who have never suffered, never been tested?"

He turned on her, gripping her arms so tightly he hurt her. "I would have preferred not to have served Him at all!" he ground out.

"But you did anyway."

"Aye, and my entire bedamned life is tied to this castle, to His cursed Treasure I am sworn to protect! Do ye not think I would have preferred to live a normal life, with a wife, and bairns?" His Scots accent was back, and thick with his anger. "I could not! The burden, and the danger, have been too great. And now —"

"Now?" she prompted, when he broke off.

He gave her a bitter smile. "Why, now He's sent Grace to me, but only as a means to lead me to another battle I must fight for Him."

She blinked, startled. "I didn't come back for that. If I could find the Treasure I was going to use it myself; if not, I knew I would have to ask for your help, but I only need your knowledge."

"Ah, no, lass," he said gently. "Ye need *me*. I'm the Guardian, and no other may use the Power."

"How does it work?" Grace asked nervously, clinging to his hand as he led her into the hidden passage. The castle slept around them. They had spent the day arguing, sometimes heatedly, over the course they would take. Huwe was dead and that threat ended, so Niall felt he could relax his defenses somewhat, and now was the perfect time for him to go. Remembering the violence of the procedure, Grace couldn't look forward to going through it again. "How do you get the electricity?"

"Electricity?" He repeated the word slowly, feeling his way along the syllables. "What is that?"

"A form of energy. Power."

"Power." He laughed, the sound humorless. "We use God's Power. The procedure is a means of *returning.*"

He walked with confidence, as if he had no need for the candle he held. Grace was less certain. She felt surrounded by the nothingness of space, of emptiness, as if the reality of Creag Dhu was already dissolving around her. Her heart pounded wildly, the pressure high in her throat. She swallowed to contain the panic, the unreasonable fear. She had been there before, and with less trepidation.

But still, now she knew. She felt the breeze, and the subtle throb of the very air against her skin. Niall led her down, down, to the deeper darkness beneath the stairs. He left the candle outside and walked into the darkness, his arm hard around her now to keep her with him.

It lay in the blacker depths, hidden from view but pulsing with that silent energy. The air should have felt dead, empty. It didn't. Though cold and dark, the chamber felt fresh, vibrant with the secrets it concealed. Treasures. Things. And yet the real treasure lay not in what they were, but what they represented.

"We have drunk the water and eaten the salt," Niall said in a low voice. "Take us."

The flash was blinding, the force like a giant blow that knocked her flat. She lay senseless for a time, deafened and blind, not even thinking. When the fog began to clear, she groaned and tried to roll over.

"Let me help you, my love," a voice crooned, and she was lifted to her feet, held upright by strong arms. Grace's head lolled back on her neck. She fought for control, won it. She opened her eyes, and stared up into Parrish's smiling face.

"Imagine my surprise when the workers found you lying in the rubble," he said conversationally. "I sent them all away, except for a few trusted men. I believe you've met Conrad, and perhaps you remember Paglione, too."

Dazed, Grace found herself staring into the cold, emotionless eyes of the man she had shot in the McDonald's parking lot. He didn't so much as blink. The other man, Paglione, looked familiar, but she couldn't quite place which assailant he had been.

A chilly wind stirred her hair, and she turned her face into it. A sea wind, blowing over where Creag Dhu had once stood. All that remained now were a few ruined stone walls, and the rubble that had been unearthed by the workers. Where was Niall? Had they already found him? Had he survived the journey?

"Looking for the gold yourself, were you?" Parrish asked. He pinched her breast, cruelly twisting the tender flesh. Grace bit off a scream, though tears started to her eyes. She didn't want to give him the satisfaction of making her cry out.

"There isn't any gold," she blurted.

He stiffened, and his eyes narrowed. "What?"

"The Treasure isn't gold. It's artifacts. There isn't any gold!"

"You're lying," he said violently, and slapped her. The force of the blow would have knocked her down if he hadn't been holding her arm. He drew back his arm again, and this time his fist was doubled.

"Aye, there's gold."

The softly burred words made them spin, Parrish dragging Grace about, wrenching her arm. She bit her lip, and tasted blood where Parrish's blow had cut her. Niall stood relaxed, the wind lifting his hair, ruffling the ends of his plaid. A faint smile was on his lips, and he leaned negligently on the claymore which he had driven into the ground. He looked wild and barbaric and wonderful, a splendid savage who possessed a sophistication of manner and experience most modern men would never come close to achieving.

"Who are you?" Parrish asked. "Not that it matters." Conrad and Paglione had already spread out, one going wide on each side of Niall, and both of them had guns in their hands.

"Niall of Scotland. And I fear it does matter, for the gold is mine."

Parrish's eyes narrowed. "You've already found it, haven't you?"

Niall looked amused. "It was never lost." He glanced at Grace, and his glance lingered on her bloody mouth, hardened.

"Well, you are a complication," Parrish admitted. "But I don't think you've spent it all, or you wouldn't be dressed like a bag lady. Maybe you don't have it at all."

"But I do." Niall reached into his shirt, the movement prompting both Conrad and Paglione to lift their weapons. Niall's eyebrows rose, and he smiled as if they were no more than presumptuous children. "Easy, lads." He drew out his hand and slowly opened it, palm upward. A crude golden coin lay there, gleaming bright in the sun.

Parrish smiled, too, his handsome face creasing in a benevolent expression that made Grace want to vomit. "Where is the rest of it?"

"It isna here. I moved it long ago, against such a day as this."

"A pity." Parrish shrugged. "You'll tell me; Conrad will see to that. But you won't like his methods, and unfortunately you look like the stubborn type." He jerked his head at Conrad, and Paglione anticipated the order, moving toward Niall.

Something wild flared in Grace's eyes. She had watched two men she loved die; she couldn't watch another. A low, animal sound tore out of her throat and she jerked to the left so that she half faced Parrish, and drove the palm of her hand hard against his nose.

Cartilage crunched, and blood poured out of both his nostrils. He staggered back, his grip on her loosening, and Grace tore free. Paglione whirled on her, the pistol rising in his hand.

Calmly Conrad tightened the slack in the trigger and fired. Grace screamed, surging forward, only to be jerked back as Parrish recovered and grabbed her again.

Paglione hung there in surprise, not even blinking. The small round hole in his forehead was neat, bluish around the edges. He dropped bonelessly to the ground and didn't even twitch.

Parrish gaped in disbelief. "Are you fucking crazy?" he screamed at Conrad, his voice high and cracking.

"No," Conrad said, and turned to face Niall. Slowly his simian head bowed. "I serve you, Guardian," he said.

Niall acknowledged him with a single nod.

Parrish pulled out a pistol and pressed the barrel to Grace's temple. He began backing away, stumbling over the raw dirt and tumbled rocks, dragging her with him. "I'll kill her," he said viciously, the words thickened by the blood streaming from his broken nose. "I'll fucking kill her."

Niall pulled the tip of the claymore out of the ground and rested the blade on his shoulder, his hand draped negligently over the hilt. "No," he said. "You will not." He looked at

Grace and smiled, a smile so sweet and strangely radiant that her heart stopped in her chest. "Grace . . . move."

She dropped immediately, lifting her feet and simply falling out of Parrish's grip. He grabbed for her and stumbled off balance, going down on one knee in the dirt. Grace rolled, throwing herself away from him, and he fired the pistol. The bullet burned along the top of her right thigh and she cried out, grabbing her leg.

Parrish scrambled to his feet, aiming the pistol first at Niall, then at Conrad, daring either of them to make a move. Niall lifted the claymore off his shoulder, the smile on his face changing to something deadly. "Are you sorely wounded, love?" he asked in the most gentle voice Grace had ever heard him use.

"No," she said, though her voice wobbled and her thigh burned like hell. Blood seeped through her fingers, and she pressed her hand hard against the wound.

Parrish fired at him, the shot echoing with a flat metallic sound across the sea. Niall began walking toward him. Parrish fired again, and still Niall advanced.

"Ye canna kill me, servant of evil," Niall whispered.

"God damn you, you bastard," Parrish screamed, and fired again. Niall was so close Parrish couldn't have missed, yet his hand must have been shaking, the shots going wide.

Niall's gaze was distant, fixed on something both beyond Parrish and yet inside himself. He turned his head and smiled at Grace, that piercingly sweet smile again. "My own Grace," he said. "I found heaven wi' ye, lass, but that time is gone." Then he lifted the heavy claymore and rested the tip against Parrish's chest. Grace saw Parrish's handsome face go slack with shock, and a bolt of lightning split the cloudless sky. The blinding light enveloped Niall, arcing along the long blade of the claymore, and shot straight through Parrish. He screamed, lifting on his tiptoes as if hauled there by an invisible hand. He trembled and shook, and the lightning arced again. The front of Parrish's trousers went wet and dark, and steam rose from his crotch. His eyes rolled back in his head, until only the whites showed. His lips split, and his hands began to scorch. His blond hair was singed, turned to gray ash. He tried to scream, his mouth open, but no sound emerged over the roar and blast of light. The skin on his face shriveled, pulling away from his bones. Through it all Niall stood motionless, wrapped in brightness. Then with a thunderous boom it was over and Parrish collapsed like a sack of rags, lying motionless on the scorched earth.

"Niall!" Grace struggled to her feet, ignoring the pain in her leg. "Niall!"

He strode rapidly across the ruins to her,

catching her as her leg went out from under her and she started to fall. Gently he lowered her to the cool ground, lifting her skirts to bare her thigh and expose the wound.

The man called Conrad went down on one knee beside Parrish's smoking, stinking corpse. What he saw must have satisfied him, for he gave a brief nod of his apelike head, then rose and came to Niall's side.

Deftly Niall tore a strip of fabric off the hem of Grace's undergown and wrapped it around the long gouge on the top of her thigh. He glanced briefly up at Conrad. "You are of the Society?"

"Yes. We have known of the Foundation's existence for many years. Someone from the Society has always belonged to the Foundation, to monitor its activities. Only twice has it come close to finding the Power; in 1945, and today."

"You were going to kill me," Grace said, her teeth chattering with shock. She couldn't quite take in that this man with the cold, dead eyes was somehow on Niall's side, at Niall's service.

"If necessary," Conrad said unemotionally. "My concern was the papers, to retrieve them at all cost and prevent Parrish from acquiring them. Then I began to think that . . . perhaps . . . you were meant to have them. You are one of only a few people in the world who could understand what they were, who would know to go to the Guardian and bring him here."

"Be verra happy ye didna harm her," Niall said softly as he glanced up from tying the cloth around Grace's thigh. His eyes were as cold as Conrad's.

"We do what we must," Conrad replied. "As do you."

Niall's mouth twisted bitterly. "Aye." He looked down at Grace's bare thigh, at his rough hands on the silkiness of her flesh. He smoothed her skirts down, his fingers gentle. "Ye'll be all right, lass. Can ye stand?"

"I think so," she said shakily. Her leg throbbed like blue blazes now, but she had seen for herself that the wound wasn't deep. Niall helped her to her feet, holding her until her balance steadied.

He looked around, lifting his head into the breeze. His gaze lit on the two cars, English rental cars parked near where the stables had once stood. "Automobiles," he said on a note of wonder. "Before, I didna see anything, just that damnable dark little dungeon, and the madman."

"Bunker," Conrad said.

Niall shrugged his indifference at the terminology. "I think there must be many wonders now to see," he said absently. "But many evils, too."

"Yes." Conrad's eyes locked on Niall, and for once they weren't cold. Grace couldn't read his expression, but suddenly she knew that Conrad would give his life unhesitatingly for Niall, and in that moment she forgave him for everything.

Niall tilted his head down, his face calm as he studied Grace. "I must go," he said.

"Go?" She realized even as she said the word how stupid she sounded. Of course he had to go; he was the Guardian.

"I couldna stay here, even if I wished." He cupped her face in his hands, his fingers tenderly tracing her cheekbones, her lips. "My duty is there." He bent and kissed her, his lips soft, barely touching hers. Then he released her and strode away from them, and she heard him repeat the words about water and salt. She took a step forward, trying to scream his name, but panic closed her throat. The flash of light blinded her, and when she could see again, Niall was gone.

"Niall!" Too late, she had voice. She stumbled toward the spot where he had stood, a great fear welling inside her, a fear that had no name.

Conrad caught her arm. "He is gone. He is the Guardian." To him, that explained everything.

"He's a man!" Grace whirled on him, her eyes wild. "He's just like every other man!" She felt hysteria building in her, a sense of loss so sharp it was staggering. "He eats and sleeps and breathes and bleeds, he doesn't have supernatural powers or anything like that —"

"No," Conrad said, turning her away from the ruins. "But God does." He began to lead her toward one of the rental cars. "The Guardian has his work there — and we have ours here."

She stumbled, her leg crumpling under her again, and without a word Conrad lifted her in his powerful arms and carried her to the car. She sat numbly as he drove them away from the scene, but inside she was coming apart, because Niall was gone.

"That man gives me the willies," Harmony muttered, watching Conrad as he sat beside Kris, the two of them patiently pulling up Foundation files and destroying them. It was night, the building deserted except for the four of them. Conrad and Kris could have done the work on their own, but Grace had to be there, her nerves not letting her be anywhere else. Harmony had come along because she was worried about Grace, who looked as if she would shatter at the slightest touch.

"He's strange," Grace conceded. She had spent a little more than a month in Conrad's company, and she still knew little more about him than she had the day Parrish had died. He didn't talk about himself. She knew he was ruthless, that some might call him a stone killer and perhaps be right.

He had been invaluable, making arrangements, contacting Harmony to more thoroughly tend the wound on Grace's leg, doing away with Paglione's body. Parrish's body he left to be found, the victim of a freak lightning strike. Grace had moved like a marionette to his orders, so numb she wondered if she would ever feel alive again. Niall was gone. She woke in the night weeping, reaching out for him. She had spent so little time with him, and yet she felt as if he were imprinted on every cell of her body.

"There!" Kris announced in triumph, his hacker's blood excited by what he had been doing. "We can't kill the Foundation, but it's going to be in the dark for a while. All their records are gone."

Conrad nodded, and for a moment there was a gleam in his dead eyes. "Good," he said, the word filled with satisfaction.

They hadn't told Kris anything more about the situation, except that Parrish was dead, but what he knew was enough to make him willing to help out. Harmony, who still hadn't recovered from the shock of watching Grace vanish in an explosion of light the month before, was even more protective than normal.

Conrad stood, looking at the blank computer screen. "Are you certain an expert can't retrieve the files from the hard disk?"

"I'm positive. Trust me. The hard disk is wiped clean. If you're sure no floppies exist anywhere, or a hard copy, then there's no way all that information can be compiled again."

Conrad grunted. The possibility of a floppy disk floating around out there worried him. He had personally searched Parrish's house and found nothing, but such a valuable disk, if it existed, would likely be in a bank vault somewhere.

Grace had burned the papers she had worked on for so long, and ached as the flames destroyed her link to Niall. She would never again read about him, marvel at his exploits. The written accounts paled in comparison to the real man, anyway. But she didn't want anyone else to find those papers, and use them to threaten the Treasure Niall had dedicated his life to protecting.

The four of them left together but separated when they reached the street. No one talked much; there wasn't much left to say. Kris departed in his Chevelle. Conrad gave Grace an oddly old-fashioned bow, and walked off down the street. Harmony and Grace slowly walked to Grace's truck.

"What now?" Harmony asked. "No more running, no more bad guys chasing you and trying to kill you. Well, the cops are still after you, but from what I see they can't find their ass with both hands and a flashlight, so I guess you're safe enough. I'd live somewhere else, though. Take up some boring stuff, like skydiving."

Grace managed a ghost of a smile. "I don't

have any plans after tomorrow," she said.

"So what's on for tomorrow?"

"I'm going to my husband's grave."

The June morning was bright and sunny, the flowers in full bloom. Grace carried two bouquets of spring flowers, daisies and lilies and bright yellow primroses making a gay splash of color in her arms. Harmony walked silently beside her through the rows of grave markers.

Grace knew exactly where the graves were. Bryant was buried beside their parents, and Ford in the plot nearby that he and Grace had chosen. The day they had bought the plots she had looked at them and thought how many decades it would be before they were used. She had been wrong.

The two graves had markers on them. The life insurance policies would have paid for the markers, but she wondered who had ordered them. Friends, perhaps, or colleagues. It was possible Parrish had done it; he would have found the idea amusing. She didn't mind. If he had, in this case, the end did justify the means. She was glad they had markers, that these two wonderful, precious men hadn't lain for a year in unmarked graves.

Bryant's marker was simply inscribed. "Bryant Joseph St. John. Born Nov. 11, 1962 — Died April 27, 1996." That said so little. He had been thirty-three years old. Never married, but engaged once. Several serious girlfriends. Loved his work, doing crossword puzzles, an ice-cold beer and salty popcorn when he was watching a ball game. His second toes had been longer than his big toes, and he hadn't liked anything starched. She couldn't have asked for a better brother.

She placed one of the bouquets on the grave, and numbly walked on. She stumbled a little, and Harmony placed a strong supporting hand under her arm.

"Are you all right?"

"No, not really," Grace whispered. "But I have to do this."

Bryant's grave had been in partial shade; Ford's was in full sun, and the grass that covered it was thick and lush. "William Ford Wessner," the marker read. "Born Sept. 27, 1961 — Died April 27, 1996." One more line had been added: "Married with Love to Grace Elizabeth St. John."

Grace's knees buckled and she sank slowly to the grass, despite Harmony's alarmed efforts to keep her upright. She reached out a trembling hand and traced the engraved letters of his name, trying to reach the essence of the man. She missed him so much, ached to see his crooked smile, or the humor in his twinkling eyes. He had died for her, and done it willingly.

"I'll always love you," she promised him, though she could no longer read his name in the stone; everything was blurred. He was a man worth loving, and that feeling for him would never die out of her heart, any more than her love for her parents had died.

The human heart had the capacity to love many people, and none of those loves diminished it for the others. Niall had been in her heart even before Ford died, a tiny burning kernel of interest and respect. Losing Ford hadn't extinguished that spark. Instead it had grown during the long months when she was alone, giving her the strength to go on. At first she had loved him as a person, and later she had loved him as a man. It had been a banked fire when she had gone back to his time, and when he stirred the coals the fire had blazed into an inferno. How many women were so lucky as to have two such loves? They were nothing alike in personality. Ford had been cheerful, good-natured; she suspected Niall could be the very devil to live with, as accustomed to command as he was. Different times, different men — and they *were* both men, in the best sense of the word.

Harmony knelt down beside her, disregarding the effects of grass on her white pants. "Would he have minded?" she asked softly, nodding at the grave. "Or would he have wanted you to love again?"

"He would want me to love again," Grace replied, brushing her hand lightly over the grass. As she would want the same for him.

She couldn't help the small spurt of jealousy she felt, ridiculous under the circumstances, but she would want him to be happy, and he had been more generous and openhearted than she was.

She laid the bouquet on the grave and touched the marker again. Since his death she had been able to see only one image of him, that horrible last one, but the words on the marker summoned another, happier memory, that of their wedding day. She saw him in her mind, nervous and excited, the way he repeatedly swallowed, the way his voice shook when he said his vows. When the ceremony was finished a wide grin broke across his face, and it was that grin she saw, relieved and happy all at once.

Tears dripped down her cheeks, and her mouth trembled. "Oh, Ford," she said, her voice shattered. "I miss you so much, and I love you, but I have to go now."

Harmony helped her to her feet and gently led her away. Grace stumbled; the grass was springy beneath her feet, and wet with early-morning dew. She stopped, tilting her head back. It was a beautiful day. She took a deep breath, inhaling all the fresh scents, and with swimming eyes looked at the wide expanse of blue sky.

"You look like you gonna pass out any minute now," Harmony said sternly. "You eat anything yet?"

"No, not yet." Grace gathered herself and smiled. It was wobbly, but it was a real smile. She ached, but she felt at peace. She hadn't had vengeance, but Ford and Bryant had had justice, and it was enough.

"Did you even try to eat, or did you just start gagging?"

"Gagging." Morning sickness had started three days ago, hitting her early and hard. Harmony had said the worse the morning sickness was, the less likely a woman was to miscarry; if that old wives' tale was true, then Grace figured she could play ice hockey in her ninth month without any harm coming to the baby.

She touched her flat stomach. She was five weeks pregnant; she knew the exact date of conception. She would have the longest pregnancy in history, a baby conceived in 1322 and born in 1998. That was one for the record books.

At first it had seemed so unreal, that one night would result in a pregnancy, but when she remembered the night, she wondered how she couldn't have *expected* to get pregnant.

She thought of what Niall had said, of wanting a normal life, a wife and babies. Perhaps a normal life would never be his, but she carried his child and he didn't even know it. He had isolated himself, allowing himself nothing but the burden of his responsibility. Would he want his child, or would he turn away?

He would want it, she thought. There was a great tenderness in him, and great passion. He had shown both of them to her. A man like that would adore his children. It would be criminal to keep such joy from him.

"Are you going back?" Harmony asked as they drove away from the cemetery.

"I think I have to. It may be a wasted trip, he may send me here again, but if he wants me I'll stay."

"Man," Harmony breathed. "That must be luuuvvv. I mean, a woman givin' up hot water and central heat, *Chicago Hope* and Sean Connery, pizza and enchiladas — a man better have somethin' more to offer than a hot love stick, if you get my drift."

"I get it," Grace said, and found herself laughing. "He has a castle, too."

"Yeah, but it's drafty. Better make that a *big,* hot love stick. I dunno about leaving Sean Connery, but at least you're tradin' him for another Scotsman, and one you can lay hands on at that. Must be something in the water up there, growin' men like that. So, when you gonna do the deed?"

"As soon as I can get back to Scotland, and Creag Dhu."

"Reckon it'll hurt the baby?"

Grace touched her stomach again, something she often did these days. "I've thought about that. I can't think why it would. It's low voltage, and the only effect I noticed was a little muscle soreness."

"Want me to go with you to Scotland?"

"I'd like that. Have you thought about *really* going with me?"

"No way. I'll miss you, Gracie; you lead a damn interestin' life. But no way in hell am I givin' up my modern conveniences for no love stick, I don't care how big it is."

Chapter 27

"Holy Christ!"

Grace heard the yelp, the sound muted, far away. She tried to think, tried to swallow, but not even her throat seemed to work. She drifted away into darkness for an unknown time, then slowly became aware of noise again, of being gently lifted and carried. Her limbs were heavy, useless. Her head lolled like a child's.

She was placed on a bed, and she felt the softness under her. Her fingers moved, rubbing the cool linen beneath her. She managed to open her eyes a little, and a face swam before her, a strong-boned, frowning face with little braids of hair at his temples. A piercing joy spread through her. *Niall.* She didn't know what would happen in the next ten minutes but for right now she could see him, touch him, and she was happy for the first time in — how long? Had she been happy when she was there before? She frowned slightly; this seemed very important. No, she decided, she hadn't been happy the time before. She had felt torn, frantic, captivated, and many other things she couldn't quite name. Now, this moment, she was finally happy again.

"Lass?" He stroked her hair back from her face. "Can ye speak?"

The Scots accent was back, she noticed. That meant he was Niall the Scot now, not Niall the Guardian. Like Harmony, he varied accents with his mood, the effect of having seen too much and knowing too many languages. A small smile quivered on her lips.

"If ye can smile, ye can speak." The words were stern, but she heard a smile under them, and another, more serious note.

"Perhaps," she murmured, not opening her eyes.

He grunted with satisfaction. "Ye sound awake enough."

"Awake enough for what?" But even before the words were completely spoken she felt his hands moving on her, loosening laces, sliding over her legs, and lifting her gown. Her heart gave an enormous leap but she lay still, enjoying his remarkable expertise with women's clothing. In little more than fifteen seconds she was completely naked.

His own clothing took even less time. Trembling in joy and her own abrupt urgency, she opened her legs and he crawled up to settle between them, pausing along the way to distribute kisses on her stomach and gently suck both her nipples. She gasped, her fingers digging into his back, electrified by the increased sensitivity of her breasts.

"I've been more than a month without ye," he muttered, reaching down and guiding himself to her. "I canna be slow, this first time."

"I don't want you to be." She had been more than a month without him, too. She held herself still as the heavy invasion began, startled anew at the initial difficulty that wasn't quite pain, the pressure, the sense of being stretched. She breathed deeply, gripping his shoulders hard until her body adjusted.

He paused, his own breathing as deep as hers. He braced himself above her, his expression drawn, urgent. He pulled back, pushed inside her again, and shuddered as he began to climax. Grace held him, her own urgency not quite at the same peak as his and grateful that, with Niall, the second time wasn't long after the first.

He sank down heavily on her, sweating, his heart pounding against her breast and his breath catching on occasional small groans at the last small twitches of his orgasm. She slid her hands into his hair, sifting the long black strands through her fingers. "Does this mean you haven't had any — ah . . . relief — since you came back from my time?" She braced herself for his answer, trying to control the ferocious jealousy that began to burn inside her. They had parted without promises or even the expectation of being together again so she couldn't expect him to have been faithful, but she thought she might skin him alive anyway.

"If by relief ye mean have I had a woman," he answered irritably, "then nay, I have not." He lifted his head from her shoulder and glared down at her, as if his deprivation were her fault.

"Good," she said, with intense satisfaction.

A reluctant smile eased his frown. "Ye like that, do ye?"

"Very much." She arched beneath him, delighting in the rub of his belly against hers, and the way her movement made him harden slightly inside her. She stroked her hands down his back, feeling the powerful muscles flex. His buttocks were cool to the touch, and she cupped her palms over them.

He slid his arms under her and rolled, reversing their positions. Grace sat up, her face glowing with soft sensuality. How freely he gave his body for her pleasure!

He put his hands over both her breasts, tenderly fondling them, rubbing his thumbs around her nipples and making them harden. "I'm verra glad of it, but why did ye come back?"

"Because of you," she said simply. "Because I love you. If you want me, I want to stay." She took one of his hands and moved it down to her belly, flattening it over her womb. "If you want *us*." Her voice wobbled then, because there were no promises between them and she had taken such a huge chance in coming back. There hadn't been any talk of love between them, but when she thought of the night they had spent together and his tender care when she had expected much less, she had hope.

He looked at her stomach and his pupils flared wide. His expression went completely blank, as if he had been hit in the head and had no idea what had happened. He tried to speak and nothing emerged. He tried again, his voice so hoarse it was nothing more than a croak. "A bairn?" He shook his head, as if the words made no sense.

"Are you surprised, after that night?" She surprised herself by blushing, hot color rushing to her cheeks as she remembered the raw, frenzied mating.

He began to laugh, gripping her hips to hold her in place. His head arched back and he howled with laughter.

"What's so funny?" Grace demanded, frowning down at him. She was glad she was pregnant, but she didn't think it was *amusing*.

"All these years," he gasped, tears of mirth shining in his eyes. "I've held to my oath, hating the responsibility, holding myself apart from the things another man would expect — and now I've no choice! Thank God!"

The words echoed in the room and he stilled, the laughter gone as if it had never been. "Grace," he whispered.

She touched his face, her fingers tracing the beloved lines. "I don't know," she whispered in reply. "You told me yourself, we can't know." Perhaps she had been sent to him, the pain in both their lives healed by the magic that brought them together, the fever and obsession and devotion neither of them could resist.

He pulled her down, cupping her face in both hands as he kissed her, long and slow and very thoroughly. "I won't question fate," he murmured. "Mayhap I question your sanity, leaving behind the life ye did — I read the books ye left. It is a truly wondrous time."

"So is this time, in a different way. You are here, and that's wondrous enough for me. You're the Guardian; you had to come back, you have to remain. So I came back too. It was an easy decision, once — once I had said good-bye."

"To your husband?" His tone was understanding. Niall knew what it was to lose those he loved.

"To him, and my brother. I've no family left there. But the start of a new family is growing inside me, and I want to be with you . . . if you want me."

"Want ye?" he growled. "Grace — I wanted ye months before ye finally came to me. I burned for ye. How could I defend myself against a lass who wasn't there? If 'tis the words you want, then aye, I love you. Did ye doubt it? After I found ye wi' the Treasure, instead of killing ye as was my duty, I came near to killing myself loving ye! I'm glad ye came to stay, because I willna let ye go again no matter your wishes."

Startled, she realized that Niall's dereliction of duty was indeed unprecedented; why hadn't she realized that at the time? "You loved me then?"

"Of course," he said calmly. "Now, lass, I think ye should have your way wi' me."

Having her way with him took quite a long time. Alice brought food to them that night, grinning at the way Niall sprawled in his big chair, modestly covered by his plaid, but his eyes heavy-lidded and drowsy with an absolute surfeit of physical satisfaction.

Grace lay on his lap, wearing only his shirt. The garment would have reached her knees, if Niall had left it alone, but he seemed to be incapable of doing so. If he wasn't feeding her or holding a cup of wine to her lips, he was stroking her thighs, sometimes reaching a bit higher.

Her stomach was peaceful now, lulled by the plain, unseasoned food. She had had one bout with nausea, right after Niall had dragged her down to the great hall and they had pledged themselves in marriage to each other in front of all the residents of Creag Dhu, and everyone had insisted on toasting them. The second cup of spicy mulled wine had been too much. And after that, of course everyone had to toast the coming bairn.

The wine she drank now was weak and sweet, but added to the events and exertions of the day, she was exhausted and sleepy. She rested her head on his shoulder, her heart peaceful.

When a section of the wall beside the fireplace began moving, Grace merely blinked at it, thinking the wine must be stronger than she had thought. Then a man strode through the opening and stopped still, his pupils flaring. "I sent you a message," he said in French.

"Aye," Niall said drowsily in Scots. "Ye did. Ye waste your time speaking French, for she does too. And Latin. And Greek. If ye've something private to say, best do so in Gaelic; she can't speak that yet."

"Why is she here?"

"Why, because I married her." Niall smiled at Grace, his thumb tracing her lower lip. "Sweetings, my brother Robert. He's king of Scots. Robert, this is Grace, my wife and the mother of my bairn."

Robert looked startled, Grace even more so. She scrambled off Niall's lap and stood before the king of Scotland wearing nothing more than her husband's shirt, her legs and feet bare, her hair hanging loose past her hips. She blushed.

Robert the Bruce was a big, powerfully built man, though not as tall as Niall. He was ruggedly attractive, probably approaching fifty in age, and wore the look of a warrior. He eyed Grace with some appreciation, his gaze lingering on her legs. Niall scowled and came to his feet, placing himself in front of her.

"Ye've told her everything?" Robert asked disapprovingly.

"Nay, she already knew." Niall reached back and made certain Grace was still modestly tucked behind him. "Would ye like wine?"

Robert began to laugh. "Ye rogue," he said with exasperated fondness. "Ye kill a clan chieftain, decimate the clan, and ask me would I like wine? The nobles are demanding that I raise an army to rid Scotland of the renegades of Creag Dhu."

"Huwe attacked *me,*" Niall said, his voice hardening. "And I freed all those Hays who survived the battle."

"Aye, I know. I came only to ask — to beg, and me a king! — that ye try not to shed more blood for a time."

"If 'tis in my power, I'll live a verra peaceful life from this day onward," Niall said. "Will ye wish me happiness?"

"Always." Robert stepped forward and hugged his brother, and the glimpse Grace had of his face made her love him forever, for it was filled with love and an aching relief. He winked at her over Niall's shoulder, and she blushed again.

"Can ye speak, lass?" he asked.

"Yes, of course," she said, pleased that her voice was steady. "I'm pleased to meet you —" She stopped, suddenly unsure of what to call him. Sire? Your Highness? Your Majesty?

"Robert," said the king. "With family, I am Robert." He cocked his head. "Your accent is strange, not English, and not French either. Where are ye from?"

"Creag Dhu," Niall said firmly. "This is her home."

Robert nodded, accepting that here would be yet another mystery about his brother. "When did ye wed?"

"Today."

"Today!" Robert laughed again. "Then there's no wonder ye had the lass half naked on your lap! I'll leave ye to your wedding night, then, and may ye enjoy it well!"

"I will," Niall said firmly. "As soon as ye leave."

Robert was still laughing as he stepped back into the hidden passage, though he tried to muffle the noise. Grace watched as the section closed behind him. "Just how many hidden passageways does Creag Dhu have?"

"It's fair riddled with them," Niall replied, lifting her in his arms and carrying her to the bed. He lay down beside her, cradling her close against his side as if he would never let her go. "Ye feel so perfect," he whispered into her hair. "As if ye are part of me, as if ye could be nowhere else."

"I don't want to be anywhere else."

"Then tomorrow morning, love, I think I should write those papers that brought ye to me. I dinna want to chance anything going wrong." He put his hand on her belly, where his child grew, and held her close as they slept, and dreamed.

The employees of Thorndike Press hope you have enjoyed this Large Print book. All our Large Print titles are designed for easy reading, and all our books are made to last. Other Thorndike Press Large Print books are available at your library, through selected bookstores, or directly from us.

For information about titles, please call:

(800) 223-2336

To share your comments, please write:

Publisher
Thorndike Press
P.O. Box 159
Thorndike, Maine 04986